Andy Hamilton and **Alistair Beaton** both began writing professionally on Radio 4's *Week Ending* and later wrote for *The News Huddlines* on Radio 2. They were members of the original writing team for *Not the Nine O'Clock News* (BBC TV), and in 1980 wrote *The Thatcher Papers* (New English Library).

Andy Hamilton has written and performed in many series of *The Million Pound Radio Show* with Nick Revell on Radio 4. He wrote seventeen episodes of *Shelley* (Thames TV) and was a writer and producer on Channel Four's late-night comedy series *Who Dares Wins*. In 1990, with G‗‗‗ ‗‗‗‗‗‗‗ ‗‗‗‗‗‗‗‗ *the Dead Donkey*, a se‗‗‗‗‗‗‗ ‗‗‗‗‗‗‗‗‗‗‗ awards (including two‗‗‗‗‗‗‗ ‗‗‗‗‗‗‗‗‗‗‗‗FTA). He was the voice ‗‗‗‗‗‗‗‗‗‗‗‗‗‗‗ won the Oscar for Bes‗‗‗‗‗‗‗‗‗‗‗‗‗‗dy is not taking part in ‗‗‗‗‗‗‗‗‗‗‗‗‗‗‗uthfields with his wife Libby, his two sons, Pip and Robbie, and daughter, Isobel.

Alistair Beaton's television work includes *Dunrulin*, (co-written with John Wells) for BBC 2, *Downwardly Mobile*, a situation comedy series for ITV (co-written with Barry Pilton), and two comedy plays for Channel Four. He has also written for *Minder* and *Spitting Image*. In the theatre, he has written a new English version of *Die Fledermaus* for the D'Oyly Carte Company. With Ned Sherrin, he co-wrote *The Metropolitan Mikado* and *The Ratepayers' Iolanthe*, and he is currently writing a new version of Offenbach's *La Vie Parisienne*. He is the presenter of *Fourth Column* on Radio 4.

DROP THE DEAD DONKEY 2000

Andy Hamilton
and
Alistair Beaton

WARNER BOOKS

A *Warner* Book

First published in Great Britain in 1994
by Little, Brown and Company
This edition published in 1995 by Warner Books

A CIP catalogue record for this book is
available from the British Library.

ISBN 0 7515 1366 0

Typeset by M Rules
Printed and bound in Great Britain by
Clays Ltd, St. Ives plc

Warner Books
A Division of
Little, Brown and Company (UK)
Brettenham House
Lancaster Place
London WC2E 7EN

An Apology

The authors wish to apologise to any person mentioned in this book who has died. At the time of writing you were still alive.

Sorry.

Andy Hamilton and Alistair Beaton
London, August 1994

New Year's Eve, 1999

Incredibly, the twentieth century was ending on a high note. As the last hours of 1999 ticked away, mankind was experiencing a surge of global optimism. The developed countries were uniting to fight famine in Africa, world leaders were agreeing plans for a summit to end the scourge of war, and George Dent had conquered his sinuses. In the seventeen years that George had been Editor at Globelink News there had hardly been a single day when his sinuses didn't feel as if they'd been injected with liquid cement. Yet today, they were totally clear.

He breathed in deeply through his nose. It felt great. Nothing would get him down today. Even the growing financial crisis at Globelink News could not extinguish the flame of optimism which now illuminated his life. True, he still felt twinges of guilt at having spent £39.95 on a bottle of L'EGOISTE − EAU DE TOILETTE POUR HOMMES. But he couldn't very well keep using Boots Aftershave now he was buying his shirts from Gap. (Helen had told him his new shirts made him look 'almost sexy'.) George whistled 'My Way' quietly to himself as he waited for the lift to take him up to the videotape library. His newly acquired Heiss Eisen watch ('as used by the SAS') beeped discreetly. He glanced at it. Only five hours

1

left till the first bulletin of the new century. He studied the photocopied running-order he held in his hand. Yes, there was definitely hope in the air. The United Nations had at last decided to intervene in the brutal civil war in Switzerland by declaring Montreux a safe area. NATO was even threatening air strikes against the Swiss-German artillery placed on the surrounding hills. That had to be first item. Second item was harder to pick. There was the government's decision to re-open fifty-three coal mines 'in the light of new market realities'. There was Gazza's knighthood, Fergie's conversion to Buddhism, and the discovery of three live rhinos in Zimbabwe. But then, the pictures of the rhinos were a bit disappointing. What if he moved up one of the later items? There were quite a lot of feelgood stories to choose from. SCHINDLER'S LIST – THE MUSICAL was breaking all box-office records. Education Secretary Gyles Brandreth was launching his new Excellence Levels. And Sister Wendy had finally been released.

The lift was taking a long time to come. George punched at the buttons. He never seemed to have any luck with this lift. Yesterday he'd met Gus in it. Gus Hedges was not a man to meet in an enclosed space. Especially yesterday. George decided that, on balance, he didn't want to know why the Chief Executive had been making strange whimpering noises and banging his head against the wall.

Damn, would this lift never arrive? George was about to become angry when he reminded himself that anger was a negative emotion. It would only bring back his irritable bowel syndrome, and

2

irritable bowel syndrome was no way to begin a new century.

George concentrated instead on his plans to go whitewater rafting in the spring. He'd already begun the induction course at the local swimming pool. This involved hanging upside down in a canoe, 'to accustom participants to the sensation of being underwater'. George wasn't sure he much liked the sensation of being underwater. For a start, he thought he might be allergic to chlorine. And that instructor was a little unkind, the way he'd designated George as 'your role model for how not to do it'. And anyhow, what was all this talk about being underwater? Surely the whole point of rafting was to stay on top of the water? Maybe he should abandon the whitewater-rafting plan and go for a day trip to Boulogne instead, even if it meant being herded on to a cross-Channel ferry. The ferries were so crowded since the Great Channel Tunnel Disaster of 1998. Funny, it all seemed so long ago. George tried to remember the name of the little French supervisor who the enquiry had decided was to blame for the entire tragedy. George ran the story through his mind. He remembered how the Anti-Europeans in the Conservative Party had seen their chance, forcing the closure and permanent sealing of the Tunnel. 'Destiny,' Teddy Taylor MP had declared, 'clearly wishes this country to remain an island.' But no matter how hard he tried, George could not remember the name of the little supervisor. He could only remember how sorry he felt for him.

George found his thoughts drifting back to

3

Globelink's financial crisis. What if the whole station were to be closed down? No, he mustn't think about that. Why get agitated when a whole new life was beckoning to him? He felt a strange optimism flood through him. He whispered to himself, 'I can be anyone I want to be. The past is a graveyard that need never be revisited.' He gazed down at his new pair of Timberlands and reflected that they gave him quite a jaunty air. They also added two inches to his height. He was still gazing down at them when the lift doors opened. He took three paces forward and entered. He pressed the button for the top floor and turned to admire himself in the mirror on the back wall.

It was then that he saw the dead body on the floor.

As George ran screaming from the lift, he failed to notice the Coca-Cola machine, an oversight that resulted in a complicated fracture of the nose. For a few terrible seconds he flailed around desperately on the floor. Witnesses were later to swear that they heard him shouting, 'Help! That lift is out to get me. The bloody thing is cursed!'

George had first experienced the curse of the lift one month earlier. On that occasion he'd actually fainted . . .

One

December 1st, 1999

'George! George! Are you all right?' There was a distinct edge of anxiety in Helen's voice. She bent over him and loosened the collar of his beige C&A shirt. He was pale and sweating. She noted that even when unconscious, George still retained his characteristic expression of startled anxiety.

George would subsequently insist that the lurching motion of the lift had caused the mucus in his sinuses to slosh about, thus making him feel disorientated and dizzy. It was an interesting medical theory, but Helen knew why George had fainted. He had slumped to the floor just as she had finished the sentence, 'So we could all lose our jobs!' She should have known better. She had seen him faint from stress many times. It was as if his brain tripped a fuse if it heard too much bad news at once.

George groaned and came round just as the lift reached the second floor.

'It's OK,' said Helen, giving his hand a reassuring squeeze. 'You're OK.'

George sat up and waited for his senses to clear. 'You . . . you were saying, Helen?'

'No, it doesn't matter.'

'I want to know.'

Helen took a deep breath. 'The City desk has noticed an odd pattern of trading in Merchant Holdings. They

5

reckon Sir Roysten could be in big trouble and might have to sell off Globelink News.'

'Well, it's all conjecture, isn't it, Helen? The important thing is not to spread panic,' said George, fighting back the wave of panic that had started in the pit of his stomach and was now gripping his chest muscles. He struggled to his feet. He mustn't show weakness in front of his Assistant Editor. 'Best not mention it to the others.'

No one noticed George enter the newsroom, because everybody was extremely busy. Nobody was doing any work, but they were all extremely busy. Henry Davenport, the station's veteran newsreader, was tackling *The Times* crossword. He did this every morning. In recent months he had noticed that the crossword was taking longer to complete. This was obviously nothing to do with his age. The dyslexic upstarts who compiled the thing were deliberately making the clues more abstruse, that was all.

Next to Henry sat Sally Smedley, described by Globelink publicity as 'one of Britain's premier newscasters', and described by Henry Davenport as 'that posturing airhead with the personality by-pass'. Sally was shaking her head in dismay. A quick scan of that morning's newspapers had confirmed an alarming trend. There was not a single mention of her. For the third consecutive day! She would have to do something quick to get some publicity (though preferably not another appearance on *Guess Whose Laundry*). Sally noticed that Joy was grinning at her from across the office in a way that could only be described as sarcastic.

'Anything good in the papers, Sal?' called Joy, her smirk widening.

Sally toyed with the sleeve of her pink Dior jacket and wondered why Joy's insolence was tolerated. Joy was, after all, a mere slip of a PA and therefore quite dispensable. She decided to pull rank. 'I'd like a coffee, please, Joy.'

Joy just laughed.

Helen clapped her hands loudly. 'Editorial meeting!'

As if magically summoned by these words, Gus Hedges materialised in the seat just behind George's shoulder. 'Don't worry, team. I'm not here. Just want to watch the editorial unit synchromeshing with the production matrix.'

Henry muttered something about sub-titles.

Helen wearily ran a hand through her blonde hair and tried to take control. 'OK. Cyprus. Dave, what have we got?'

Dave cleared the latest odds at Chepstow from his VDU and quickly accessed Reuters. 'Um, more incidents along the Green Line. Greeks claim Turkey is secretly landing troops in Northern Cyprus. Russia's jumping up and down and making threatening noises. I'm offering three to one against war by Monday.'

'All right,' said Helen. 'So it's Cyprus first item.'

There were general murmurs of agreement round the table.

'Um, I don't want to interfere,' Gus interfered. 'As you know, I'm not a hands-on playmaker, but don't you think we should consider leading with the footage of that supermodel collapsing from hunger on the catwalk? Great visuals.'

There was a long pause.

'Gus,' said Helen. 'She died.'

'Exactly,' replied Gus, beaming. 'On camera.' He

sensed a certain disapproval in the air. 'Obviously we angle it towards . . .' Gus floundered momentarily '. . . towards the ethical . . . angle. Yes, that's it. The ethics of the fashion business, which peddles a dangerous image of thinness to innocent young girls.' Gus sat back in his chair, pleased at having seized the moral high ground.

Helen remained firm. 'I'm sorry, Gus, there's no contest. Russia is threatening to invade Cyprus.'

'Hmm,' said Gus. 'Not a lot of good pictures there. Now if they'd actually invaded, and we had some good war footage, then that would be different. Obviously.'

George shifted uneasily. He sensed a confrontation looming, and George hated confrontations. 'I do tend to agree with Helen, actually, Gus. And we've got that profile of President Zhirinovsky that Dave has been preparing. We could use some footage from that.'

'Oh, fantastic!' Gus exploded. 'Show some pictures of a fat drunken Russian and elbow the last moments of a telegenic young sex symbol. And then watch the ratings collapse. Will you people please try to interface with the real world, for God's sake!'

'Great,' thought Dave. 'Gus is cracking up.'

Helen stood up and started quoting guidelines laid down by The Broadcasting Ethics Council. This did not have a calming effect on Gus.

'Now, now, everybody. Let's not . . .' But George's placatory words were drowned out by the raging argument that ensued. An argument so loud and heated that nobody noticed the arrival of the three Japanese men in dark suits.

Damien was hacked off. Damien was seriously hacked off. Getting from London to Brecon by public transport was no easy matter. The woman behind the desk at the Paddington office of Badger Trains had failed to tell him that his ticket was non-interchangeable. As a result, he'd been put off the train at Reading. 'Sorry, sir,' the Red Roller Travel Hostess had told him, 'you are in possession of a non-viable ticket and are thereby obligated to detrain at the next station.'

Of course, Damien ought to have known about non-interchangeability of tickets between rail companies. But then Damien wasn't used to slumming it on trains. Damien was a Porsche owner, for God's sake! A Porsche owner, but not a Porsche driver. Having been given his licence back in mid-June, he'd lost it again in early July. That magistrate had no sense of proportion. Probably drove an old Fiat Uno. OK, so doing ninety-two in a built-up area was an error of judgement. But it wasn't as if he'd actually *hit* the lollipop lady, was it?

Losing his licence was bad enough, but he'd also been sentenced to a hundred hours of community service planting bluebells on motorway verges. Then, of course, Gus had found out about it, pulled Damien into his office and subjected him to a mind-numbing diatribe about the need to protect the station from 'an ethical downsizing of its popular image at a time of ruthless competitive struggle in the televisual marketplace'. Damien had reckoned that half an hour of strategic grovelling would be enough to get him rehabilitated. He was wrong. Gus had 'grounded' him. No foreign travel for at least two months, just as he was about to be smuggled into Switzerland to report on the siege of Montreux. Damien was devastated. Nowhere else in Europe offered the same potential for atrocity exclusives. He'd already bought a new flak jacket. And a girl he knew at BBC Drama had nicked a very convincing stick-on wound for him. He'd noticed that wounded reporters who bravely continued to bring you the story were a virtual cert for a BAFTA award. No one gave BAFTA's for stories from Brecon.

Damien paced impatiently up and down the platform at Reading, drawing his sheepskin coat tightly against the wind which whipped the litter from the ground and sent it eddying in sinister vortices round his feet. The waiting room was for Red Roller passengers only. He kept a wary eye on his camera bag. The introduction of multi-skilling and one-man camera crews at Globelink was meant to make reporters more flexible and responsive. As a result they now went round weighed down like bloody pack-horses.

Damien sighed. He didn't want to be in Reading. He wanted even less to be in Brecon, and yet he had to go. Gus had assigned him to recce a piece on the imminent privatisation of the recently revived South Wales Borderers (who had briefly been the South Wales Tourist Board Borderers until it had been decided to elbow sponsorship in favour of outright privatisation).

'It's a military subject, Damien,' Gus had sniggered. 'Very much up your journalistic alley.'

The station loudspeaker crackled into life. Damien listened for details of the next Badger Train to Cardiff. But the only trains announced were Red Rollers. It slowly dawned on him that Badger Trains didn't stop at Reading. Damien kicked viciously at an empty Coca-Cola tin and imagined it was Gus's head. Bugger it, thought Damien. This poxy, boring story isn't worth five minutes of my time.

But Damien was wrong. He had never been more wrong. Because this poxy, boring story would lead to a corpse in the lift at Globelink News and the nastiest government cover-up of the century.

Still, we all make mistakes.

The editorial meeting was going much better now, mainly because Gus wasn't there any more.

Helen was skilfully juggling the running order to accommodate some new footage of President North re-opening Los Angeles.

'So that means we move "record beef exports" to the end and we drop the kitten that fell down a well.'

The others nodded agreement. Helen always cut the fluffy news item at the end, and Gus invariably put it back.

'Anything we've missed?' asked Helen. 'No? Good. Meeting over.'

Henry's voice suddenly boomed out across the room. 'According to the City desk, we're all buggered. It seems our beloved proprietor Sir Roysten Fatbastard is about to flog off Globelink News. God knows who'll want to buy it. We'll probably all be boiled down for glue.'

'Oh God,' thought George, 'they've all heard,' forgetting that everyone always knew everything long before he did. Even when his wife Margaret decided to divorce him, he had been the last in the office to know. In the end, he had heard it from a cleaner.

A terrible chill descended on the newsroom. Ever since Gus's economy drive, persistent rumours had swept the building that Globelink was in deep financial trouble. Dave was currently offering odds of two to one against a programme of voluntary redundancies, and five to one against complete closure of the station. This was felt to be in poor taste, and for the first time he was finding no takers. Even Henry, whom Dave saw as the

11

bookie's best friend, could not be induced to risk as much as 50p.

Dave looked at his watch. 'How come the three sinister Japanese characters have been in with Gus for half an hour now?'

'I expect they're here to arrange an interview with me,' simpered Sally. 'I'm very big in Japan. I'm planning to go there in the spring.'

'Poor sods,' muttered Henry. 'Just when they were getting over Hiroshima.'

Sally took out her compact and checked her make-up. 'I'm a worldwide cultural icon, you know, Henry. Only last week I received a fan letter from Reykjavik.'

George raised his head. 'From some geyser,' he said, pleased to lighten the atmosphere with a little judicious banter.

Five people stared at him in silent pity. George mistook this for incomprehension. 'Some geyser . . .' he repeated, the first scintilla of doubt entering his mind. 'You see, Iceland is very famous for its geysers . . . and . . . geyser is also a synonym for a person, like . . . some bloke and so . . . on.' He paused. 'Perhaps it wasn't a very good joke.'

George bowed his head over his work and wished the earth would swallow him up. Five other people shared this wish.

'In my opinion,' said Henry, 'the Nips are here to buy Globelink.'

An even more terrible chill descended on the newsroom. George decided to exercise leadership. He stood up. 'Now listen here, everybody. I am sick and tired of all these stupid comments. There is no evidence whatsoever that Globelink is going to be sold off, or closed, or

12

slimmed down, or anything else. As Editor I would obviously be informed immediately of any such plans, and I can promise you that I have heard nothing. So . . .' Here George slammed his right fist into his left hand in a poignantly unconvincing impersonation of a born leader. 'So, come on, team, let's get this show on the road!' He stood there for a moment longer, surveying his troops with what he hoped was an eagle eye.

'George . . .' said Joy.

'Yes, Joy?'

'Your flies are undone.'

Helen looked up from her VDU, where a Reuters flash had just appeared. 'Change of running order,' she shouted out. 'Russian troops have landed in Cyprus. Zhirinovsky says Holy Mother Russia cannot stand aside while atrocities are perpetrated against Orthodox Christians.'

George swung into action, grateful to President Zhirinovsky for this diversion from the question of his trouser buttons. It was these chinos he had bought at Gap, that was the problem. He had only ever worn trousers with zips before, and was beginning to think that buttons were too high a price to pay for looking stylish. He ran his eyes over the agency report. 'Yes, we'll definitely lead on Cyprus,' he announced.

Sally was reading over George's shoulder. 'This could mean war. NATO certainly isn't going to take it lying down.'

Henry glowered at her. 'Russia's a member of NATO, pin-brain! Has been for two years. But then I don't suppose one can expect an international cultural icon to know anything about foreign affairs. Unless by foreign affairs one means exchanging body fluids with French truck drivers.'

Sally drew in her breath sharply. 'That was cheap, Henry. Cheap and vulgar. I know you find me attractive, but I would ask you to keep your libidinous fantasies to yourself.'

Dave leaped to his feet with a roar of triumph. 'Lib-id-in-ous!' he shouted, counting off the syllables on his fingers. 'Henry, you owe me a tenner!'

'I do?'

'Yes,' said Dave. 'You bet me ten quid that Sally wouldn't come out with a word longer than three syllables today.'

Henry groaned, and handed over the money.

Suddenly they all became aware of three sets of oriental eyes peering at them from between the blinds of Gus's office.

Damien got off the Red Roller Intercity at Newport. He was now £36.70 poorer. There was no way Gus would cough up for a Red Roller *and* a Badger Train ticket. Not in view of his new economy measures. Damien sighed, and thought wistfully of the time when expense claims were an exercise in creative writing. He and Henry had spent years building up a strategic national network of restaurants which would obligingly add fictional starters, salads, and cover charges. Now there was a flat rate of £25 a day for meals. Twenty-five quid! That would hardly cover the price of egg and chips in a Happy Muncher. Damien checked the timetable for the next train to Abergavenny. This timetable was easier to understand, as there was only one company on the Abergavenny line. Thank God for that.

Damien settled down on a platform bench, pulled up his collar against the icy wind, and began to itemise his grievances. Why did no one appreciate him? In order to survive commercially, Globelink News needed punchy, sexy stories, and Damien always delivered. But did he get any thanks? Did he hell! Only last week his stunning piece on patients at risk in under-staffed hospitals had been met with irritating quibbles about exactly how a drip had come to be disconnected. And why was Gus giving him such a bad time? Gus had always stood by Damien as his 'front-line news warrior'. But in recent weeks Gus's manner had become decidedly frosty. Especially since Damien's dramatic footage of the Mystery Puma of Bodmin Moor. OK, with hindsight, Damien conceded, maybe he ought not to have provided the puma. But it wasn't his fault the bloody thing had got away. Sure, everyone in the area had been ordered to stay indoors, but no one had been hurt and none of it had been traced back to Damien, so what was the problem, for God's sake?

Damien moved on to his next grievance. Why did nobody in the office like him? This line of thought was interrupted by the scrape of forty-year-old brakes as the Dragon Express to Brecon inched along the platform. Damien boarded and found a window seat, grateful to be out of the bitter cold. A steward approached, pushing a trolley. Damien felt ravenous. So ravenous that even the prospect of Dragonsnax Kwikbite Catering was quite attractive. Damien eyed the trolley, which was groaning with burgers in buns. The burgers were huge and Damien guessed they'd been made from cows whose growth had been artificially stimulated by the wonder drug Bovactilax. In normal circumstances, this might have put Damien off. But his stomach was aching with hunger, so he bought two. He had just wolfed down the first one when the train began to creep out of the station.

Damien sank his teeth into the second burger and decided things were looking up.

Then the train shuddered arthritically to a halt. A loud-speaker announcement from the Customer Coordinator informed passengers that the train was delayed 'due to operational difficulties'. Unknown to the passengers, the operational difficulty in this case was Dragon Line's rental arrears to Intertrak, who controlled all movements on the line. As a result, the signal had been turned to red just outside Newport. There the train was to remain while a messenger from Dragon Line HQ was sent to the Intertrak office with a banker's draft for £40,000.

The door of Gus's office flew open and the Chief Executive of Globelink News strode into the newsroom. 'Just seen the agency wires! George, I presume we're going to impact live with a newsflash on the Cyprus story?'

'Um, well . . . yes, I suppose that would be a good idea.'

'You suppose? Come on, George! Let's get out there on to the cutting edge of a breaking story!'

Behind Gus, three Japanese faces appeared in the doorway. They watched with puzzled interest as Gus attempted to whip his team into a fervour of action.

Sally was in deep distress. 'Gus, I'm sorry. I can't pos-sibly appear live on air just because somebody's invaded somebody. I'm due to have my hair done in half an hour.'

'Fine,' said Gus. 'Henry, you do the newsflash.'

'Perhaps my hair's all right,' said Sally quickly.

And so Globelink went on to red alert in preparation for the newsflash. As the minutes ticked by, the working tempo picked up. In fact, it had been some time since the newsroom had seen such an outbreak of enthusiasm.

This was not altogether unconnected to the three Japanese observers, who had fanned out round the newsroom bearing clipboards.

'Your name, please?'

'Sorry?' Dave looked up at a smiling Japanese face. 'Dave Charnley,' he added quickly.

'Thank you, Mr Charnley.'

Dave shot a quick glance at the man's lapel-badge.

'You're welcome, Mr Sakimoto.' It was as well to be polite. For all he knew, he could be talking to his future boss. Mind you, he couldn't quite understand why this high-powered Japanese executive was wearing bicycle clips. Just as Mr Sakimoto couldn't quite understand why Gus was paying him £7.50 an hour merely to walk around in a suit and write down people's names.

The Privatisation Coordinator of the South Wales Borderers came out from behind his desk as Damien entered the room.

'Mr Day. Great to see you. The name's Farquhar. But call me Tom. Have a seat.' Damien sat down. 'How was the journey?'

Damien decided not to go into his true feelings about the journey. 'Um, it was . . . fine.'

'Good, good. Coffee?'

'Yes, please.'

Farquhar pressed a button on his intercom. 'Coffee, please, Corporal.' He leaned back in his chair. Farquhar was in his early thirties and studiedly lean and elegant. He gazed at Damien. Farquhar had learned there was nothing more flattering than giving someone your undivided attention. He was at his best at buffet suppers and receptions. Where others desultorily chatted, their eyes flicking round the room for other more important contacts, Farquhar would fix his gaze on the person he was speaking to, nodding sagely whenever the other made some point, however banal. This technique had served him well over the years, not only in his chosen profession, but also in his personal life. There was nothing women liked better than a man with listening skills. Yes, Farquhar told himself, he was good with people.

'So, Damien. I gather you're planning to do a feature on the forthcoming privatisation of the regiment?'

'That's right.'

'Good, good. Well, I'm here to provide you with whatever facilities you need. Perhaps a little background would be useful?' Farquhar slid a glossy press pack across the desk. Damien picked it up. It must have weighed at least half a kilo.

'I think you'll find all the facts and figures you need in there. It's a very tempting investment, of course. I think we've pitched the flotation price at quite an attractive level. There shouldn't be any shortage of investors.'

Damien was not so sure. The public had become rather bored with share flotations. Hardly anyone had opted to buy a piece of British Palaces plc.

The corporal entered with the coffee.

'Ah, Corporal,' said Farquhar. 'Let our friend here have a good look at the new regimental uniform.'

An embarrassed corporal put down the coffee and stood in front of Damien.

'And turn,' said Farquhar.

The corporal turned round once.

Damien stared in horror at the bright blue uniform, with its scarlet epaulettes, its gold braid and its plumed helmet. The man looked like a gay hussar from a nineteenth-century operetta.

'We got Vaclav Havel to design them for us,' Farquhar declared proudly. 'The hottest couturier in Paris, you know. Thank you, Corporal.'

The corporal clumped out of the room.

'Yes, I know,' said Farquhar. 'Not ideal for the modern battlefield, but useful in creating a high profile for the flotation. Echoes of imperial glory. The Heritage Army. It's what people want.' Farquhar poured the coffee, then leaned intimately towards Damien. 'I have a suggestion. As you know, we haven't actually unveiled these new uniforms to the public yet. How would Globelink like an exclusive? Say, twenty-four hours prior to the official press launch? I could allow your cameras access to the parade ground. Three hundred and fifty troops marching past in the new uniforms. Plus regimental band. Very attractive visuals for you. Could be quite a scoop.'

This was not Damien's idea of a scoop. This was more Damien's idea of a free commercial. On the other hand, it was better than nothing, and it was the kind of cheerful flim-flam that might get him back into Gus's good books.

'That sounds brilliant, Tom.' Damien put down his cup of coffee. 'Of course, we'd like to do a few interviews.'

'Of course, of course.' Farquhar smiled benignly. 'I'm available for interview virtually any time that suits you. And I'm sure I could also arrange an interview with the Commanding Officer.'

'Actually, I'd quite like to talk to some of the ordinary soldiers. And maybe a couple of the officers. Just to see how they feel about the flotation.'

Farquhar's smile became à little more fixed. 'I think

you'll find the CO and I will be able to give you all the information you need.'

Damien's journalistic antennae began to twitch. Why block such a harmless request? What was the man afraid of? He probed a little. 'Just a few of the men. You know, sort of military vox pops. To give it a bit more energy. Otherwise it might turn into a boring piece. And you wouldn't want that, would you, Tom?'

For the first time, Farquhar looked away. He had put his hands together, and was examining his carefully manicured nails.

'No. Sorry. Logistical problems, you understand.' He finally looked up, fixing Damien with his pale blue eyes. 'I presume you still feel there's a piece worth doing?'

'Oh, yes,' replied Damien. 'I'm sure there is.'

Gus's anger was terrible to behold. 'Don't try to wriggle out of this one, George!'

'I'm not wriggling,' said George, as he wriggled in the seat facing Gus's desk.

Gus came round behind George and thrust a sheet of paper into his hands. 'Look. 11.22, the BBC interrupts programmes to announce the invasion of Cyprus. 11.27, CNN runs its newsflash. 11.29, Channel Four runs the story complete with hi-tech graphics. 11.33, CNN starts running live pictures of Russian planes bombing Famagusta. 12.03, Globelink runs a newsflash. Except it's not a newsflash any more, is it, George? It's a history lesson! Now what went wrong?'

George blew his nose.

'Stop playing for time!'

'I'm not playing for time. All this stress is very bad for my sinuses and—'

'Fuck your sinuses, George! I've had Sir Roysten on the phone. This is a testicles-in-the-toaster scenario!'

George swallowed hard. He had never heard Gus use the F-word before. This could be serious. 'We were only . . .' George counted mentally. 'We were only forty-one minutes behind the Beeb.'

'Oh. And that's all right, is it?'

'No, perhaps it's not entirely satisfactory, but . . .' George blew his nose for a second time.

Gus pulled himself up to his full height. 'You do know, don't you, that Globelink's facing a negative cash-flow? You know what that means? We could all end up on a workfare scheme. Scraping dog mess off pavements for five pounds a day!'

George looked up. He began to feel faint again.

'You chew on that, Mister,' Gus shouted, jabbing a sun-tanned finger at George. Then he turned and swept out of the office, leaving George seated in a daze.

George couldn't remember the last time he'd felt so low. This would set his rodent ulcer off for sure. He looked at Gus's tank of Burmese fighting fish, and envied them. No cares, no responsibility. His eye came to rest on the wastepaper bin. There was a book in it. George picked it up. The cover design showed a large red bird rising from some flames. He read the title: *Self-Rebirth Made Easy.* Along the bottom of the cover a shout-line screamed, 'This book will change your life!'

How silly, thought George.

An anxious Helen looked up as Gus crossed the news-room. 'Excuse me. Who exactly were the Japanese gentlemen?'

21

'Oh, that's big-league stuff, Helen. You don't want to bother your pretty little head with that.' Gus smiled. It was good to see that his Japanese hirelings had successfully intimidated the staff. He smiled, adjusted his tie, and breezed out of the newsroom.

Helen struggled to concentrate on her work. But her mind kept being invaded by dark possibilities. Like a Japanese takeover of Globelink. What would she do if she got made redundant? How would she continue to pay for her daughter's education? Chloë was in her last year at school, sitting her Excellence Levels in Team Sports. It cost Helen a minimum of £12,000 a year in teacher sponsorship fees. Not to mention extras, like books. She finished the spreadsheet she had been working on and pressed Save. Dammit, she thought, they couldn't fire me. I'm the most efficient person in this building. I'm surrounded by lazy, ligging, skiving hacks. Let them be the ones who get the push. Without me this place would fall apart.

Dave was sitting minding his own business when Helen came over and ripped off his virtual-reality helmet.

'Hey!' he protested. 'Do you mind?'

'I've told you before,' said Helen, 'no virtual-reality games during office hours.'

Dave glared at her. 'This is work, Helen. I was following today's debate in the House of Lords. Sitting right next to Lord Skinner of Bolsover. Do you think I'd do that for the fun of it?'

Helen looked dubious. She put on the virtual-reality helmet and found herself stroking the breasts of a girl from Thailand.

Helen quickly removed the helmet. 'Since when are

22

there naked women in the House of Lords?'

'Oh. Yes. Right. Um, you must have accessed the debate on pornography. Which is, er, under way. At this moment. In the Lords. Currently.' He paused. 'This isn't very convincing, is it?'

'Correct. I'm docking an hour's pay.' Helen walked away, helmet in hand.

Dave ran after her. 'Hey. My helmet.'

'I'm confiscating it. You'll get it back at the end of the week.' She wheeled and fixed Dave with her intense blue eyes. 'You know your trouble, don't you, Dave?'

'He's useless,' said Joy, without looking up.

'Yes, thank you, Joy, but I can deal with this.' Helen turned back to Dave. 'Your trouble is, you're useless.'

Sally Smedley was staring hard at her computer screen when she became aware of Helen standing over her.

Helen's voice was icy. 'What are you doing?'

'I'm doing a projection of my earnings from commercials, business conferences and supermarket openings. And I would appreciate if you would not pry into my private affairs.' Sally stabbed at the keyboard, removing the figures from the screen. This was not because she really regarded them as private, but because they had turned out to be disappointingly small.

'Sally, you are not paid to sit here planning your extra-curricular activities.'

'I'm sorry, Helen, I couldn't possibly live on the pittance I am paid by Globelink.'

'The rest of us seem to manage on our salaries. You don't see Henry moonlighting.'

'Wrong, Helen,' trilled Sally. 'As always. On the sly, Henry does after-dinner speaking. Or should I say

23

after-dinner slurring?' Sally decided to twist the knife. 'I know what this is all about, Helen. Envy. You envy me my full, glamorous life because it contrasts so starkly with your own humdrum lot as a struggling single parent.'

Helen began to boil.

But Sally was hitting her stride. 'However, you chose that road, Helen, so don't blame me. You chose to flout the norm of the nuclear family. Of course, that's not to say I don't feel sorry for you.'

Helen came to the boil. But she was damned if she was going to let it show. 'You feel sorry for me?' she said, with a slight quiver detectable in her voice.

'Yes,' said Sally, tipping her head coyly to one side in a way that momentarily reminded Helen of Princess Diana.

'Why?'

'Because of the dreadful burden you carry.'

Joy looked over and noticed that Helen's knuckles had gone white.

'The burden?' Helen asked. 'What burden would that be exactly?'

'Why the burden of being the way you are. You know, your sexual leanings. It causes an inner sadness. I've seen it so many times among people of your . . . persuasion. But you must excuse me, I'm due for my shiatsu.'

Sally got up and sailed serenely towards the exit, a thin smile on her lips. Helen watched her go. She heard Joy's voice from behind her.

'Stab her, Helen. We'll all swear it was an accident.'

Damien was staring at a severed human finger. It was pickled in formaldehyde in a glass jar which bore the label, 'Finger of Argy, Port Stanley, 1982'. It had been given pride of place on a shelf above the bar. And Damien rather liked it.

He turned and looked around the near-empty pub. He'd been told that the Green Boar was where all the squaddies went drinking. Of course, he didn't want to hang about in Brecon, who would? But he couldn't get rid of the feeling that Farquhar had something to hide. Damien reckoned the other ranks were probably pissed off about privatisation. He'd deliberately given Farquhar the impression that Globelink would do a supportive little piece. But Damien would happily renege on that if it turned out there was a sexier angle to the story. It wasn't exactly war reporting, but a sensational piece to camera on the lines of 'British troops lash privatisation deal' would at least be more fun than footage of a bunch of military wankers in Royal Opera costumes.

Where were the squaddies? Damien wondered. In one corner of the pub a bunch of farmers were drinking vodka martinis and raising a toast, 'To Bovactilax – God bless it!' Over by the far wall, a gnarled old man in a silver tracksuit was playing Serial Killer III. At the bar, two middle-aged women were munching Camembert-and-onion crisps and watching the evening repeat of Michael Portillo's daytime chat show. Today it was all about period pain, and Michael was struggling a bit.

'Excuse me,' said Damien to the barman, 'what time do the guys from the South Wales Borderers normally turn up?'

'Oh, you won't see any of them in here tonight,' the barman replied, wiping a glass on a filthy tea-towel. 'They'll all be down the brasserie, see? Big celebration tonight.'

'Oh, yes? What's the occasion?'

25

'The regiment's just won the franchise for the Gulf War Experience. You're not from round here, are you?'

'No,' said Damien with feeling. 'Where's this brasserie?'

What a total waste of time, thought Damien, as he zipped his lightweight video camera back into its blue bag. He had just finished eight consecutive interviews with squaddies in the mock art nouveau setting of the Brecon Brasserie. To Damien's intense irritation, the squaddies had not attacked the privatisation plans. They had expressed no views on privatisation whatsoever. At least, he didn't think they had. Three of them had been so sloshed that their syntax had disappeared completely, to be replaced by a random selection of nouns and verbs. Another had seemed very angry about something. But Damien was unable to tell quite what it was, due largely to an impenetrable Glaswegian accent. The whole thing was a fiasco. There was no story here after all. He'd have to resort to a humiliating feature on the poncey new uniforms.

Damien perched himself on a bar stool and ordered an alcohol-free Pineapple Wallbanger. A young soldier staggered to the bar alongside him.

'Double Calvados there, please, barman, ta,' the soldier called out with a strong Scouse twang. He turned and smiled a boozy smile at Damien. 'So you're off the telly, like? Brian over there says you're off the telly.'

'Yes,' said Damien, trying not to get involved in a conversation. 'I'm off the telly.'

'Brian says you're a weather man.'

Damien bristled. 'I am not a weather man. I'm a reporter.'

'Oh, right. Sorry, pal. We're all a bit bladdered, like.

Celebrating. Got the franchise for the Gulf War Experience.'

'Yes. I've heard.'

'UK's first military theme park. We'll make a bloody fortune. Hordes of kiddies and their dads paying twenty quid a head to fire a few pretend Patriot missiles. Bloody brilliant! You should put it on the telly, you should.'

Damien realised that this deal would greatly boost the privatisation package. The regiment seemed to have secured a healthy financial future for itself. Shareholders would be attracted by that. He sipped at his Pineapple Wallbanger, and pulled a face. He watched the soldier sink the double Calvados. The man was only in his early twenties, but he was clearly a seasoned drinker. He put a sweaty hand on Damien's shoulder. 'Have a drink on us, eh? We can afford it, pal. We're all in for a significant slice of the action, see?'

Damien found this hard to believe. 'I bet the really big money will be creamed off by the officers.'

'Maybe,' said the soldier, signalling for another double Calvados. 'Them that's still alive.'

Damien frowned. 'How do you mean, exactly?'

'I mean, exactly, that the officers, like, are snuffing it faster than we can bloody bury them.'

'What? They're dying?'

'In considerable numbers.'

Damien experienced a definite rush of adrenalin. 'Let me buy you another drink.'

By the time George had finished reading the book about self-rebirth, it had changed his life. From the moment he'd set eyes on the opening sentence ('Do you feel your life is one long car crash, happening in slow motion?') George felt as if it had been written specifically with him in mind. He carefully put down the book in the middle of his kitchen table and marvelled for a moment at the miracle of personal renewal. He picked up the pad on which, as instructed by the book, he had compiled a tally of his successes and failures. Unfortunately, he hadn't been able to itemise his successes yet, as he'd used up all the pad on his failures. But it didn't matter; he'd found the process strangely healing. The simple act of writing it all down had somehow given him a genuine sense of putting things behind him, just like the book had promised it would. He was converted. If only he could focus his energies he could rebirth himself using his untapped inner resources. Yes, the millennium would see a new George.

He poured a cup of tea, then decided to have a couple of Hob-nobs, just to keep up his blood sugar level. He ought really to be making himself a proper supper, but he'd become so hooked on the book that he just couldn't be bothered. He found a new pad and prepared to list his successes. The break-up of his marriage to Margaret had gone quite smoothly; maybe that could be counted as a success. In fact, they had managed to retain quite a civilised relationship. Margaret positively encouraged him to call round from time to time, especially if there were things that needed fixing. Some women would have felt threatened by the idea of their ex-husband pottering about in the home they'd once shared, but not Margaret. Last weekend she'd let him fix a dripping tap, rewire the electric kettle, put a new plug on the toaster, replace a couple of broken roof tiles, and unblock the waste pipe in the lavatory. It was a pity she hadn't asked him to stay on for the dinner party she was having, but he quite understood that her friends would have found his presence a bit awkward. Yes, all in all he felt they were both making their divorce work.

He picked up the book again and read the last two lines: 'You can be anything you want to be. The past is a graveyard that need never be revisited.'

Gus sat alone in his Barbican flat and poured out his second large Rémy Martin of the evening. Someone had once asked him whether he was lonely. Gus Hedges, lonely? He was much too busy to be lonely. What better way to end a busy day at the helm of one of Britain's premier news-gathering operations than to get home to a blissfully empty home, kick off your shoes, and pour out a drink? Gus examined the bottle of brandy. Perhaps he was drinking too much . . . He pushed the thought away. Nonsense. At forty-seven he was still in peak form, played squash three times a week, did ninety press-ups every morning. A few drinks were a harmless relaxant for a top-flight motivator. There was a buzz on his doorbell. That would be the takeaway delivery. He'd ordered pizza for the third time that week. Was he getting in a rut?

Gus waited by the door for the delivery boy to emerge from the lift. The delivery boy finally arrived, took off his motorcycle helmet, and revealed himself to be a delivery girl. She shook out her long blonde hair and Gus felt a vague stirring. The sensation frightened him.

'That'll be twelve-fifty, please,' said the girl.

'Sorry, young lady.' Gus tapped at his watch. 'You've got a customer guarantee of delivery within thirty minutes or fifty per cent off the price. You've taken exactly thirty-three minutes.'

29

The girl protested loudly. 'Someone tried to mug me as I came in.'

'In a Vigilante-patrolled Sleepeezie Zone? I don't think so.' Gus smiled and handed over £6.25. 'Goodbye.'

Gus sat down with his pizza. Had he been a bit mean to the girl? Perhaps he should have invited her in for a drink? No, that was a ridiculous thought. Besides, he had seen too many executives fall for some grasping temptress. Sex had a habit of wrecking people's lives. And it was such a messy procedure. Gus drained his glass, poured out another large brandy, and went over to his home computer. He would call someone up on the Internet. The information superhighway was a much safer and cleaner place to meet people. Perhaps he'd reach that oil executive in Houston; he was usually good for a computer chat. Last night they'd spent an hour discussing how to motivate a team. THERE IS NO FAILURE, ONLY FEEDBACK is what had come up on Gus's screen. Gus liked that a lot. He'd noted it down. Yes, this guy in Houston really understood what made people tick.

Gus gazed at the screen and munched on his last slice of pizza as he waited for the connection to come through. Why was it taking so long? Truth was, the info super-highway was full of electronic tailbacks nowadays. The interractive paradise promised by the big manufacturers back in the early nineties had proved to be a bit unreli-able. Last week Gus had ordered up a video game called *Sonic The Hedgehog Breaks Into Top Management* and found to his horror a pornographic movie appearing on his screen. He'd stabbed Exit immediately, but the screen refused to clear. In a frenzy of disgust, Gus had pulled the power plug out of the wall, resulting in the loss of all his secret documents on 'Financial options for Globelink'.

Gus was just typing in the password to get him through to his soulmate in Houston when the videophone rang. Oh damn! He hated having a videophone at home, but nobody took you seriously if you only had one of the old audio ones. He hurriedly checked himself in the mirror, put on his jacket, straightened his tie, and went over to the phone. He'd positioned it carefully, so that the camera was trained on a chair behind which several media awards were carefully arranged. He was about to pick up the phone when he realised that the brandy bottle would be in shot. He moved it, picked up the phone. A bleary Damien appeared on the screen. Oh God, what did he want at this time of night?

'Gus. It's Damien.'

'Yes, I can see that,' Gus replied drily. Would people never get the hang of using these things?

'Gus, I need an overnight in Brecon. There's something I want to check out here in the morning.'

'I'm afraid that's not a viable option, Damien. You'll be over budget.'

'But I think I'm on to a really good story. An army scandal. Several mysterious deaths.'

Gus was sceptical. 'And your source is . . . ?'

Damien hesitated. 'A . . . a squaddie.'

'A squaddie,' repeated Gus. 'In a pub, presumably?'

'No, actually, it was in a brasserie.'

'A squaddie. In a brasserie. Of course.'

'Honestly, Gus. I reckon it could be a very tasty exclusive.'

'What, like the puma?'

Damien fell silent.

Gus's voice took on a vicious edge. 'Get your arse

back to base, all right?' Gus slammed down the phone. He moved across to the window, gazed out at the London skyline and tried not to think about the delivery girl's hair.

Damien stood in the video phonebox of the Brecon Arms Inn and decided to defy Gus. Full of resolve, he booked a room. When he actually saw the room he felt a little less resolved. He undressed quickly and slid into bed. Oh God, nylon sheets. There was a faint crackle of static as he pulled up the covers to his chin. The smell of damp in the room mingled gently with the fumes from the paraffin stove. Still, he'd known worse than this. Discomfort was the price a front-line journo often had to pay in order to pursue the truth. Sod Gus. This was story worth chasing. It could be big. Could be mega.

Damien fell asleep rehearsing his BAFTA acceptance speech.

Two
December 2nd, 1999

The archive room of the *Brecon & Radnor Clarion* was a time-warp. Dark brown walls, ancient green metal filing cabinets, and bare electric bulbs. Damien lugged a huge file of newspapers over to the ink-stained desk. They covered the period January to October 1999. He turned to the births and deaths column.

Two hours later, Damien closed the file thoughtfully. Eleven officers from the local regiment had died in the previous five months. Their ages ranged from twenty-three to fifty-eight. But the announcements of their deaths were curiously brief. No 'after a long illness', or 'peacefully at home'. No mention of hospitals. No mention of the circumstances at all. Odd. He stood up and pulled on his coat.

'That'll be twenty-five pounds access fee,' said a voice. Damien turned to see a smiling young man in a suit. Damien groaned; the *Brecon & Radnor Clarion* was not as old-fashioned as it looked.

The Coroner's Office, on the other hand, was every bit as old-fashioned as it looked. The stooped old lady behind the enquiries desk appeared to be in the early stages of rigor mortis. She stared blankly at the list of names Damien had given her.

'Dead, are they?'

'Yes,' said Damien, gritting his teeth.

'What did they die of?'

'I don't know. That's what I'm here to find out.'

The old lady was racked by a bout of coughing. She spat copiously into a paper handkerchief. Damien took a step back and waited. The old lady recovered her breath. 'We won't have any record of them here if they died of natural causes.'

'I'm aware of that,' said Damien with forced politeness.

'Well, did they die of natural causes?'

'I don't know. That's what I'd like to find out,' Damien repeated.

'I see.' She stared again at the list for a long time. 'They won't have been murdered. We don't get a lot of murders in this part of the country. Unless you count the Birdwatcher of Llandefaelog Fach. Terrible that was. Man in an old Barbour jacket went into a council meeting and shot dead five people. Said they hadn't been doing enough to protect wildlife. Turned out he was a comedy writer.'

'How interesting. Um . . . my list?'

'Oh, yes,' said the old lady. 'Are these people dead?'

Damien took a deep breath. 'Yes.'

'Hmmm. Did they die of natural causes?'

'I DON'T KNOW!' roared Damien.

The old lady stared at him malevolently. 'You'll have to wait. Take a seat over there.'

Damien sighed and sat down on a hard wooden bench in the chilly entrance hall. A poster on the wall opposite detailed one's rights under the new Victim's Charter. If you were the victim of a criminal act, it listed the target response deadlines for the police, the legal profession and the aftercarers.

He heard another grotesque spasm of coughing from the old lady and recalled, with a shiver, that TB was now rife throughout Wales.

'What do you mean, Sir Roysten's not available?' Gus asked plaintively. This was the third time in as many days that he'd failed to get through to the owner of Globelink. 'Of course I realise he has a busy schedule. But I would be most grateful if he could find a window at the earliest opportunity. Thank you.' Gus put down the phone. What was happening? Why was Sir Roysten being so remote? Gus hero-worshipped Sir Roysten and desperately wanted to be his best friend. Gus was loyal. He was Sir Roysten's main man. He looked up as Helen strode into his office.

'Take a look at this,' she said, and put a newspaper on the table.

Gus found himself looking at the City pages of *The Times*. 'Merchant Holdings' was circled in red. Sir Roysten's interests were extensive. They covered everything from gravel mining to film-making, from fertilisers to hamburgers, from Personal Rubber Products Plc to Globelink News International. Gus studied the figures carefully.

'There's been another burst of frantic trading in Merchant Holdings. What's that mean for us?' asked Helen.

Gus looked up, his face a smiling mask. 'I'm not entirely with you on this one, Helen. Does the post of Assistant Editor include a watching brief on the share price of Merchant Holdings? Only I don't recall that being in your job description. Or am I mistaken?'

'Please don't patronise me, Gus! Our jobs could be

on the line here. People have a right to know what is happening with their future. We are not just pawns in some high-rolling game of financial roulette!'

'I think you'll find that pawns are not used in roulette, Helen.' Gus leaned casually back in his chair, savouring his riposte.

'Has Sir Roysten discussed it with you?' asked Helen.

'Are there birds in the sky?' said Gus, feigning nonchalance.

'And what did Sir Roysten say?'

Gus got out his silver Relax-U-Balls. 'Well, Helen, I really can't divulge the content of a confidential conversation, now can I?'

'But it affects everybody here,' said Helen, thumping the desk for emphasis.

Gus thought she was pushing her luck. Perhaps he would get the gentlemen from the Oriental Casting Agency back tomorrow and tell them just to follow Helen around. He slowly rotated the Relax-U-Balls in the palm of his hand. 'The thing is, Helen, and you must try to get your head round this, in the business jungle, information equals power. If I gave you the slightest hint of Sir Roysten's intentions, that data would be profit-sensitive.'

Helen jabbed a finger at him. 'People matter more than profits. Employees have rights, you know.'

'Dear, oh dear,' chuckled Gus, 'living in the past a bit, aren't we?'

'Yeah, well you want to be careful. If people feel they're being kept in the dark, you might end up with a strike on your hands.'

Gus burst out laughing.

Helen felt embarrassed. It would be very difficult to

organise a strike. The NUJ had disbanded eighteen months earlier, due to lack of members.

'Thank you for that, Helen. I love a good laugh.'

Helen responded to her embarrassment, as always, by upping the stridency. 'Sir Roysten can't just treat people like dirt, Gus.'

'Want to bet?' Gus said to himself.

Helen went for a bluff. 'We may just write Sir Roysten a letter, expressing our grave—'

Gus sprang to his feet. 'You'll do no such thing! Need I remind you, Ms Cooper, that without Sir Roysten's vision, his energy, his entrepreneurial nous, *none* of us would have a job. So let's have a little bit of gratitude feedback, eh?'

Gus's phone rang. He picked it up. 'Gus Hedges . . . Ah, right. Hold on one moment, will you?' He covered the phone and looked pointedly at Helen. 'It's Sir Roysten. For me.'

Helen took the hint and left the room.

Gus waited till she had closed the door behind her. Then he took the call from the dry-cleaners about his silk tie which had gone missing the previous week.

It was Dave's job to sift through the day's news stories and select ones that might be worth a place in the next bulletin. When Dave had started doing the job, ten years ago, it had seemed quite exciting. Now he was seriously considering a change of career, or even a change of country.

To cap it all, now he'd been given a *really* boring job, looking back through the film archives to choose suitable footage for Globelink's *Millennium Special – The Twentieth Century Remembered,* which was scheduled for transmission in the final hours of 1999. For the next few weeks he would have to spend endless stints in this tiny edit suite, wading through tons of bloody videotape.

He'd already watched what felt like the entire First World War. He had fast-forwarded through the Depression. He'd picked the usual bits of the Second World War, like the Blitz, Dunkirk, Hiroshima. He'd also gone for Suez. The Cuban crisis. Profumo, because he fancied Christine Keeler. Kennedy's death. Moon landing. Watergate. Gulf War. Overthrow of apartheid. Fall of Gorbachev. Robert Maxwell's death, because that was funny. Maastricht. The massacre in Tiananmen Square. The Pergau Dam disaster. He had now reached 1998, the year of the horrendous nuclear accident at Thorp. Staring out from the small monitor was the frozen image of the technician whom the Enquiry had blamed for everything.

Dave hit Rewind, leaned back in his chair, and watched images of the Nineties dance past. A decade soon flashes by, he thought. Ten years ago his hair was brown, not brown with occasional silver highlights. And his boyish good looks had been exactly that – boyish. Last week a woman friend had told Dave that his face had become 'more interesting'. Dave knew what she meant. And he didn't like the sound of it. He hit Pause. Yes, Leon Brittan was as ugly as he remembered. He spooled back some more, looking for anything that might lighten the tone a little. He caught a fleeting glimpse of Concorde and hit Pause again. Whatever happened to supersonic passenger flight? According to the predictions of the seventies, we were all supposed to be whizzing around in thousands of commuter Concordes by now. Instead, the last Concorde had just had a preservation order slapped on it.

Dave heard the discreet beep of his portable video-phone. Dave was the only person at Globelink with a See-u-Fone. He'd paid for it himself. It had seemed a good investment at the time. It meant every time he spoke to a woman caller he could check her out. Dave picked up the phone. A dark-haired woman with high cheekbones appeared on the screen. 'Hi, Dave,' she said archly.

'Hi!' said Dave.

'It's been ages. You said you'd call me.'

'Right,' Dave replied vaguely. The face was familiar. But what the hell was she called? That was the trouble with videophones. With the old audio ones, callers auto-matically gave you their name. Now you were expected to put a name to a face the minute the phone rang. He'd have to get rid of the damned thing. He stared at the videophone screen. She had great bone definition, he'd give her that.

'So, how's tricks?'

'Great,' Dave replied. 'And you?'

'Ace. How about we do supper at Lou Pescadou tomorrow? I'm inviting.'

Then it all came flooding back. She was that brigadier's daughter he'd met at a party in Knights-bridge. They'd smoked some dope (not so much fun now it was legal) and ended up screwing in the room where all the coats were put. Yes, that was her.

'We can relive our adventures in sunny Dorset,' she said.

Shit, it wasn't her. Dorset, Dorset, he couldn't even remember visiting Dorset. Hang on though, yes, Dorset, the weekend course at Lyme Regis, yes, of course, the researcher from the Beeb with the rather nice little rose tattoo on her left buttock. Dave was unaware of Joy standing behind him. There was contempt in her eyes as she observed the conversation.

'You haven't forgotten me, have you, Dave?' asked the dark-haired woman.

Wendy! That was her name. Thank God. 'Course not, Wendy. How could I?' Dave wondered whether or not he wanted to see her again. He'd been going out with a nice Scottish girl called Maisie for the last two months, and he'd sworn to be faithful. On the other hand, those cheekbones . . . He moved closer to the screen.

'Listen, I, er, I'm a bit busy at the moment. Can I call you next week?'

Wendy shrugged. 'Fair enough. If you really mean it.'

'Sure I mean it. We'll go dancing or something. I know a great new Latino club.'

'OK,' said Wendy, with a hint of scepticism.

'You're a very beautiful woman.'

'Yes, I know.'

Dave felt a frisson of excitement. At that moment Joy leaned over him and held a sheet of paper in front of the videophone lens. On it were written the words 'DAVE SCREWS AROUND'.

Furious, Dave grabbed the paper. 'Piss off, Joy!' He turned his attention back to Wendy. 'Look, I'm sorry, there's a sick woman here who thinks it's funny to—'

The screen went blank. That settled it. He was definitely getting rid of the videophone.

Joy plonked some more tapes in front of him and went out. Henry came in. 'Why's Joy laughing?'

'Because she's just humiliated somebody.'

'Oh, right,' said Henry sitting down. 'I've redrafted the voice-over for the 1998 bit.'

Dave moved to an adjoining machine and fast-forwarded to the one sequence he'd already edited. There was still masses to do. And Gus insisted he wanted it finished inside three weeks. Not long ago he would have told Gus the schedule was impossible. But the fear engendered by the mysterious Japanese visitors was producing a miraculous transformation in working practices. Dave stopped spooling.

'Here we are. 1998.'

'Try this,' said Henry. He cleared his throat. ' "March 1998. And in the wake of Portillogate, the Conservative government looks set to lose a crucial vote of confidence. In an eleventh-hour deal with the Liberal Democrats, the government agrees to bring in Proportional Representation. A year later, in Britain's first PR election, eighteen different parties win seats at Westminster. After four weeks of negotiation, a government is formed: a rainbow coalition of the Conservatives, the Pensioners' Power Party, the BNP and the Keep Sunday Special Party. On 3 April, 1999, crowds in Downing Street hail the new Prime Minister, Sebastian Coe. The famous athlete's rise to power is—" '

'Best not say that,' Dave interrupted.

'Best not say what?'

'Athlete. Sounds slightly suggestive, doesn't it, y'know? Athlete. Sexual athlete. Best call him a runner.'

'Oh for Christ's sake.'

'You know how touchy Gus gets. Why risk it?'

Henry tore up his draft of the voice-over. Everyone was so mealy-mouthed these days. He looked at the pictures of Seb Coe smiling and waving on the steps of 10 Downing Street.

'I used to like him,' Henry said. 'How can someone

41

who ran with elegance and style be such a noxious little tightarse?' He shook his head. Thirty-seven years as a journalist had failed to excise his sense of wonder at the unpredictabilities of politics. Who would have predicted in 1985 that communism would be abolished within a few years? Who would have thought at the start of 1990 that Margaret Thatcher would be shafted by her own party? Who would have forecast Mandela as President of South Africa? And who would have predicted that in 1999 Britain would be led by a man whose only significant achievement was to make David Coleman look intelligent on *A Question of Sport*?

'Oh, sod it,' said Henry, 'let's voice the juicy stuff. You know, 1994. Back-to-basics. All that self-righteousness and kinky sex.'

'Oh, all right then,' said Dave.

He spooled backwards from 1998 towards 1994. More images flashed past at speed. Wars. Earthquakes. Domestic stories. Every ten seconds or so, in a succession of dazzling outfits, Princess Di would appear, announcing her retirement from public life. Another recurrent image was David Mellor. Every news story that broke, there he was, banging on about the barbarism of the media.

Henry hit Pause and caught Mellor in a particularly sanctimonious expression. Henry hated Mellor. And with good reason. Mellor was the enemy. He fiddled with the keys of the caption generator.

The face of the Chairman of the Broadcasting Ethics Commission was acquiring the caption 'David Mellor: Waste of Space', when George entered the edit suite.

'Oh, honestly,' George groaned. 'When are you two going to grow up?'

42

'I don't know,' said Henry. 'When are we two going to grow up, David?'

'Hard to say really, Henry. But I'm definitely looking forward to puberty.'

'Yes, me too.'

George shook his head sadly. 'You really are pathetic sometimes.'

Henry leaned back in his chair and stared hard at the Editor of Globelink News. 'George, I feel "pathetic" is a word you should use sparingly, given your choice of cardigans.'

George winced a little inwardly. But then he remembered the book's advice. 'You only get jibes from stunted lives'. Besides, George was aware that his dress sense was not all it might be. But he was going to do something about that. He would dress with more élan. From now on he would be a stranger to Milletts.

'What can we do for you, George?' asked Dave.

'I just came to see how you were getting on,' said George.

'Why?' said Henry.

It's not easy being supportive, thought George.

'We're getting on fine, George,' said Dave. 'Though obviously we'll get on a bit quicker if people stop dropping in and asking us how we're getting on.'

George thought this was a fraction rich, considering that he'd arrived to find Henry sticking graffiti on to David Mellor. 'Well maybe I'll just sit in with you for a bit,' he said. 'Maybe bounce a few ideas around.'

Henry and Dave exchanged weary looks.

'Talk me through what you've got,' said George, perching himself casually on the edge of the table.

'All right, eyes down,' said Dave. 'I'll show you where

43

we've got to on our "back-to-basics" montage. You know, Shirley Porter and friends. Tim Yeo spending more time with his families. Stuff like that. No problem if we include all that, is there, George?'

'Oh, I shouldn't think so.' George folded his arms. 'Roll it for me, Dave!' George liked being in the tiny edit suite with Dave and Henry. It made him feel like one of the lads.

Three
December 3rd, 1999

'And then guess what I found at the Brecon coroner's office?' Damien stopped pacing for a moment and looked round the newsroom. Helen was tapping away at her terminal. George was binning several bottles of pills. Dave was betting Henry £50 that he could remain completely faithful to Maisie till the end of the year.

Damien raised his voice. 'Listen, will you? OK? Eleven officers from the same regiment died in the last six months. And those eleven officers all died in the same way. They all committed suicide. Now is that peculiar, or what?'

Joy walked past, distributing the post. Damien felt he wasn't getting the attention he deserved. 'Helen, are you taking this in?'

'Yes, Damien.'

Damien moved closer. 'Well, I reckon, right, that these guys who've all topped themselves must have something in common. Apart from being dead, I mean. You see, my theory is, there's got to be some sort of connection.'

'Yes, but we can't broadcast a theory about a connection, can we?' said Helen.

'Well, no, obviously. Thank you for that insight. Look, we have to convince Gus to let me go follow this up. I need time, resources.'

Joy handed Damien a letter. 'From that nutter in Droitwich who thinks you're the Anti-Christ.'

'Look,' said Damien, tearing up the letter without reading it, 'this is worth chasing. I can feel it in my bones.'

'We'll discuss it later.' Helen clapped her hands. 'OK, people. Running order!'

Gus appeared and took a seat in the corner. 'Right,' said Helen.

'OK, this is what we've got so far. Lead item. UN resolution condemning Russian attack on Cyprus. Got some good pics of the shelling of Larnaca. Then we've got the growing incidence of piracy in the English Channel.'

Dave and Henry burst into a quick chorus of buccanneering 'ooh-ahs' and 'Shiver me timbers, laddie'. George joined in with a belated 'ooh-ah'.

'Yes, yes, very good,' said Helen, without even bothering to look up. 'There's decent footage of the Russian pirates sentenced for hijacking that Sealink ferry. Then it's the piece on Prozac, you know, this new claim that it might be linked to personality problems.'

Gus shifted uneasily. He'd been on Prozac for the last two years, and never felt better. What was all this nonsense about personality problems?

'Let's see. Middle of the running order still a bit open,' Helen continued, 'but final item looks like the woman who went into hospital for a tonsil operation and had both her legs amputated.'

Gus stood up. 'It's all a bit . . . downbeat, isn't it? Not exactly designed to zap our viewers full of feelgood factor. Now, is it? Tell you what . . .' Gus came over to George, putting an arm round his shoulder. 'Let's downsize the Prozac item. No point in getting people alarmed. And instead of the legless woman I think we might end on something light and bright, don't you?'

Sally gave a deep sigh. 'Things haven't been the same since they got rid of the monarchy. I used to love doing those little tail-pieces on what Princess Di was wearing on her ski holiday.' She shook her head and went back to counting her fan mail.

Gus was rummaging through a pile of tabloid newspapers on the desk. 'Here we go. Look. "Giant Chicken Found in Powys". So big its legs collapsed under its own weight. Perfect! Keep the tone light. You know the sort of thing – "Fowl Deeds in Powys". And what about – this? "Vicar to Eat a Hundred Tulips to Raise Money for Children's Charity". That's the perfect Globelink story – zany yet heart-warming.'

Damien couldn't take any more. 'Oh for God's sake!' he exploded. 'Here we are talking about running items on fat chickens and tulip-eating vicars, and you won't let me follow up what could be a very big story down in Brecon.'

Gus hooded his eyes in irritation. 'People committing suicide is not a story,' he intoned wearily. 'People commit suicide all the time in this country. In increasing numbers, in fact.'

'Yes, but—'

'But me no buts, mister,' Gus snapped. 'Or else I may raise the question of why you stayed on an overnight when you'd already received executive instructions to the contrary and why instead of a report on army privatisation, we end up with sweet zippidy-dip!'

'The privatisation story was crap,' yelled Damien. 'You should see the uniforms, they're laughable. It's an insult to send a front-line reporter like me to cover a poxy little whocares story in the middle of the backside of bloody beyond!'

Gus wondered for a moment whether he should fire

47

Damien on the spot. He decided he would cut a better figure by being above the fray. He beamed his most benign smile. 'We're obviously not making full use of Damien's incredible energies, George. Put him on to the vicar story.' Gus then announced that he was going for his powernap. He'd read about powernapping in a magazine. Fifteen-minute breaks in a darkened 'sleep module' were de rigueur among management high-fliers in Japan and the US. Though Gus found he could never sleep. So he just used to draw the blinds, take the phones off the hook and pretend he was having a snooze.

Once Gus was gone, the rest of the running order soon took shape. The police being issued with cattle prods was given a place. So was the latest outbreak of malaria in Norfolk. The other health story – the Minister for Energy denying that electromagnetic waves from power cables were harmful – found itself in direct competition with the Prozac item. So it got elbowed. To keep Gus happy, the giant chicken was squeezed in (though Henry threatened to refuse to read it out) as was the tulip-eating vicar.

There was ninety minutes to go to the lunchtime bulletin. So nobody was showing any real urgency, apart perhaps from Helen. She asked herself for the millionth time why so many of them did bugger all for a couple of hours and then subjected themselves to short bursts of blind panic just before the bulletins hit the air. That weekend time-management course in Lyme Regis had been a complete waste. Nobody had remembered anything. Nobody paid attention to her wallchart showing all the micro-deadlines throughout the day. She looked around. Dave was on the phone putting £50 on Hitachi Lad. Sally was nagging George about the harshness of the lighting in the news studio (it made her look severe and less feminine). And Henry was leaning back in his chair, yawning. 'Anyone fancy a bite to eat in the canteen?'

'It's only eleven thirty, Henry,' said Helen.

'Yes, but it's Friday, after all. I've got a hard weekend's sailing in front of me, so I feel a proper hot lunch and a glass of vino would build me up a bit. Had nothing but sandwiches all week.'

'You don't need building up. You need slimming down,' said Joy. 'Oh, and you owe the biscuit kitty one pound fifty.' Joy rattled the tin in front of him.

Henry put the money in the tin and slid a hand over his paunch. Joy was right. Though she was cruel, Joy was always right. God, was there anything more depressing in this world than a woman who was always right? Mind you, that young Polish piece he'd met at the sailing club two weeks before hadn't seemed to mind his belly. In fact, she had slapped it and said, 'What a big belly. I suppose with you the woman always has to be on top?' It had seemed safe to regard this as a green light, albeit a faintly insulting one. In response, he had leaned over and said, 'I am reliably informed that size of belly doesn't matter. It's what you do with it that counts.' She'd turned a bit chilly after that. Perhaps he had gone too far too fast. He'd had to settle for a date two weeks later. And now the two weeks were almost up. Yes, thought Henry, as he decided to defer lunch for a token ten minutes, there were still young women around who appreciated the wisdom and maturity of the older man. Though not, he had to admit, as many as there used to be.

Henry became aware of Damien hovering beside him. Damien had 'hidden agenda' written all over him.

'Um, er, are you, um, doing anything this weekend, Henry?'

49

'I'm on a promise, old boy. Polish filly. Gorgeous. Can't keep her hands off me.'

'Oh, right,' said Damien, disappointed. Damien crossed to Dave, who was filling out his Littlewoods Fantasy Football Form. 'Um, Da-ve.'

'Ye-es,' answered Dave warily.

'You agree with me, don't you, that Gus is wrong, that there is something in this Brecon thing?'

'Yeah, well you know what Gus is like. He hates stories about death. Unless it involves thousands of foreigners and a lot of telegenic rubble. He also hates stories that might upset people in high places.'

'Why should people in high places be upset by a story about a few army officers topping themselves?'

'Don't be naïve, the army's in the middle of a very tricky privatisation.'

Damien sat down next to Dave and looked round to make sure no one was listening. 'I'm going back to Brecon this weekend. In my own time. Want to come?'

Dave cackled. 'What?'

'We could drive down in your car.'

'Oh, I get it. You need a chauffeur.'

'I just thought you might like to come.'

'To Brecon?' said Dave. 'In Wales. In December. I'd rather spend the weekend snorkelling in a septic tank.'

'Come on, be a pal. I need help.'

'Look, it's not my fault you got yourself banned.'

'Aw, come on, that was blown up out of all proportion. All right, so the lollipop lady was a bit shaken.'

'Damien, she had to retire.'

'It's only three hours' drive, Dave.'

'No way.'

'You'll like Brecon.'

50

Dave cackled again.

'Please, Dave.'

'N-O equals No.'

George came over, with a slightly awkward smile on his face.

'Dave, I wonder whether you'd like to come to my house for supper tomorrow night. I'm preparing a dish from my new Italian cookbook.' Dave blinked. 'Yes, I know I don't exactly have the reputation of being a bon viveur, but well, you know, I feel I have to start living a little more . . . expansively. And it should be rather a pleasant little evening. I've invited the couple next door. He's in office stationery retailing. And I've asked Helen and Joy, they really seem quite excited by the idea.' George turned to Damien. 'Now, Damien, I don't want you to feel you're being left out' – Damien didn't feel left out. Damien felt relieved – 'only I don't feel quite confident about cooking for too many people at once. This is all rather new for me. But I'd like to do this on a regular basis over the next few Saturdays, so everyone's turn will come round. I think it will be good for the team spirit if we all start socialising together a little more, don't you? So, Dave, what do you say?'

Dave could think of no worse way of spending a Saturday night than at a dinner party hosted by George. It would be excruciating. 'Um, I . . . It's very nice of you, George, but . . . but . . . but I'm . . .' Dave found himself floundering. 'But I'm going for a hillwalking weekend with Damien,' he heard himself say.

'Oh, really? I've been thinking I could do with branching out a little myself in that area. I've written off for some brochures about whitewater rafting. One can so easily get into a rut, can't one?'

Dave and Damien struggled to come to terms with the idea of George going whitewater rafting.

'Well, never mind, Dave. You two enjoy yourselves. You're both young, and there's nothing worse than finding your youth has gone by and you haven't done the things you wanted to do. But I insist you come round soon. I'd like to experiment with a recipe for Hungarian bean stew that I saw in last Sunday's *Observer*.'

'Right,' said Dave. 'Look forward to it.'

George moved off.

'I blame the millennium,' said Dave. 'It's having a very odd effect on people.'

Damien was grinning. 'Right. So it's a weekend's hill-walking in Brecon, then.'

Dave began to protest.

'Uh-uh-uh,' said Damien, wagging a finger. 'Otherwise I tell George you told him a fib and he is mortally offended, which is it to be?'

Dave's shoulders slumped.

'Good,' said Damien. 'We'll leave at seven. Soon as I've banged off the vicar story.'

Damien checked that the little church of St Botolph's was in shot behind him and then looked into the lens. He would give Gus exactly the kind of pap he wanted. He took a deep breath. 'In an age of crime, violence and cynicism, it's heartwarming to find someone who still cares about the poor and disadvantaged. Here in the heart of Surrey, the Reverend Thomas Hedley is about to consume one hundred tulips to raise money for the tens of thousands of Dutch people who were made homeless in March when the North Sea overwhelmed so many of Holland's coastal dykes. Thanks to the generous intervention of Interflora, the tulips are already . . .'

The cameraman pulled back to reveal the Reverend Hedley standing beside an enormous pile of tulips. An Interflora banner flapped gently in the wind. The poor man looked rather pale. At a signal from Damien, the small crowd of parishioners began the countdown. 'Ten. Nine. Eight. Seven . . .'

Gus kicked off his shoes and paced up and down his living room, watching Damien's report as it climaxed to a backing track of 'Tulips from Amsterdam'. Yes, that was what he called a final item. And Damien had done an excellent job. He'd managed to mention Interflora no less than seven times in the space of three minutes. Discreet product placement was making an increasing contribution to Globelink's revenue.

The bulletin came to an end (with the synthesized fanfare Gus had commissioned) and the weather girl appeared. She had a bright girl-next-door manner and good teeth. Gus marked her down as a potential newsreader. She ran through the prospects for the weekend. Raining again, thanks to the volcanoes in Iceland. Then she informed the viewer, very cheerfully, that the ozone warning was only amber and that the benzine count was average. Gus picked up the remote and adjusted the flat's air filtration system to high. He liked to breathe purified air. He didn't want any toxins polluting his body and deadening his mental reflexes. He set his remote to TV and then pressed Scan. The remote automatically blipped from channel to channel, changing every ten seconds. Gus smiled to himself when he thought how people used to get up and walk to the TV to change channels. What an inefficient use of time that was.

As the blipper hopped to Channel Fourplus (the station aimed exclusively at high-income viewers) Gus straightened in his armchair. The screen was filled with a picture of Sir Roysten's face. He cancelled the Scan function and concentrated hard on the details of the report. In essence, it was saying that Sir Roysten was rumoured to be re-financing, in a desperate bid to save his commercial empire. An alarming graph appeared on the screen and Gus hit the off button on his remote.

'Tittle tattle,' he said, the words resonating around the vast expanse of his flat.

Gus did some stretching exercises. He felt strangely on edge. Maybe he'd ring up the agency and hire a late-night squash partner. Or perhaps he'd ring for a pizza.

He got up and crossed to the enormous windows which faced on to the centre of the Barbican Piazza. A shadow flashed past the window. Probably an eagle. Eagles had been introduced as a way of keeping down the rats. Away to his left, Gus could see the blue-white aura hovering above the Tower of London. It was the Son et Lumière. 'London's Millennium – a pageant of 2000 years'. Every evening, around eleven, it would climax with a noisy re-enactment of the Blitz. Gus was fed up with it. He was fed up with seeing holograms of Spitfires chasing holograms of Messerschmitts past his window. To be honest, he was fed up with the whole build-up to the millennium. It seemed to have been dragging on for years. He didn't feel particularly thrilled by the approach of a new century. In fact the thought of it gave him a leaden feeling in the pit of his stomach. It would just be more of the same. Another eagle flew past the window. Gus drew the curtains and rang for a pizza.

* * *

Sally almost went past the junction. She braked sharply and swung the wheel to the left. The car behind hooted loudly. She breathed a sigh of relief at leaving the motorway behind. As she emerged on to the A303 she switched to full-beam. She quite liked driving in the dark. There was something faintly illicit and exciting about it.

She continued along the dual carriageway, keeping an eye open for the sign to Andover. The meeting was due to start at ten the next day. The organisers had tried to persuade her to drive up on Saturday morning, but Sally had insisted on overnight accommodation. Didn't they realise she needed at least two hours to get dressed and do her make-up? She had no intention of rising at six o'clock on a Saturday morning merely to chair the press launch of a new charity. And all for a miserable £200. It was demeaning. Almost as demeaning as opening supermarkets. But then she had to maintain her profile somehow. Things were not looking good on the career front. She had failed to get the *Newsnight* job (which she couldn't understand). She had even failed to get that three-week holiday stand-in for Lady Porter on her afternoon talk show.

Sally flinched as she heard the roar of a juggernaut overtaking her. The juggernaut drew level with her. It was left-hand drive. An unshaven, olive-skinned man with very black hair leaned out of the window and blew her a kiss. Sally quickly looked away. As the truck passed her, she saw the Italian number plates. That explained it. An English driver would have made an obscene gesture. But the Italians had style – their shoes, their clothes. She wore lots of Italian stuff.

She was still a good twenty miles from Andover when the landscape was illuminated by a flash of lightning. Seconds later, the windscreen wipers could hardly cope with the sudden rainstorm. She screwed up her eyes as the lights of a vehicle behind filled the driving mirror. This journey was going to take longer than she'd hoped. She wanted a coffee. Gratefully, she caught sight of thirty-foot-high neon-lit Frenchman waving a four-foot baguette.

Sally pulled into the crowded car park. The café was designed to look like a château – only smaller. It looked very vulgar, but Sally really needed that coffee. She slammed shut the car door, bent into the driving rain and ran towards the entrance. Thank heavens she had brought that umbrella. Ten seconds in this rain would have destroyed yesterday's three hours at the hairdresser.

Sally recoiled when she saw the queue at the counter. Oh God, a coach party. But she craved the caffeine. She disdainfully pushed her way past the noisy, jostling crowd, who appeared to be putting in a mass order for boeuf en croûte. They would realise she was in a hurry. 'One filter coffee, please, black, no sugar. In a clean cup, if you don't mind.' Sally knew the level of hygiene in these places was quite beyond the pale. She heard a gruff male voice behind her.

'Here. Aren't you Sally Smedley?'

Sally looked around. It was always gratifying to be recognised. She found herself looking at a small, plump man in a shell suit.

'That's right, yes.'

'From Globelink News?'

'Quite correct.' She waited to be asked for her autograph.

'You're crap.'

Sally struggled for breath. Was there no limit to the vileness of the common man?

'You're also jumping the queue, darling.'

Sally felt it would be too humiliating to argue. She tossed her head in the air and walked away. Oh damn, damn, damn! Now she couldn't have a coffee. She was certainly not going to go to the back of the queue. One had one's status to think of.

The rain had become even heavier by the time Sally emerged from the building. She took a deep breath and ran towards her car. The lights of a nearby juggernaut flashed on and off. And then she saw him again. He was leaning out of his cab, smiling down at her, a flask of coffee in his hand. 'You are wishing a coffee?'

Sally hesitated. It would be foolhardy in the extreme to get in with him. God only knows what he had in mind. On the other hand, he had a lovely smile. And she did desperately want a coffee. And it was probably rather good Italian coffee . . .

It was warm in the cab. The driver smiled as he handed her a cup of thick, black espresso. 'My name is Sergio.'

Sally nodded and reached out to take the cup. She was careful to keep a two-foot space between them. She sipped gratefully at her coffee.

'And your name?'

'Jane,' said Sally, watching for any sudden movement. Her eye travelled up his jean-clad legs.

'I am seeing you earlier on the road, I think?'

God, what a beautiful accent. Sally nodded again. She risked a sideways glance at him. He had a dangerous gypsy quality about him. And his designer stubble reminded her of that Albanian crane driver she'd once met. She smiled at him, noticing the small cobra tattoo on his forearm.

'Sometimes my job it is very lonely.'

'Yes,' said Sally, trying to suppress a little tremble in her voice. 'So is mine.'

Sergio looked at her a little more, then reached out and gently touched her on the arm. '*Lei è una donna molto bella. Molto bella. Anche molto simpatica.*'

Sally's head began to swirl. Oh, that sensuous, languorous language of love. He was staring at her again. Please don't touch me again, she prayed to herself, at the very edge of the abyss.

'You know, I am a big fan of yours, Sally.'

Sally tried to focus on his words. What was he saying? How did he know her real name? Oh, heavens, was this going to be some sort of blackmail?

Sergio laughed. 'I understand. You are having so much of the public adulation, you must keep the name secret. But in Italy I am seeing you on satellite every night. With you I am improving my English.'

'Oh,' said Sally.

Sergio was scrabbling in the glove compartment; he pulled out a pen and notebook. 'Please, I am so happy if you are giving me your autograph.' He bestowed another dazzling smile. 'Ah, yes, you are beautiful. You remind me of my mother.'

'Oh,' said Sally.

'It is not for me,' said Sergio, handing her a pen.

'For your son? Your daughter?'

'For my boyfriend.'

Sally wailed inwardly. And gave him her autograph.

By the time Dave's car reached the centre of Brecon the rain was coming down hard. Dave scowled at Damien. 'Where now?'

'Widows,' Damien replied.

'Widows?'

'Yuh. I took a list of the officers who committed suicide. Eight were married. We track down the widows. We pump them for information.'

'We?'

'Yeah.'

'It's not my story, pal.' Dave drew up outside the Brecon and Bavaria Building Society. 'You do the sniffing. I'm just the chauffeur, remember?'

'All right then,' said Damien. 'I just thought you might be interested in meeting the widows, that's all.'

'I'll just book us into a hotel.'

'Fair enough,' said Damien, preparing to get out of the car. 'You book lodgings. I'll find the young widows.'

'Yeah, you find the young widows.'

Damien waited for the inevitable.

'When you say young widows, Damien, exactly . . . how young?'

'Six of the officers were in their mid-twenties.'

'Uh-huh.' Dave drummed the steering wheel pensively with his fingers. 'Oh, all right then, if you insist, I'll help you out.'

'That's very big of you,' Damien smirked.

'Well, why not?' said Dave. If he was going to spend the weekend in this rain-lashed town he could at least try to enjoy himself. Maisie would understand that. He was helping Damien, that was all. Yeah, she'd understand. 'Right, what are we waiting for?' said Dave.

It was obvious that Amanda had got over the death of her husband. She leaned over towards Dave. 'Shall we have a bottle of champagne?'

Why the hell not? thought Dave. He glanced over at

Damien, who was sitting nervously on the edge of his leather armchair. Damien hadn't really wanted to stay at the Lloyd George Hotel, because it was so bloody expensive. In fact, the prices were so outrageous that they'd had to take a double room, which pleased neither of them very much. Still, Dave was confident the hotel was the right setting to put the widows at their ease. Amanda was certainly at her ease. She'd accepted their invitation to drinks with alacrity. A bit too much alacrity, in Damien's view.

'You're looking bushed, Damien.'

'No, no, I'm fine.'

Dave realised he would have to be more direct. 'Didn't you say something about wanting an early night?'

'Oh! Yes. Right, I think I'll um . . . I think I'll just have an early night.' He stood up. 'So. See you in the morning, then?'

Dave nodded. 'Good night, Damien.'

Damien gestured discreetly in Amanda's direction, indicating that Dave should get information out of her.

'Good night, Damien,' Amanda said, pushing back her long auburn hair and flashing him a glossy smile.

You wear far too much lipstick, thought Damien, and headed for the door.

'He's a real sweetie,' Amanda said when he'd gone.

'Yeah, yeah. He's . . . OK, I suppose.' The waiter came by. 'Excuse me,' Dave called out.

The waiter grudgingly approached.

'What?' he asked, looking Dave over suspiciously.

Dave knew how to put waiters in their place. Especially when he was in the company of an attractive woman. 'I'm sorry, did I hear you say, "Yes, sir, what would you like, sir?"?'

'No, you didn't.'

'Well, I'd like a bottle of Bollinger, please.'

The waiter ran his eyes over Dave's leather jacket and designer jeans. He detested these flash young Englishmen who swanned around Wales snapping up the best women and the best country cottages.

'It's fifty-three pounds fifty a bottle.'

Dave gulped. But he couldn't back off now. 'I'm not terribly interested in the price, actually.'

Amanda giggled. He was definitely making a good impression.

The waiter trudged off. Dave leaned back in his chair with a mischievous grin. She was gorgeous.

'So,' said Dave, 'tell me a bit about yourself.'

Amanda began to open up.

Damien hadn't gone to bed. He resented Dave casting him in the role of wallflower. He would go to bed in his own good time, thank you. When he was sleepy. And not before. So, as he walked out of the restaurant, he had turned left into the Tom Jones Gala Ballroom.

The ballroom was not really a ballroom. It was just a large room with a bar in it. A plastic chandelier hung from the ceiling, throwing out a greasy yellow light. The dark brown carpet was sticky from decades of spilled beer. And in front of a big dusty bay window was a podium with a four-piece jazz band on it. Luckily, they were not playing. Damien hated jazz. It was music for people who couldn't be bothered to remember the tune.

He crossed to the bar and ordered a Branson's tonic water with ice. He felt a light tap on his left shoulder and turned to find himself facing a shortish, well-built man in his late thirties.

'Excuse me,' said the man, 'only this room is booked

61

for a private function. Sorry about that.' The man had obviously been drinking. He was holding his pint of beer at a sixty-degree angle so that it was slopping over the side of his glass. 'It's my stag night, see.'

'Congratulations,' said Damien. 'I just want to buy a tonic water, then I'll leave you to it. I'll take it up to my room.'

'No, no, no,' said the man, swaying backwards. 'No, you don't understand, I've paid for the room, see. Exclusive use thereof. Seven till twelve. And if people I don't know come in for a drink, then it's not exclusive use, is it? Do you see my point?'

'I'm Damien Day. How do you do? See, you know me now, so that's OK, isn't it?' Damien tried to catch the barman's eye, but the barman just turned away; he didn't want to get involved.

'No, no, you don't understand,' the man repeated, raising his voice and lurching slightly to his left. 'This room is booked in the name of Gareth Pugh. That's me, see? Booked for my stag night, it is. For me and my friends. And I don't know you. Now I'm asking you, polite like, to please leave.'

'I will leave,' said Damien, with a smile.

'Good chap.'

'After I've got my drink.' Damien turned away from the drunk. If there was one thing worse than being told to leave by Dave, it was being told to leave by an irritating Welsh squirt.

Suddenly Damien felt a sharp poke behind the left shoulder blade.

'OK, Sonny Jim,' yelled the drunk, 'if that's how you want to play it. Come on, I'll bloody have you!'

A gaggle of friends rushed over to restrain him.

'All right, Gareth, calm down, now,' said one.

'Yes, Gareth, do calm down,' mocked Damien.

'I think you'd better just go, mate,' said a huge friend with a cauliflower ear.

'I just want a drink.'

'Oh, give him his bloody drink,' muttered Gareth. 'Then he can bugger off.'

The barman poured Damien his tonic water.

'Thank you, Gareth,' said Damien, 'that's very big of you.'

This last remark had an extraordinary effect on Gareth.

'And what's that supposed to mean, sunbeam?'

'Sorry?'

'That's very big of you, what's that supposed to mean, eh? Eh?' Gareth thrust his head towards Damien, his little glazed eyes trying to focus. Again, his friends held him back.

'Sorry,' said the huge friend with the sprouting ear. 'He's a bit touchy about his height, see.'

'Oh, I see. He's touchy about being a bit of a shortarse, is he?'

'That's it,' shouted Gareth. 'I can have him! I can! Let go of me! I can have him!'

'Here,' said another friend, 'aren't you on the telly?'

With this magic phrase, Gareth stopped struggling. All the aggression went out of him. 'On the telly?' he said, with a small bubble of saliva coming out of his mouth.

'Yes. Damien Day. Globelink News.'

'Oh, yes, I know,' said the cauliflower ear, 'always running around war-zones in safari jackets. What are you doing in Brecon, then?'

'You took the words right out of my mouth,' said Damien.

'No, no,' said Gareth, pointing a wobbly forefinger at Damien's nose, 'he's that comedian, isn't he? Thingummybob with the catchphrase.'

'No. I'm Damien Day. Front-line reporter. See?' Damien produced a crumpled business card and tucked it into Gareth's top pocket.

'There, if ever you're lying critically injured in a motor-way pile-up or trapped in a pit disaster, please don't hesitate to call me.'

'Cheers,' said Gareth, with a burp.

'My pleasure.'

Gareth's face was a bleary moon of vacantness. Damien had a desperate urge to punch it.

'Well, good night all,' said Damien, paying for his drink, 'and, Gareth, I wish you well. Good luck on your wedding day.'

'Cheers, pal!'

'And don't forget your words,' Damien laughed.

Gareth and his friends laughed.

'And don't forget the ring.'

They all laughed some more.

'And on your wedding night . . .' The laughter turned boozy and lecherous, 'don't forget your stepladder.'

They all roared with laughter. Damien gave a raffish wave and strode jauntily out of the bar. By the time Gareth realised he'd been insulted, Damien was gone.

Damien woke with the sound of Dave's voice in his ear. He sat up.

'What's going on? What time is it?'

'About one thirty. You couldn't bunk down in the

bathroom, could you?'

'No, I bloody well couldn't.'

'Shhh! Amanda's outside in the corridor.'

'Good. Because she's not coming in here.'

'Oh, come on, Damien. Don't be so mean.'

Damien switched on the light. 'I am not being mean. I am being reasonable. Go back to her place. It's not as if she has a husband, is it?'

'Her mother's staying for the weekend. And she's got a three-year-old kid.'

'Tough shit!'

Damien pounded his pillow and prepared to go back to sleep.

Dave was desperate. 'Look. This is all research. I'll get lots of information out of her. Bed's the best place for that. I'm not doing this for myself, you know. I'm doing it for us.'

'Oh, yeah,' Damien sneered.

A soft voice came from the corridor. 'Dave? What's happening?'

'Hang on! Be with you in a minute. Just clearing up a bit. I left this room in a terrible mess.' He turned to Damien. 'Fine. We'll just have to do it in the next bed, then.' He was sure that would work. He was right.

Damien leaped out of bed, grabbing his duvet and a pillow, and marched into the bathroom. He hissed at Dave. 'You'd better get something out of her, Charnley.'

'Oh, I will,' said Dave.

Four
December 4th, 1999

Breakfast next day was a tense affair. Damien nibbled on the soggy toast, his head buried in the *Guardian*, while Dave tucked into egg, bacon, tomatoes, mushrooms and fried bread and gave thanks for the revival of the traditional English breakfast.

'Aren't you going to ask me how I got on?' asked Dave.

'No.' Damien continued to read about the escalating conflict in Cyprus, got bored and turned to the back page. It looked like the Pope might be about to sanction the use of condoms, provided they were Vatican-approved brands.

Dave crunched on the fried bread. 'It went quite well, actually. Hungry lady.'

Damien's lip curled in distaste. 'Well, she would be, wouldn't she? Her husband's been dead for six months.'

'Yeah and before that he'd turned impotent. It seems that's why he topped himself.'

'How disloyal can you get? Going around telling strangers about your dead husband's sexual problems. It's disgusting.'

'Women always confide in me. I think they trust me.'

'Only very stupid ones.' Damien put down his paper. 'Why should he top himself just because he's impotent?'

'I would. Wouldn't you?'

'No.'

'Yeah, well it would be less of a loss in your case, wouldn't it?'

Damien ignored the provocation. 'Suicide's a bit of an over-reaction, wouldn't you say?'

'Maybe not if you're in the army. Pretty macho outfit, right? I mean it's probably a bit demoralising to go out and bayonet foreigners to death when your willy's a limp rag.'

Damien looked at him. God, Dave could be tacky sometimes.

Dave kept on eating. He wasn't going to admit it to Damien, but in reality he felt a bit depressed. These one-night stands were beginning to make him feel ridiculous. He'd been giving serious thought to settling down with Maisie. She wanted them to live together. Maybe that would be quite nice. Solid domestic routine. Children. Nappies. Mortgage. Home at the same time each night. Goodbye to wild adventures in hotel rooms. No, perhaps he wasn't quite ready for it yet.

Damien poured some more tea and picked up the *Brecon & Radnor Clarion*. NEW TOILETS TO BE FINISHED SOON, roared the front page.

'So,' said Dave, mopping up a pool of fat with a slice of toast, 'what's the plan of action for today?'

Damien looked glum. 'I dunno. Talk to more army widows, I suppose.'

'Right.' Dave flashed a lascivious grin. 'Maybe I'll order another breakfast.'

Sally turned her head slightly to the right so the photographers would get her best profile. Frankly, she was

67

astonished by the turnout. Who'd have predicted such a crowd for the launch of a new charity? Mobile Phone Addiction Stress Disorder was obviously the coming illness. She looked around the hall. At least four national newspapers had sent reporters and photographers. There was even a crew from Berlusconi Weekend Television. Oh, dear, Gus wouldn't be too happy about that. Technically, it was a breach of her contract. Oh, to hell with Gus! Globelink was on its uppers anyway. More cameras flashed. She realised a question was being addressed to her.

'May I ask Sally Smedley whether she is herself a sufferer from this new syndrome?'

Sally thought quickly. She rarely used mobile phones, she thought they were common. She cleared her throat. 'Yes, I have gone through a great deal of pain because of this disorder. I have experienced the characteristic panic attacks if I have tried to do without my mobile phone. The fear of being isolated, cut off. In fact there was a period when I was unable to sleep unless I was clutching my mobile, like a teddy bear. But you know,' here Sally lowered her voice to add a certain timbre of compassion, 'there are so many people worse off than myself. I'm here because I want to do whatever I can to help. In my own small way.' With tremendous skill she pursed her top lip and then let it quiver, as if she were holding back the tears. A fusillade of camera shutters echoed through the hall. God, this felt good.

As Sally was leaving, the organiser came up to her. He shook Sally's hand and handed her an envelope. 'Thank you so much, Miss Smedley. I think we got off to an excellent start.'

Sally noticed a television camera pointing in their

direction. She put up a hand in a gesture of refusal. 'No, please, I couldn't possibly accept any fee. Not even expenses. I did this because I care.'

It was a gamble. Normally she would never refuse a cheque. And two hundred pounds was two hundred pounds. But, in the greater scheme of things, she felt it could turn out to be the smartest investment of her life. She had spotted a way of raising her rather neglected public profile. She would move into the caring game. She would find a cause and become its media angel. That would get her more screen time, more good crits, and more full-page spreads in *Hello!*. All good for her brand-image.

A fat man in a suit appeared at her shoulder. On his lapel was a little badge – 'Get off the phone, get in touch with yourself'. He smiled warmly at Sally.

'Could I have your autograph please, Miss Smedley?'

Yes, it was starting already.

Henry felt humiliated. Going aground on a falling tide was an elementary error. How could he have been so stupid? Now it was beginning to get dark, and he faced the prospect of spending the best part of the night having to cook, sleep and shit at an angle of forty-five degrees. As if that wasn't bad enough, he was going to miss his date with lovely Polish Lissa, whom he'd arranged to meet that evening in the Bull's Head.

Henry clambered up on to the sloping deck of *The Bosanquet*. The sun was setting behind Osea Island, throwing out a subtle changing blend of greens, reds and yellows. That's the upside of air pollution, thought Henry, it does make for nice sunsets. He could hear the shrill buzz of the jet-skiers as they sliced back and forth across the Blackwater Estuary. They were mad, of course. Horrible, mad upwardly mobile oiks, who'd reduced Henry's unassuming little sailing paradise into a shell-suit hell of discos, ghastly seafood restaurants and Ford Warrior GTs. Sailing, Henry reflected, was not what it once was. He remembered a time when the waters around Maldon more or less belonged to the Old Gaffers' Association, of which Henry had been a proud member for over twenty years. He gazed lovingly at the teak deck of his gaff-rig double-ender, built in 1930 by Albert Strange, probably the best boat-builder England had ever known. Now the world was all fibre-glass hulls and Bermudan rigs and naff little Hunter Horizons, which looked like floating caravans. It had all become so horrible that Henry now preferred to sail in the winter. Most of the wankers in designer outfits were too wimp-ish to venture out in the winter gales. Even if the jet-skiers were a pain in the arse, at least there was nobody water-skiing. Water-skiers really were a boil on the backside of humanity. A few summers back, Henry had discovered that a long rope dragged behind his yacht would lie just below the surface and be invisible to an approaching skier. It was hugely gratifying to watch the bastards flip face down at twenty knots, and come gasping to the surface wondering what on earth had hit them.

The raw wind cuffed Henry around the ears. It was great to be alone, to be breathing sea air. He felt it was blowing away all the clog and clutter that filled his brain after a week in that damned office. Hell's bells, the office was depressing these days. Short tempers. Long faces. Strange Japanese visitors. This boat was his therapy, his salvation.

A flight of Brent geese crossed the sky above him. It

70

always amazed Henry that geese flew in formation. How did they work out which goose went at the front? And why bother with a formation? Did it help aerodynamically? Was it just habit? Why were geese so organised in the air and such an unruly rabble on the ground? He would ask David Attenborough next time they were having a few lagers.

Henry lowered his gaze and wondered whether he really needed to put out the anchor. To do so would entail wading through twenty yards of mud to the seaward side of the boat. She was hard on – there didn't seem to be any danger of her being blown off in the next few hours. And right in front of him he'd spotted a sandspit which led to the shore. Which led to Maldon. Which led to the Bull's Head. Wherein waited the lovely Lissa.

Mrs Macedo's bungalow on the outskirts of Brecon was the very model of taste. Damien eyed the Laura Ashley wallpaper, the little glass animals on the mantelpiece, and the collection of enamelled eggcups by the window. He stretched out his hands to warm them at the gas flames of the imitation coal fire. Mrs Macedo came back into the room, carrying a tray. Damien watched as she laid out the delicate bone china on the low table in front of them. She was in her early forties, with darting brown eyes set in a small child-like face. Her movements were swift and precise. She reminded Damien of a sparrow.

It hadn't been difficult to track her down. Armed with his list of the dead officers' names, he had combed the local telephone directory. It seemed unlikely there would be a huge number of Macedos in Brecon. Damien had half expected to get the brush-off when he phoned, but she'd been very chatty, and immediately invited him to

71

come to her home. You could never tell how people would respond to the media. Some of them treated you like the Black Death, while others couldn't wait to tell you their life story. For a moment he wondered how Dave was getting on. Dave had volunteered to check out a Mrs Torrington-Evans, widow of Captain Torrington-Evans, aged twenty-eight.

'Milk and sugar?'

'Er, neither, thanks.' Mrs Macedo handed Damien his cup. The handle was too tiny to get any kind of a grip on it. He gingerly cradled the cup in his right hand. He considered how he was going to approach the question of her husband's death. Trouble was, he didn't really know what he was after. All he could hope for was to establish some kind of common factor in the demise of these officers.

Mrs Macedo sat back in her Parker-Knoll and smoothed her frock. 'So. You'd like to know about my husband's death?'

Damien nodded. She didn't beat about the bush, did she?

'He killed himself,' she said, picking at a loose thread on the armchair.

'Yes . . . Do you have any idea why?'

'He was depressed. But he wouldn't tell me what was worrying him. Bloody annoying really.'

Damien sipped at his tea. How could she be so matter-of-fact about her husband's death? 'When did the depression start?'

'About six months before his death. Just after our wedding anniversary. Not that we celebrated our wedding anniversary. No, no, sadly it clashed with a regimental dinner. Officers only. He was obsessed with

72

the regiment. Kept scrapbooks full of regimental trivia. Pictures of mascots. Four pages of goats in frocks.'

Damien sipped at his tea some more. 'How did this depression manifest itself?'

'Oh, all kind of ways. Became strangely withdrawn at home. Wouldn't talk much. Not that we ever really talked a great deal, anyway. I never quite understood why he married me in the first place. Sex, I suppose. About the only thing Tom was any good at. Surprising, really, considering his public-school background. They're all homosexual at heart, you know. They don't really care for women. Too complicated for them. Toasted crumpet?' She held out the plate. Damien, grateful for the pause, took one. Mrs Macedo carefully removed a crumb from her lower lip. 'So, of course, when Tom became impotent, there wasn't really much left of our marriage.'

Damien swallowed hard. This was really embarrassing. He felt sorry for Tom Macedo. He even felt a bit sorry for her. She obviously hadn't had much of a marriage. Come to think of it, that widow Dave had screwed last night, what was her name? Amanda, yes. She obviously hadn't had much of a marriage either. Was it something about army wives that made their husband impotent?

'Will you be making a programme about army marriages?'

Damien stared into his cup. 'Um . . . it's a bit early to say. We're still very much at the research stage.'

'I see.' Mrs Macedo adjusted her string of pearls. 'If you do, will you promise me you'll show them to be the bastards that they really are?'

At this point Mrs Macedo burst into tears.

* * *

Helen looked apprehensively at the bowl of plain spaghetti in front of her. It was quickly congealing into one huge sticky lump. She wondered whether she should tell George that it was a mistake to leave spaghetti for so long without putting the sauce on it, but she didn't want to hurt his feelings. And judging by the desperate clatter coming from the kitchen, George was already stretched to the limit.

Joy broke the silence. 'This was a mistake, wasn't it? What a way to spend a Saturday night.'

'Keep your voice down,' said Helen. 'It means a lot to George and—'

'Why do we always have to defer to men's feelings? That's what I'd like to know.'

Helen poured herself a glass of the Valpolicella laid on by George. It was an ominous dark purple colour. 'Do you defer to men's feelings? I hadn't noticed.'

Joy sipped at her mineral water. 'Well, it's not a problem you have, is it?' She noticed a frown cross Helen's brow. 'Oh, I'm not being critical. I'm very pro-lesbian. Sex without men, great idea.' Joy toyed with her fork. 'I've been thinking about having a baby. On my own, of course. It's dead easy. Just get some remotely intelligent and good-looking bloke to jerk off into a jar, pop the contents into a Sainsbury's basting syringe, one quick squirt and you're banged up without all the problems of relating to a man.' Joy pronounced the word man in a curious tone, as if it were a synonym for 'worm'.

They stopped talking as George came in. The merits of artificial insemination was not the kind of topic to put George at his ease. And he seemed quite nervous enough already. George hurried over and placed a steaming pot on a large plastic table mat which 'celebrated the British Hedgerow'.

'Here we go,' he said brightly, and poured the sauce over the spaghetti. 'It's called *Spaghetti alla Putanesca*.'

'Tart's spaghetti,' said Joy.

'Yes, I believe it does mean that,' said George, colouring slightly. 'It's a Neapolitan dish. So, I . . . I suppose there are quite a lot of ladies of the night in Naples.'

'Looks delicious,' Helen said.

Joy shot her a quick glance.

George was having trouble stirring the sauce into the spaghetti, which now resembled a glutinous football. 'Oh, dear,' he said glumly. 'It seems to have gone a bit wrong. It said it was a simple peasant recipe.'

Helen touched him on the arm. 'It'll be fine, George.'

George smiled and started spooning aggregated lumps of pasta on to Helen's plate. Joy couldn't look.

'I'm sorry it's just the three of us tonight. The couple next door were going to join. But his back's playing up and she's gone down with this Belgian flu. So . . .' George's next sentence was completely drowned out by the staccato roar of a pneumatic drill. 'Sorry about that,' George shouted above the din. 'Cable company are working all hours digging up the street.'

'Yes, we had to climb over their trench,' Helen shouted back. George grimaced. 'Little bit irritating really.'

The drill stopped and, for a second, George found himself shouting unnecessarily. 'Quite bothersome.' He adjusted his volume. 'They've taken ages.'

Joy stared at the ominous zigzaggy crack in the dining-room wall. 'Did they cause that?'

George glanced over his shoulder. 'Hm? Oh, yes. They've accepted liability, but as they've destabilised all the houses in the street, they said it would be some months before they could get round to fixing me. So, in the meantime I've got my own builders coming in on Monday to underpin the house.'

'How much is that going to cost you?' Helen asked.

'Oh, I'll claim it back from the cable company. Anyway, I'm not letting it get to me, that's the important thing. I've the book to thank for that. It's shown me how to put things in perspective. So I've got a few problems with my house; there are people in this world with no house at all.' George spread his hands in a carefree Mediterranean way and attempted an Italian accent. 'So, tuck in, *amici*. After this, it's *Saltimbocca alla Romana* and an *Insalata mista*.'

'Lovely,' said Helen.

Dave was getting information from Mrs Torrington-Evans. So far he had found out that she was a Gemini and that she liked to experiment with frightening sexual positions. He was exhausted. They were now lying, naked and sweating, on the living-room floor. Dave had suggested, at quite an early stage, retiring to the bedroom. But Mrs Torrington-Evans had started kissing him so vigorously that it rendered further conversation impossible. She kissed him so hard that his lips hurt. She also tore his shirt.

'I hope I wasn't too rough,' she sighed, her face glowing pink.

'No, no,' said Dave, wondering how he would explain the love-bites to Maisie.

'It's just I was feeling a bit pent-up, you know.'

'I understand.'

'It's been a long time.'

'Really, I do understand. When did your husband . . . pass away?'

She clambered on top of him. Oh no, thought Dave.

'It had been a long time, even before he died, actually.'

'Oh . . . I see,' said Dave, experiencing a moment of *déjà vu*.

'Oh, well, not his fault,' she said. 'Seems to be a pretty common problem. I kept telling him not to get so depressed about it. But, well, I suppose it's important to a man really, isn't it?'

'Yes, I suppose so,' said Dave, worried by the look in her eye.

'Now then,' she whispered, cupping his testicles in her hand, 'second helpings.'

'No honestly, George, it was delicious,' said Helen, 'but I'm totally full up. Very generous portion. Couldn't eat another bite.'

'Me neither,' said Joy, hurriedly.

'Oh, right,' said George, and cleared away the half-eaten Saltimbocca alla Romana. He turned at the kitchen door. 'Never mind. Soon we eez eating zee dolce!'

Helen and Joy exchanged a glance of quiet despair.

George came back with a bowl of rather sinister tiramisu. The pneumatic drill gave a quick ten-second blast outside the window, which left their glasses tinkling gently on the table. George spooned out generous helpings of dessert. The two women watched in silence.

'Well,' said George, 'this is nice. Two colleagues round for dinner. Exotic food. Fine wines. We must do this more often.'

Helen smiled. Joy toyed with the tiramisu.

'So,' said George, reaching for a topic, 'how's that young daughter of yours, Helen?'

'Oh, Chloë's fine.'

'Any boyfriends on the horizon?'

'Yes. Yes, she's going steady.'

'Isn't that nice! What's he like?'

Helen hesitated. 'Well, he's called Martin. And . . . and she's fond of him. Which is all that matters, I suppose.'

'Absolutely,' agreed George. 'Quite right. When you're keen on someone it doesn't matter what other people think, does it?'

Both Helen and Joy wondered whether George was making a veiled reference to Alison. He'd been engaged to Alison a year earlier. They'd met in the doctor's waiting room. George was soon going around introducing her to people as 'Miss Right'. The engagement party was an enormous success. But the following day Alison had mysteriously changed her mind and posted back the ring. Since that day no one had heard George mention her name.

George topped up their wine glasses and tried to keep the conversation going. 'It's hard for a parent though, isn't it? You must never make them feel like you're interfering. I remember I criticised my Deborah's choice of boyfriend once. She was furious. Made miniature effigies of me and her mother with little spears through our chests.' George chuckled nostalgically. 'We came home and found them on the Christmas tree.'

Helen looked at George, appalled.

There was another silence. Joy began to long for the pneumatic drill to start up again.

'So, Joy,' asked George brightly, 'did your dad ever disapprove of any of your boyfriends?'

Joy's eyes blazed. 'That's none of your business, George.'

78

George blinked. 'Sorry.'

'All right, Joy, steady on,' said Helen.

'We're not at work, Helen, so please don't boss me around, OK?'

'God, why are you so angry about everything?' Helen asked.

Joy's spoon clattered as it flew into the serving dish. 'Don't try to psychoanalyse me, for God's sake!'

'All George asked was—'

'I know what he asked, and I've said it's nobody's business, do I have to spell it out in blood, for Christ's sake?'

George made a conscious decision to distance himself from all this conflict ('Do not carry the baggage of others', Chapter Eight).

The drill started up again.

What a bloody unmitigated disaster! Henry tore savagely at the branch in front of him. Where the hell was the path back to the estuary? Everything had gone wrong from the minute he'd stepped on to that sandspit. Because it wasn't a sandspit. It just looked like a sandspit. He had got to the Bull's Head caked in mud up to his waist. Everyone had given him a round of applause when he marched into the bar. He'd tried to look nonchalant, of course. It wouldn't do to let Lissa think he was troubled by a little bit of estuary mud. Real sailors didn't mind about stuff like that.

Unfortunately, Lissa minded. She found the mud 'disgusting' and 'smelly' and 'frankly a bit off-putting'. God, she was stuck-up. Over his fifth litre of Theakstons, Henry had watched her walk out on the arm of an odious young poseur in an Italian football shirt.

Henry gave a sigh of relief as he finally broke through on to the shore. He shone his flashlight out across the mudflats. Damn! The batteries were going. The feeble beam finally picked out his boat. He gave a great sigh of relief and flicked off the flashlight to preserve what was left of its power. The tide had turned but – thank God – there was still too little water in the estuary to have floated her off. It wasn't going to be easy getting out there, though. He swayed slightly. He shouldn't have drunk so much, he couldn't hold it like he used to. And he was getting too old for chasing women in bars. Tomorrow, he resolved, he would spend the entire day sailing on his own, let the wind blow the toxins and the wenches out of his system.

Christ, the water was cold! Only halfway out to the boat, and it was up to his knees. The estuary mud sucked greedily at his feet with each step. He paused, fighting for breath. Was that a pain in his chest? If he had a heart attack here, he was definitely a goner. He'd already had a coronary ten years ago. The doctors had told him to change his lifestyle. He'd told the doctors he would cut down to just four acts of excess per day.

He leaped with fright as a mallard lifted noisily out of the water a couple of feet in front of him. He took a few more laboured steps. The tide was running fiercely against his legs. Must be careful not to fall. What was that noise? He stopped and listened, but could hear nothing now. He switched on the flashlight. The beam flickered and died. But he had glimpsed the outline of his boat. Not far now.

The water was up to his waist by the time he reached her. He was gathering his remaining strength to hoist himself up on to the deck when he heard voices. They seemed to be coming from his boat.

'Hey!' he bellowed. There was a scrabbling from inside the cabin and a figure suddenly loomed on the deck above him. He found himself blinded by the beam from a powerful torch.

'Who the fuck are you?' Henry enquired fiercely.

'Might ask you the same question, mate.' There was the sound of muffled laughter. Hell! There were two of them. He grabbed the rail and hoisted himself up. A hand pushed him in the chest and he fell backwards. He came up gasping with the shock of the icy water.

'Get off my bloody boat, you bastards!'

'Sorry. You see, it's not actually your bloody boat. Technically speaking. Not any more.'

'We'll see about that,' Henry answered.

'We're claiming salvage.'

'No, you bloody are not.' Henry slowly moved round to the other side of the boat. He found his way blocked by a jet-ski.

'Did you put out the anchor, then?'

'No, I . . .' Henry stopped. Oh Christ! In law, any boat found below high tide without an anchor out was, technically speaking, a wreck. Anyone finding it had the right to claim salvage. Which meant the bastards on the deck above him could lay claim to maybe a quarter of the boat's value.

Henry sensed he wasn't going to win this one by brute force.

'Look,' he said, adopting a tone as reasonable as possible in the circumstances. 'Let me come on board and we'll talk about this. And take that bloody light out of my eyes!'

'OK. But no violence, all right?' Again the two men sniggered.

81

Henry laboriously pulled himself on to the deck. 'Now,' he said, fighting for breath, 'please get off my boat and we'll discuss this in the morning.'

'Sorry, mate. 'Fraid we'll have to discuss it now.'

Henry fought back waves of rage. Was there a chance of pushing them both into the sea and then bashing them on the head with a marlin-spike? He shielded his eyes against the glare of the torch and tried to gauge how big they were. They sounded young. And tough.

'Tell you what,' he said. 'I'll give you fifty quid. Fair enough?'

'No. Not nearly enough, grandad. We were thinking more about . . . say, ooh, a couple of grand?'

Henry gasped. 'Go fuck yourself!'

'OK, then. We'll file for salvage.'

'Look. I'll make it sixty quid. That's all the cash I've got on me.'

'No problem. We'll take a cheque.'

'Yeah, we'll take a cheque,' said the other. 'Only if it bounces, next time you come looking for your boat, you'll find it very badly damaged.'

Henry sneezed. The sound echoed across the estuary. He was shivering with cold and trembling with impotent rage. He sneezed again.

One of the men laughed. 'Not really worth getting pneumonia for the sake of a couple of grand, is it?'

Henry grimaced. The same thought had just occurred to him.

'Damien! Damien! Wake up!'

Damien struggled awake, reached out for the light. He stared up blankly at Dave. He turned to the bedside clock. It was two in the morning.

'Damien, listen, I—'

Damien went berserk. 'No, Dave, I will NOT bunk down in the bathroom! And I am NEVER EVER going to share a hotel room with you again! And why don't you grow up, and stop screwing anything that's got a pulse!' Damien switched off the light and pulled the duvet over his head.

Dave switched the light back on again. 'Damien, listen—'

'Je-sus!'

'Damien, I'm going back to London. Now!'

Damien blinked, and for the first time registered Dave's pale sweating face. 'What's going on?'

Dave grasped him by the shoulder. 'Mrs Torrington-thingy, we, were, y'know, and she starts saying let's do it again because she really needs it and it's been such a long time since she—'

'I don't want all the details, thank you.'

'OK, OK, the point is her husband couldn't manage it either. Like Amanda's husband.'

Damien sat up in bed. 'So bloody what?'

'But it gets worse, OK. After she and I have done it a couple of times—'

'I said, cut the details.'

'OK, OK, she starts talking, right, she says when hubby lost the ability she felt unfulfilled and lonely and all that and pulled one of his army mates, another captain. At least she thinks she's pulled, because when they get down to it, nothing happens, he can't cut it either. A while later, after the husband's died, an officer comes round on behalf of the regiment to see if there's anything she needs. She says she's feeling—'

'Unfulfilled and lonely.'

83

'Correct,' said Dave. 'Anyway, they start kissing, one thing leads to another, then it stops. He can't manage it either. So, of course, the poor girl's been thinking it's all her fault, right, that she's got this weird ability to turn willies to water. Until tonight.'

'You always have to boast.'

'Shut up and listen! The point is, I don't think it's anything to do with her.' Dave paused, out of breath. He gave Damien a sideways look. 'Did your Mrs Macedo tell you anything?'

'Well,' said Damien, 'um, by an extraordinary coincidence . . .'

'Oh no,' groaned Dave. 'Right.' He picked up his suitcase and started packing at extraordinary speed. 'This place spells erection-killer. I'm out of here.'

'You're kidding!'

'It gives me the creeps.'

'Be rational.'

'Sod rational. There's a pattern. Something in the air, in the water. I dunno. Anyhow, I'm off, before I find out.'

'Hang on. So a few blokes are impotent. Probably just a coincidence. Or maybe the army attracts sexual inadequates.'

'I think not,' said Dave, slamming shut the lid of his suitcase. 'We've been here twenty-four hours and we've already found five cases. And that's just the ones we know about. How many more are out there? I mean, impotent blokes don't stroll around saying, "Good morning how are you oh by the way I can't get it up!" '

Damien stared at him. 'Are you seriously tying to suggest you can get impotent just by being in Brecon?'

'That's how it looks to me,' said Dave. 'And I'm not chancing it.' He headed towards the door.

84

Damien leaped out of bed, protesting. 'You can't leave me here. You're my wheels!'

'You can come with me if you want.'

'But I need to check out these suicides!'

'Fine. Bye then.' The door closed and Dave was gone.

Damien sat down on the bed and punched the pillow. What a jumpy little prat Dave was. He slid under the duvet and stared at the ceiling for a bit. He heard the engine of Dave's car cough into life. He switched off the bedside lamp and lay thinking about Dave's theory. After a few minutes' careful deliberation he formed the considered view that it was bollocks.

Five
December 6th, 1999

On Mondays, Gus always got into the office at seven thirty. He felt invigorated to be back in the front-line, brimming with energy, and ready to interface with the real world. He could never understand why everybody else seemed to hate Monday mornings. Still, other people's inadequacies weren't his problem.

He breezed past the uniformed security guard in the lobby. 'Good morning, Tim!' he boomed.

'Morning, sir,' answered the security man, without looking up from his portable television. He was absorbed in the BBC's Rolling News Channel. Terry Dicks, the Heritage Minister, was being questioned by Paul Boateng. On the screen were two sets of constantly changing scores. A klaxon sounded and Terry Dicks started putting on a bra. Tim loved these infotainment spots. He became aware that Gus had come back and was looking over his shoulder.

Gus smiled an icy smile. 'Enjoying the programme, are we?'

Poor Tim registered the smile but missed the icy. 'Yeah. Smashing fun. You seen it, Mr Hedges? They have this political argument, right, and after each one-minute round people phone in and vote for who's winning. And whoever's losing has to pay a forfeit.'

Another klaxon sounded. Gus reached out and switched off the television, as a bucket was put over Paul Boateng's head.

Gus drew close to Tim, and asked very quietly, 'Do you know who I am?'

Tim sensed he was in trouble. His figure slumped into grovel posture. 'Yes, Mr Hedges. Course I do, Mr Hedges. You're Chief Executive . . . Sir.'

'How do you know? I mean, how do you know I am not a terrorist and that in this very briefcase I am carrying a bomb?'

'Well, I know, don't I? I know 'cause I know your face.'

'I see. Are people allowed into this building without showing their security passes?'

'No, Mr Hedges, they certainly are not. I see to that.'

'Oh, good. So why was I not asked for my pass this morning?'

Tim blinked. 'Well, you're different, Mr Hedges, I mean, you're the guv'nor. And I know your face, don't I?'

Gus pointed a finger at a notice behind Tim. 'What does that say?'

'Um, it says, "All passes to be shown".'

'Very good. Does it say "All passes to be shown unless it's the guv'nor and I know his face"?'

'No, Mr Hedges, it don't, I'm very sorry, Mr Hedges.'

Gus tapped on the man's lapel. 'You are here to ensure that no thieves, lunatics or terrorists penetrate this building. That means you ask EVERYONE for their pass. ALWAYS. No exceptions. Not even me. Understood?'

'Yes, sir.'

Gus relaxed, took a pace back. 'Excellent. I'm glad we

synergised on that one, Tim. I don't want you to feel you've been reproached. You have just been for a short ride on a learning curve. My pass.' Gus flashed his security pass at Tim and, whistling, disappeared in the direction of the lifts.

'Git,' mouthed Tim.

Gus reached his office and was surprised to find Sally waiting for him. She was clutching a green folder.

'Good morning, Sally. Are we in motivation mode today?'

'Oh, absolutely, Gus, you bet,' Sally gushed.

This uncharacteristic show of enthusiasm made Gus suspicious. 'And what can I do for you?'

Sally handed him the folder.

'What is it?' asked Gus.

'It's a proposal for a new programme.'

Gus picked up the folder and riffled through it. 'It's thirty-five pages long, Sally! I don't have time to read thirty-five pages.'

'I do realise that. Which is why there's a two-page summary at the front.'

Gus glanced at it. 'Still too long. You clearly don't understand the pressures that a top executive is under. Give me a summary of the summary.'

'What, now?'

'Yes.' Gus sat down and put his feet up on the desk. 'You've got two minutes. Pitch.' Gus knew this was how they did things in Hollywood. He liked the feel of it. There was something satisfying about watching a supplicant supplicate on the other side of his desk.

Sally felt she wasn't really ready for this. She'd stayed up late last night finishing the proposal. She hoped there weren't bags under her eyes. But Gus was waiting. There was no way back.

She smoothed down the lapels of her vermilion Lacroix jacket and took a deep breath. 'Right. It's a nightly programme. Five minutes long. It's called *Globelink Cares*. It will deal with major issues of concern in our society, e.g. homelessness, drugs, crime, as well as more neglected issues, e.g. Mobile Phone Addiction Stress Disorder. It will avoid the visually unappealing, e.g. pictures of famine victims, which only depress people . . .' She was aware of Gus nodding at this point. '. . . and concentrate instead on the visually compelling. So if we show a still of a sick child, it will be an *attractive* sick child, with beautiful eyes. Not because we only want to help the attractive ones, but because only the visually appealing can help us reach out to the hearts and minds of the viewers.'

Sally leaned forward and flipped open a page in front of Gus. 'You'll find it on page eighteen under "Compassion – The Televisual Opportunities". At the end of each programme we will give the *Globelink Cares* phone number, which viewers can call with their credit-card donations. *Globelink Cares* will deal exclusively with our own native problems. Viewers are fed up with sob stories from Africa. *Globelink Cares* will care about Britain. Its slogan will be "Go on – give a damn!" Oh, and *Globelink Cares* will be presented by me.'

Sally folded her arms, tilted her head, and waited for a response from Gus. She felt quite exhilarated. She had never 'pitched' before in her life. But she obviously had a talent for it.

Gus was looking carefully opaque. That usually meant he was interested.

He stood up, playing with his Relax-U-Balls. The silver spheres emitted a delicate tinkling sound as he rolled one in each hand. 'Not unimpressive, Sally. I always felt there was a motivator in there, struggling to get out.'

Sally smiled. 'Thank you, Gus.'

'But,' he added, 'how could I clear the airtime?'

Sally had anticipated this objection. 'You won't have to. It will go out on the end of the evening bulletin. Which will simply be five minutes shorter.'

Gus looked up with a gleam in his eye. He paced up and down, squeezing hard on his Chinese Relax-U-Balls, forgetting the instruction leaflet which had told him 'to roll gentlywards your balls to induce the heavenly harmony and the sublime transcension over the daily stress'. Gus stopped pacing, wheeled round and smiled. 'Sally, I like it! It's popular. It's accessible. But are we talking financial viability here? For example, how many operators would we need for the credit-card calls?'

Sally remained unflustered. 'None. We do it all on automatic 0891 numbers. Currently costing two pounds per minute cheap rate. Let's assume twenty thousand callers a night, averaging two minutes a call. Five nights a week, and we're grossing four hundred thousand pounds a week. Half goes to Telecom, of course, but that still leaves around two hundred thousand pounds for Globelink. Less expenses, which I estimate at eighty thousand pounds and, of course, we'd have to discuss my fee. You'll find a detailed budget breakdown on page thirty-four.'

Gus examined the budget. He had to admit, it all looked pretty damned good. Yes, he would definitely go for this.

He looked up at Sally. 'Well, I'm not sure,' he said,

shaking his head grimly. 'And I really don't think we could pay you an additional fee. After all, since the bulletin would be five minutes shorter, you wouldn't actually be doing any more work than before. And given our financially straitened circumstances, I could hardly go to Sir Roysten and justify extra expenditure, could I?'

Sally gave a nervous little cough. 'I don't think we need get bogged down in any vulgar discussions about fees at this stage, Gus. Though I think you'll find that you could pay me, say, ten thousand and still make a very substantial profit.'

Gus laughed. 'Tell me, Sally, how many people recognise you in the supermarket?'

'I don't know, Gus. I'm not a Sainsbury's sort of person.'

'One in a hundred? One in two hundred?'

Sally shrugged.

'Put it this way, Sally. You're not exactly a major player in the celebrity league. On current form I'd say you rated somewhere between Jill Dando and Judith Chalmers.'

Sally winced. Sometimes Gus could be so cruel.

The young man in charge of the archive room at the *Brecon & Radnor Clarion* was, on balance, even less friendly than before. This time he demanded the £25 access fee in advance. Damien handed over the money, asked for a receipt, and started on the tedious task of ploughing through all the local news for the first few months of 1999. He wasn't sure what he was looking for. Something, anything, which might connect up with the officers who'd committed suicide. OK, so it was a long-shot, but right now long-shots were the only option.

91

Suddenly all the other widows were refusing to speak to him. Had they been got at by Farquhar?

As Damien scanned the pages of the back numbers, he found his thoughts wandering to Dave's theory that Brecon was Impotence Gulch. It was silly and irrational, of course, but rather disquieting. Not that Damien rated sex very highly. His libido had long ago been enlisted in the service of his profession. But he didn't like the thought of any unseen force interfering with his body. He would leave Brecon as soon as he could.

Damien was growing increasingly irritated by the presence of the young man, who hovered behind him like some kind of prison warder.

'I can manage this on my own, you know. I mean, presumably you've got other work to get on with?' Damien looked him up and down, wondering how the guy could afford an Armani suit.

'I'll just stay here.'

'What's your name?'

'Trevor. My friends call me Trev.'

'Then I'll call you Trevor. Listen, Trevor, please go and hover some place else. You're making me nervous.'

Trevor adjusted his silk tie. 'Can't do that, sorry. You might vandalise the archives. It's happened before.'

Damien sighed and turned back to the joys of the *Brecon & Radnor Clarion*. He hadn't realised that people still won prizes for the biggest onion, the longest carrot and the tastiest chutney.

He ploughed on grimly, struck by the number of murky photographs of people shaking hands for reasons not immediately clear to the reader. Horrible memories of his first steps in journalism began to infiltrate Damien's brain. He'd only been on the *Accrington*

Leader three months when he was put on to doorstepping the relatives of the recently deceased 'Damien! RTA! Two fatals!' the sub-editor would shout. This translated as two people dead in a road traffic accident. Damien would then turn up at the house of a grieving mother/father/daughter/son/husband/wife. He quickly became rather good at it. He used to tell them he was writing a tribute. This normally got him invited in for a cup of tea. Within ten minutes they began to feel that the *Accrington Leader* was their friend. Within twenty minutes they were unloading happy memories and handing over photographs. Within thirty minutes they were admitting that the dear departed was less than perfect. This normally gave Damien enough to run a story on the lines of CAR-CRAZY YOUTH DIES IN GLUE-SNIFFING MOTORWAY NIGHTMARE. There were quite a lot of complaints, circulation soared, and Damien was given a bonus.

The *Brecon & Radnor Clarion* for 26 February 1999 was different from all the others in one crucial respect. A hole had been neatly cut in page seven. Damien examined it with interest.

'See what I mean?' said Trevor. 'Bloody vandals.'

'This is your idea of vandalism, is it?'

'What else would you call it?'

Damien examined the page again. It was obvious that one particular story had been carefully excised. 'Very neat, the vandals round here, wouldn't you say?'

Trevor shrugged.

'I'd like to see a copy of this page. You've got another set of archives somewhere, right?'

'Suppose so. But they're not public access, are they?'

'No sweat. I'm a journo too. You can let me see them.'

93

Trevor shook his head firmly. 'That's impossible. Sorry.'

Damien stood up. 'What story is it that's been removed? And who removed it?'

'How would I know?'

'I just have a feeling that you might.'

'Well, I don't. And if I did, I've forgotten.' Trevor gave Damien a sly look. ''Course, I might remember. If you wanted to come to some arrangement.'

The breath flew out of Trevor's lungs as he found himself slammed hard against a metal filing cabinet. Damien rarely resorted to violence. Unless provoked by skinny little weasels who got on his nerves. Trevor struggled for breath.

'How's the memory now, Trevor? Or shall I call you Trev? I'd like to be your friend. In fact I'll be your friend for life if you give me the information I need.' Damien's forearm pressed a little harder against Trevor's windpipe. 'Only I'm not contributing any money to your Armani fund, all right?' Trevor made a nasty choking noise. Damien eased the pressure. 'OK, Trevor, what story was removed from that edition?'

Trevor pulled in grateful draughts of oxygen. 'It was . . . it was dead boring.'

'I'm not asking you to score it for dramatic content, Trev, I just want to know what it was about.'

'It was . . . a report on the annual dinner of, you know, the local regiment.'

'Very good, Trev. And who removed it?'

'I can't tell you that, he warned me that if—'

'WHO REMOVED IT?'

Trevor yelped in pain as Damien stabbed two fingers in the region of his kidneys. 'A bloke from the regiment. New bloke. In charge of privatisation.'

'Name?'

'I can't remember.'

Damien put his face very close to Trevor's. 'How would you feel about your eyeballs popping out of their sockets, Trev? It's incredibly easy, if you know how. And I know how.'

'Farquhar,' said Trevor quickly. 'Tom Farquhar.'

'Thank you,' said Damien, slipping his hand into Trevor's jacket pocket and taking out a wallet. Damien opened it and removed fifty quid. 'There isn't an access fee, is there, Trev?'

As he handed back the wallet, a little shower of business cards fell to the ground. Damien picked one up and read it out. 'Young Filipino brides available now.' He looked at Trevor. 'So that's how you can afford the Armani suits.'

Trevor adjusted his tie. 'You interested?'

'No thanks, Trev. I'm not sad, inadequate and Welsh.'

As soon as the corporal in the Ruritanian uniform had brought them coffee, Farquhar began to confess.

'The wrong way to do things, I know. Censorship, and all that. But not an easy flotation, this one. Well, none of them are nowadays, I suppose. And bad publicity doesn't help.'

'What bad publicity?'

Damien waited.

Farquhar carefully stirred his coffee. He seemed, unusually, lost for words. When he finally spoke, he was careful not to look Damien in the eye. 'What happened was, the colonel made an after-dinner speech which was . . . how shall I put it? Well, it could have been construed as offensive to women.'

'You mean he told dirty jokes?'

'Dirty joke. Singular. He'd drunk rather too much. Not like him, really, but I believe his marriage has been under some strain recently.'

'Oh?'

'You know the local rag. Not much going on down here, so they made a bit of a meal of it. Even Brecon is politically correct these days, you know.'

'I see. And that's why you clipped the article out of the archives?'

'Yes.'

'Could I see it?'

'Sorry. I'm afraid I destroyed it.'

'Ah. Right.' Damien adopted his most relaxed tone. 'But what was the point of cutting the piece out of the archives? I mean, the damage had been done, hadn't it? Not that I remember any of the nationals picking it up.'

Farquhar stirred his coffee again. Damien felt that, on the whole, Farquhar was stirring his coffee far too much. And what had happened to the carefully cultivated eye contact?

'Damien, I'm going to be perfectly frank with you. The officers are pretty demoralised at the moment.'

'Especially the dead ones.'

Farquhar heaved a deep sigh and stared at the floor. 'Yes, the deaths were very unfortunate.'

'They were all suicides, weren't they?'

'So you know about that?'

'Yes.'

'Hmm.' Farquhar pulled at his earlobe, and finally looked up.

'The thing is, the army's a pretty stressful environment for officers these days, what with performance-related pay and worries about privatisation. I know it was foolish to destroy that article, but it was just one more bloody pressure we didn't need.' Farquhar suddenly adopted a jocular tone. 'Can't have the great British shareholder alienated by stories of drunken regimental dinners, can we?'

Damien felt that the great British shareholder was an altogether hardier breed than Farquhar was making out.

'So there you have it, Damien, the whole story. And very foolish it makes me feel.'

'You've been very helpful.'

Farquhar accompanied Damien to the door. 'If there's any other information you require.'

'Thank you. But I don't think there's anything here I really need pursue further.'

Farquhar's handshake was firm and sincere. 'I appreciate that, Damien. Thank you.'

Damien left feeling determined to track down the missing article.

The editorial meeting had been underway for five minutes, but Dave had taken hardly anything in. His thoughts kept drifting back to the curse of Brecon. When he woke that morning, the first thing he'd done was check he had an erection. He had encountered only sleepy softness. Oh, no! He always woke with a hard-on, didn't he? Or did he? He wasn't sure any more. In the shower he'd closed his eyes and tried to visualise that girl out of the jeans advert. But instead all he kept seeing was a man with a stethoscope who looked at him and shook his head sadly.

Dave suddenly felt a stinging pain behind his ear. Joy had flicked an elastic band at him. 'Planet Earth calling Dave Charnley,' she hissed.

Dave realised that a lot of people were looking at him. Oh God, someone must have asked him a question.

'Well?' said Helen.

'Erm . . .' He was saved by a loud entrance from Gus.

'Morning team! Are we all goal-orientated today? Are we pushing out the parameters of the possible? I hope so. Because the stiff breeze of the market place is blowing our way and nobody wants to get left out in the cold, do they? Where's Damien?'

'He rang in sick,' said Helen.

'Yes,' said George. 'Gone down with this Belgian flu thing, he reckons.'

'Send him my very best wishes, George.'

George, pleasantly surprised, nodded. 'I'm sure he'll appreciate that, Gus.'

'Wish him a speedy recovery. Forty-eight hours at the most. After that he's out of a job. Sorry, team, but this train doesn't carry passengers. Not any more.'

'Oh Christ,' muttered Henry rather too loudly, 'he's turning into the Fat Controller now.'

Gus beamed extravagantly. 'Office humour. Like it.' He unfolded a sheet of paper. 'I've been looking at the proposed running order for the lunchtime bulletin. Just a few *bijou* changettes perhaps. I wouldn't dream of interfering but I do wonder if we're realising the full potential of the gerbil story. Pretty fascinating when you come to think of it. Lost gerbil walks sixty miles to be reunited with owner. Yet we've only allocated it twenty seconds! Let's get a crew out there, George. Let's get pictures, first-hand accounts. Dave, call computer graphics and get them to do us a really sexy map of the gerbil's journey home. You know, animated paw-prints, that kind of thing.'

Henry stood up and threw his notepad on the floor. 'Why not have the whole bloody news read by a sodding gerbil hand-puppet! Bong! Nuclear holocaust in Korea – two gerbils feared dead. Bong! Gerbil outsider wins the Grand National. Hell's Bloody Bells! Are we a news station any more, or are we just jelloid triviamongers?' Henry sat down, his face verging on crimson.

Gus smiled. Henry was obviously feeling insecure. That was the way Gus liked him.

'I don't think the gerbil's worth a place at all,' said Helen.

Now Gus smiled at Helen. 'Don't tell me. The staff are all prepared to strike over it.'

Sally looked up from her copy of *Hello!* ('Fergie Talks Exclusively About Her New Spiritual Advisor!') 'Well,' said Sally, flicking some fluff off the sleeve of her blazer, 'it is a well-known fact that Joseph Public likes stories about small, furry mammals. We're a nation of animal lovers.' This was an entirely political intervention. Gus had still not committed to *Globelink Cares*.

'Nice input, Sally,' said Gus. Helen prepared to dig her heels in over the gerbil. But as she drew breath to speak, Gus played his trump card. 'All I will plug into your collective matrix is that Sir Roysten Merchant himself pointed out this story to me. He feels it's the kind of viewer-friendly item we need to win the ratings war.'

Everyone in the newsroom suspected this was all a lie. But no one was going to risk a challenge.

'I'll get a crew sent out,' sighed George.

The Brecon bookshop wasn't Damien's idea of fun, but it was the only place to shelter till the rain eased. Well, not the only place, exactly, but he would rather have run naked through a swarm of killer bees than spend five minutes in the Crinkley Bottom Heritage Theme Pub. Anyhow, maybe he could buy a few books and solve his Christmas present problem.

He wandered past an enormous dumpbin displaying the winner of the Edwina Currie Award for Literature, drifted alongside a wall of Melvyn Bragg's *Lust of the Lakes*, and squeezed past the awesome bosom of an inflatable Andrea Dworkin promoting her new book, *Why I Like Men Now*. He was about to flip through *The Punt and Dennis Millennium Comedy Scrapbook*, when the word 'scrapbook' leaped out at him.

Mrs Macedo was horribly pleased to see Damien. Damien had one simple question to ask her, but he could hardly get a word in edgeways as she twittered pleasantly about the weather while lighting the imitation coal fire. Damien resigned himself to 'a nice pot of Earl Grey'. With darting, bird-like movements, Mrs Macedo laid out the tea things.

'It's extremely kind of you to come and see me, Mr Day. No sugar, no milk, if I remember rightly?'

Damien nodded.

'Would you find it very forward of me if I were to call you Damien?'

Damien shifted uneasily on the edge of the sofa. 'Um . . . No, no, of course not.'

'Oh, good. I'm Charlotte, by the way.'

Damien decided he'd better get to the point as swiftly as possible.

'When I was here last time—'

'You were wonderful. Such a good listener. After Tom died the vicar came round, you know. And the chaplain

100

from the regiment. They were both rubbish, of course.'

Damien frowned. He couldn't quite get used to Mrs Macedo's unexpected turns of phrase.

'Both complete rubbish.'

Damien noticed a tremor in her voice. He hoped she wasn't going to repeat her previous performance and burst into tears. 'Um, you mentioned that your husband kept a scrapbook, and I wondered—'

'They both kept saying that time was a great healer. Oh, yes, and God moves in mysterious ways. And Tom has gone to a better place. No wonder the churches are empty. Didn't listen to a word I was saying. Unlike you, Damien.'

'This scrapbook – was it just photographs, or did your husband collect things like . . . newspaper clippings, for example?'

She didn't seem to have registered his question. 'You know, Damien, at my age it's hard to face the thought that one has wasted most of one's life.'

At this point Mrs Macedo repeated her previous performance and burst into tears.

Damien gazed in dismay at the bus timetable. There was only one bus a week between Brecon and the nearest rail station at Abergavenny. Bloody Dave, leaving him without wheels! It would have to be a minicab to Abergavenny. He lugged his bags over to a grubby café. He needed something to eat before setting off.

Damien picked at the plate of bubble'n'squeak. Ah well, at least he'd got what he wanted out of Mrs Macedo. Mind you, it had taken two hours of tea and sympathy before he'd persuaded her to hand over the clipping from the *Brecon & Radnor Clarion*. Damien unfolded it. It didn't seem to get him very far. He shook his head and read it for the umpteenth time:

OFFICERS OF SOUTH WALES BORDERERS HOLD ANNUAL DINNER.

On Tuesday evening, the officers of the South Wales Borderers gathered at their regimental HQ for the purpose of holding their annual dinner. The hall itself was a delight to behold, being decorated as it was with flowers in many hues of pink. Following a splendid starter of consommé, the guests relished the pleasure of some excellent beef Wellington, supplied by Heslop's of Brecon, following which there was a particularly fine dessert. But perhaps the highlight of the evening was a speech from the regiment's Commander-in-Chief, Colonel Pemberton. Colonel Pemberton gave a detailed account of the challenges facing the regiment in the coming years, and wittily regaled his guests with a number of entertaining anecdotes, the fancy of those present being perhaps most taken with a daring story concerning a chorus girl, a pussy cat and a Gurkha. The colonel sat down to prolonged applause and it was generally agreed that a thoroughly enjoyable time had been had by all.

And that was it. Hardly the stuff of scandal. What was Farquhar playing at? Why the hell did he want to prevent people reading the article? The man was obviously trying to keep something under wraps. But what? The colour of the bloody flowers at the regimental dinner? And then there was Farquhar's explanation of the suicides. The introduction of performance-related pay didn't seem to have produced suicidal tendencies in other fields. Apart from the medical profession, of course.

Damien pushed aside the remains of the questionable bubble'n'squeak and worried for a moment about Dave's impotence theory. His mind was whirling. All he had so far was a tangled web of conjecture.

But in Damien's book that very nearly constituted a story.

Mrs W.E. Grindlay was wearily putting the final touches to the Minister's speech. It was getting damned difficult to make this material sound fresh. For the fourth time in three weeks the Minister for Energy was to deny that electro-magnetic fields could have any adverse effects on health. As far as Mrs Grindlay could tell, the evidence, though not conclusive, pointed pretty firmly in the opposite direction. You certainly wouldn't catch her buying a house within a mile of an electricity pylon.

Still, the facts of the matter were not her department. As head of the Flexible Response Unit her role was basically one of damage limitation. Whenever a minister screwed up, or got caught telling bare-faced lies, Mrs Grindlay's task was to come in and clear up the mess. Among the inner circle the unit was colloquially known as the Pooper Scooper.

Eleven years ago, when she'd first been offered the job, she'd felt very uneasy, and hesitated for weeks. Not only was the existence of the new department to be a tightly guarded secret (she didn't even appear in the internal phone directory), but it was clear she would have to abandon her few remaining scruples. She'd spent all her working life in the civil service, and she still recalled with affection the balmy days when civil servants were not yet the personal playthings of the Prime Minister. Since 1988, Mrs Grindlay had scooped several tons of government poop. Sometimes the scale of corruption and/or incompetence had been so great that she had toyed with the idea of just letting the truth come out in all its embarrassing glory. But somewhere deep inside she got a thrill from all the manipulations. All the feints and dummies and decoys. She had a talent for it. She enjoyed it. At least she used to. Now she only wanted to coast downhill to early retirement. In two years' time, as a sprightly fifty-year-old, she would cash her pension and head for somewhere hot. Somewhere that grew oranges and lemons and available young men.

She glanced up at the television screen flickering silently in the corner of the room. It was football. Liverpool versus Crystal Park Rangers. She liked to watch football, but couldn't bear listening to Paul Gascoigne's inane commentary. It looked like a pretty dull game anyway. She turned off the television with the remote and caught a glimpse of her reflection in the screen. She'd always known she wasn't a beautiful woman. Her chin was too prominent, and she never really liked that sallow complexion of hers. But she took comfort from her best feature: her spectacularly beautiful eyes. They were a deep liquid brown, not unlike Sophia Loren's – as her husband had often remarked. Although his admiration for her eyes hadn't stopped him leaving her after only two years of marriage. For his secretary! Even his adultery was unimaginative.

She leaned back in her chair and read the latest draft of the speech. It was still horrendously dull. The Minister would hit the roof if he didn't make it on to the news, so she would have to juice it up a bit. Perhaps she'd throw in a spirited attack on media scaremongering. Yes, the Minister would like that. Lots of jibes at 'so-called experts'.

She was just scribbling a few notes when she heard the lift doors close. That would be Mitchell going home. At last! She got up from her desk. It was almost nine o'clock. She guessed that, apart from Security, she was now the last person left in the building. But she had to be certain.

She crossed to the heavy mahogany door of her office, opened it, and looked up and down the corridor. She felt the usual icy draught on her face. Opposite her, a murky oil portrait of W.E. Gladstone frowned down at her. She'd always had a bit of a soft spot for old William Ewart, maybe something to do with the man's basic decency, maybe something to do with his murky private life. Or perhaps it was just because they shared the same initials. In any case, the first thing she'd done after being appointed was to get Gladstone's portrait hung outside her office door. In eleven years she had never once gone home in the evenings without nodding good night to him.

She looked down the corridor towards Mitchell's room. Good. There was no light showing under his door. Pity that Mitchell always worked so late. It meant she had to be extra careful in the evenings. The man had a nasty tendency to drop into her office for, as he put it, 'a chinwag'. She could never figure out why Mitchell's vocabulary was locked in a 1940s time-warp. He was only thirty-seven, yet every time he opened his mouth she felt she was meeting Trevor Howard in *Brief Encounter*.

Mrs Grindlay held open the door and listened carefully for a few moments. Complete silence. She stepped back into her office, quietly closed the door, and locked it. She switched off her anglepoise. A pale wash of light from the Whitehall streetlamps splashed across her desk. With quiet urgency she crossed to the far corner of the room and dropped to her knees. She rolled back a corner of the dark red Persian carpet and inserted a pencil into a small hole in the third floorboard from the wall. A practised twist of the pencil and the board lifted. She slipped a hand into the gap. For one awful moment she thought it had gone. Then she felt it. With one hand she wiped away a bead of sweat from her forehead, while with the other she slowly pulled out her pack of Marlboro Lights.

Crouched very low on the tiny balcony outside her office, Mrs Grindlay knew that she was invisible to anyone in the buildings opposite. Of course, there was always the risk that someone would spot the little clouds of blue smoke being tugged away by the December wind, but that was a chance that had to be taken. It would have been sheer folly to smoke in the room itself. She'd learned how to disable the smoke detectors, but that still left the risk of somebody noticing the smell the next day. Only last month a cleaner had been given a £50 reward for denouncing a smoker in the Ministry of Defence. The poor man was jailed for two months and, of course, lost his job.

The cold wind blew Mrs Grindlay's ash-blonde hair across her face. She drew deeply on her cigarette and listened to the steady roar of idling engines in the streets below. Sometimes she wondered whether society had got its priorities entirely right. Surely car pollution killed more people than smoking ever did? And you couldn't walk up to someone going past in their Volvo estate, knock on their window and say, 'Excuse me, would you mind putting your engine out?' It all made her feel very angry. Especially now smoking had been criminalised. Mrs Grindlay was no radical, but she was prepared to defy a law which she saw as an infringement of individual liberties. The Tobacco Products and Allied Substances (Restriction) Act of 1997 had made smoking in any place outside the home a criminal offence punishable by up to six months' imprisonment. What enraged her most was the total hypocrisy of the government's position. She happened to know that Number 10 had never intended the bill to make it on to the statute book. It had only been introduced in order to counter growing criticism of the intimate relationship between the government and the tobacco barons. The government had confidently expected it to be voted down with the convenient help of twenty backbench rebels. But at the last moment, and without any warning, the Pensioners' Power Party and the Cornish Independents had swung behind the bill, and the Act had been carried by four votes. The new Draconian anti-smoking measures had prompted millions of smokers to give up the weed. The Chancellor was soon faced with a revenue loss of three billion pounds. He'd been obliged to put VAT up to thirty-five per cent, increase national insurance contributions to £28 a week, and sell three Trident nuclear submarines.

The wintry air was now beginning to nip at her ears. Her fingers were going numb. But she didn't care. Her whole day had been a build-up to these moments of solitary vice. The phone started to ring. At ten past nine in the evening? She decided to ignore it. She would finish her precious cigarette. But the phone kept ringing. It became intrusive. It was ruining the moment. Then she realised the call was coming through on her green line. That phone, sadly, could not be ignored.

She clambered back in through the window, closing it carefully behind her. She didn't want to leave Mitchell any little clues. She hesitated before picking up the phone. She hated the green line, because calls on this line always presented particularly messy problems. This one was no exception. A familiar voice briefed her at length, and within a few minutes she had a full page of scribbled notes. With a heavy sigh she replaced the phone, sat down at her computer terminal and accessed the datafile on the Chief Executive of Globelink News.

Six
December 7th, 1999

Henry was angry. You could tell he was angry because he had just kicked a chihuahua. The dog squealed loudly, much to Henry's satisfaction.

He pushed his way grimly along the crowded pavement. Thanks to the latest tunnel collapse on the London Underground the entire service had been shut down at a moment's notice. So the streets were swarming with displaced tube travellers. And Henry was an hour late for work. And he was still two miles from the Globelink building. He was about to make yet another attempt to hail a taxi when the dog's owner, a large florid lady in her sixties, grabbed him by the elbow. Her voice was trembling.

'You have just kicked my dog.'

'Yes, madam, that is correct. And if you continue to delay me I shall jump up and down on it until it resembles a strawberry ice-lolly on a very hot day. TAXI!'

That day's work started without Henry. In a way it also started without Joy. Although she was there in body, she was certainly not there in spirit. She just sat at her desk and doodled with a horrible intensity.

George felt concerned. 'Is there anything the matter, Joy?'

'Yes,' said Joy, turning her back on him.

'Right. I did enjoy our little meal on Saturday. I was wondering if you could come to another one?'

'No,' said Joy.

'Right. Sorry.' George retreated.

Dave looked up from his VDU. 'More on this London Transport chaos. LT have described the tunnel collapse as an incident on the line which necessitated a roof relocation strategy.'

'Should we send out a crew to record some passenger opinions?' asked George.

'Won't be broadcastable,' answered Dave with a shrug. 'Remember the last lot of commuter vox-pops? We had to bleep every other word.'

'Yes,' said George, recalling a little old lady they'd filmed spitting at a London Transport apologies board. 'Maybe we won't bother.'

'There is one quite fruity item,' offered Dave. 'Press release. Another bunch of religious nutters who say the world will end on the first of January. "Vegetarians for Jesus". They're all going to gather on the slopes of Mount Ararat.'

'To do what?' asked George.

'Dunno, they'll probably sacrifice a carrot or something.'

'I thought the Pope had already booked Mount Ararat for his millennium TV special.'

'Well, let's face it, there's hardly a mountain top from here to the Himalayas that hasn't been booked by some bunch of loonies.'

'Well,' said George, 'I suppose they might be right ("Always Be Open to Possibilities", Chapter Three).'

'Nah, George,' said Dave, folding his arms behind his head. 'If there was any chance of the world ending on

New Year's Eve, Ladbroke's would be taking bets on it. Mind you, they did accept my bet that Seb Coe would have to resign because of a sex scandal. Fantastic odds. 200,000 to 1. Definitely worth a punt. Well, you never know, do you?'

George wondered whether Dave was mentally ill. Certainly his compulsion to gamble seemed to be getting stronger. Only last week he had bought two hundred tickets for the National Lottery on the grounds that he felt lucky. But George noticed that Dave never seemed to be lucky. His 'sure things' invariably fell at the first, or stayed in the stalls, or, as on one occasion, bit the jockey and ran away. In fact, the only time George could remember Dave's horse finishing first was in the aborted Grand National of 1993. Dave would have won two thousand pounds if that race had counted (he had taken it very badly and was off work for two weeks).

Some belligerent grunting in George's right ear signalled that Henry had at last arrived for work. Henry glared at everybody in general and then sat down. He was very careful not to fulminate about the traffic. He was only too aware that Dave regularly took bets on what Henry's opening line would be. This was something Henry resented. He hated being seen as predictable.

However, Henry's anger this particular morning went far beyond any ire at being used as a game of chance. It was a general cumulative anger, triggered by those young bastards on his boat, not to mention the incompetent bastards who ran the trains, the rude bastards who ran his local off-licence, and all the unspeakable bastards he had to work with. Henry couldn't free himself of a pervasive certainty that he was heading into the twilight, both personally and professionally. So it was unfortunate

111

that Dave chose this particular morning to tease him about his age.

'Trains are crap nowadays, eh, Henry?'

Henry grunted.

'Not like the good old days, eh? The age of the train. Must have been great. What was it like travelling on Stephenson's Rocket, Henry?'

It was only a silly piece of office banter. But Henry responded with a volley of magnificent abuse. Dave tried to back off, but Henry insisted in a pointless comparison of their sexual prowess. A comparison which Henry felt worked in his favour. Dave became irritated and made a misjudged comment about Henry needing to take along a younger man and a set of jump-leads. Seconds later Henry had bet Dave that he could pull the new South African receptionist before the new century dawned.

George thought the whole conversation was a bit off-putting. A few minutes later, as Henry made himself a cup of Bransonblend coffee, he also felt it had been pretty tacky. He'd got carried away. But vanity stopped him from cancelling the wager. He noticed Sally's seat was empty. She was empire-building, he could sense it, and he felt he was in grave danger of being geriatrically cleansed from the face of Globelink News. Or perhaps he was being irrational. Yes, there was nothing to worry about. It was time he calmed down and stopped being so paranoid.

The conversation taking place at that moment in Gus's office proved that Henry was not being paranoid.

Sally smiled at Gus. 'So you see, since the main bulletin will now be five minutes shorter, I think it would have a greater sense of unity if there were only one newsreader, don't you?'

Gus thought about this for a moment. 'You mean – you?'

'Of course I mean me. I don't wish to be pushy, Gus, but Henry *is* getting on a bit. I don't think it helps our image to have our bulletin fronted by old buffers with broken veins in their noses, do you?'

Gus didn't answer immediately. He was mentally calculating how much Globelink would save by having only one newsreader. On the other hand, he didn't want to be entirely dependent on Sally. Having two presenters who hated each other was quite useful – it allowed Gus to play off one against the other.

Sally wondered whether she had gone too far too fast. 'Of course, I do understand it's not my job to decide whether Globelink hangs on to people who're past their best. I suppose I just care about quality broadcasting, that's all. Which is why I came up with the idea about *Globelink Cares*.' Sally sat back and felt she had moved the conversation on quite neatly. The silence which ensued went on a little longer than she anticipated. Gus had stood up and was staring out of the window. She assumed he was pondering the points she had made.

In fact, Gus was experiencing a warm, gratifying glow. In less than two hours from now he would be lunching with a very senior government figure. He wasn't sure what it was all about. Mrs Grindlay's secretary had implied that it had to be all very discreet and off-the-record. Gus had readily agreed. He loved the feeling of being trusted by authority. As a schoolboy, he used to get his essays read out in class, not because they were particularly good, but because he always managed to write exactly what the teachers wanted to read.

'Gus?'

113

Gus snapped out of his reverie and turned to face Sally. 'I've thought of a better title for the new segment, Sally. *Globelink Cares* lacks impact, drama. So we're going to call it *Crisis 2000*.'

'Gus, that's absolutely brilliant!' Sally actually thought her own title much better, but she knew the crucial importance of allowing Gus to feel he was at the creative cutting edge.

Gus looked pleased. 'Thank you, Sally. But I'm afraid it's not going to be a five-minute programme.'

Sally's mouth tightened. What was he going to suggest? Three minutes? *Two* minutes? That would be an insult. She would not tolerate that.

Gus enjoyed watching Sally squirm. He waited a moment longer. 'It's going to be a ten-minute programme.'

Helen pulled herself up to her full height, threw back her head with pride and said, 'Chloë, your mother is a lesbian and . . .' she faltered for a moment, '. . . and I want to move in with my lover, Gail. You haven't met Gail. She's a warm and loving and loyal person and, well, I've tried my best to be a good mum, really I have, but you'll be leaving home soon and . . . You know I'll always love you very much, but I think now is a time when perhaps it's fair if I, well, if I put *my* feelings first . . .' Helen's blue eyes glistened with tears. It was a very affecting speech. It was just a shame that Chloë was not there to hear it.

Helen reached for the tissue dispenser. As always, it was empty. She took a toilet roll from one of the cubicles and set about repairing her make-up.

Helen's reflection stared back at her from the ladies' room mirror. Every day now for three weeks she had rehearsed her speech and every time it had upset her. She dabbed her eyes with a wad of toilet paper. Why did she feel so guilty about everything? Why was she programmed to imagine everything was her fault? It was ludicrous. As a working single mum she constantly felt she was short-changing her daughter, short-changing herself, in fact, short-changing everybody. If only she could make up her mind what she wanted in life. She needed to be a lot more focused. Focusing on what was really important would get rid of these ridiculous guilt feelings. Why did she find it so hard to focus?

Helen was starting to feel guilty about finding it so hard to focus, when Sally breezed into the ladies' room. Helen snapped into a brittle smile.

'Are you all right, Helen?' enquired Sally, with a regal tip of the head. 'Only your face is rather puffy. Or is it just tiredness? You should try mudpacks. They work wonders with problem skin.'

'I'm fine,' said Helen. 'Thank you for your concern.' She walked out of the ladies' room and headed for the canteen. One day, she swore, she would head-butt Sally. Right on her stuck-up little nose.

The canteen was virtually empty. Helen chose a ham roll that looked faintly edible and set off for a seat by the window. To her surprise she saw Joy sitting at a table, stabbing her fork into a plate of lasagne.

'Hi, Joy, you don't usually slum it in the canteen.'

Joy didn't look up, because she didn't want company. Helen sensed this, but with all the other tables empty, it would look ridiculous if she went and sat anywhere else. 'Do you mind if I sit here?'

'Please yourself.'

Helen sat down and peeled the cellophane from her roll. 'How's things?' she said casually.

'Crap as always.'

Even by Joy's standards this response was unusually aggressive. Something was up. Should Helen try to help? Helen's sensible half told her not to get involved. Unfortunately she listened to the other half. 'Look, what's the problem, Joy, eh? You've been in this godawful mood all . . .' Helen broke off because Joy was now stabbing more vigorously at her lasagne. Where, wondered Helen, did all that rage come from? Joy could be so intimidating. She had a reputation for occasional moments of awesome physical violence, but always against men. Usually they were men who sort of deserved it, which was why she was so popular with the female members of staff. In fact the girls had given Joy a standing ovation when she'd hung the groper from Accounts out of the fifth-floor window.

Joy looked up. 'It's my dad.' Her voice had gone curiously quiet. 'It's bloody awful.'

Helen looked at Joy's grim expression and feared the worst kind of news. 'What . . . what about your dad?'

'He's . . .' Joy struggled to find the words. 'He's sent me a postcard.'

'Oh.'

Helen jumped as Joy smashed her fork down on her plate. 'How *dare* he? I mean, how *dare* he! He buggers off when I'm seven, I don't see hide nor hair of him for twenty-odd years and then he sends me a bloody . . .' she glanced at the card, 'a bloody mosaic of some blond pretty boy with wings on his sandals.'

'That's Hermes,' said Helen, regretting it the moment she said it.

'I don't give a fuck who he is, little Miss University Challenge.' Joy tore up the card into little pieces.

Helen wondered what to say next. 'Um, do you want your father to—?'

'I don't want anything from him and I certainly don't want photos of some dead Greek's floor, thank you very much!'

Helen nibbled at her ham roll.

Joy surveyed her lasagne. 'This is revolting. I've half a mind to leave it in Gus's in-tray again.'

Helen ignored her sensible half for a second time. 'What did your father say in the card?'

'That he was sorry. That he knew he'd hurt me. That he wanted to see me. That he loved me. The usual male bollocks. You know, tons of indefensible behaviour followed by a token nano-second of guilt. It must be a chromosome they have or something. Women don't do that.'

Helen pondered the theory. 'Sally does the indefensible behaviour, but without the nano-second of guilt.'

'Yeah,' countered Joy. 'Well I was talking about women. Not some alien robot from the Planet Smug.'

Helen smiled. That was more like it. Bad-mouthing Sally was guaranteed to cheer a girl up. 'Would you like a coffee?' Helen asked.

'Yeah, ta.'

But as Helen got to her feet, George arrived, out of breath and agitated.

'Helen, I need you in the green room. Sir Titus Granby has arrived and needs some hand-holding. You're the best at that.'

Helen sighed. 'All right, then.'

'Can't get my breath,' George gasped. 'Ran up the stairs; lift's broken.'

Joy looked up. 'It was fine a few minutes ago. It must be you, George.'

'Yes,' laughed George, unconvincingly.

La Grasserie was *the* hot restaurant of 1999. It appeared every week in glossy colour supplements. It served the high-quality greasy fry-ups that had become so fashionable since scientists had proved that high cholesterol intake actually increased life expectancy. The décor was all optimistic blues and pinks (the colours of 1999) and its tables presented a pageant of the rich and famous. People off the telly, actresses from the movies, business high-fliers, Channel Four executives, advertising people with loud voices drawing things on the tablecloths, they were all there. Anybody who was anybody ate at La Grasserie and that, thought Gus, as he sat waiting for his chip-butty starter, makes me an anybody. Of course he was used to power-lunching in swanky restaurants, but this was the one patronised by the *faces*, the glamorous young talent-base. No number-crunching going on here, thought Gus, these are all creatives.

'Have you been here before?' asked his lunch date.

'Oh, yes, Mrs Grindlay,' Gus lied. Truth was Gus had always felt too nervous to book a table here. But she seemed at home, so he was starting to relax.

The *sommelier* handed Gus the wine-list. It was forty-two pages long.

Mrs Grindlay spread the napkin on her lap. 'They do a splendid house red here.'

'I know.' Gus turned to the *sommelier*. 'The splendid house red, please.'

Mrs Grindlay leaned across the table towards Gus and for a moment he thought he detected a faint waft of nicotine.

118

'Mr Hedges . . . Gus, I know that you are a man of immense ability and discretion.'

Gus smiled. She'd obviously been checking up on him.

'I spoke to Sir Roysten about you the other day and he said you were the perfect Chief Executive.' Sir Roysten had indeed said these very words, though the full sentence ran: 'the perfect Chief Executive, a totally malleable crawler'.

'Sir Roysten spoke in glowing terms of your flexibility and loyalty,' she went on. Gus felt a wave of relief. Sir Roysten might not be returning his calls, but Gus was still his number one boy.

'The thing is . . .' Mrs Grindlay paused so that the waiter could deposit her Fried Eggs au Mossiman.

'The chip-butty for monsieur?' said the waiter.

Gus nodded. The waiter slid the oval Meissen platter in front of him and glided away.

'The thing is,' Mrs Grindlay continued, 'a delicate situation has arisen. You have a reporter, Damien Day. The puma liberator.'

Gus's fork stopped halfway to his mouth. How the hell did she know about that?

'And,' she paused for effect, 'he has been in Brecon, pursuing a rather sad story. Some officers in a regiment have committed suicide and, well, there's a pattern. I must compliment Globelink on getting on to it so quickly; no one else in the media spotted it.'

'Right,' said Gus, completely lost. 'Well I always say we're the rapid-response unit of the global news-gathering task force.'

'Do you?'

'Oh, yes.'

This is going to be a long lunch, thought Mrs

Grindlay. She watched Gus pretending to enjoy his chip-butty. She changed tack. 'Have you noticed that our Minister for Energy has gone rather freelance recently?'

'Oh, yes, indeed,' chuckled Gus, without the faintest idea of what she was talking about.

Mrs Grindlay felt a moment of despair. Manipulating people was tiring enough, but manipulating idiots was horribly laborious. Now the man was gawping at Sinead O'Connor MP, who was sitting three tables away. Mrs Grindlay called the waiter over and asked for fried bread soldiers.

She gazed at Gus's vacuous smile. It never ceased to amaze her how people with no talent and no intelligence could rise to positions of responsibility. In her career she had met countless government ministers who could barely string two thoughts together. The women were the worst. Pushy little soundbite specialists who couldn't organise an argument to save their lives. She remembered, with a shudder, a minister called Bottomley. Victoria? Vanessa? God, she'd been the thickest of the lot. Her only talent had been for finding the shortest distance between two platitudes.

Mrs Grindlay's thoughts were interrupted by the arrival of four fried bread soldiers, on a bed of lettuce, and flanked by two lychees.

'So, Mrs Grindlay, what exactly is your role within the governmental network?' fished Gus with all the finesse of a Japanese supertrawler.

'I'm, um, in charge of presentational downloading of core activity at an executive level.'

'Ah,' smiled Gus. 'Snap.'

'It's a consultancy basically. Arm's length interactive crenellation.'

'Uh-huh, uh-huh.'

'With hands-on point-of-use curlicues.'

'Uh-huh, I get you.'

Mrs Grindlay decided to stop playing this game, even though it was a lot of fun. She'd better not bewilder Gus too much. She needed him to remember the important bit. 'Now, Gus, this is vitally important and extremely confidential. I know I can trust you with this. Your boy Damien is on to something. And frankly the story he's chasing could be terminally embarrassing for a government minister. So what we want from you is cooperation.'

Gus's face lit with sudden comprehension. 'No problem. You want the story hushed up.'

'Not exactly,' said Mrs Grindlay, mopping up her last puddle of egg yolk.

Sir Titus Granby had just been sick. He had been in the green room for only twenty-two minutes but in that time he had got through half a bottle of vodka. Helen had tried to stop him, but he was in a foul temper and had physically prised her fingers from the bottle. He'd quickly become so drunk that Helen had told him it would now be inappropriate to record an interview with him for the next bulletin. Especially as the subject of the interview was new drink-driving legislation. At this point Sir Titus had become abusive, accusing Helen of politically motivated censorship. Halfway through a comparison between Helen and Joseph Stalin, he had suddenly gone very still. With a composed 'Excuse me', he'd walked, with meticulous steadiness, towards the door, which, sadly, was the door to a cupboard. Sir Titus had run out of time and had vomited all down his trousers. Now he was sitting on a sofa, sobbing with self-disgust.

'It's all right,' comforted Helen. 'Don't worry, it could happen to anyone.' Helen wondered why she was trying to make him feel better. He was a pig. A sad pig. A sad, lonely pig. Like so many of the politicians she'd had to mother in this green room.

Sir Titus looked up at the ceiling and groaned. 'It's the life, you see, Westminster life. All the pressure. And your wife and kids are miles away, so you drink, and you fool around, consorting with young ladies.'

Consorting with young ladies? God this one's really creepy, thought Helen. Sir Titus's face was slowly recovering that familiar shade of vermilion which testifies to a lifetime on the sauce.

'I was Junior Minister for Employment once,' he muttered, gazing somewhere into the middle distance. 'Long time ago now. I was a high-flier, oh, yes, tipped for stardom. They used to love me at conference. Mrs T . . .' he sighed nostalgically, 'Mrs T stood as close to me as you are now . . .'

'Was she cleaning the sick off your trousers?'

'Sorry?'

'Nothing.'

'Mrs T said, "Titus, you are a warrior and I will need warriors." That was before . . .' his expression darkened, 'before . . . well, you know what I mean.'

Helen knew exactly what he meant. He meant the unfortunate incident with the Danish 'researcher' and the builders' skip. Sir Titus had only survived because the story was pushed off the front pages by the Prince Charles love-child scandal.

'You know,' said Sir Titus wistfully, 'my problem is . . .'

Oh no, Helen thought, his wife doesn't understand him.

'. . . my wife doesn't understand me. If only I'd met someone, someone kind, like you.' He took her hand in his sweaty palm. 'You've got lovely eyes.'

'Thank you,' said Helen. 'I'll call you a taxi.'

As George walked down the corridor he could feel the new bounce in his step. The self-help book had made him feel stronger and younger. For instance, normally he would have been a little thrown by Joy informing him his builders had rung with a problem. And he'd have been even more thrown by the news that a partition wall had turned out to be load-bearing. But Wayne the foreman had sounded unruffled, so George wasn't going to let it worry him.

'After all, what's the worst that can happen?' he had asked Joy, blithely.

'Your house could fall down and crush you to death,' she'd replied.

No, thought George, leave it to Wayne. All that talk of pins and buttresses had sounded pretty reassuring.

He strode on confidently down the corridor. Past the coffee machine, which only dispensed cups of boiling hot water, past the graffiti saying 'Due to management cutbacks, the light at the end of the tunnel has now been switched off', and past an open-plan office where Jenny, Head of Audience Research, was alone in the corner rubbing her temples and staring into space. He gave her a cheery wave, but she didn't seem to notice.

George knocked on the door marked Edit Suite B.

'Enter,' said Henry from inside, in his richest actor-manager tones.

George stepped into the murk of the tiny edit suite. A small monitor was glowing with slightly fuzzy images.

Dave and Henry were watching the pictures intently, giving an occasional whoop of astonishment.

'How's it going, troops?' asked George in a chummy way, designed to boost morale. Nobody answered.

'How far have you got?' George enquired.

'We've just reached one of the most significant events of 1997,' Dave replied.

George examined the picture closely. 'It, um, seems to be a, um, a pair of male buttocks . . . moving.'

'Correct,' said Dave.

'Well, what's significant about it?'

'This is the only known footage of Sally in full flagrante. The engineers stashed a camera in her dressing room and filmed this encounter with Toby, the sound man. We're splicing it into the office Christmas tape.'

George was appalled. 'I can't believe my eyes!' he cried.

'Yes, he must have very strong thigh muscles,' said Henry.

George switched off the monitor. 'Honestly! How can two grown men stoop to invading a colleague's privacy like that? I think it's very tacky indeed, the way you keep humiliating Sally.'

'What else are we meant to do with her?' enquired Henry.

'That's not very funny!'

Dave lolled back in his chair. 'Oh, lighten up, George! It's just the Christmas tape. Old office tradition. Bit of fun, that's all.'

George hesitated. Had he overreacted? He'd got upset, the way the old George would have done. The new George, he decided, would rise above it. 'I'm not going to argue about it,' he said imperiously. 'Is the millennium retrospective finished?'

'Not really,' sighed Dave. 'Gus asked us to add on a section with lots of disaster stuff. You know, the R 101, Aberfan, Hillsborough, the mystery fire at EuroDisney. I'll show you where we're up to.'

Dave cued up an adjoining monitor. Images of the Mexico City earthquake appeared. Children crying, a house falling down. George didn't much want to watch a house falling down, and was relieved when Dave spooled forward to graphic pictures of an oil spill.

'Which oil spill's this?' George asked. He was worried it might be the oil spill Damien had covered in '93. He had come back with award-winning pictures of oil-soaked seabirds. It was only later they'd learned that Damien, frustrated by an absence of distressed wildlife, had obtained several cormorants and dunked them in barrels of pitch. Since then they had never used that footage, in case the truth got out.

'Don't worry,' said Dave. 'It's not that oil spill.'

'And have you finished writing the voice-over yet, Henry?'

'Give me a break, George. It takes time. I'm a craftsman, a wordsmith.'

'Would you mind if Sally narrated some of it, only she keeps nagging me.'

Henry gave a charming smile. 'George, this piece will require a style of narration that is resonant and authoritative. A style, say, like that of the late Richard Burton. I share many characteristics with Burton. Rolling cadences, clear diction.'

'Enlarged liver,' added Dave.

'Sally, on the other hand,' Henry continued, 'has a voice with all the poetry of Formica. I rest my case.'

'Oh, well,' shrugged George, 'perhaps she'll drop it

now Gus has given her this programme of her own.'

'What?' snapped Henry, the air suddenly filling with electricity.

George sensed danger. 'Oh, it's nothing, Henry. I received a memo from Gus. It's just some silly little teensy-weensy thing of a problems slot.'

'A programme of her own?' bellowed Henry.

'Don't get worked up,' soothed George. 'She's just diversifying a bit, that's all. Don't forget, she has to build her career, that's not a problem for you,' said George.

Dave closed his eyes and groaned quietly.

'Meaning what exactly?' Henry rumbled. 'Tell me why I don't have to worry about building a career.'

'Well,' stammered George, 'because your career, you know, a lot of it is . . . You're well established. Yes. That's what I meant. You're totally established.'

'You mean old!' Henry exploded. 'We'll soon see about that. Come on then, you bastard! Come on!'

'Oh no,' sighed George, 'not arm-wrestling again. Henry, I wish you'd just come to terms with growing—'

'Growing what?' growled Henry, rolling up his sleeve.

'Nothing.'

Henry won the arm-wrestling, three out of three. Which meant he was in quite a sunny mood as he waited for the afternoon editorial conference to begin. He had lost his sense of outrage at the idea of Sally getting her own programme. On reflection, the naffness of the concept probably spelled disaster. With luck Sally's career would be buried rather than diversified. There was always a silver lining. He busied himself with Nine Across and tried to ignore Damien, who'd just arrived back from Wales and was gibbering wildly.

126

'Don't you see,' he was shouting, 'there's a cover-up!'

'A cover-up of what?' asked George, nursing his arm.

'I don't know. But why did this bloke Farquhar try to steer me away from the suicide story? And who told him to flog me the claptrap about why he removed the newspaper article?'

'George,' called Joy, 'cable company on the phone for you. Something about limited liability.'

'Oh, right,' said George, taking the call.

'Look, this is important!' Damien yelled. 'For Christ's sake, call yourself journalists! This is big! I can smell it.'

'Big enough to justify going AWOL, mister?' It was Gus. He'd come in without anyone noticing. He had a real talent for that. 'Recovered from the Belgian flu, I see.'

'Yes but I was on to something!'

'And what have you got?' questioned Gus, with a strange, smug grin.

'Well, nothing concrete,' Damien conceded. 'But I'm telling you, these suicides are a real mystery!'

'Oh, to some maybe,' Gus said, sitting with studied nonchalance on Helen's empty desk. 'But I think you'll find,' Gus peered at his fingernails, 'that the suicides were caused by depression. Depression caused by electromagnetic pulses from power cables which converge directly beneath the officers' mess in Brecon. You see, they affect the brain's sensitive circuitry.' Gus had everyone's attention now. It was a good feeling.

'Bollocks,' Damien said. 'Who told you that?'

'Let's just say I got it from a high government source. Sometimes, Damien, it is not necessary to yomp across obscure parts of Britain. You just need to network with the right players. I've got all the details.' Gus waved a slim green folder triumphantly.

Dave had his hand in the air. 'Excuse me, but the Minister for Energy, whatshisname, with the basin hair-cut and the very ugly wife, he has repeatedly denied that electro-magnetic pulses from power lines can cause health problems. So why would a government source give you all this? The Minister will be crucified.'

Gus relished the moment. Over the suet puddings in La Grasserie, Mrs Grindlay had made it clear to Gus that Number 10 would smile on the crucifixion of the Minister for Energy. At that point, Gus had virtually fallen in love with Mrs Grindlay. She had made him an insider in the corridors of power.

Dave watched Gus's smile go to full-beam. 'Don't you worry your little head about the government's response, David. Just tell me, is it a hot story newswise or not?'

Dave floundered. 'Well, yes, but . . .'

'Then let's run it. Let's whip the opposition's arse till it bleeds!' Gus wondered where that particular image had sprung from. For a split second he visualised the tumbling locks of the pizza delivery girl.

Damien exploded. 'Look, you can't just swan in here with all this masonic bullshit about sources close to government! For God's sake! This is MY story!'

'And you shall front it, my boy,' said Gus, placing a fatherly hand on Damien's shoulder. 'Another Damien Day exclusive. "CREAM OF BRITISH ARMY CUT DOWN IN ITS PRIME!" "GOVERNMENT MINISTER LIES TO THE PEOPLE!" Sensational stuff. Probably win you a BAFTA. At last. And don't worry, I'll downplay my crucial role in all this. I'm not here.' Gus squeezed Damien's shoulder and handed him the green folder. 'I think you'll find everything you need in there.' Gus strolled whistling towards his office.

Damien slumped into his seat. He was dazed.

'Well, well,' said Joy. 'Beaten to a story by Gus. I'd call that humiliating.'

'Incredibly humiliating,' added Henry.

'Yeah, well it still doesn't explain the newspaper article,' pouted Damien. 'And cutting it out, and the supposed dirty joke, and the impotence! Tell them about the impotence, Dave!'

'Excuse me,' protested Dave.

'Dave slept with two of the widows, and both their husbands had been impotent, isn't that right, Dave?'

Dave gave a watery smile. He was aware that he was not coming out of this very well. 'I comforted them, that's all. They just wanted physical companionship.' Everyone else was staring at him hard. He heard himself say, 'It was a form of grief counselling.' Joy's stare became particularly intense and Dave remembered her reputation. 'I didn't plan any of it.' Dave shuffled some papers on his desk. To be honest he did feel ashamed and he hoped none of this would get back to Maisie. 'It just happened,' he muttered. There was a moment's silence.

'Dave,' boomed Henry, 'please convey my heartfelt gratitude to the aforementioned widows. They have just won me fifty quid.'

'Eh?'

'You remember? The Dave-Charnley-I-can-be-faithful-to-Maisie-Challenge?'

'Well,' said George brightly as he came off the phone. 'Wayne is on top of that. Did I miss anything? . . . Are you all right, Dave?'

Henry put his wig in its box and got into bed. It had been a difficult day and he knew he would have trouble

129

getting to sleep. He stretched across to the bedside table and picked up his hot toddy. He liked a hot toddy of a night-time. It helped him to unwind.

He sat in bed sipping the comforting beverage and struggled to do up the top button on his striped flannelette pyjamas. In the distance he heard a long, deep rumble. Probably another sewer collapsing. That would mean another morning of bloody transport chaos. God! London was disintegrating faster than Michael Jackson's face. Henry gazed at the wall-painting on the wall opposite. It was a picture of his beloved yacht, *The Bosanquet*. That old artist fellow from Maldon had done it for him. *The Bosanquet* was depicted riding a moody, magnificent sea, a plume of silvery spray breaking over her polished teak foredeck. He loved that painting. After the yacht itself, it was his most prized possession.

He drained the last of the hot toddy, switched off the light, and nestled down under the covers. He felt edgy. Thoughts richocheted around inside his head. Not very nice thoughts. He couldn't get comfortable. He rolled over and made eye contact with a bedside photo of his first wife, Lauren, the only one of his wives whom he had really loved. She was a glamorous, highly intelligent American, and they'd been wonderfully happy for three years. But then it had all gone wrong. Henry didn't blame Lauren for the break-up of their marriage. He blamed Israel. If the Israelis hadn't invaded Lebanon in '78, Henry wouldn't have been sent to report from Beirut, and he wouldn't have met that spectacular French interpreter with whom he'd had a torrid eight-month affair. Bloody Israelis.

Henry rolled over on to his left side. How stupid he had been to lose Lauren. He could feel his heart fluttering inside his chest. He was anxious. And he was angry. Angry about feeling anxious. Anxiety was the kind of thing George went in for, but not Henry Davenport, the man who'd been everywhere and done everything. The thump of his heartbeat quickened. There was no getting away from it. He was very worried. The worries were queueing up.

The first worry was that Damien had dominated the late bulletin with his piece on army brains being buggered by power cables. Henry acknowledged that the Minister for Energy's duplicity on the matter made the story a terrific scoop, but Henry didn't like to see Damien doing so well. Damien was a ruthless little upstart, and Henry felt threatened by him. He felt even more threatened by the malignant spread of Sally Smedley. How the hell had she persuaded Gus to give her a programme of her own? Henry knew her game. She was trying to squeeze him out. No doubt about it. Why was the bloody pillow suddenly so lumpy! He sat up, thumped the pillow viciously a few times, lay down again, and moved on to his next worry.

He'd been summoned to a disciplinary hearing of the Broadcasting Ethics Commission. They were going to haul him over the coals about an interview with the Minister for Transport in September. The Minister had complained that one of Henry's questions ('Why is it, Minister, that the only things moving on our motorways today are hedgehogs?') was offensive. Henry accepted that it was rude. It was meant to be. The Minister was a toad and Henry had relished making him squirm. In fact, he hadn't enjoyed an interview so much since the time he'd made John Patten develop a nervous skin condition on camera. Though he could hardly say that to the

Broadcasting Ethics Commission. No, he'd just have to eat humble pie and promise to be a good boy. Otherwise those tightarsed bastards would fine him again. Or worse. Look what they'd done to Paxman.

All these worries were quite enough to prevent Henry drifting into a good night's sleep. But, even in aggregate, they could hardly compare with The Big One: the deafening approach of time's wingèd chariot. Henry groaned quietly. George's comments about how 'established' Henry was had triggered something dark and terrible in Henry's psyche. Henry's career in TV news was drawing to a close. He didn't belong any more. He was a throwback to the days when to be a newsreader you had to have presence, personality and a drink problem. Nowadays they were all anodyne androids, smiling nonentities. Maybe he'd jump before he was pushed, get the hell out of it, take early retirement.

Retirement. The very word made Henry's blood run cold. What would he do? Who would he be? He couldn't sail his yacht seven days a week. He needed to work. Work was the only thing that gave his life shape and meaning. Henry contemplated a nightmarish future as an occasional contributor to radio programmes hosted by Ned Sherrin.

The bedroom seemed to have turned very cold. He pulled up the duvet beneath his chin and thought about that desperate little bet he'd made with Dave – that he could pull that South African receptionist before Big Ben chimed in the millennium. Oh God, why did he allow himself to get drawn into teenage stuff like that? What would Lauren think? Henry decided that he hated the millennium. He wanted it to be cancelled. It was making people either pathetically morbid or nauseatingly optimistic. It was just another year, for God's sake! Why all the fuss? He particularly resented having to help put together Globelink's *Review of the Century*. Not only was it a lot of extra work, it was also extremely depressing. The century didn't make very pleasant viewing.

A wailing pack of sirens drifted past and then faded slowly on the cold night air. Henry felt very tired, but at the same time totally awake. He stared at the ceiling and tried to think of a single human activity where the century had seen undeniable progress. Medicine, perhaps? Yes, positive progress there. At least Henry would have said so a few years back. But now antibiotics were proving less and less effective. New mutant strains of bacteria were giving technology a good thrashing. As a result, people were losing their faith in science and turning to ludicrous mystical alternatives. Only the previous week, Globelink had carried a news item on Druid oncologists who claimed that cancer could be cured by dancing inside a stone circle at the summer solstice. Off-air, Henry had ridiculed the piece as 'mindless mumbo-jumbo', but to his dismay, Globelink's phones had rung for days as viewers asked for further details. Henry rolled over on to his left side.

Telecommunications. Surely that was an exemplar of progress? Mankind could swap information every minute of the day thanks to the info-superhighway. Not that it changed anything. There still seemed to be the same capacity for godawful bloody cock-ups. More so, in fact. Stock exchanges could now crash in seconds. Computers could fire missiles at friendly targets. The ether was polluted with the chaotic oscillations of zillions of radio waves. The whole atmosphere was jiggling with frenetic activity. Henry could almost feel it right here in his bedroom.

He remembered something his dad used to tell him. His dad said that the more moving parts something had, the more chance there was of something going wrong. In Henry's eyes, this theory went a long way to explaining the state of the world. Nothing stayed put any more. Too many moving parts.

As the millennium drew near, Henry had found himself thinking more and more about his father. Doctor Hugo Davenport had been a big man, a Cambridge blue at rugby and a captain in the Hampshire and Dorset Regiment. He'd been wounded on D-Day. He'd fought his way up the beach at Arromanches. And for what? For a country where everything carried a price tag. A country where patients were called clients, where headmasters were called Managing Directors, and where milk and bread and bingo cards and God knows what were sold in post offices! God, it made Henry livid to think about it.

He leaped out of bed. Dammit, he'd never get to sleep now! He stomped across to the dressing table and found a half-empty bottle of Benylin. He swigged the lot. That should give the sandman a good kick up the arse, he thought, and climbed back into bed.

The minutes ticked by. The worries came creeping back. He'd have to watch himself with the Broadcasting Ethics Commission. Have to curb his temper. Have to give Lauren a ring some time . . . His eyelids began to droop. Have to watch Sally. Have to watch Damien. Have to . . . Henry was asleep. He snored gently. For a moment he spluttered and rolled over. Then the snoring continued. Between two loud snores, he muttered, 'Sorry, Lauren.'

Seven
December 8th, 1999

At precisely nine fifteen the following morning the news came through on the wires that the Minister for Energy had resigned. Globelink was able to broadcast live coverage of the Minister at home, with his arm round his plucky wife, explaining how for some time he had wanted to quit public life so that he could see more of his children. His children, Marcus and Seraphina, stared at the camera and looked less than thrilled by the prospect.

In the Globelink office some lukewarm champagne was produced and Damien was heartily congratulated. His exposé of how the Minister had ignored scientific warnings and implicitly caused the deaths of innocent men was generally acclaimed, across the media, as a devastating piece of journalism. From somewhere, Damien had come up with dates, details and confidential documents which unquestionably fingered the Minister. The rest of the government had immediately distanced themselves from their ex-colleague. In off-the-record briefings they branded him a dangerous maverick who'd concealed the facts from the Cabinet. The story was huge and made the front pages of all the papers. It had been years since a government minister had resigned over anything political.

Damien refused all offers of more champagne and

threw the cardboard beaker into the waste bin. He didn't share everybody's excitement. Sure, this was the kind of acclaim that he'd always dreamed about, yet somehow he felt cheated. The story belonged to Gus really. That green folder had contained every bit of evidence he'd required. It had all been too easy. What's more, he knew in his bones that the story didn't quite add up. Somebody in high office had clearly wanted to shaft the Minister for Energy. But it was still an embarrassing moment for the government. Their friends in the City were hopping mad; share prices in the electricity companies had collapsed within minutes of the Stock Exchange opening. Was there some other motive in feeding Gus the story? And where did the Brecon newspaper article fit in? Why had Farquhar been so keen to remove it from circulation? Not that Damien was an idealistic seeker after truth. He was, after all, a man who'd been known to help a story along if the facts were disappointing. No, what he didn't like was the feeling that someone had been jerking him around. He didn't like being used. And he didn't like the knowing way Gus kept smiling at him.

George plonked himself down in the empty seat next to Damien.

'Well done, Damien,' he said, 'really well done. I know I've questioned your methods in the past but, well, well done.'

'Thanks,' said Damien flatly.

'Someone said you got the whole thing chapter and verse from Gus, is that right?'

'Yes.'

'Gosh,' said George. 'Not like him to promote an anti-government story. Perhaps he's developing a bit of a social conscience.'

136

'Oh, yeah,' said Joy, 'and perhaps Bernard Manning is anorexic.' Out of the corner of her eye Joy saw Dave shuffling into the office. 'Oh, hello, it's the widowmaker,' she called. 'You're late. What happened? Don't tell me, problems on the tube, you were delayed because someone threw himself in front of your train, so you had to nip round to his place and fuck his wife.'

Dave looked at Joy. He could see she was going to string this one out for months. 'Yeah, well actually, Joy, before you or any other bugger beat me to it, I've told Maisie everything, OK?'

'And how did she take it?' asked Joy.

'She took it very well if you must know,' replied Dave. In fact, Maisie had ditched him on the spot. It was the first time he'd been totally honest with a woman and, he decided, the last.

The editorial meeting was about to start, but there was a brief hiatus while George took a call about insurance and Helen fielded a call from Sir Titus Granby. Sally was reading a book entitled *People in Pain*. On a piece of paper she was jotting down phrases applicable to various emotional problems. Next to the word 'bulimia' she had written 'anguished flight from the fear of growing up'.

'What are you doing?' asked Henry, intrigued by the unusual combination of Sally and a book.

'These are my compassion crib notes,' she twittered. 'For when these poor troubled souls ring me for solace.'

For once Henry found no sarcastic rejoinder. He was just too sick at heart. He contemplated the appalling prospect of some desperately damaged individual phoning Sally as an emotional lifeline. The suicide rate was going to shoot up overnight.

Helen slammed down her phone. 'Honestly! Of all the bloody barefaced nerve. He only asked me for a date. Can you believe that? Sir Titus Granby, piss artist extraordinaire and champion vomiter wonders if I'd go to the opera with him! "No hanky panky, just an intelligent woman on my arm for once." I mean, which rotten piece of woodwork do these people crawl out of?'

'So you're not keen then?' said George.

Joy weighed in with the view that Helen should accept the dinner date, get Sir Titus totally smashed and then steal his wallet.

'Listen,' said Helen, 'even if he had a million pounds in cash it wouldn't compensate me for the hours of self-pitying crap I'd have to sit through. You should have heard him yesterday.' Helen began to imitate Sir Titus's drink-sodden bass. ' "I'm lonely, I'm overworked, I've become impotent." '

'He's impotent?' said Damien.

'Oh, well, that's something,' said Joy.

The wheels in Damien's head started to turn. 'What's his constituency?'

'Brecon and Radnor,' Helen replied. She was blessed with a superb memory for facts. Dave was always trying to persuade her to appear on quiz shows so he could place bets on her and make a real killing.

Damien was now deep in thought, his wheels spinning fast. 'He's MP for Brecon and Radnor . . . and he's been struck impotent?'

'Yeah yeah.' Helen went back into her Sir Titus impression. ' "God knows what's gone wrong, used to get erections like Nelson's column. It's the wife, I reckon." '

Damien knitted his brows. 'Where's he live in Brecon?'

Helen laughed. 'Why would he live there? He's the

138

MP. He hates the place. "Mother Nature's rectum", he called it. Said he'd only been there once in the last year and that was some godawful army dinner which was totally inedible apart from some steak pie or something.'

'An army dinner?' said Damien, fighting to conceal his excitement.

'Yes, why?'

Damien paused to gather his thoughts. Should he tell Helen about the link she'd just made for him? He had no hard evidence yet. And if it got back to Gus, the story would get spiked for sure. Why did someone put up that smoke screen about the brain damage and the power cables? It was all very titillating. Damien opted for a spot of fact-checking. 'Do you mean, he only ate the steak pie thingie?' asked Damien as casually as possible.

'That's what he said.' Helen was puzzled by the question. 'Why?'

'No reason.' Damien changed the subject. 'So what do we reckon's first item, then? I mean after the resignation.'

On the words 'first item' Gus appeared from his office. 'OK, team, I'm not here.'

Helen glanced at her notes. 'It has to be the by-election at Hastings. Sixty-eight per cent of the vote to the Pensioners' Power Party.'

'That should please you, Henry,' said Sally, without looking up.

Henry's eyes bulged. 'Yes, well sadly for you, my dear, there isn't a party that represents the interests of people whose only brain cell is dying from agoraphobia.'

As Henry and Sally engaged in their morning spat, Helen typed the words 'Item 2 – Pensioners' victory' in to her computer. The words appeared instantly on all the

VDUs in the newsroom. And on the VDU belonging to Mrs Grindlay.

Mrs Grindlay hated snooping. At an emotional and intellectual level she thought that an individual had an indisputable right to privacy. For the state to invade that privacy was totally indefensible. On the other hand it did save her huge amounts of time. She'd asked Spooks Division to hook her into Globelink's mainframe, so now at the flick of a switch she could check what was happening on any computer in that building. At that moment, she was keyed into Damien's terminal. Thanks to the dummy she'd sold Gus, Damien probably no longer posed a threat. But Mrs Grindlay was a thorough person; she wanted to be one hundred per cent sure that Damien had let the story drop. The reports she'd received from Brecon had been typically unclear. How much had Damien really found out? And had he talked to anyone else at Globelink? Whenever she buried a problem, she liked to be sure that the corpse wasn't capable of making a surprise comeback.

Nothing was happening on Damien's terminal, so she went on a little electronic tour. As she flicked from computer to computer she became increasingly amazed that Globelink News ever made it on to the air. No one seemed to do any work. She accessed Dave Charnley. He appeared to be composing a letter to a girl named Maisie. She watched in fascination as seven opening sentences were typed and deleted in succession, leaving only the words 'Dear Maisie'.

She switched to Henry Davenport's terminal. He was calling up the test score. England's tour was going from bad to worse. The middle order had collapsed again and

England were 72 all out. Burma were 204 for 1.

She continued her computer walkabout. Sally Smedley was, for some reason, studying the career biography of Esther Rantzen. Helen Cooper was compiling a running order. Helen was obviously the one who kept things going. Mrs Grindlay warmed to her. She knew the feeling. Mrs Grindlay sat back and watched Helen moving items around on the running order. She watched as 'Teachers' dispute over oath of alliegance' moved from Item 6 down to Item 11 and then back up to 9. Mrs Grindlay became intrigued by the process. The Russian attack on Turkey was down at 7. Well, people were probably getting a bit bored with Russian invasions. An item on Charles Windsor (as he now was) starting up a small business called Arcadian Village Crafts Ltd was moved down from 18 to 21.

Suddenly, an unnumbered item appeared. 'Lady Bienvenida Buck Weds Sex-Change Colonel'. It hovered for a moment beneath the bottom of the running order, and then climbed rapidly to Item 3. Gus must have come into the room.

Mrs Grindlay drummed her fingers on her desk and wondered whether she could risk a cigarette. She had disabled the smoke alarm. But the smell would give her away. What if Mitchell came in? No, she couldn't risk it. She chewed on a pencil. Maybe tapping into Globelink was an unnecessary precaution. It all looked pretty quiet. Her thoughts turned to lunch. She'd jut have one last scamper round the Globelink terminals and then head off for that little Greek place with the fishing nets and the Adonis-like waiter.

A second check on Damien's terminal revealed that he was studying updates on the siege of Montreux. Fine.

Maybe he'll get sent there. Then the screen cleared and up came the RAC Happytravel Dataguide. 'Oh, dear,' muttered Mrs Grindlay, as Damien accessed the low-budget motorway routes to Brecon.

Mrs Grindlay reached for her roll-on Nicotino stick and applied it liberally to her forearm.

Damien entered the dingy little edit suite and locked the door behind him. He sat down, took out a pen, and made a list on a clean sheet of paper:

> BRECON
> SUICIDES
> ARMY OFFICERS
> REGIMENTAL DINNER
> STEAK PIE
> ELECTRO-MAGNETIC FIELDS???
> IMPOTENCE

He stared at the list for a few moments, and then carefully ringed the words 'steak pie'. He fumbled in his inside pocket and pulled out the clipping from the *Brecon & Radnor Clarion*. He read it slowly and carefully. Then he went back to his list, deleted 'steak pie' and wrote in 'beef Wellington – supplied by Heslop's'.

Someone hammered on the door.

'Who's in there?' yelled Henry.

Damien quickly pocketed the papers and flicked the door-catch. The door flew open and Henry marched in, followed by Dave.

'What are you up to, Day?' bellowed Henry.

'Can't say. But I need your help. I want you to lie for me.'

'Why would we lie for you?' laughed Dave. 'Give us one good reason.'

'Because if you don't, I'll tell Gus who put the Superglue on his running machine. That'd be instant dismissal, I reckon.'

Dave feigned indifference. 'That was two years ago.'

'He still talks about it,' countered Damien.

'We were drunk,' protested Henry. 'It was only meant as a bit of fun. How were we to know he'd decide to run barefoot?'

'Well, maybe he'd understand,' said Damien, twiddling with his pen. 'He didn't lose that much skin, after all.'

Dave hesitated. 'You wouldn't tell him. You're bluffing.'

Damien moved to the door. 'Fine. If you're prepared to take that risk.'

Dave and Henry looked at each other and decided they weren't prepared to take that risk.

'Damien's what?' Gus shouted.

'Collapsed,' replied Dave.

'That's right, collapsed,' echoed Henry.

'Just talking one second, then bent double the next, clutching his stomach.'

'His stomach, yes.' Henry clutched his stomach in illustration.

'We sent him up the doctor's straight away.'

'Up the doctor's,' Henry echoed.

Gus stared at them both. From the moment they'd marched into his office, he knew something was going on, but what? Well, he'd find out soon enough. 'Go on, get out,' he snapped. Dave and Henry scuttled out. Gus

143

slumped into his chair and let out a low groan. How fickle fate was. Twenty minutes ago, a bike messenger had delivered a letter from Sir Roysten. Gus had opened it quickly, expecting a pat on the back for Globelink's big scoop. Instead he'd got a kick in the balls.

Gus took the letter out of his pocket and read it again at speed. It informed Gus baldly that Sir Roysten's business empire had experienced several bodyblows. Roysten Films had made a £26 million loss on the quarter, thanks mainly to the disastrous performance of its blockbuster movie *Total Predator*. They had been caught cold by the moral backlash. Critics condemned its mindless scenes of violence. Local church groups picketed cinemas. Finally, and perhaps most influential of all, it was crap. Even Gus, who had sat through the entire film out of loyalty, could see it was awful. Gus knew nothing about films, but he knew that people walking out saying 'This is crap' was a bad commercial indicator. And they had started walking out as early as the second scene, where Hugh Grant decapitated the nymphomaniac android. Sir Roysten had totally misread the market. Gus was deeply shaken. He'd always seen Sir Roysten as infallible.

The letter from Sir Roysten listed his other disasters (or 'glitches' as they were termed) including the foray into liposuction home-kits, which had resulted in several law suits. Gus cursed himself. He'd seen the signs. He'd heard the gossip. But he'd found it all just too scary to contemplate.

The second page laid out the terms on which Sir Roysten would agree to keep Globelink open. If these terms weren't met then Sir Roysten would shut down the whole operation overnight, or, as the letter put it, 'immediately return the workforce to the market place'.

The terms were simple – a fifty per cent reduction in staff levels and a cut in wages for those who remained.

Gus read the paragraph again, then scrabbled around in his top drawer, looking for his Relax-U-Balls. He found them and started clanking them around rapidly in one hand. It was clear that even after these Draconian measures Globelink's future would not be assured. The letter said Sir Roysten would only commit to a probationary period. Gus rotated the silver balls a bit faster. He walked over to his fish tank. One of the fish was trying to fight its own reflection. Gus watched it swim at speed towards the side of the tank, waggle its body aggressively at the imagined intruder and then dart away.

For the first time in his life Gus had bad thoughts about Sir Roysten. He'd always admired Sir Roysten so much, worshipped him even, as the ultimate achiever. But now Sir Roysten was letting him down. All the sweat Gus had put into this place, and now it looked doomed.

Gus gazed out through the glass partition wall of his office at the workforce he was expected to halve. George was talking to Helen. He looked relaxed. Odd that. And he was wearing a yellow polo-neck which didn't quite fit. Could Gus really fire George? That would be like drowning your pet hamster. At the far end of the office Gus could see Henry chatting to Connie, the new South African receptionist. Why wasn't she on the front desk? She would have to go. Last in, first out. Dave was on the phone, presumably to a betting shop or a married woman.

Gus recalled the incompetent way Dave and Henry had lied to him a few minutes earlier. Yes, they had definitely stepped forward for voluntary redundancy. And Damien, of course. He was just too much trouble these days, the way he kept disappearing. He had it coming to him. But one question kept coming back. What did the future hold for Gus himself? At best he'd be leading a chronically damaged operation. Understaffed and under-resourced, Globelink would probably limp along for a few months before expiring with a whimper. Then Gus would be stained with failure. No, no, no, that was not acceptable to his career curve. He would have to keep an eye open for an alternative opportunity. After all, he could walk into a job anywhere. Of course he could. Yes, indeedy! There were still plenty of hands-on executive roles for a serial achiever like himself. What was it that Texan on the Internet had said . . .? 'There is no failure, only feedback'. Yes, that was it. He picked up the phone. It was time for action. He'd give his old mate Alan Yentob a bell. Alan would give his right arm to have Gus on board. Unfortunately, Alan's secretary told him that Alan was in a meeting. No sweat. He'd ring Michael Grade instead. Mike was in a meeting too. So were John Birt, Greg Dyke and Chris Evans. Gus glanced into the newsroom and had the distinct impression people were staring at him. He closed the blinds, and picked up the phone again. There were plenty of other mates he could call.

George looked up from his terminal and glanced across at Gus's office. He wondered why Gus had drawn his blinds. George shrugged and went back to work. Ten minutes went by. Then the newsroom was rocked by the crash of two silver balls smashing through a fish tank.

Damien was driving very carefully. He was doing a steady forty in the slow lane of the M129. He was driving with this new-found caution because he was breaking the law by driving at all. He was banned, and the last thing he wanted to do was draw attention to himself. Besides, he was in a stolen car. Damien had thought long and hard about the risks of stealing a car, but in the end he'd decided any risk was acceptable if it meant not having to use the rail network again. So he'd hotwired the Granada which belonged to Gerry, the cameraman with the bit of shrapnel lodged in his head. The shrapnel caused Gerry to suffer occasional memory lapses. So, if challenged, Damien would simply maintain that Gerry had forgotten giving him permission to borrow the car.

A signpost appeared signalling the turn-off for Brecon. Damien had happy memories of this stretch of motorway. He'd covered a massive pile-up here in 1997. Forty-nine killed. Thirteen drivers trapped in their cars. A blood-stained child's teddy bear lying poignantly in the road. Damien always kept a blood-stained teddy bear on him. It often came in handy. The pile-up had been a good result for Damien. The pictures had been so brilliant they'd had to be prefaced by a warning that viewers might find them distressing (the ultimate accolade in Damien's book).

Damien slowed gently as he approached the slip road. It had been a trouble-free journey. True, it was a little humiliating for a Porsche driver to be driving a lime green Granada, but what the hell. He eased to a halt just in front of the toll gate. A small speaker crackled and a computerised voice addressed him.

'Wel-come-to-Ex-it-9-2-Please-in-sert-your-toll-point-card-now.'

Damien took out the plastic toll-card (which Gerry wouldn't remember lending him) and put it in the slot.

There was a click and a whirr and the card came back out again.

'We-re-gret-that-your-toll-point-card-is-over-drawn-Please-pull-in-to-the-en-quir-ies-lane-where-one-of-our-op-er-at-ives-will-ass-ist.'

'Shit,' said Damien. He heard the whine of a video camera turning to film him. Bloody Gerry! He'd probably forgotten to pay the bloody bill! Shit! Damien knew he couldn't be caught behind the wheel of a car flouting a driving ban. That meant prison. Not to mention months of compulsory counselling from psychotherapists. He heard a furious beeping from behind. The driver of a red Renault Challenger was gesturing for him to get a move on. Two Group 4 operatives in their canary yellow uniforms emerged from a kiosk and ambled towards him. Other cars further back joined in the beeping. The man in the red Challenger was shouting obscenities. The Group 4 men were only ten yards away now. Damien threw open the car door, leaped out, and raced up the grass embankment.

An hour later, Damien was standing in Brecon High Street, his arm in the grip of a huge Welshwoman.

'You are, aren't you, you're him, aren't you?' she was saying with deafening enthusiasm. 'Off the telly. I knew you were him.'

This was all Damien needed. Normally he loved being recognised but right now he wanted to be incognito. People were less likely to open up once they knew they were talking to Britain's foremost investigative TV reporter.

'I said you were him,' bellowed the giantess, letting go of his arm. 'Oh, yes. We like you around here! Very big in Brecon you are.'

'Thank you. Actually, I'm looking for Heslop's the butcher's. Can you help me?'

'Just up there, look. On the right, past the building society.'

'Great.'

'You look differently than on the box.'

'Yes,' said Damien, 'my trousers aren't usually spattered with mud.' He had made his way across country from the motorway, and it had not been easy country. 'Anyway, thanks for the directions.'

'Here. You couldn't say it, could you?'

'Say what?' asked Damien.

'That thing you always say. It's so funny. We always laugh when you say it.'

For a moment Damien stood bewildered.

'Go on,' she said. 'You know.' She stood with one enormous arm in the air and said, 'That's my arm, that is.'

Oh no, this was totally humiliating. Damien had been mistaken for Simon Simpleton, the young comedian who was inescapable on British TV. Damien hated him. The man's entire act consisted entirely of inane *non sequiturs* delivered in a childish squeak. The *Guardian* had called him 'a genius who has injected surrealism into mainstream comedy'. Damien called him 'that tosser with the lisp'.

'That's my arm, that is,' the woman squeaked again, before her massive lumpy frame doubled up in hysterics.

'I'm not him,' said Damien.

' 'Course not,' said the woman, winking.

'I don't even look like him,' Damien insisted.

'That's my arm, that is.' The woman dissolved with laughter again. Damien seized the opportunity to sprint up the road and duck into Heslop's the butcher's.

'Hallo there,' said a spotty-faced man, without, mercifully, the slightest flicker of recognition. 'What can I do for you, sir?'

'Um, I'd like some beef, please.'

'And what kind of beef will it be, sir? Topside? Silverside? Fillet? Rump? Sirloin?'

'I'm . . . I'm not sure, really.'

'Ah-ha, the little lady at home has sent hubbie out shopping, am I right, sir?' The butcher leaned towards him. 'Now did she tell you what kind of meal she had in mind?'

Damien struggled to remember the name of the dish on the regimental menu. 'It's that flaky pie thing, you know . . . Oh yeah, beef Wellington!'

'Ah, well for your beef Wellington, I'd say you ought to go for a decent bit of fillet.'

'Right. Some fillet.'

'Okey-dokey.' The butcher wiped his hands on his apron and, whistling the theme from *Jurassic Park 4*, stretched up and brought the fillet down from its hook. The butcher sharpened his knife.

Damien leaned casually across the counter. 'A friend of mine was at a big regimental dinner, you know, officers' bash, and he said you'd supplied the beef for that.' Damien pointed at the fillet. 'This is the same sort of beef, is it?'

The butcher stopped sharpening his knife. 'Officers' bash . . . Oh, yes, I remember now. The South Wales Borderers. A very smart function, that was. But what they had was my special.'

'Could you get me some?'

The butcher sucked in his breath.

'Oh, not worth my while to do it by the pound. It's so expensive, you see, I normally only take orders for group catering, you know, special occasions, like.'

Damien thought quickly. 'Oh, I'm sorry. Didn't I make it clear? It's not one fillet I want. The little lady at home is organising a big charity dinner.'

A gleam came into the butcher's eye. 'How big?'

'Thirty people.'

The butcher looked doubtful.

'Sorry, forty. I meant forty.'

'Forty? Hm. Could you come back tomorrow?'

Damien shook his head. 'No. I live in Swansea, you see. I've got to get back tonight.'

'That'll push the price up a bit. I'll have to organise a special delivery from my suppliers.'

'Oh, who are your suppliers?' asked Damien casually.

The butcher turned his eyes to the window. 'Good God, here comes the rain again! Would you credit it? They reckon it's these volcanoes in Iceland. Now look, I can do you this beef if you come back at six.'

'OK.'

The butcher was scribbling figures on a sheet of greaseproof paper. He looked up at Damien. 'Enough for forty beef Wellingtons . . . that'll be four hundred and eighteen quid. Call it four hundred, since it's for charity.'

Damien swallowed hard. 'No problem.'

'Has to be cash, no credit cards. Not with the way the banks keep going under.'

'Fine. I'll pay you when I collect it.'

'Only if you leave a deposit, sir. Fifty pounds'll be fine.'

Damien took out his wallet. This was ludicrous. He was about to buy his own personal beef mountain, when

151

all he needed was a few grammes to send to a lab for analysis. And he very much doubted whether Gus would allow him to put forty beef Wellingtons on expenses. He handed over the money. This story had better bloody lead somewhere.

The butcher slipped the £50 into his apron pocket.

'Cheers. See you at six. And tonight you'll be going home to a very happy little lady.'

Oh, shut your face, thought Damien, as he headed for the door.

A shortish, depressed-looking Welshman by the name of Gareth Pugh came out of an Indian restaurant, trudged along John Redwood Road and turned into Brecon High Street. He drew his coat around him as the December wind whipped at his thinning hair. The street was crowded with afternoon shoppers, but Gareth scarcely noticed them. His misery was so intense that a troupe of naked dancers could have passed him by and he would scarcely have noticed them. His unhappiness separated him from the rest of humanity. How could all one's hopes be fulfilled and then destroyed again within twenty-four hours, wondered Gareth?

Gareth trudged past the Bingley and Berlin Building Society, sidestepped two policemen dragging a beggar off to jail, and found himself staring into the window of an electronics shop. A mass of television sets was showing pictures from Berlusconi Weekend Television, Brecon Cable, BBC Rolling News, Bransonvision, and MTV. But that wasn't what interested Gareth. Because in one corner of the window, a dozen TV sets showed the face of the Globelink newsreader Sally Smedley. Gareth had always had a soft spot for Sally Smedley.

Her commanding presence somehow comforted him. He'd always liked women with confidence and presence. What a pity he couldn't hear what she was saying. Gareth moved closer to the window. The news bulletin was obviously ending, because a caption had appeared, 'Crisis 2000', followed by a phone number. A series of brightly coloured 'Globelink Cares' slogans flashed across the screen in rapid succession. Gareth frowned. This must be a new programme. Then he saw the face of Sally again. She had a look of such compassion on her face that he almost burst into tears. Sally seemed to be introducing a panel of experts. The captions revealed them to be a doctor, a psychotherapist and a stress counsellor. The phone number came up on the screen again. Then Gareth suddenly understood. He took out his pocket phone. He needed to speak to somebody about his troubles, needed to express the misery he felt. Surely Sally and her helpers would be able to offer some kind of advice?

Passers-by didn't pay any attention to the sight of a small man in a grey raincoat talking into his mobile phone in front of a television shop. Gareth waited to be put through. A recorded voice had told him he was on a stacking system. He hoped it wouldn't be too long; these 0891 numbers cost an absolute fortune. Gareth watched the screen. The caption now read 'On line: Sandra from Glasgow'. Sally was nodding intently. It was clear to Gareth that here was a woman who really wanted to help people. The experts took turns to chip in. Oh God, please put me through, thought Gareth. Don't let the programme end without— At that moment, he heard Sally's voice in his ear. He gazed at the TV screens in the window. Sally seemed to be looking straight at him, looking straight into the dark pit of his unhappiness. The voice in his ear was slightly out of synch with the lip movements on the screen. Sally was asking him something.

Gareth answered quickly. 'Um, Gareth. Gareth from Brecon.'

A second later, a new caption appeared: 'On line: Gareth from Brecon'. By God, this was bloody brilliant.

'And how can we help you, Gareth?' cooed Sally down the phone.

Gareth gulped. 'Um, well you see, Sally, a few days ago I married the woman of my dreams . . . but, but then, on our wedding night . . .' Gareth wiped his eyes. 'It's a bit personal, like. Embarrassing, really.'

Sally suddenly looked more interested. 'That doesn't matter, Gareth. You can be perfectly frank with us.'

'The thing is see, that . . . well, on our wedding night, I was unable to fulfil my duties as a husband.' He gazed at the screen. Was he imagining it, or did Sally look a little bored?

'Just first-night nerves, I imagine, Gareth. Did anything else occur? Our panel is quite unshockable, you know.' The cameras cut to the three experts looking very solemn.

Gareth sniffed miserably. 'No. Just that. But you see, that's really awful for me because—' At that point Gareth got cut off. He banged his phone. Was there something wrong with the bloody thing? He looked up at the screens again. Now the caption read: 'On line: Ms X (Trans-sexual from Norwich)'.

Damien slid into the back seat of the Toyota minicab. 'Heslop's the butcher's, please.'

The driver pulled a face. 'You could walk that.'

'Yes, I know,' snapped Damien. 'But once we get there, I want to wait outside for a while. Then there'll be another journey.'

'Where to?'

'No idea. Can we please get moving?'

The driver pushed the greying fringe of hair out of her eyes, and started the engine. Damien gave an exhausted sigh and flopped back in the seat. He hoped he'd have enough money to pay for the cab. His cash card had just been confiscated by the automatic dispenser at Bransonbank. 'Insufficient funds', the screen had flashed at him. Several passers-by had stopped to stare at the sight of that comedy bloke Simon Simpleton pummelling the machine and shouting, 'Give me my money, you fucking Dalek!' Now Damien didn't have enough money to buy the beef. That left only one option: to hang around outside the shop and see who delivered the bloody stuff. Then he'd follow the suppliers and with a bit of luck find out where it came from.

After a ninety-second drive, the cab pulled up opposite the butcher's.

'Can you reverse up a bit, please?' said Damien quickly.

'You're the boss.' She reversed a bit quickly, throwing Damien forward in his seat. She switched off the engine.

'And would you mind switching your lights off?' asked Damien.

She shrugged. 'All right, then.'

Damien peered out of the window and thought how dark the night was in Brecon.

His driver noticed him squinting. 'Council's in receivership, see. No streetlights for weeks now.'

The only significant source of light was the glow from the butcher's window. Mr Heslop appeared in the doorway and looked up and down the street, glanced down at his watch and then went back inside.

Damien and the driver sat silently in the darkness for a few minutes.

'I wonder if we might have the radio on?' asked the driver.

'Sure,' said Damien, his eyes fixed on the butcher's shop.

She tuned into a local station. The car filled with the belligerent vocal of Bad Boyos, the Welsh rap band.

> *'We don't want unemployment,*
> *We just want some enjoyment,*
> *We all got bags of hwyl,*
> *We don't want—'*

She stabbed at the station pre-set button. The World Service news was ending with an instrumental from a Meatloaf track. Then a voice started shouting about sport. 'Tonight, live on BBC World Service! Basketball from Atlanta, Georgia!'

'No, thank you,' said the driver, switching it off. She was quite elderly as cab drivers go.

'Been driving a cab long?'

'Not long,' she said, turning round. 'I only do evenings, you know, when I can.' A car drove past, illuminating the genial sparkle in the driver's eyes.

'I have to fit it in with my proper job.'

'Oh, right. What is your proper job?' asked Damien, still looking at the shop.

'I'm a priest.'

A priest? She had to be one tough cookie. Women priests were having a terrible time of it. The High

156

Church extremists had got very organised. 'Not an easy road, eh?'

'Oh, I don't know, I've got off quite lightly, really. Just the odd phone call in the night, you know. "Get out of God's house, you bitch", that sort of thing. And the local Gummerites have stopped picketing the vicarage. It's not so bad. I've always got my faith.'

Damien had never understood the notion of faith. Fancy placing your trust in some abstract being. Only mental weaklings needed an invisible crutch like that. All Damien trusted in was number one.

A loud beep marked the arrival of a large green van as it pulled up outside the butcher's. Damien watched intently as a man in a green uniform leaped out of the van. Heslop the butcher came scuttling out of the shop, and helped the man open the back doors. Together they unloaded a carcas. It was huge. They had difficulty carrying it into the shop. Damien read the logo on the side of the van: 'The Alert Patrol'.

'Security firm. All ex-Group Four,' his driver informed him. 'Got kicked out of Group Four after that Dartmoor business.'

The two men came back out and huddled in the doorway for a moment. Money was changing hands now, though Damien could tell from the animated gestures that the amount was at issue.

'Now, Reverend, when this van pulls away I would like you to follow it as craftily as possible.'

'Oh, right,' she said, with considerable relish. 'Are you the police, then?'

'No,' said Damien. 'I'm just a seeker after truth.'

The man in the green uniform climbed into the van and pulled away. The priest's hand reached for the ignition.

'Wait a sec,' said Damien. 'Let's not make it too obvious.' He waited for a couple of beats. 'OK, now!'

She turned the ignition key, slammed the Toyota into
first gear and stalled the car with a lurch.

'Jesus!' hissed Damien.

The reverend shot him a look. She re-started the
engine and the Toyota pulled away at unnerving speed.

It was going-home time. The newsroom was slowly emp-
tying as staff picked up their things, and headed for the
door.

' 'Night, 'night,' said George, as each one passed.
' 'Night, 'night, Helen.'

Helen was struggling to pull on her coat as she walked
to the door. George thought she looked tired. 'Put your
feet up this evening, eh? It's not been an easy day.'

No, thought Helen, it had certainly not been an easy
day. Gus's Burmese fighting fish had died a slow death,
flopping about among shards of glass on the carpet.
Then the newly elected MP for the Pensioners' Power
Party had had a nasty turn live on air during the early
evening bulletin. They had been forced to cut away early
to the weather girl, who wasn't ready and was caught on
camera picking the wax out of her ears. That was just
before the police arrived and tried to arrest Gerry the
cameraman for road-toll evasion. Helen was still struggling with her coat; she'd put her arm into the wrong
sleeve, so George hurried over to give her a hand.

'So, what'll it be?' asked George. 'Nice relaxing
evening in front of the telly?'

'No. Me and Chloë are having dinner at home
together.'

'Oh, that'll be nice.'

'Yes,' said Helen with barely concealed trepidation, 'I'm sure it'll be very nice. Bye.'

'Good God Almighty!' exclaimed Henry, who was huddled over a tape machine in the corner of the newsroom, watching a recording of Sally's programme. It was the bit where Sally was fielding the call from Gareth. Joy was watching it too, with a morbid fascination.

'This is nauseating,' yelled Henry. 'A repulsive slush-fest! I can't believe we actually broadcast this. Globelink has finally hit the gutter.'

George didn't know why Henry kept watching it if it upset him so much. He squeezed past Joy and switched off the tape machine.

'Time to go home. We don't really want to watch this, do we?'

Joy switched it back on. 'Speak for yourself.'

'It's just some sad little man bleating on about being impotent.'

'Exactly. Hugely entertaining.' Joy turned up the volume.

Dave drifted past, his leather jacket slung over his shoulder. ' 'Night all.'

'No date tonight, then?' said George in a chirpy, laddish way.

Dave fixed George with a weary stare. 'No. Sorry to disappoint you. I know you all have this image of me as some vacuous Lothario who keeps his brains in his crotch, but I am actually going home.'

Joy glanced over her shoulder. 'A likely story. He's going out on the pull. He'll put on his tightest Levis and hang around outside the hospice.'

'Oh, very droll!' Dave shouted, and stormed out of the office.

Oh, dear, thought George, that wasn't like Dave. Henry grabbed his coat and hat.

' 'Night, 'night, Henry!'

Henry grunted and swept past with a desultory wave.

Sally bustled into the newsroom and saw her own nodding face on the monitor. 'Came across very well, didn't I? I think the format of the programme allows me to show my human side.'

'Are there humans in your family, then?' enquired Joy. 'What, you mean, way back several generations, presumably?'

'Joy, I will not have my family insulted, do you hear?'

'You're right. I'm sorry. They've suffered enough.'

Sally resolved to write to Gus demanding Joy's dismissal. After all, Sally was the star of Globelink now. She threw back her head and swanned out.

' 'Night, 'night, Sally,' called George after her.

Joy switched off the tape machine. George watched as she packed away her things with jerky, aggressive movements. Joy often reminded George of his daughter Deborah. He smiled at the thought of Deborah. Like a lot of girls, she could be difficult sometimes, but to George she would always be his little Debbie, the chubby-faced two-year-old who used to call him 'Dadabops' and throw cutlery at him. She'd stopped calling him 'Dadabops' now, of course, though she still occasionally threw cutlery on her rare visits home. He hadn't heard from her for a while. Not since that card from the Hezbollah training camp.

George heard the slam of a drawer as Joy finished packing up. She did seem particularly edgy.

'Are you all right, Joy? No problems or anything?'

'Nothing that can't be solved by my slashing an artery.

Goodnight, George.'

' 'Night, 'night, Joy.' George found himself alone in the newsroom. Thanks to that wonderful book, he no longer felt panicky when left on his own ('You Are Your Own Best Friend', Chapter Twenty-one). He took his new blue raincoat off the coat-stand, crossed to the door and switched off the newsroom lights. He paused. Light still glowed from behind the blinds in Gus's office. A shadowy figure could be made out seated motionless at the desk. ' 'Night, 'night, Gus!' called out George.

There was no reply.

Damien sat in the darkness of the Toyota and pondered his next move. They had followed the green van through a warren of dark country lanes for about twenty miles. The reverend had driven with the reckless abandon of someone with a firm belief in the afterlife. Road markings had been largely ignored or treated as very loose guidelines. So it was with a sense of relief that Damien had seen the van pull into a fenced compound.

The Toyota was now parked at the top of a rise which offered a good view of what resembled a brightly lit internment camp. The fence, which was topped with gleaming razor wire, must have been at least twenty feet high, with video cameras mounted on it at fifty-yard intervals. Behind the fence, Damien could make out a complex of low prefabricated buildings.

'Where are we?' he asked. 'Have you got a map?'

'This place isn't on the map,' replied the reverend. 'It's the experimental farm. Creepy place. Loads of stories.'

'What sort of stories?'

'Well,' she said, 'old Hwyel who keeps his sheep on that hillside over there, he reckons one of his dogs was

161

attacked by something that got out of this place. Said it looked like a giant goat. Looked like Satan himself, he said.' There was a long pause. 'Mind you, old Hywel's the one who told Sky News he was raped in a corn circle by aliens.'

'What sort of experimental farm is it, then?' asked Damien, producing an Autofocus Bransonmatic.

'Search me.'

Damien decided to take a closer look. No men in green uniforms were in evidence so he felt the risk was worth taking. He turned to the reverend. 'Wait for me here, OK? Don't go away.'

She glanced at the meter. It stood at £28.60. 'Don't worry.'

Damien quietly closed the car door behind him and crept down through a thicket of ferns and brambles until he was just a few yards from the fence. He could see a couple of sheds. Outside the sheds were sacks of grain and some crates bearing the name 'Phabox UK'. Next to the shed were animal pens. There were no animals in sight, though he could hear a faint mooing. Somewhere near there were chickens, clucking gently. And somewhere very close he could hear a dog growling. A big dog. Very close. Behind him in fact. He turned and found himself confronted by a Dobermann, its teeth showing beneath a snarling top lip.

Damien looked around for a green uniform. Surely they weren't letting dogs roam around loose outside the fence? Obviously they were. Damien tried to remember everything he'd read about what do if confronted by an aggressive dog. Number one, he recalled, was 'Don't look the dog in the eye'. Otherwise the dog will feel it is being challenged. Two was 'Don't run'. If you ran you became prey and would trigger the dog's deepest hunting instincts. Three was 'Don't shout'. There was one more tip, but Damien couldn't remember exactly what it was – something to do with behaving in a dominant way which would convince the dog you were its pack leader. Maybe if he barked commandingly at the Dobermann. He certainly had no hope of out-running it. Yes, it was worth a try.

Damien's first few barks had an immediate effect on the Dobermann. It stopped growling instantly. Then it hurled itself at Damien's throat. He instinctively ducked and threw up his right forearm to protect his face. His elbow caught the airborne Dobermann's jaw with a dull clunk and the dog tumbled through the air and landed on all fours just behind Damien. It crouched close to the ground, snarling and growling some more. Damien, ignoring previous advice, turned and ran, shouting like a lunatic.

He felt a whack in the back and the ground came up to meet him. The impact jolted the air from his lungs, he rolled over quickly and kicked out at the thing as it came for him again. The kick missed. The dog lunged at his face and Damien's arm shot up again. He felt the Dobermann's jaws clamp around his forearm. 'Oh shit!' screamed Damien, as he felt the teeth start to puncture the skin. Then the dog's jaws slackened, and the creature crumpled into an unconscious heap beside him. Damien looked up to see the reverend holding a wheel-jack. Damien thought she looked beautiful.

She bent down, her brow furrowed with concern. 'Poor doggie,' she said.

Helen could not remember feeling so scared in her entire life. She cursed herself for feeling so scared. What was there to be scared of? She was simply going to tell her teenage daughter that she was a lesbian and wanted to set up home with her lover. Nothing scary about that. She took a corner of tablecloth and wiped the sweat from her hands.

'More ratatouille, Chloë?'

'Cheers, Mum.'

Helen ladled ratatouille on to Chloë's plate. 'Nice to have an evening together,' Helen said. 'Hardly ever see each other these days. Either I'm working late or you're out with Martin.' Helen smiled when she said the word 'Martin', because she didn't want Chloë to sense how much she loathed him. Martin was Chloë's choice, for now, and that was Chloë's business. If she chose to waste her time with a nineteen-year-old who wore silk cravats and voted Conservative, then so be it. It would soon pass. And it would end all the quicker if Mother didn't stick her oar in.

'Martin's coming round later, Mum, if that's OK,' said Chloë.

'Of course it's OK, darling,' replied Helen. 'How is he?'

'Oh, he's fine. He's got over four hundred signatures for his petition.'

'What petition is that?'

'Clearing up the vagrants.'

Helen watched Chloë finishing off the ratatouille. Why couldn't she get herself some interesting clothes? That Laura Ashley print frock made her look so frumpy. She was seventeen. She should be out enjoying life, going to all-night parties, hanging about with bikers, not attending public meetings and sending out circulars.

If Martin was coming round, Helen would have to

take her courage in her hands and spring the whole lot on Chloë now. Helen wished she'd told Chloë about being a lesbian years ago. Just as she wished she'd told her parents (who still asked her every week if there were any 'nice men' in the picture). Why did she fear disapproval so much? But Chloë wouldn't disapprove, surely? Chloë wouldn't judge her. Chloë loved her.

Helen started to ease gently towards the moment of truth. 'Chloë, there's a friend of mine I'd really like you to meet. You'll like her. Her name's Gail. She's a great friend. A very special friend.'

'Is she from work?'

'No. She's . . . Well, when I say she's a special friend, actually she's—'

Chloë interrupted, raising her hand. 'Mum, stop. I've got to say this.'

Helen's heart leaped into her mouth.

Chloë's voice wavered. 'I don't want to hear about this Gail person. I've something to tell you. I'm pregnant.'

Helen's jaw dropped.

'I'm pregnant. Three months in, actually. I'm sorry. I've been meaning to tell you.'

Helen exhaled slowly. 'Right . . . OK . . . Well . . . right.' She cleared her throat. 'Is the baby Martin's?'

'Of course, Mum.'

Helen wanted to scream. 'Right, and it was an accident, presumably?'

'Yes, but it doesn't matter. We were planning to get married anyway. This will just bring it forward a bit, that's all.'

Helen put her hand to her forehead. She glimpsed an image of a toddler in a cravat.

'I would have told you earlier, but I was scared you'd

165

disapprove. It'll be a lovely wedding. In church. We've already got our eye on a flat, and we're enquiring about a mortgage. Martin says there are some very attractive endowment policies available.'

Helen struggled to survive this nightmarish avalanche of news.

Chloë came round the table and took her mother by the hand. 'We just want to be a family, Mum. You know, a proper family with two parents and kids and a nice house.'

Helen felt an invisible force yank her to her feet. From somewhere deep inside came rage, pure undiluted rage. Her voice dropped by an octave. 'How *dare* you? How dare you keep all that from me! How could you be so secretive! How could you live a lie like that, making small talk over the ratatouille, coming and going for months and months and all the time *knowing, knowing,* that you were carrying the spawn of that, that, that . . . Nazi!'

Chloë remained calm beyond her years. 'You're upset, Mum.'

'Upset!' Helen shrieked. 'Upset! There isn't a word that describes how I feel! My daughter announces that she is having a baby, marrying a stormtrooper and going to create "a proper family", whatever that is! Presumably it's not a family where a single mother goes out to slave her tits off for seventeen years so that her daughter can have a decent education which the daughter then throws away by marrying a walking cravat!'

'Please Mum, don't judge us.'

'You're not even eighteen, for God's sake!'

Chloë beat her hands on the table. 'We want to settle down, we want something permanent.'

166

'Permanent brain damage. That's what you'll get living with him!'

Chloë headed for the door. 'It's no use, Mum, we'll discuss this when you've calmed down.' The door slammed, and Chloë was gone.

Helen hurled the bowl of ratatouille against the wall, crossed to the fridge, took out a half-kilo tub of double-whip chocolate fudge ice cream, and ate it.

The moment Henry had left work that evening, he had got in his car and headed for the Blackwater. He wasn't sure why he'd done it. He'd just felt the need to get away. And somewhere inside there'd been a lingering anxiety about the boat. He had stopped the cheque he'd given those two bastards who'd tried to claim salvage.

The drive had taken over three hours, thanks to a tail-back caused by a slow-moving convoy of vehicles transporting reprocessed nuclear waste to Harwich. So by the time Henry reached Maldon, it was almost chucking-out time. His body was crying out for food and alcohol. He parked his Rover outside the Maldon Arms, charged into the warm hubbub, squeezed through to the bar and ordered a double Scotch and two Cornish pasties.

'Henry!'

Oh no, that sounded horribly like Jim Bliss. Henry turned. It *was* Jim Bliss. There were worse members of the Old Gaffers' Association, but not many. The man was a twenty-four-carat arselicker, a PR wizard with thousands of contacts but no friends.

'Jim!' cried Henry. 'Nice to see you.'

'Nice to see *you*, Henry. I hear you're up before the Broadcasting Ethics Commission again, you naughty

167

boy, you!' Jim laughed. The skin of his face was tanned and extremely taut, the result of an overambitious facelift a few years back. 'Good result for your lot, Henry, nailing the Minister for Energy like that.'

'Yes, thank you.' Henry's eyes drifted longingly towards his pasties, which the barman had just tossed into the microwave.

'Very good result,' Jim repeated.

'Yes.'

'Yes.'

Henry's Scotch arrived. He downed it in one. 'Must dash, Jim! Enjoyed the chat.'

'Me too. We must do lunch some time.'

'Yes, why not?'

'Why not, indeed?'

'Absolutely.'

The barman slammed Henry's pasties on to the bar. Henry wrapped them in his handkerchief and elbowed his way towards the door. As he was leaving, he noticed Jim Bliss taking a drink over to an attractive young blonde woman. She didn't look very much like his wife.

Henry stepped out into the night air and trotted across the car park. Safely inside his Rover, he wolfed down the hot pasties. He didn't much like eating in his car, but it was better than suffering an endless exchange of banalities with Jim Bliss. He swept the pastie crumbs off his lap, started the engine, and drove off. It was only a couple of miles to the spot on the sea wall where he could park his car. He should be able to see *The Bosanquet* on its mooring, and go home reassured that it was safe and well.

Henry parked his car and walked along the sea wall.

168

The whole estuary was drenched in moonlight. He certainly wouldn't need the headlamps. He breathed in the salty air. Soon he would round the point and see his yacht moored in the creek. A lone curlew welcomed him back to the sea. He stumbled over something. It was a' piece of wood. He bent down to pick it up. It looked vaguely familiar. It looked like his boom crutch. He examined it carefully. It was indeed a piece of his boat. He recognised the worn piece of leather he had nailed into the carved wood to cushion his boom. He ran towards the shore. He peered out into the moonlit creek, trying to pick out his mast from the others moored nearby. He couldn't find it. His boat must have broken free. He scanned the shoreline but could see no sign of it. He closed his eyes and opened them again. He aligned himself with known features of the landscape. He performed mental trigonometry, lining up the telegraph pole with the beacon. His eyes swivelled twenty degrees North, and came to rest on the spot where his boat should be. He sat down in the damp grass and stared at the spot for a long time.

As the tide slowly receded, the tip of his yacht's mast appeared. A short while later the crosstrees appeared, glinting in the moonlight. Still Henry sat there. Finally, five hours later, the boat lay high and dry on the mud. Henry made his way across the saltings. He hoped there would not be too much damage from her submersion. The inside of the boat might just need pumping out. There would be a layer of mud over everything. Nothing that a high pressure hose couldn't put right.

As he approached her he could hear the little fountains of water pouring out of the seams. With every step he heard ominous creakings echoing from the yacht's timbers. The truth was beginning to dawn on him. His boat was designed to keep water out. It was not designed to keep it in. A few tons of water were now exerting pressure on the planking from the inside. Each rifle shot he heard was the snapping of a fastening. He hurried impatiently towards the boat, the mud sucking at his boots with unusual tenacity. If only he could reach her in time, he could pump her out.

It was as if the boat had been suddenly detonated. The planks sprang in unison from the frames. One moment she was recognisably a boat, the next she resembled the carcass of a Christmas turkey. Somehow Henry felt that if only he could find out how this had happened he could put her back together again. He took a torch from the pocket of his Barbour and flashed it into the splintered maw of the only thing he had ever loved. The beam came to rest on the inlet valve of the head. The arrow on the valve pointed forward. Someone had opened it. *The Bosanquet* was history.

Eight
December 9th, 1999

It was nine fifteen in the morning and George was reading a 1989 copy of *Punch*. The waiting room was full and Dr Pendry was behind on his appointments, because his computer had gone down, temporarily transporting his patients' records into electronic limbo. Not that the patients were called patients any more, of course. A notice on the wall read: 'Clients are requested to assist the doctor's throughput by appearing promptly for appointments'. Dr Pendry's receptionist was doing her best to keep on top of things, but her task was far from easy. Since the practice had gone public the clients were a lot stroppier. At least the ones who'd become shareholders were stroppier. A horsy woman at the counter was loudly threatening to take her complaints to OFFDOC.

George was not one of Dr Pendry's shareholding clients, but that didn't stop George being his most regular client. On George's last visit Dr Pendry had greeted him with the words, 'What is it today, George, a phantom pregnancy?' On another occasion, he'd suggested that George could save time and money by just faxing in his symptoms every morning. George felt safe with Dr Pendry. He'd been his GP for thirteen years and done his utmost to get to the bottom of George's sinuses. George particularly appreciated the way Dr Pendry always tried to jolly him along to make him feel better. Once when the doctor had joked, 'Tell you what, George, why don't we fill your nostrils with Semtex and then blow your head to smithereens? That'll cure your sinuses,' George had chuckled to himself for hours afterwards.

An old man came coughing and wheezing into the waiting room. The poor man was very distressed. He explained to the receptionist that he'd been waiting for a chest X-ray at the local hospital when the Resources Manager had appeared and informed him he fell outside their target parameters. The old boy had no idea what he meant. And nobody was keen to explain it to him. Least of all the receptionist, who was on the phone trying to close a deal on a hip replacement. The old man started shouting about El Alamein. George was relieved when the buzzer sounded and the receptionist nodded to him that it was his turn.

George walked down the familiar corridor and into Dr Pendry's surgery. 'Hallo there,' he said breezily. Dr Pendry was filling out some forms. He didn't look up. George sat down. Dr Pendry went on doing the forms. George looked out of the window. Dr Pendry's head slumped on to the desk with a weary groan.

'Everything all right, Doctor?'

Dr Pendry looked up with manic intensity. 'All right? Yes, of course I'm all right, why shouldn't I be all right? I lead such a full life. The government sends me all these lovely forms to fill in. Look, for every male patient – sorry, client – that I see I have to complete this health profile, isn't that fun? Yes, great fun, lots of lovely questions. Look. 14b, Does the client experience episodes of sleep disturbance? Tick box for yes. Does the client have bouts of depression, stomach upsets, sore throats,

172

nervous illness?' The doctor was shouting now. 'Anthrax, distemper, swamp fever? You're no problem, George, we just tick every bloody box for yes, don't we!'

George found the doctor's tone a little unsettling.

'Here's one: 39a, Has the patient complained of erectile dysfunction? If so, give dates. Well, George, well? Come on, dates of last bout of erectile dysfunction, hm?' The doctor was pacing up and down the room now.

'They're very thorough, aren't they?'

'Pointlessly thorough, George.' Suddenly all the air seemed to go out of Dr Pendry. He subsided into his leather chair and stared up at the ceiling. 'OK, George,' he intoned wearily. 'What is it this time? What symptom have you brought in order to help me widen the frontiers of medical science?'

'Actually, I've come about my sinuses.'

'Ah! A golden oldie. What news, pray, of your sinuses?'

'Well,' said George, 'they've completely cleared up.'

'Sorry?'

'My sinuses have completely cleared up.'

Dr Pendry sat bolt upright in his chair and rubbed his eyes. 'I'm sorry, George, I can't quite get my head round this.'

'All my symptoms have disappeared, and I just wanted to tell you how wonderful I feel.'

Dr Pendry struggled to put the pieces together. 'You came in . . . to see me . . . a doctor . . .'

'Yes.'

'. . . to tell me . . . the doctor . . . that you feel perfectly OK?'

'Yes,' said George.

'My busiest morning of the week, and you come in just to tell me you're not ill?'

'That's right,' said George. 'I thought you deserved the satisfaction of knowing you'd helped me through, thanks to all your time and support. I've cracked the mental side, you see. The past is a graveyard I need never revisit.'

'Really?' said Dr Pendry, losing the will to live.

'Oh, yes. It's in this book . . .' George read aloud from the first page: ' "Does your life feel like one long car crash happening in slow motion?" '

The doctor nodded robotically.

'Then this book is for you.' George slipped the book under the doctor's limp hand. 'Please. Take it. I went out and bought an extra copy. It's my way of giving you something back.' George got up and walked to the door. 'Don't overdo it, Doctor.' George left the room. He was glad he had done that. Doctors were shown so little appreciation. He smiled as he walked out through the waiting room. It was good to bring a little sunshine into other people's lives ('Sharing the Good News', Chapter Eleven).

'Gareth from Brecon' was now in Builth Wells. He was standing under an oak tree, plucking up courage to cross the road and ring the doorbell of his wife, Megan. If only that nice Sally Smedley hadn't been cut off, he was sure she would have advised him to do what he was about to do now. He'd been married to Megan for just over a week, but in that period they had spent only seventy-two hours together, before parting in a blaze of acrimony. Now was the time to heal the wounds.

Gareth shivered. The oak tree wasn't giving him much protection from the rain. It was nine forty-five. She was late setting off for work. Perhaps she wasn't going to work, perhaps she was too upset to go to work. Same as he was. That was it. The poor girl was in her flat crying her eyes out. Well, he would go and explain and everything would be OK again. He would tell her how he'd loved her from the moment she'd come to work at the lab. He would tell her how, for nine years, he had worshipped her from afar. He would tell her how he had been too scared to approach her because he was so very short and she was so tall and beautiful. (In fact, Megan was only five foot nine, but that's quite tall in the eyes of a man who's exactly five foot. Or used to be. Gareth had mysteriously grown three inches in the last year, which is rare at the age of forty-three.)

Gareth strode out from under the tree. He would tell her everything. Above all, he would tell her the *real* reason why their wedding night had been such a disaster.

He was just about to cross the road when the front door opened. It was Megan. She wasn't crying though, she was laughing. She was with someone. It was Mr Parmenter, his boss. Mr Parmenter, Gareth's big, burly, six foot four, rugby-playing bastard of a boss!

Megan and Mr Parmenter kissed and then got into their separate cars. It was a kiss that was to alter the course of history, a kiss that would lead to murder. It filled Gareth with fury, the kind of blind, consuming rage that only lurks in the hearts of short men. Short men who hate being short have shaped human destiny. Attila the Hun, Napoleon, Lenin, Menachem Begin, Lee Harvey Oswald, they all compensated for their lack of inches by cutting the rest of the world down to size. Gareth Boyce Pugh resolved to add his name to this roll-call of influential shortarses.

* * *

Dave's eyes drifted back to his VDU. He wondered how much longer Henry would drone on with his lament for *The Bosanquet*. It was mid-morning, the time Dave normally checked for important breakthroughs at Ladbroke's.

Henry went silent.

Dave's spirits rose, then sank, as Henry started up again. 'God, how I loved that boat. Double-ender she was. Well, she had a canoe stern, of course, as opposed to a counter stern or a transom stern, so it would be more correct to call her canoe-sterned. But doesn't matter what you call her, she was beautiful. And by God, how she moved. She sailed like a witch, slicing to windward, showing those fibre-glass caravans the way home. I didn't have to bother with new-fangled telltales, oh no, I'd sail her on the trembling of her luff, slipping along the edges of the wind, making five knots. In light airs I used to take the tension off the peak of the gaff, induce a little hollow in the sail, then slacken the foot to help the air escape off the leech. Off the wind I used to set a balloon staysail on a twenty-foot pole. The old girl used to get the foam beneath her bit and romp along. I'd put up the jackyard topsail for a little extra speed, and we'd surf along with the trailing log reading seven knots, steady as you like, hour after hour, day after day.'

Dave felt himself slipping into a coma. Henry rambled on for what felt like a couple of hours about jibs and tacks and binnacles. At last the tide of his grief subsided, and he sat gazing forlornly into the middle distance.

Dave wanted to say, 'It's only a boat, for Christ's sake!' but realised that this would be insensitive. 'Cheer up, Henry. There'll be other boats. Not the first one you've lost, is it? What about that one you wrote off a few years back?'

Henry did not respond.

176

'You remember, you got completely rat-arsed and somehow managed to sail her into a sewage works.'

Normally this reminder would have prompted a small chuckle, at least. But Henry remained impassive.

'Come on, mate,' said Dave. He became aware of Sally eavesdropping. She was hovering behind them, pretending to study the noticeboard. If Henry was in distress, she wanted all the glorious details. Dave put a protective arm round Henry and gave Sally a sideways glare.

At the same moment, in the adjoining office, George was putting a fatherly arm round Helen. As he did so, he was pleased to note that he did not feel a single pang of desire. There had been a time, a while back, when he had wanted her desperately. But now he could cuddle her and not feel the slightest bead of sweat form on his forehead. He was in control. He had grown.

George was so busy congratulating himself on his epic spiritual journey that he heard less than half of what Helen was telling him. In halting bursts she was describing how her ludicrously young daughter was carrying the child of the dreadful Martin. She lambasted Martin's politics, his attitudes, his dress sense (which sounded fine to George). Helen said she felt scorned and betrayed and then she burst into tears.

George squeezed her shoulder and searched for something to say. 'Come on,' he offered finally, 'babies are such fun. And you'll make a lovely granny.' Helen began to wail like a widow at an Arab funeral. George squeezed her shoulder a bit harder. He knew the tears were part of the healing process, but he couldn't help feeling embarrassed. He had never liked seeing women cry. It reminded him of his mother, who often used to look at George and just start crying.

'I'm sorry,' sobbed Helen. 'So sorry.'

George mentally scanned his self-help book. Various passages sprang to mind, but in the end he opted for 'I'll make a nice cup of tea.'

George left their office and headed into the newsroom. He went to the kettle, which was already half full, and plugged it into the electric point by Joy's desk.

Sally materialised at George's shoulder. 'Is poor Helen all right?' she enquired. 'Only I heard her wailing.'

'She'll be fine,' said George.

'It must wear her down. Being the way she is.'

George looked at her blankly.

'The way she is. You know? Handicapped by her hormones.'

George quickly changed the subject. 'Any sign of Gus yet?'

'No,' said Dave. 'Probably in therapy. Shares in Merchant Holdings hit their all-time low yesterday and Sir Roysten is "unavailable for comment".'

George played it upbeat. 'No point in fretting. You know the markets. Up, down, up, down, that's all they do. Up, down, up, down.'

'George?' said Henry.

'Yes?' said George.

'Shut up.'

George thought Henry's look was particularly thunderous, and wished the kettle would boil.

Sally sat down next to Henry and checked her rigidly lacquered hair. 'I can't say I'm bothered by the fate of Sir Roysten. My future's assured. *Crisis 2000* is making such an impact. I shall be the white Oprah Winfrey. Just look at these overnight figures for yesterday's programme,

Henry. Really rather impressive, don't you think?'

Henry ignored the statistics Sally had placed before him. 'Yes, well the world is full of sad wankers,' he boomed. 'And even more cruel bastards who want to listen to sad wankers.' Then Henry disappeared behind his newspaper.

'You must watch my special this afternoon, Henry,' Sally said. 'It'll interest you. It's all about the anguish of growing old.' Sally waited for a response, but Henry's newspaper didn't even twitch. 'You know, the feeling that one is sailing against the tide of life, the realisation that you're sinking fast, that time has holed you beneath the waterline.'

George wondered why Sally was labouring these clumsy nautical metaphors. She was halfway through one about the undertow of senility when suddenly the newspaper flew across the room and Henry exploded on to his feet. Everyone braced themselves for one of Henry's spectacular eruptions of invective, ablaze with invention and wit, a dazzling Krakatoa of spleen. Instead, Henry just put his face up against Sally's and roared. A long, threatening, animal roar. Then he closed his gaping mouth, folded up his newspaper, and strode out of the office.

Oo-er, thought George. Henry was obviously bottling something up. He'd have to have a little chat with him.

A thin whistling told him the kettle had boiled. George fished a Bransonbrew tea-bag out of a jar marked 'Tea Kitty Members Only'. He was just about to drop the tea-bag into a blue 'Chelsea Champions '96–'97' mug when Joy tapped him on the shoulder. 'Phone message, George. Margaret rang, can you nip round and paint the cellar. And Dave . . .' Dave looked up. 'Reception just rang. Maisie's on her way up.'

179

'Maisie?'

'Yes.'

'Oh God,' said Dave, hurriedly combing his hair. 'She might have warned me. How do I look?'

'Fine,' said a warm Scots voice. It was Maisie. George thought she looked very nice. With her short red hair and vivacious eyes, she reminded him of Lulu, whom he had always rather admired. Maisie held out a small plastic washbag. 'You left this.'

'Oh, right,' replied Dave. 'Thanks.'

'No trouble.'

Dave glanced self-consciously at George, who was hovering at his shoulder. George gave Dave one of his fatherly smiles.

'Won't Helen be wanting that tea, George?'

'Right. Yes,' said George. 'Nice to meet you, Maisie.' Then he slid through into his office with a mug of tea and some digestives.

As he closed the door with his foot, Helen took the tea from his hand. 'What was that roar?'

'Oh, Henry's just feeling a little bit moody.'

'Oh no. He's up before the Ethics Commission this afternoon.'

'He'll be OK,' said George, putting his arm round her again, purely to reassure her.

The nearby coffee bar where Dave had taken Maisie was pretty grim, but it was better than trying to have a private conversation in the bloody Globelink building. They sat by the window and watched the rain as it bounced off the umbrellas of passers-by.

Dave tried frantically to marshall his thoughts. He presumed the return of the toilet bag was meant as the final kiss-off. On the other hand, Maisie could easily have posted it back to him. Or just chucked it in the bin. Maybe there was hope after all. Maybe he was being given one last chance. He took a deep breath. 'Maisie, I . . . I . . .'

Two cappuccinos were plonked on the table by a man with coalminers' fingernails.

'Thank you,' said Dave lamely. 'Maisie, I . . . when I told you that I'd cheated on you . . .'

'Twice,' prompted Maisie.

'Cheated on you twice, well I—'

'With two widows.'

'Yes, with, um, with two widows, well I—'

'On two consecutive nights.'

'Well, let's not get bogged down on the details, let's just say that when I told you all that, I was being honest with you, wasn't I?'

'Oh. That makes it all right, does it?' Maisie's eyes flashed.

'No, of course not. But you see, it was the first time I'd ever told a woman that I, that I'd been unfaithful. Sometimes they'd find out, of course, but, I, er, I never told them, as such, like I told you.'

Maisie's eyes burned into him like lasers. She sipped her cappuccino. 'Do you want me to thank you for being honest, or what?'

Dave leaned forward and took her hand. She pulled it away again. Christ, she wasn't making it easy, was she?

'Look, Maisie, what I'm saying is, I was honest to you because I think you're special.'

'Gosh. I feel incredibly privileged. Special?'

'Yes. Special in the sense you're the kind of person I could imagine making a commitment to.'

181

'And screwing two Welsh widows on the trot? That qualifies you to talk about commitment, does it?'

Dave heaved a huge sigh. He wasn't used to this kind of conversation. Normally he'd bugger off the minute they started putting on pressure. But Maisie was definitely special. 'I'm not defending what I did. I'm just saying I think I could, you know, put my past behind me and move towards a commitment now.'

Maisie shook her head with incredulity. 'Dave, I asked you to make that commitment months ago. I said, let's move in together, and you were terrified. The nearest you came to commitment was moving in a washbag containing a flannel, a toothbrush and a packet of condoms.'

'I left two pairs of underpants as well.'

She stared grimly at him. Maybe it wasn't the moment to be flip. He stared into his cappuccino. 'Yes, yes, I know, yes, I admit I was scared. I've never really had um, a sustained . . . relationship with anyone. I've always been a bit unlucky in the women I chose. There was someone who I, er, once, long time ago, wanted to have a long-term relationship with, but that proved impractical because she turned out to be a lesbian.'

Maisie snorted with laughter in mid-sip, and cappuccino came down her nose.

Dave couldn't find the memory of his disastrous encounter with Helen quite so amusing. 'What's so funny?'

'Just your incredible ability to choose women who're not really available. It's nothing to do with being unlucky. That's what scared you about me, isn't it? That I really was available. That's why you went widow-shopping. So as to destroy our chances together.'

'No. It was just . . . bad luck, that was all. And bad

182

judgement too, of course,' Dave added hastily.

Maisie smiled. She had a lovely warm smile and Dave felt his hopes rising.

'Dave, in many ways, you're a very nice man. But you're not serious relationship material.'

Dave protested.

Maisie raised a forefinger. 'Let me finish now . . . You can't help it. It's an affliction. You're a martyr to your groin.'

'I can change.'

'Not without surgery.'

Dave suppressed his annoyance and stared out of the window. A buzzard landed in a skip outside the Globelink building and emerged moments later with a small tail hanging out of its beak.

'I still think I could change.'

'Well, I'd rather not be your test flight, if that's all the same to you.' She put her hand on his. 'Don't be so glum. Maybe someone else would take that chance.'

Dave tried to smile. 'Oh, well,' he said. 'So marriage is out of the question?'

Maisie burst out laughing. 'I presume that's a joke?'

Dave shrugged. He hadn't actually meant it as a joke.

Gus had never fed the ducks before. Not even as a kid. But here he was, in St James's Park, lobbing bits of loaf at a scrum of mallards, mandarins and those funny little black ones with the tuft at the back of their head. Gus was enjoying the politics of the experience. You have the bread, the ducks come to you. Total power. They quack and squawk and fight just to snatch any crumb you might throw them. Gus liked being the God of Crumbs. It was a bit like being Sir Roysten.

This was also the first time in Gus's life when he had woken up and been unable to face going into work. In fact he'd lain in bed, just staring at the ceiling, for forty-five minutes. That was so unlike him. Perhaps he was going down with some wasting disease.

He looked at his watch. Eleven thirty. They'd be having an editorial conference and he wasn't there to say, 'I'm not here.' What's more, he didn't care. Gus was frightened by the realisation that he didn't care. He shook the last of the crumbs out of the bag and his feet disappeared in a cloud of ducks. He stepped carefully out of the gaggle and walked up towards Buckingham Palace.

The sky was a low ceiling of grey. As he walked, Gus initiated an option-rehearsal strategy. If he accepted Sir Roysten's terms, and halved the staff, he would be the most hated man at Globelink. (In fact, Gus had enjoyed this title for many years, but had always imagined that his staff liked him for his approachable manner.) And after the massacre, what then? Gus wasn't sure if he could carry on. But what was the alternative for him? Gus kicked an empty coke can and shouted the F-word. 'Failure!' Nobody heard him because his shout was drowned out by a loud whoosh from a Westminster Council patrol van which was hosing down the vagrants. No, Gus couldn't resign. He wouldn't be able to cope with the fear, the uncertainty. He wouldn't be able to face the total loss of self-esteem. Most of all, he wouldn't be able to face his smug bastard of a brother, Julian, the bloody wonderboy. The family darling. The talented, good-looking, popular, happy smarmball.

Gus had no choice but to hang on by his fingernails and just hope he would survive. He would have to meet Sir Roysten's terms. But who would have to go? That

184

truant Damien, obviously. The newsreaders would have to be downsized to just Sally. Gus winced at the thought of being reliant on Sally. She would exploit the situation horribly. But Henry was getting no younger. He no longer received those suggestive letters from housewives (well, hardly any, just a couple in what looked suspiciously like Henry's handwriting). So, it had to be Henry. It would be an unpopular decision, but at least the broadcasting regulators would approve. Gus knew he had to retain Joy. Much as he would love to lose her, her efficiency was crucial. She might be terrifying and prone to bouts of vengeful violence, but her work was quick and accurate. Similarly Helen was pivotal to the station's core activity. Dave was not pivotal to anything, so he could go. That left George. Gus weighed up George's contribution to Globelink. It didn't take very long.

Gus's deliberations were interrupted by a Tannoy announcement.

'Will those customers wishing to be knighted by the animatronic Queen Elizabeth, please enter by Gate F. Thank you.'

Gus had reached the Palace. A long crocodile of tourists, in brightly coloured cagoules, was queueing beneath a garish sign, all pinks and yellows, which proclaimed: 'The Living Museum of Windsor'. Even Gus found the marketing slightly vulgar. Some American children were tickling a life-sized cut-out of ex-Prince Charles with a speech bubble that said 'One's thrilled to see you'.

Gus gazed up at the freshly painted Palace façade and reflected on the transience of things. No dynasty lasts for ever, he thought. All empires crumble in the end. Maybe even Sir Roysten's.

Gus glided by these thoughts as quickly as possible and chose to concentrate on specifics. Sir Roysten's letter had insisted on fifty per cent staff cuts by 1 January, 2000. So Gus would announce the sackings, the 'human resource reallocation programme', on New Year's Eve. Admittedly it might put a bit of a damper on the New Year's Eve party. But despatching the victims quickly would be kinder. If Gus dismissed them now there would be three weeks of pointless arguments, and recriminations. Gus felt he didn't have the emotional energy to go through all that. Besides, since the removal of all the red tape constraining British industry, workers were not entitled to more than eight hours' notice.

An excited murmur passed along the queue of tourists. Word was spreading that today all visitors would be personally greeted by former Prince Edward, Managing Director of British Palaces Plc. Gus glanced at his watch. Eleven thirty-five. He really should go to work now. He set off with leaden steps. He crossed the road and joined the end of the queue.

The chairperson of the Broadcasting Ethics Commission tapped on the table with her pen. Then she leaned across to confer with the pale, bespectacled man on her left. They whispered, which Helen thought a little rude, and nodded to each other. Then the woman leaned across to the other side and repeated the performance with the young man in the bow tie.

Helen glanced across at Henry to see how he was coping. Henry gave her a lovely smile. He was showing admirable composure. Helen noticed that the chairwoman, Lady Sylvia Tench, bore a remarkable resemblance to Richard Nixon, shortly before his death.

The woman was, undoubtedly, the ugliest female she had ever seen. Helen wasn't being bitchy. She was being factual. As a feminist, Helen hated the way plain women's looks were held against them. But this woman was hideous and there was no point denying that. She ought not to be allowed out in public.

Lady Tench looked up and approximated a smile. 'I'm dreadfully sorry, but our President, Sir David Mellor, is unable to attend this hearing as he was called away at short notice to make a guest appearance on *Masterchef*.'

Helen prayed that Henry would not make any wry observations.

Lady Tench's piggy eyes shifted towards Helen. 'The Commission was given to understand that your Mr Gus Hedges, your Chief Executive, would be present here today.'

'Yes,' said Helen, 'yes, um, he's been unavoidably detained.' (I must try to be more convincing, thought Helen.) 'Yes, he's um . . .' (God knows where). 'He's had a bereavement.' (Oh hell, why did I go for that? I wish I knew how to lie.)

'Oh, we're sorry,' said the bespectacled man. 'Family?'

'Yes,' said Helen, a fraction too quickly.

'Right,' said Lady Tench. 'To business. The Commission has now viewed the offending material several times. It seems to us that throughout the interview the Minister for Transport remained civil and courteous while you, Mr Davenport, became increasingly offensive in tone.'

'If I might say something,' Henry interjected.

'In a moment,' snapped Lady Tench. 'Apart from the sarcastic reference to the hedgehogs, there were several questions where your tone was most rude. For instance,

187

the questions, "You say our trains are excellent, Minister, but when did you last travel by train? Or have you merely observed their excellence from the comfort of your limo?" ' Lady Tench's turkey neck wobbled in indignation. 'Defend the personal animus in that, if you can.'

Henry put his fingers to his lips and thought for a moment. Then he started to speak in smooth, measured tones. Helen loved Henry's speaking voice. It had an old-fashioned mellifluous quality. Except when he ranted, of course.

'If the Commission will recall,' Henry began, 'this interview took place on a day when the government had announced the total de-regulation of transport. This prospect raises considerable public alarm. Already the quality of life of the average citizen is diminished on a daily basis by the collapse of our rail network, the absence of viable alternatives to private cars, the congestion which turns ring roads into circular car parks, and the levels of stress which result in apoplectic workers arriving home with a psychopathic urge to kill.'

A slight edge had crept into Henry's voice. He smiled and softened his tone. 'In the light of those circumstances, I endeavoured to speak for the travelling public. I asked the Minister why his government, indeed why any recent government, had failed to come up with a coherent policy for transport in this country. He replied evasively. I pressed him again. He quoted some obscure statistics and called me by my Christian name to make it seem he was responsive. To try to elicit a more meaningful response, I put the question again in slightly more colourful language. He refused to answer the question and instead answered a question I had not asked him. I then put it to the Minister that there was perhaps a gap in perception between a politician's view of things and real life.'

'Yes,' said the young man in the bow tie, slowly reading aloud from a transcript. '"With respect, Minister, as you drive from ivory tower to ivory tower, with your motorcycle escorts clearing a path, can you ever expect to know what life is really like for people in this country? You can't experience it any more. You could imagine it, of course. But only if you had an imagination. So no luck there. Would you agree that you have lost touch with the people who've voted for you?"'

Henry stuck his chest out. 'I stand by every word of that.'

Helen thought he was doing brilliantly.

The hideous Lady Tench leaned alarmingly across the table. 'Mr Davenport,' she intoned, 'all across the country we see a lack of respect for our most cherished institutions. How can we reverse that trend if you show no respect on television towards a government minister?'

'Respect has to be earned,' answered Henry calmly.

'He's a minister. He automatically commands respect.'

'Not if he dodges the question,' Henry maintained.

The three members of the commission regrouped and whispered to each other.

Helen winked at Henry.

The man in glasses cleared his throat and fixed Henry with grave intensity. 'You will recall, Mr Davenport, that you were summoned before this Commission just a few months ago, subsequent to your having been abusive while conducting an interview with an anti-drinking campaigner.'

Helen dived in. 'The Commission accepted that Mr

189

Davenport's behaviour during that interview was due to an adverse reaction to some medication.'

'Indeed,' said the man. 'But the Commission feels that Mr Davenport has a tendency on air to sacrifice good manners.'

'With respect,' Henry butted in, 'my manners are only sacrificed when I encounter arrogance!'

'The Minister was polite.'

'Ministers buy time by being polite. I have to cut through that.'

The bespectacled man turned to his two colleagues. There was a great deal of whispering and nodding.

Henry's won this one hands down, thought Helen. Intellectually he had won every argument. No contest.

Lady Tench tapped her pen on the table. 'Globelink News is fined two hundred thousand pounds,' she said, 'and you, Mr Davenport, are personally fined ten thousand pounds. You will be sent a full copy of the ruling.'

Henry went white. He's going to blow, thought Helen. He'd been controlling his anger all through this hearing but now she knew he'd bury them with a firestorm of devastating invective.

'Thank you,' said Henry meekly.

A massive roar went up as the tall blond German defender crashed into the Arsenal striker. The striker collapsed in a heap. Thirty-five thousand voices shouted, 'Off! Off! Off!' and Mrs Grindlay found herself joining in. 'Off! Off!' she screamed, her shrill voice resounding around the characterless interior of the hospitality box. She felt a moment's embarrassment at behaving in such an unladylike manner, but luckily she was alone.

She rummaged inside her handbag and fished out her

pack of cigarettes, ignoring the bottle of Krug '49 that was sitting in the ice-bucket next to her. She hated champagne. A crescendo of booing battered against the Perspex windows of the box. The ref had not sent the Hamburg defender off; he had merely subjected him to a long, prissy, finger-waving lecture.

'Tosspot,' said Mrs Grindlay as she lit up. Excitement always made her crave nicotine. As did stress. Or depression. Or the weather. There were so many good reasons to reach for the weed. She didn't like being addicted. She wasn't one of those smokers who went around saying, 'My Uncle Herbert smoked sixty a day and he lived till he was a hundred and four.' No, she knew full well what a deadly habit it was. In fact, she felt she had been duped. It was now clear that as early as the 1950s the manufacturers had known their product was harmful and addictive. Test results had been hushed up, documents destroyed, nods and winks exchanged with the government. Now, forty years later, the anti-smoking backlash meant she was an addict *and* a pariah. She remembered the ads of her youth. 'You're never alone with a Strand'. Well you would be nowadays, you'd be at home with the curtains closed. Perhaps she could sue. In the United States there were more than 50,000 such cases going through the courts. A man in Baltimore who'd shot nine people dead in a shopping mall had claimed it was due to 'smokers' rage'. Psychiatrists had testified that the frustration at failing to give up smoking, coupled with feelings of persecution, had driven the man to random murder. The court had awarded him $23 million in damages. Hmm, she thought, perhaps if she random-murdered Mitchell.

A klaxon sounded the quarter and the players trotted

to the touchline. Mrs Grindlay hated these stoppages. They'd been introduced to allow more commercial breaks, but they killed the flow of the game.

Her thoughts turned to Damien Day. She'd spent an hour that morning accessing everything State Security had on him. She'd read the summary which concluded that Damien was 'not psychotic in the clinical sense'. She wasn't so sure. Some parts of the detailed biography were alarming. She'd felt quite nauseous at the account of how he'd once asked a South American death squad to repeat an execution, using a propped-up corpse, because the first take had not looked very good. All in all, she was mildly concerned about Damien. Spooks Division were supposed to be following him, but had mistakenly tailed his next-door neighbour instead. Which as far as Spooks Division was concerned, was pretty much par for the course. She guessed Damien had gone back down to Brecon. She was sure he wasn't bright enough to unravel it all. But he was an obsessive, and she knew from working with politicians that an obsessive's blinkered drive often carried them much further than their intelligence could ever do. Maybe Damien had already talked to other people at Globelink. Maybe he knew more than her tap into the Globelink mainframe was revealing.

Mrs Grindlay stubbed out her cigarette in the little travelling ashtray she always carried with her and slid open the window to let the smoke clear. Maybe she needed a pair of ears in the Globelink newsroom.

She heard a voice outside the door and opened the window a bit more. Jim Bliss breezed into the box, his tubby frame encased in one of those shiny green suits which were all the rage. His manner was confident and urbane or, as some put it, insensitive and smug. He was fifty, but saw himself as twenty-five.

'Bit nippy in here, Mrs G,' Bliss barked, and slid shut the window. 'Oh, don't worry, I shan't tell.' He sat down with a loud swish from his trousers. 'Enjoying the game?'

'Looks like a nil-nil to me. Arsenal's final ball is letting them down.'

The blank look on Bliss's face revealed that he knew nothing of football. This box was for corporate hospitality, not watching the game. 'I'm a rugby man myself,' he said.

Mrs Grindlay had never seen the point of rugby. Just a lot of overweight men treading on one another's faces. And that oval ball seemed to bounce off in completely arbitrary directions, so it was really more a game of luck than judgement. Whereas football, when played properly, was a game all about judgement. She loved football. She especially loved the drama of evening matches. Something about the cauldron of warm, packed humanity and the noise and the blaze of floodlights against the inky black sky. At least that's how she remembered it, as a little girl standing with her dad on the terraces of Stamford Bridge. She used to get up on to a little folding stool that he'd made for her. But now the terraces had all disappeared. Everybody sat now. Nobody drank Bovril. Nobody wore bobble hats in their team's colours, and nobody swung noisy, brightly painted rattles. Football just wasn't what it was.

She realised she'd better pay a little attention to Bliss. She hadn't come here merely to watch football. 'This is a tremendous treat for me, Jim. I'm really very grateful.'

Bliss smoothed back his hair. 'No problem. I get this box free. As a thank-you for helping the club out on the PR front. You remember, over that Page Three girl?'

Mrs Grindlay remembered all right. Bubbly busty Barbara had claimed to have worked her way through the entire Arsenal midfield on the night before the Cup Final. Though Mrs Grindlay doubted whether Barbara could have enjoyed the experience; the Arsenal midfield were notoriously unimaginative.

The klaxon sounded and the players came back on to the pitch.

Arsenal kicked off and the play soon got bogged down in a patch of bad passing and mistimed tackles. The German defenders clattered persistently into the back of the young Arsenal striker whom the media were hailing as the next Jimmy Greaves. In Mrs Grindlay's eyes, this amounted to sacrilege. Greaves could not be replicated.

An angry roar signalled another foul. Players from both sides surrounded the referee and jostled the little man around. The Arsenal manager ran on to the field, waving his arms wildly. The game was degenerating into a brawl. Mrs Grindlay lost interest.

Jim saw that it was the right moment to move to business. 'So, Mrs G, that little chat you had in mind?' He smiled, to the limit that his facelift would allow.

Mrs Grindlay turned to him. 'I won't bore you with all the details, Jim. In a nutshell, the manufacturers of a certain wonder drug which stimulates the growth hormone in cattle—'

'Bovactilax?' asked Bliss.

'Correct. Well, they've dropped something of a goolie. A consignment of beef from an experimental herd, never intended for human consumption, was sold by some spivvy little security man and ended up being eaten by a bunch of army officers at a regimental dinner.'

'Oh, dear,' chuckled Bliss, 'naughty.'

'Quite. And unfortunately the large amounts of the drug ingested by these men resulted in certain side-effects.'

'Such as?'

'Impotence. Then depression. And, in some cases, suicide.'

Bliss shuffled his feet. 'I see. Um, how many suicides?'

'Eleven so far, including two decorated war heroes.'

'Bloody hell!'

Mrs Grindlay's attention drifted momentarily back to the game, which had restarted.

Bliss frowned. 'It all sounds a bit like that Brecon story. You know, the electro-magnetic fields. Didn't that also lead to army suicides?'

'It's the same incident, Jim.'

'Oh, I see. Well I must say the electro-magnetic stuff was a very nice piece of news management. Couldn't have done better myself.'

'Thank you. Unfortunately – that was never a goal kick – sorry, unfortunately, a pushy reporter is now starting to turn over a few stones.'

Bliss suddenly understood the purpose of their meeting. 'I can fix that for you. I'll spread the word that if this reporter starts touting anything round, there should be liberal use of the sterilised barge pole.' He poured another glass of Krug and relished how important he felt. He liked feeling important. He was a specialist. He did it partly for the money, but mostly for the importance.

Mrs Grindlay smiled at him and refused another glass of champagne. She thought he was pathetic. Useful, but pathetic.

195

'That would be a great help, Jim.'

'All part of the service.'

The crowd was now whistling derisively. A German forward was rolling on the ground in a ludicrously over-acted display of agony.

'Still sailing?' asked Mrs Grindlay, purely as some-thing to say.

'Not really keen on winter sailing, unless it's in the Med, of course.'

'And how's Melanie?' (She had almost said Melissa, but then she'd remembered that Melissa was his mistress in Maldon.)

'Very well. Taking a quiet break in Monaco.'

(Yes, with the Portuguese male model.)

'Putting her feet up.'

(Well, you could call it that.)

It amused Mrs Grindlay to think that his wife was having fun with her toyboy while Bliss fondly pictured the old girl sitting in a deck chair with a cup of tea in her hand.

'Actually, Jim, what I'd most appreciate from you is a sort of fire-fighting document, in case all this blows up in everyone's face. I'd like you to propose, in PR terms, what the government's response might be.'

'Yes. The government's response to what, exactly?'

'The government's response to evidence that it covered up events which led to the poisoning of army officers who subsequently became impotent and died.'

'Right,' said Bliss.

Mrs Grindlay's noticed that his sunlamp-orange face had paled a little. 'This is a real just-in-case job, you understand? I'm sure we'll all keep the lid on. But I believe in covering every conceivable contingency.

OH YES! Brilliant goal!' Mrs Grindlay was on her feet, punching the air.

Jim Bliss poured himself another glass of Krug.

Nine
December 10th, 1999

It was eight forty-five in the morning and Sally was copulating with the sound man. She was copulating with the sound man on all twelve screens in the Engineering Department. A small, bored technician watched all the screens simultaneously, checking each picture for quality. Dave hovered behind him, nervously glancing at his watch as he waited for the copies to be run off. Sally's cries suddenly grew louder. 'Whoops,' said the technician, twiddling down the volume slightly. The sound man's buttocks shifted to a quicker tempo. 'Neat little bum,' murmured the technician. 'What's his name?'

'His name's Toby,' Dave answered. 'But there's no hope for you there, Graham, because, a) he's two hundred per cent hetero, and, b) he left Globelink and went to Australia nine months ago.'

'Pity,' sighed Graham. He chewed on a cheese sandwich as Sally shouted a series of detailed instructions. 'By the way, I'll be wanting some copies of this for my friends. We think La Smedley is a star.'

Dave recalled that Sally was something of a gay icon. In fact, once a year, the gay bars of Soho combined to stage a SallyFest, where hundreds of men spent the evening dressed as Sally Smedley, with immaculate sculpted hair and startlingly severe jackets. It was a real carnival evening, though Sally had repeatedly attempted legal action to get the event banned.

'What are you charging for these tapes?' asked Graham.

'The Bumper End of the Century Christmas tape is remarkable value at only five ninety-nine.'

'What, and it all goes to you?'

'And why not? I've spent hours working on this. There's some great stuff on it. As well as Sally's legendary knee-trembler, there's Henry mispronouncing the word Shi-ite live on air.'

'Oh, yes,' laughed Graham nostalgically.

'And there's the video of the charity tournament where Gus got a bit competitive and shouted "Eat dirt, scum!" every time he took a point off Harry Secombe. There's George blacking out on *Right to Reply*, and Damien's Amazon rainforest piece where Gerry the Cameraman has the unfortunate encounter with the piranha.'

Graham shifted uneasily. 'How long's it going to take to dub these off, then? Only I don't want to get caught. You know what it's like round here. They're looking for the slightest excuse to sack people.'

'Yeah, yeah. Just fifteen minutes or so. No problem,' said Dave, glancing through the porthole window in the door. 'I've got a clear view down the corridor.'

Sally's volume increased again. 'Oh yes!' she gasped.

'Oh no,' groaned Dave, as he spotted a familiar lemon polo-neck approaching. He hurtled into the corridor, slamming shut the door behind him. 'Hi, George!'

'You're in early, Dave.'

'Oh, just putting in a bit more work on the *Review of the Century*.'

George was impressed. 'And how's it going?'

'Oh, pretty well. Got up to 1990. John Major becoming PM.'

'John Major,' said George wistfully. 'I wonder where he is now?'

'I wonder,' said Dave, moving to block George's view into the VT edit suit.

'Do you want to show me what you've done?'

'Later, George. All the machines are tied up at the moment. We'd best go up to the newsroom and get cracking on today's stories, eh? Come on.'

George was troubled. 'I can hear a woman yelling.'

'Can you? I can't. Come on, there's all that Cyprus stuff to decide on.'

'Something about "not yet",' puzzled George, as Dave led him to the stairs. 'Are you sure you didn't hear it?'

'Positive.'

'Oh.'

They walked up the stairs from the basement and got in the lift on the ground floor. George pressed the button for the newsroom. The door glided shut. A few seconds later, the lift juddered to a halt. Dave stabbed at various buttons. Nothing happened. 'Shit!' he said. They looked at each other for a moment, then George pressed the emergency button and waited for the alarm bell to ring. There was only silence.

Dave kicked the wall of the lift. 'We're stuck in this bloody thing!'

George patted him on the arm. 'Don't worry. The team will soon notice I'm missing.'

An hour and a half later, nobody in the newsroom had noticed that George was missing. Helen was staring at the artist's impressions lying on the desk in front of her. It was always hard to find an artist capable of providing decent visuals for these judicial enquiries. She examined the drawing of the Minister for Northern Ireland. He'd been portrayed as a double-chinned lardball with a huge red nose and protruding ears. This was no good at all. It would have to go back. It was far too realistic. She didn't want any hassle.

Oh God, thought Helen, I hate this enquiry. It had been sitting for eighteen months now, and with every day that passed, the story became more and more impenetrable. Public interest had died months ago. Lord Justice Grey had done his best, but with the evidence of the 490th expert witness, even he was having difficulty concealing his complete bafflement. So far, not one incontrovertible fact had been established other than the fact that in 1998, elements in British Intelligence had sold twenty-two Patriot missiles to the IRA. Nobody knew why. And nobody cared any more.

Helen looked up at the sound of ironic applause from Joy. Damien had returned. He swept through the newsroom towards Helen.

Joy jeered, hands on hips. 'You're in deep shit, boy. Gus wants your gonads for cufflinks. I'm telling you, you are dead.'

Damien looked around the office. 'Is Gus in?'

'No,' said Helen. 'Second morning in a row that he hasn't showed. Where have you been?'

Damien seized Helen by the arm, and led her quickly across the office to the small hospitality room.

'What the hell do you think you're doing?' demanded Helen. Damien locked the door behind them.

She pointed at his bandaged hand. 'What happened?'

201

'A Dobermann wanted to play with it. Now listen, Helen, I need everything you know about a company called Phabox UK.'

'What for?'

'Please, I'll explain later.'

'Phabox UK?'

'Yes!'

Helen trawled through her mental files. 'They manufacture drugs.'

'Go on.'

'They're the second biggest drug manufacturers in Europe. Very big in tranquillisers. But their real money-spinner is Bovactilax.'

'The drug for cattle.'

'Yes.'

'What does Bovactilax do exactly?'

'They give it to new-born cattle; it stimulates the pituitary gland to release more growth hormones. The calves grow to maturity twice as fast and have a high meat-to-fat ratio. Farmers worship the stuff. Especially since cows raised on Bovactilax have an accelerated metabolism, so they're able to calve two, maybe even three times a year.'

Damien jangled his keys in his pocket and hopped from foot to foot.

'Right, OK, yes! What else do you know about it?'

'What is this? *Mastermind*?'

'Come on, Helen, you're great on facts and figures and all that.'

Helen wondered for a moment whether this was a euphemism for boring. 'Er, that's about all I know, actually. Oh, the Chairman is Sir Terence Huntleigh.'

'What, the guy who cleaned up flogging condoms to China?'

'Yes, before he went to Phabox. I've heard he's very ill and rapidly turning gaga. Why are your clothes so dirty?'

Damien glanced down at his mud-splattered trousers. 'That's six hours' worth of standing by a Welsh roadside trying to hitch a sodding lift to London.'

Helen became intrigued. Her blue eyes followed Damien as he paced compulsively back and forth like a polar bear in a zoo.

'Why were you hitching?' she asked. 'Didn't you have any money?'

'Oodles of it, Helen. I just thought I would hitch from Brecon to London as a way of seeing the glories of the countryside and increasing my spiritual fucking karma! Of course I had no bloody money!'

'No need to shout.'

'I'm sorry,' said Damien, spreading his arms. 'I'm sorry. OK? I'm a bit worked up. Listen. Have there been any health scares about Bovactilax?'

'What's all this about, Damien?'

'I think the business with those officers in Brecon is somehow connected to Bovactilax.' To Damien's relief, Helen looked like she was taking this seriously. 'I reckon we're looking at a tasty little scandal.'

'All right,' Helen conceded. 'Tell me more.'

While Damien was telling Helen everything he knew, George was coming to terms with being stuck in the lift. He was putting it nicely in perspective as part of a learning process.

'You see, the old George,' he explained to Dave, 'the old anxious George, with his claustrophobia, would be panicking by now. Probably hyperventilating. But the new George just sails through it.'

203

Dave was sitting on the floor of the lift with his head in his hands. 'Yeah, the new George does go on a bit though, doesn't he?'

'Sorry?'

'We've been stuck in this thing for an hour and a half now and all you've done is witter on about your bloody rebirth.'

'Well, it is a very good book. It's changed my whole way of looking at things. I lent it to Joy this morning. She said she was getting through it very quickly.'

'That's because she put it through the shredder, George,' said Dave in measured tones.

George laughed, assuming Dave was joking, and whistled tunelessly for a bit. 'Amazing,' he said. 'All this time in a metal coffin and yet I don't feel the slightest bit scared. Yup. Not a flicker. The walls don't feel as if they're closing in or anything.'

Dave muttered something and looked at his watch.

'Dave, there's something I'd just like to say.'

'Go on.'

'Thanks.'

Dave was puzzled.

'Thanks for everything you've done for me over the years.'

Dave couldn't remember ever doing anything for George.

'Friends are jewels who must be treasured,' George quoted from Chapter Four.

'Quite.'

'I particularly appreciated the way you stood by me after that business when Alison left me the day after our engagement party.'

Oh no, thought Dave. Alison!

'In those dark days,' continued George, 'after Alison had run off and I felt so vulnerable, you were tremendously supportive.'

Dave felt like a heel. He'd been tremendously supportive only to assuage an overpowering sense of guilt. Perhaps it was time to be honest with George. But Dave's recent experience with Maisie had placed a huge question mark over the advisability of being honest with people.

'You were great, Dave.'

Oh, this made him feel awful.

'You really came through for me.'

Dave could take no more. He looked up. 'George, I've got a confession to make.'

'Fire away,' said George, pleased to be party to another healing process.

Dave fiddled with a shoelace. 'You remember last year, when you got engaged.'

'To Alison.'

'Yes, Alison. How do you feel about all that now?'

'Oh, I'm comfortable about Alison.'

Dave brightened a little. Maybe this wouldn't be so bad. 'The thing is, George, it's been preying on my mind for over a year now. But that night, after your engagement party, you know, when I drove Alison home, well, I, um, I didn't just drive her home . . .'

George turned pale.

'I'm so sorry, George, it just happened. I'm really sorry. It was . . . well, I'm ashamed, I'm deeply ashamed.'

George spoke in a robotic tone. 'Alison told me that we'd grown apart emotionally.'

'Oh, I think that's true, George. I'm sure the break-up

would have happened anyway. And what I did with Alison had nothing to do with it at all really.'

Dave went on justifying himself but George didn't hear a word. He just stared at the walls of the lift, which were hurtling towards him.

All things considered, George's panic attack was not really that bad. He was panting rather rapidly when the lift was winched up to the second floor. But by the time he was in the familiar surroundings of the newsroom his breathing was calmer. Half an hour later he was explaining how airless the lift had become. So airless in fact that *anyone* would have struggled for breath. Dave agreed that he too had felt desperately short of oxygen. He hadn't. He just said it to make George feel better.

'Are you sure you're OK now?' Helen enquired.

'Oh, yes, fit as a flea,' chirped George, feeling a tremor of gastric anxiety.

'You sure?'

'Yes.'

'It's just that Damien's got something interesting to tell us.'

Damien took centre-stage. 'There's something weird going on.'

'There certainly is,' said Sally, slamming down her copy of *Hello!* magazine. 'Two hours they interview me and all I get . . .' she took out a ruler, '. . . all I get is one and a half column inches.'

Damien ploughed on. 'I don't know the whole picture yet. But here's what I do know.'

Mrs Grindlay was surprised at how much Damien had found out in Brecon. She was listening via a tiny transmitter which had been hidden on the underside of George's desk in the centre of the newsroom. It should have been hidden on the underside of Damien's desk, but as usual Spooks Division had failed to master a small but crucial detail.

This was the first time Mrs Grindlay had listened in live, as it were. Damien's account of his recent investigation was rapid and accurate (apart from the single Dobermann multiplying into a vicious pack). He took them through what he saw as the key elements: the deaths in Brecon, the spooky experimental farm, Sir Titus Granby's impotence, the butcher's special beef and, of course, Bovactilax.

To Mrs Grindlay's relief, Damien couldn't complete the connections. But he was scoring the occasional direct hit.

'The power-lines explanation that Gus was bowled, that is total bollocks!'

Mrs Grindlay found herself straining to hear Damien's words, which were momentarily drowned out by gurglings from George's stomach. Then she made out a woman's voice.

'What could we broadcast though?' Helen was asking. 'It's just a series of mysterious links. There's nothing that's hard fact.'

'Absolutely right!' Damien's voice rose in volume. 'So here's what we do. We fly a kite. Try and smoke the buggers out by running part of the story.'

Henry looked up from his crossword. He liked the sound of this.

'Go on,' said Dave.

'Well, I present a health-scare job. You know, speculation is mounting.'

'Where's it mounting?' interrupted George.

'We mount our own speculation, dimmy.'

George didn't like being called dimmy and it meant Mrs Grindlay was half deafened by a particularly loud colonic rumble. Normal service was resumed. To her alarm Damien was refining his text.

'There are growing fears . . .' He glanced across at his Editor. 'See, George? Creative use of the passive. There are growing fears that the deaths of military personnel in Brecon may be linked to harmful effects caused by eating beef from an experimental farm. The farm, which it's believed is used for research by the makers of Bovactilax, is a . . .'

Damien was cut off by a doom-laden voice.

'You . . . must . . . be . . . fucking . . . mad.'

It was Gus. He looked awful. His face was grey and his hair looked as if it hadn't been combed for days. Normally every hair on Gus's head was totally controlled.

Gus walked towards them slowly, his voice low and menacing.

'Are you seriously contemplating running a health scare on Bovactilax? Bovactilax has revolutionised meat production. It has given us bigger, beefier cattle. Jucier, meatier meat.'

It was hard to see where Gus was heading, but the rabid look in his eye ensured no one was going to interrupt.

'Let me spell it out.' Gus broke into song.

' "Come along and sink your teeth

In our bigger better beef!" '

Oh dear, thought George, he's gone.

' "It's a fun time for your tum

208

With a Brunchieburger bun".'

Everyone stared at Gus. Gus *never* sang. And the little dance had been very peculiar.

Gus smashed his fist down on a desk. 'Don't you see? Bovactilax helps make the beef that's used to make Brunchieburgers!'

Helen completed the circle. 'And Brunchieburgers is Sir Roysten's largest company.'

'Give that girl a coconut!' yelled Gus. 'Brunchieburger is the core-lynchpin factor in Sir Roysten's empire. His ailing empire!'

Mrs Grindlay's earpiece was zapped by a resounding fart, as George experienced a surge of stress. Never before had Gus admitted to anyone that Sir Roysten was in financial difficulties. If Gus said things were bad, then they must really be appallingly bad.

For a moment Mrs Grindlay wondered whether her receiver had packed up, but in fact the newsroom had fallen completely silent.

Sally frowned. 'Gus, could you possibly recap? I got a little lost around the coconut section.'

'Now listen, you people.' Gus raised his hand. He held his forefinger a millimetre from his thumb. 'This close,' he whispered, 'Sir Roysten is this close to shutting down Globelink. And, he'd do it just like that. The ruthless bastard wouldn't hesitate.' Gus's tone became even more funereal. 'Only the other day Sir Roysten interracted with me by E-mail. He threatened immediate closure of our entire operation unless . . .' Gus hesitated. Should he divulge Sir Roysten's terms? No, it would only stir up anger. What he needed now was collective fear. 'Unless our general performance improves to a target-attaining standard. Needless to say, any speculation about

Bovactilax would be intolerable in his eyes. We would be endangering his very survival. He would cut our throats.'

Mrs Grindlay was grateful for Gus's intervention. It was bound to work. She knew, from extensive experience, that fear of redundancy was a primal human instinct. She'd often exploited it herself to persuade potential troublemakers to keep their heads down. She waited for someone to speak.

'Of course,' said Gus, 'it's an editorial decision.'

All eyes turned to George. 'Well,' he said, pausing to burp, 'I think I'd be prepared to be guided by the feeling of the majority.'

Henry spoke up with an air of detachment. 'Yes, well, this story of Damien's is, I suppose, mildly intriguing, but objectively one has to say that it is all entirely unsubstantiated. And I've always maintained that responsible journalism has to be built on the bedrock of fact.'

'Hear, hear,' said Dave quickly.

'Hang on,' Damien protested. 'There's a principle at stake here. We can't censor ourselves.'

'Oh, don't be so bloody sanctimonious!' roared Henry, contemplating how many weeks' old age pension it would take to pay off his £10,000 fine from the Broadcasting Ethics Commission.

Damien jabbed Henry in the chest. 'Look! There's a story here that the public ought to know about. The public has a right to know.'

'Rubbish,' said Sally. 'The public has no rights. Just privileges.'

Damien tried desperately to remember a speech from a Spencer Tracy film. 'The truth has to be given wings,' said Damien to general puzzlement.

'You don't know the truth,' snapped Gus.

'The press mustn't be muzzled,' yelled Damien, sensing that his BAFTA-winning story was disappearing down the toilet. 'It's our duty to follow the story up. Isn't that right, Helen?'

Helen thought about Chloë. She still nursed a faint hope that she could persuade her daughter to ditch Martin and go to university. But it would be expensive. There'd be the university fees and the cost of looking after the baby.

'Of course, in principle . . .' Helen said, 'I agree with you, Damien, but it, um, at the moment, it's very much a flier and there are practical considerations to be considered.' Helen looked at her feet.

'Quisling,' said Damien. In desperation, he turned to Joy for support.

Joy replied that she wasn't paid enough to care.

Gus, suddenly his old self again, came over to Damien and put a fatherly hand on his shoulder.

'Damien, I know you're in disappointment-mode, but I've an exciting opportunity to kick between your goalposts. What do you say we get you into Montreux? I hear the Swiss Germans are planning an artillery assault.'

'Montreux?'

'Yup, Flak city, Your natural habitat.'

Damien pulled at his ear lobe, 'What, with a full crew? Not just me and half a ton of lightweight equipment?'

'Full crew. Live satellite hook-ups. Nightly reports from the front.'

Damien hesitated. He was aware that the whole newsroom was watching.

Gus squeezed his shoulder, and leaned close to his ear. 'And, of course, first-class air travel and special

211

war-zone expenses supplement of two hundred pounds a day.'

Damien drew himself up to his full height. 'I'll have to think about it, Gus.'

'Of course, Damien.' Gus smiled. He knew the fish was hooked.

'I thought you'd grounded the little bastard.' Henry was on his feet.

Gus adopted his most honeyed tones, 'What, and waste Globelink's most distinguished front-line warrior?'

Mrs Grindlay removed her earpiece. Self-interest had triumphed again.

Five hours later Mrs Grindlay got a call informing her that Damien Day had just boarded Swissair flight SR 207 to Basle. She went straight over to the bright red steel data cabinet marked 'Authorised Personnel Only', pressed the palm of her hand against the electronic sensor, waited for the drawer to glide forward, reached into an unmarked section at the back, and took out a SoloSunFun holiday brochure. Now she could finally take that Christmas break in Antigua she'd been promising herself. Three weeks of sun, sand, sex and all the ciggies she could smoke. No more hours of tedium spent burying the bodies from the Bovactilax cock-up in Brecon.

Because, thank God, that story was now well and truly dead.

Part Two

Ten
Boxing Day, 1999

Damien ducked as a shell exploded a hundred metres away. God, that was bloody close! There was the dull crack of a sniper's rifle and splinters of wood erupted from the tree behind him. That was even closer! He mopped his face with the back of his sleeve. Damien was worried, extremely worried. Because in five minutes' time a ceasefire was due to start. He still hadn't filed his report to London. He heard the whine of a second shell and threw himself to the ground. That one was even closer. A few metres away from Damien, the white camera-van with the satellite dish on its roof gave off a volley of pinging noises as tiny bits of shrapnel bounced off it. Inside the van cowered two ashen-faced Swiss technicians.

Damien sprang to his feet, dusted himself down, and prepared to do a piece to camera. Except where was the bloody camera? He shouted in the direction of the van. A technician climbed out warily, clutching his camera. He froze for a moment as a burst of automatic fire raked the nearby park. The Swiss Germans were giving Montreux a terrible pasting. Damien watched as the bullets chewed up the makeshift wooden crosses which filled the park. Damn! That would have made a great shot. And what a commentary: 'Even in death there is no

215

escape from the deadly fire of men whose hatred, etc . . .'
He waved frantically at the cameraman, 'Move it! Else
we'll lose the satellite booking!'

As the man nervously framed Damien in his
viewfinder, he could see how tense the reporter was.
Crump! The roof of a sedate villa fifty yards away disappeared in a cloud of smoke and debris. Damien was
sweating. 'Come on, let's get this done. Quick!'

Back in London, George sat in Globelink's Engineering
Section waiting for Damien to come through on the
satellite hook-up. Next to George was a bored technician, gnawing on a cheese sandwich and reading a new
biography of Liza Minnelli.

'Christmas present, Graham?' asked George, indicating the book.

'Hmm? Oh, yeah. Big fan of Liza's I am.'

'I used to like her mum. *Wizard of Oz* is my favourite
film.'

George chuckled quietly to himself. 'As a kid, I just
loved the straw man.'

'That figures,' mumbled Graham, his mouth full of
sandwich.

George gazed at the token Christmas decorations
hanging above the monitors. Funny how they always
looked so sad and pathetic immediately Christmas Day
was over. Above the head of the little Mr Blobby dressed
as Santa Claus was a red home-made paper chain which
spelled out the yuletide greeting: 'Merry Xmas to one
and all, except those bastards in management'. Morale
was definitely a bit of a problem at Globelink, George
decided. Gus's revelations that Sir Roysten was close to
shutting down Globelink had knocked everybody

216

sideways. Everybody except George, that is. He had resolutely refused to get down-hearted. Armed with a new copy of *Self-Rebirth Made Easy* to replace the one Joy had shredded, George had put Chapter Nine ('Setbacks Equal Springboards') into action. He had signed up for a whitewater rafting expedition next summer. He had taken up badminton. He had started, in a modest way, pumping iron in the gym. He'd bought a double-breasted blazer in a rather extrovert cinnamon. He'd lashed out on a Cerruti tie. He'd thrown away his hush puppies and bought a pair of Timberlands. Most important of all, he had resolved not to worry about the future. In response to the standard greeting, 'Morning, George, how are you?' he now replied, 'I'm very well and living in the moment, thank you.' And so he was.

Damien's voice suddenly filled the room. 'Are you recording? Come on, somebody talk to me!' Damien appeared on a monitor. Behind him, thick black smoke was billowing out of a ruined villa. His voice was momentarily drowned out by the chatter of automatic fire. Graham handed George the satellite phone.

'Are you all right, Damien? It all looks a bit hairy.'

'Is that you, George?' shouted Damien, clutching at his earpiece.

'Yes, I didn't want Helen's Christmas spoiled by having to come in, so I'm holding the fort.'

Damien got agitated. 'Are you recording?'

'Oh, yes,' said George.

'OK, because this ceasefire's supposed to begin any minute.'

'I know. Great news, isn't it?'

Damien shook his head and muttered. There was a massive explosion from a mortar shell and the camera lurched to one side. This meant that, on the screen, Damien was now standing at an angle of forty-five degrees. He walked towards the camera till his shirt filled the picture.

'What are you doing?' called George.

'I'm straightening the sodding camera, what do you think I'm bloody doing, George!'

'Can't your camera crew do it?'

'No, George, they can't.' Damien was struggling to adjust the camera on its tripod and, for a moment, the picture filled with bright blue sky.

'Why can't they?' asked George.

'Because they're hiding in the bloody camera-van, that's why!' yelled Damien. The camera straightened and Damien stepped back into shot. 'Pathetic, isn't it? One tiny bit of shrapnel happens to hit one of them in the thigh and they're hiding like a bunch of girlies. Now come on! Let's do this!'

George and Graham exchanged a look. It really was extraordinary how often crews got hurt when they went filming with Damien. Yet Damien himself just strode through artillery barrages and deadly crossfire and never even got a scratch. Joy's theory was that the bullets bounced off an invisible force generated by Damien's ego.

'OK in three,' called Damien. Three seconds passed and Damien switched on an earnest frown. 'Here on the outskirts of Montreux, forces from both sides are heralding the ceasefire with a final fanfare of death. The . . .' He stopped as George's voice came through on his earpiece.

'Hold it, Damien. Problems on vision. Don't worry, Graham's on to it.' George looked over at Graham whacking the console with his fist.

Damien's pleading tones drifted out of a blank screen. 'Here I am, reporting from the most fantastic firefight of the whole bloody war, and you're poncing around like a bunch of—' Damien was interrupted by the sound of more explosions. '— like a bunch of sodding amateurs.'

Graham viciously jammed a lead deeper into its socket and Damien re-appeared on the monitor.

'Loose connection,' explained George.

'Just start recording, OK? In three . . .'

A muffled voice spoke to Damien.

'What?' snapped Damien, looking off camera.

The voice said something not quite audible to Graham and George.

'Yes, yes, yes,' Damien shouted in exasperation, 'I told you, we'll take him to hospital *in a minute*. OK? Now shut up! Right, George, in three . . .'

A ground-to-air missile screeched over his head. Oh yes! thought Damien. This is orgasmic! This is what reporting is all about! You can't get this sort of high from chasing a poxy little scandal in Wales! This is sexy! sexy! sexy! He adopted a pained expression and stared portentously down the lens. 'Here, on the outskirts of Montreux, forces from both sides are heralding the ceasefire with a final fanfare of death. The most devastating firefight of the war so far is engulfing the whole area in a terrifying inferno of . . .' Damien stopped. He looked around. Something was wrong. What was it? Then he realised. It had gone very quiet. All that could be heard on the silent air was the distant clank of cowbells. The ceasefire had come into force. Damien threw back his head and howled like a wounded animal. Then he slumped to his knees.

George and Graham couldn't see Damien any more,

because he'd disappeared out of the bottom of frame. But they could hear him sobbing.

George gave Graham an anxious look. 'I think we'd better get Damien back home soon.'

Like George, Sally had volunteered to work on Boxing Day. She'd told Gus she was prepared to come in 'out of a strong sense of duty'. But the truth was she hated the Christmas holiday. She had no one to spend it with. In previous years, she had resorted to buying herself Christmas presents, wrapping them, placing them under the tree, and then opening them on Christmas morning. But this year she hadn't even bothered to do that.

She sat down at her desk in the newsroom and wondered what to do. It was teatime. She'd fronted the only newscast of the day, a slimmed-down ten-minute bulletin featuring a rather dull report from Damien in Switzerland. So it was time to go home, really. No, Sally couldn't face that. She pulled a heap of mail towards her. It was mail from troubled viewers who wanted her advice. She'd been getting quite a lot of this since *Crisis 2000* had started going out. Many of the letters were clearly from madmen, who wrote in green ink, with lots of underlinings, capital letters, and multiple exclamation marks. With a sigh, she pushed the letters to one side. Her resident experts could deal with that lot. She massaged her forehead with the heel of her hand. Tension was building up. Her skin felt taut and dry. She would sleep with the mudpack on her face again tonight.

Perhaps she would stop doing *Crisis 2000*. Her heart wasn't really in it any more. In the last two weeks she had grown increasingly irritated by the class of caller. They were mostly weirdos, especially that little Welshman, who'd repeatedly tried to get through in order to flaunt his sexual ineptitude. Very few callers had the kind of fashionable problems that would boost Sally's profile as TV's most caring person. What's more, the viewing figures were creeping inexorably downwards. Sally was at a loss as to what the next leap forward in her career would be. She would continue to be the patron saint of Mobile Phone Abusers. That was an AB affliction. But it wasn't enough. A new career direction was definitely needed, preferably one that involved lucrative secondary markets.

Sally got our her compact and examined her complexion closely. Yes, moisturising was definitely called for.

'Hallo, Sal.'

Joy's face appeared at her shoulder. Sally jumped. 'You could have given me a heart attack.'

'I couldn't get that lucky,' said Joy.

Sally wondered why Joy was staring at her with such undisguised hatred. She tilted her head. 'I didn't think you'd be coming in today.'

'No, neither did I.'

In fact, Joy had come in partly to escape the creepy phone calls from her father, but mostly to use the phones in the Globelink office. She had friends in the USA, Australia and Hong Kong whom she always rang at Christmas time.

Joy held up a typed memo. 'I know using the photocopier represents something of an intellectual Everest for you, but I thought even you would know you're supposed to take the copy *and* the original.'

Sally's back stiffened, She wasn't going to take lip from someone who, after all, was not much more than a skivvy. This was exactly the sort of insolence that had prompted her to send a memo to Gus demanding Joy's dismissal. Oh my God! That was the memo in Joy's hand!

Joy waved the piece of paper very close to Sally's face. So close, in fact, that Sally could read the paragraph where she'd provided Gus with a meticulously itemised list of all Joy's most poisonous jibes going as far back as 1995.

'You're dead meat, Smedley.'

Sally felt cornered, so she lashed out. 'You know, you really are a deeply unpleasant individual. It's little wonder your father walked out on you.'

Joy stared hard at Sally for a moment, then turned on her heel and left the newsroom.

Sally felt a frisson of anxiety. Joy wasn't one to forgive and forget.

Eleven
December 28th, 1999

Gareth Pugh was sitting on a black leather sofa in Parmenter's luxury flat in Builth Wells, waiting for Parmenter to come home. At which point he would kill him. The man had it coming to him; he had stolen the affections of Gareth's beloved Megan.

Gareth ached when he thought of Megan. From the moment he'd seen her, he'd wanted her. For nine years he'd wanted her. But she was so slender, tall and elegant. Just looking at her made Gareth feel stumpy and stupid. He was so ridiculously short. Or had been, until he'd started taking the Bovactilax.

As a laboratory assistant with Phabox UK, he'd seen at first hand that Bovactilax accelerated the growth cycle of rats and mice. Later, on visits to the experimental farm, he'd seen cows the size of camels and chickens so huge that their legs snapped under their own weight. He knew that, in large doses, Bovactilax seemed to produce a kind of metabolic overdrive. He'd seen a copy of the licence application, which stated definitively that there were no side-effects. Of course, it wasn't designed to be administered by mouth to human beings, but it sounded pretty safe. And Megan was worth the risk.

Gareth had been 'Employee of the Month' on several occasions, so he'd had no difficulty in convincing his boss Parmenter that he was the best man to be given the job of keeping the drug inventories. The rest was a doddle. Over six weeks Gareth stole a tiny amount of Bovactilax each day and swallowed it in granule form. He began to grow like Topsy. Within three weeks his frame was wider and considerably more muscular. Every day he stood against the kitchen wall and drew a pencil mark in line with the top of his head. And every week the mark got higher. By the time he'd stopped taking the Bovactilax he had grown a remarkable one and a half inches. In the nine months after that, he kept growing until he was five foot four inches tall. Not exactly a basketball player, but when you've been five foot all your life, those four inches, well they made all the difference,

Gareth became charming, assertive, confident. He swept Megan off her feet. True, she did once comment that he seemed to have put on a bit of a spurt lately, but Gareth explained that he'd found an excellent chiropractor who'd radically improved his posture. There'd been a couple of inches of slack in his spine, you see.

Megan was too much in love to question Gareth. Their wedding day was perfect. Their wedding night had begun with champagne and caviar. She had gone off to the bathroom and returned in a babydoll nightie she'd ordered by catalogue. Gareth, who'd already slipped under the covers, watched as Megan provocatively peeled off the nightie, got into bed and pressed her soft yielding body against his. This was the moment he had dreamed of all these years. He became excited. Very excited. Or at least part of him was excited. His mind. But not, strangely, the part of him that ought to be excited. Megan was loving and tender and reassuring

224

but after forty-five minutes of kissing, caressing and tongues in ears, his penis remained totally inanimate.

'It doesn't matter,' she said.

'Yes it does,' he said.

'Well it doesn't matter to me. You're probably just feeling a bit stressed.'

'I am not stressed, OK?'

'It's normal to be stressed on your wedding night.'

'I just said, I'm not stressed.'

'Don't worry about it. Relax.'

'I am relaxed, relaxed, *very* relaxed. The only thing making me less relaxed is you telling me to relax all the time.'

'. . . I'm sorry.'

'Don't be sorry.'

'OK . . . It really doesn't matter to me, you know. The physical side's not that important.'

'And what's that supposed to mean?'

'Well, it wasn't just your body that attracted me, it was your lovely personality.'

'. . . You're saying I'm short, aren't you?'

That night had been the beginning of the end. After a couple of ill-tempered days and disastrously flaccid nights, Gareth had run away. He felt overwhelmed with shame. He couldn't face going to work. Megan would be there. He couldn't go home. Megan would be there too. He'd stayed with friends for a while, but their cheerful supportiveness had been more than he could bear. He was now staying in a seedy B&B populated almost entirely by Albanian guest workers. He was quickly becoming a forgotten person. Megan certainly seemed to be forgetting him. She was being consoled by Denzil bloody Parmenter. Who might be a foot taller than

Gareth, but knew damn all about anything and had only got that management post with Phabox because he was the Chairman's bloody nephew! Well, Denzil Parmenter would soon be history.

The broken glass! Parmenter might go into the kitchen first and see the broken glass! Gareth leaped up from the sofa, hurried through to the kitchen, and pulled a curtain across the shattered window. He opened a drawer and found a very long Sabatier carving knife.

Gareth went back into the living room and carefully placed the knife on a little table by the door. Mentally rehearsing how he'd despatch Parmenter with one deft slice across the jugular, he prowled back and forth in front of the Home Auto-Management Centre. He found the remote control and pressed buttons at random until the drinks unit bleeped and opened. Gareth grabbed a bottle of Rémy Martin and headed back to the sofa. He caught sight of himself in a mirror. God, he'd let himself go! His hair was matted, and he hadn't shaved since the wedding night, so now he had the beginnings of a wispy beard.

He stretched out on the sofa, kicked off his damp shoes, swigged from the brandy bottle, and hit a few more buttons on the remote. The telly came on. He channel-hopped. There was nothing decent on, just some stupid game shows, *Guess Whose Laundry* and *Three in the Bed*, and a repeat showing of the mini-series about the life of Alan Clark. Gareth pressed another button and found himself looking at the menu for the Videopaedia Britannica. He blipped again. It was the Supersport Channel. Frank Bruno was being inter-viewed about his forthcoming fight. Frank burst into his deep infectious laugh and Gareth soon found himself laughing too. For the first time in weeks, he was actually laughing. Then the loud bleeps started. Across Frank's mouth the words 'Incoming Videocall' flashed in neon orange. Gareth stabbed at the buttons on the remote in an attempt to remove this graffiti from Frank's face. To his intense annoyance, Frank now disappeared entirely from the screen. A gentle hum told Gareth that the video answerphone had cut in. He punched furiously at the remote, trying to get Frank back. Instead the screen fizzed with electronic shash for a few moments before slowly clearing to reveal the skeletal face of a dying man.

Gareth knew he was dying the moment he saw him. He looked just like his grandfather had looked in his final hours. That cordite grey tinge to the skin. The dullness in the eyes, sunk deep in their sockets. The shallow, rapid breathing. Gareth sat up. He knew this man! It was Sir Terence Huntleigh, Chairman of Phabox UK. At least, it was what was left of him.

It was several moments before Sir Terence could summon the strength to speak. His voice was a dry, low rasp. 'Denzil, this is your Uncle Terence . . . Sorry, never could get the hang of these video answerphone thingies. I'm afraid that . . . that by the time you see this, I shall be dead . . . But I want to tell you the whole story.'

He stopped to get his breath back. Gareth watched, riveted.

'You're the only one I can trust, Denzil. If those bastards try to blacken me after I'm gone . . .'

Gareth turned up the volume.

'You're a good lad . . . the only one in the family who really bothered . . . If it gets out, they'll pin it on me, I know they will. Dead men are so convenient.'

His wasted frame was shaken violently by a burst of

227

coughing. When it abated, the breathing was even faster. 'This is it, I'm relying on you. The whole story . . . It's a huge bloody mess, and if those bastards in Whitehall dump it all on me, they'll find I can bugger them up from beyond the grave . . . Here it comes, Denzil, chapter and verse.'

Gareth sat motionless on the sofa and received Sir Terence's confession. He could barely believe the things Sir Terence was telling him. The whole story was obscene.

Mrs Grindlay stared wistfully at her holiday snaps. The photos of the West Indian waiter lying naked on her bed had come out very well, even though in some of them she had cut his head off. Still, that had been his least interesting part.

She had planned to stay in Antigua for Christmas and the New Year, but the British government's plans for celebrating the millennium were in such chaos that she'd received a phone call asking her to come back early and do a bit of yuletide poop-scooping. The PM's speech about 'the dying days of the old century' had been denounced as ageist by three members of the Pensioners' Power Party, who were threatening to resign and bring down the coalition. Now Mrs Grindlay would have to patch things up by drafting a new speech for the PM, revealing his profound affection and respect for all senior members of the community. She heaved a sigh. She hated writing speeches for this PM. No matter how clever, witty and lively she made it, Seb Coe always managed to make it sound boring. And he invariably messed around with the text at the last minute, adding the most appalling clichés in a doomed attempt 'to give it the personal touch'.

At that moment the gods smiled on Mrs Grindlay by providing her with some Seb Coe displacement activity. The message blinking at her from the top corner of her VDU announced 'Sir Terence using videophone'. She'd ordered a tap on Sir Terence after getting reports that he was turning a bit gaga. On his sick bed he'd been saying some rather wild things about friends in high places. In his dotage the old boy was turning into a bit of a loose cannon, and Mrs Grindlay didn't like loose canons. Sir Terence's face appeared on her screen. My God, he looked awful, like a spectre. She frowned. This seemed to be a bit of a one-way conversation, virtually a monologue. Then she realised Sir Terence must be talking to a video answerphone.

Mrs Grindlay only started giving Sir Terence her full attention when he reached the words, 'Here it comes, Denzil, chapter and verse . . .' Like Gareth, she found the whole story obscene. Obscenely detailed. Names. Places. Dates. More names. Ministers' names! Bribes. And something about the Home Secretary that even she didn't know about. Good God, with every sentence the old fool was unravelling all her hard work of the previous weeks. Fortunately, the life seemed to be draining out of him. The old man paused for breath. What he proceeded to say next filled Mrs Grindlay with horror. She fumbled for a cigarette. Sir Terence continued. Mrs Grindlay sat as still as a statue. She even forgot to light her cigarette. If what she was hearing was true, somebody in government had been concealing the full story from her. She very much hoped these were the ramblings of a man in the last stages of senile dementia. But everything he said was remarkably detailed and coherent. His long message finally came to an end with a poignant,

'Bless you, Denzil . . . Goodbye.' Then the screen went blank.

Mrs Grindlay sat in silence for a few moments, then realised she had no time to lose. The first priority was to get hold of that answerphone tape before anyone saw it. Who the hell was Denzil? She stabbed at her keyboard, and the screen immediately displayed the number that Sir Terence had been ringing. She pressed a few more keys and up came the name 'Denzil Parmenter' and an address in Builth Wells.

As she picked up the yellow phone and waited to be put through to Spooks Division, Mrs Grindlay reached for a pad, scribbled 'health survey', and underlined it three times. She urgently needed independent corroboration of what Sir Terence was claiming. Or better still, proof that it was all nonsense. But she had a dark foreboding that it wasn't nonsense.

Gus's heart leaped as he saw Sir Roysten's name along the top of the incoming fax. This was what he'd been waiting for. He put his hands together in silent prayer. He had sent Sir Roysten one desperate last plea for a less Draconian solution to Globelink's financial problems. He had suggested, very respectfully, that the fifty per cent job cuts might not be necessary if Globelink implemented other money-saving measures, such as selling off its prime Central London site and moving into cheaper premises in somewhere like Deptford. Gus had also proposed more sponsorship, more commercial breaks, more use of agency footage. In fact, he had thrown in any suggestion that might appeal to Sir Roysten's greed. Gus had stressed how he and his staff (or 'co-achievers' as he called them) would happily work longer hours for no more money to try to 'boost our viability quotient'.

The fax was spooling through now. It consisted of a single sheet with the word 'No!' written on it.

Gus threw the fax in his wastepaper bin and wandered, glassy-eyed, into the newsroom to join his colleagues, half of whom were now unquestionably doomed. George was clapping his hands to get everyone's attention. Gus slumped into the chair next to Helen.

'All right, all right,' called George. 'Listen up, people. Since we didn't really bother with a Christmas party this year, I've had a chat with Gus, and he's kindly agreed that we should push the boat out a bit for our office millennium party. Which means you can all bring your partners. Isn't that nice?'

Judging by the stares, nobody else found it nice.

'So, Helen you can bring . . . your partner, and, um . . .' George realised, a little belatedly, that none of the rest actually had a partner.

'Oh dear,' said Sally. 'It's a little hard for me to choose one admirer to bring. I don't want to break any hearts. I'll just come on my ownsome.'

George noticed morale was so low that no one could be bothered making a snide remark at Sally's expense.

'OK, team,' said George, bouncing from toe to toe on his springy Timberlands, 'it's onwards and upwards. Let's get stuck into this running order. Another day, another challenge.'

'Listen, Jimminy Cricket,' sneered Henry, 'just cut the bollocks and go through the bloody items, OK?'

God, what was the matter with everyone today? thought George. So much gloom and doom. Christmas didn't seem to have cheered people up much.

'Right,' said George, rising above it. 'Lead story looks to me like the negotiations to stop the war in Switzerland. Damien's going to do a "What Prospects for Peace" number, then he's flying home. Second item, well, not easy. Helen, any thoughts?'

Helen shrugged. 'Not really. Not a lot happening, is there?'

Oh, dear, even Helen was showing negativity. She was normally so helpful. Never mind, he would just seize the helm himself and run through all the possible news items. As he did so, he felt there was a definite theme of optimism around the globe, probably something to do with the approaching millennium. In Cyprus, Zhirinovsky had called a halt to the Russian advance. No one knew why. But then no one knew why Zhirinovsky did anything, least of all Zhirinovsky. In Brazil, the timber companies had agreed to a total ban on logging in the Amazon. To mark the millennium, the Chinese were releasing five thousand political prisoners from Hong Kong's jails. The UN had called a World Peace Conference. And there was the heartening news that this year the hole in the ozone layer had grown less rapidly than in previous years.

But as George went through this catalogue of hope, he received not the slightest flicker of enthusiasm from any of his team. He tried Helen again. 'So, Any thoughts now, Helen?'

'Na.'

Dave looked up from a book about Australia. 'I suppose,' he sighed, 'we could do something on the return of you-know-who.'

'Yes,' said George, 'I suppose that's a possibility.' He called up the relevant press release on his computer and read how Lady Thatcher was due to be discharged from the exclusive clinic where she'd spent the last three years being treated 'for nervous exhaustion'. She was coming out at eleven thirty. His thoughts drifted back to the last time he'd seen her in the flesh.

She had come to record an interview on France's decision to quit the European Union, and had seemed in fine fettle. Unfortunately, she'd brought along Mark, which meant half an hour wasted talking about the merits of fuel-injection engines. George had been sitting with Lady Thatcher in the green room just getting her approval for the questions she would be asked, when rain started to patter against the windows. Lady Thatcher had walked over to the window, stared up at the darkening sky and casually remarked that, once again, the clouds were betraying her. She went on to explain that, during her last months as Prime Minister, she had wanted to introduce legislation to outlaw clouds but had been thwarted by the fainthearts in the Cabinet. Everyone in the room had waited politely for her to finish talking. Then Mark had stepped forward and quietly led her away. She had not been seen in public since.

George felt a momentary shudder. He never liked the thought of illness. Especially that sort of illness. Still, the story could be presented in a positive light, woman rebuilding her life, etc.

'OK, penultimate item,' affirmed George.

'What I want to know,' boomed Henry from behind his paper, 'is why we never find out our Prime Ministers are psychos until after they leave office.'

'But we always knew she was strange,' said Helen.

'In what way was she strange?' asked Sally, puzzled.

'Maybe we could get a crew there to film the moment

she leaves the clinic?' suggested George. 'It should be quite an emotional scene.'

'Out of the question,' droned Gus. 'Mark is asking for twenty grand up front.' It was virtually the first thing Gus had said all morning. He sounded very tired.

'Perhaps we'll just do a straight report with some footage of her in better times,' George offered.

The phone on Damien's desk rang. Dave answered it wearily.

'Miserable Bastards Productions, can I help you?'

Joy was going round lobbing post into people's in-trays. But when she came to Sally's desk, she laid the mail neatly on the desk in front of her and gave Sally a bright cheery smile. Sally felt relieved. It was obvious Joy wasn't harbouring any thoughts of revenge over the unfortunate memo incident. Dave came off the phone with a sigh.

'Some Welsh bloke looking for Damien. That's the third time he's called.'

George was about to raise the question of what should be next item when Helen let out a piercing shriek. Eyes wide with horror, she was holding a white card out in front of her at arm's length, as if it were contaminated. In gold letters it bore the words: 'Mr and Mrs Gerald Tiptree cordially invite you to the wedding of their son Martin to Chloë Cooper'.

Mrs Grindlay was doodling on her blotter, which showed a man's bald head with an axe stuck in it. This was Mrs Grindlay's impression of the Operations Director of Spooks Division. She knew him only as 'John', and had never actually met him. She had no desire to do so; his tired Oxbridge drawl at the end of a phone line was quite unpleasant enough, thank you very much. She picked up the buff-coloured file on her desk and read, for the second time, how a team of operatives had been despatched to the home of Denzil Parmenter, nephew of Sir Terence Huntleigh (now, fortunately, the late Sir Terence Huntleigh). She read with mounting anger how the team had initially raided a house four streets away. By the time they reached Parmenter's address, the local police had beaten them to it. Parmenter had reported a break-in. Nothing had been taken, except a bottle of brandy and the tape from his video answerphone. The operatives had struggled to explain their presence to the local constabulary. But at least they had possessed enough brain cells between them to get an ID on the culprit. On the walls of the living room, written in large letters, were the words: 'Hands Off Megan, you lofty bastard!' From this, Denzil Parmenter had deduced that the intruder was Gareth Pugh.

Mrs Grindlay closed her eyes and groaned quietly. Finding a short, obsessive Welshman would not be easy. Especially given the rampant incompetence of the people who would be tracking him down.

There was a brisk knock at the door which she recognised as Mitchell's.

'Come in,' she called.

Mitchell came in smiling, though his smile always seemed like the beginning of a cocky grin. God, she disliked him. He was pushy and shifty. Experience had taught her never to trust a man who put styling gel on his hair. This simple rule had never let her down. And Mitchell's hair was gelled flat to the top of his head.

He waved a CD-ROM at her. 'All the data from that

nationwide health survey you asked for.' He handed her the disk.

She thanked him perfunctorily.

Then he hovered, 'Um, I could collate some of it for you, if you like.'

'That won't be necessary, thank you.'

Still he was hovering. What did he want?

'Health surveys aren't your usual field, are they? What's it all in aid of, anyway? Massive thing, I'm amazed the Department of Health undertook it.'

Well, she thought, it hadn't been easy to convince them, She'd had to resort to rattling the many skeletons in the Minister's closet.

Mitchell leaned chummily on her desk. 'What's it about, old girl? You can tell me.'

Old girl? Old girl! 'That'll be all thanks,' she said coldly.

Mitchell straightened up. An unpleasant gleam came into his eye. 'Strong smell of air freshener in here.'

'Is there?' she answered casually.

'Yes.'

'Well, I use it to freshen up the air a bit.' She used it to smother the stale smell of cigarette smoke. He knew that. And she knew he knew.

'Toodle pip,' he said.

Once he had left the room, Mrs Grindlay crossed to her main computer, the one with the relational database. She inserted the CD-ROM, and typed in the heading 'Erectile Dysfunction', followed by the instruction, 'Collate and Compare'.

'Searching,' announced the screen.

She waited for a moment. She needed a diagram that would reveal at a glance the incidence of a whole range

236

of complaints reported to GPs over the last few months. Maybe a bar chart? No, she'd go for a 3D block diagram. She typed in a few more instructions and watched as the diagram built up on the screen. It looked a bit like a row of skycrapers. And one particular skyscraper was much, much taller than the others. For one crazy moment she saw the skyscrapers turn into erect penises. Mrs Grindlay blinked and the erect penises were gone. This job was definitely getting to her. Maybe she was reading the data wrongly. She instructed the computer to present the figures as a pie chart. The computer obliged. Sadly, one slice of the pie was much larger than any of the others. She felt a little wave of panic sweep over her. Whichever way the computer presented the figures, the conclusion was inescapable. These statistics were confirming everything that the dying Sir Terence had claimed.

Now her panic was turning to anger. This was going to mean bloody weeks of working ridiculous hours to try and keep the lid on. I mean she had poop-scooped some enormous dungpiles in the past, God knows she had, but this was a belter, this took the biscuit. During the Scott Enquiry she'd been asked to 'lose' the 'thank you' note from Saddam Hussein. After the accident at Thorp in '98 she'd had to lead journalists away from the accident's real cause and convince them it had been the result of sudden subsidence. And when a BBC documentary had asked why the wife of the Transport Minister had such extensive holdings in road construction companies, she'd arranged for the Director General to be reminded of a lively conference in Bangkok. She had got her hands dirty again and again to save a procession of dullards, incompetents and crooks. And for

237

what? How ever much shit you dug them out of they always found a bigger heap to go and play in. If that tape from the video answerphone found its way to the press, there were going to be resignations. Lots of them. Well, this time maybe she'd let them stew. Yes, maybe she would do just that.

Two cigarettes later, Mrs Grindlay had calmed down enough to realise that she could not afford to let anyone stew. They all shared too many secrets. With a quick mental addition she had calculated that, technically, she was guilty of about thirty criminal offences over the last eight years, mostly attempting to pervert the course of justice. She could not let anyone be thrown to the wolves, because she would certainly be lobbed in after them. She looked at the phone. She didn't want to see Jim Bliss again, but there was really no choice.

Gus and George were sharing the lift up to the restaurant area. They were both staring at the floor numbers as they lit up in turn, because they couldn't think of anything to say to each other. This made them both feel embarrassed. George thought how silly it was that he should feel embarrassed. Why did lifts generate instant embarrassment the moment you stepped inside them? It was ridiculous. He'd known Gus for ten years. They were workmates. They had lots of topics in common. George smiled reassuringly at Gus. Gus half-smiled back. Then he let out a long despairing groan and banged his head rhythmically against the wall of he lift. Five times he banged it. Then he stopped and watched the floor numbers again.

'What's up, Gus?'

'Nothing,' said Gus with hooded eyes.

George cleared his throat. 'Gus, a few weeks back I found this book in your bin all about self-rebirthing and, well, I read it, and it's brilliant. I was just wondering why you threw it away?'

'I'll tell you why I threw it away, George,' said Gus in a strangely distant sing-song voice. 'Because it's rubbish. It's all about how you can change. Change for the better. And that's a cruel lie. People never change. They just . . . deteriorate.'

George looked down at his new Timberlands. 'With respect, Gus, I can't agree. I've changed.'

Gus grunted.

'And Paul Gascoigne's calmed down a lot these days. People can change for the better.'

'Well, perhaps there's hope for us all, George,' said Gus bitterly. 'Perhaps Mr Zhirinovsky will give up invading people and take up macramé. Perhaps Pol Pot will join the Sally Army, and maybe Sir Roysten will stop sending me threatening faxes demanding full details of who I am going to—' Gus stopped himself just in time.

'Who you're going to what?' asked George.

The lift doors opened. They'd reached the restaurant area. Gus strode briskly out of the lift. George went to follow but noticed the buttons of his chinos were gaping open. He quickly fiddled them shut, but as he did so the lift doors began to close. George knew what to do. Halfway up the frame of the doors was a small glowing sensor. If anything passed in front of the sensor the doors automatically re-opened. So George quickly thrust his arm in front of the sensor. Inexplicably the sensor failed to acknowledge the existence of George's arm. The heavy lift doors kept trundling across and trapped George's arm just above the elbow. George let out a yelp and tried desperately to claw the doors away from his arm. But the angle at which his arm was trapped meant he was turned square on, so he could not achieve any real leverage. What made the situation even more alarming was that the lift was still refusing to recognise the presence of George's arm. The doors were continuing to close, like some manic sci-fi robot, crushing George's arm with ever increasing pounds per square inch. He was now crying out with pain. The arm was tingling as the circulation was remorselessly cut off by the door. A gallery of images flashed through George's mind, including photos of gangrene victims that he'd see in his medical dictionaries. Suddenly, thank God, there was help. A couple of staff were hauling back the doors to release George's arm. They pulled George through the gap. As the doors closed George gasped with relief.

Dave, who had been one of George's rescuers, stepped forward.

'Are you all right, George? Really went for you, didn't it?'

George nodded lamely.

Dave pressed the call button and the doors re-opened. He waited for them to start closing again.

'Next time, George, just stick your arm in front of the sensor. Like this.'

Dave illustrated. And the sensor worked perfectly.

'On the line now we have Morag from Perth. Morag, what seems to be the problem?'

Sally's tones were hushed and reverent, her face a picture of concern. Helen, who was watching the monitor in the newsroom, found it all deeply tacky.

Morag's quavering voice drifted down the phone line.

Sally marked the end of each hesitant clause with an exaggerated nod of the head. The three resident experts sitting under the *Crisis 2000* logo were listening carefully. Sometimes they wondered why they were on the programme. Sally very rarely let them get a word in.

'I'm not sure . . . I can go on like this,' said Morag softly.

Sally nodded again. 'Take your time, Morag.'

'It's . . . it's a compulsion. I have this compulsion.'

Sally nodded some more. She hoped it was something good.

'A sexual compulsion.'

Excellent. Oprah had achieved fame and fortune with stuff like this.

The lilting Perthshire accent was almost musical. 'I have this compulsion . . . to sleep with men . . . men of a certain kind . . . lorry drivers mostly.'

Sally coloured visibly.

'Or workmen. Any rough trade, basically.'

Sally was shifting in her seat.

'Especially with tattoos.'

Helen thought she saw Sally sway in her seat. This was more like it. She called George over to watch the monitor.

'George, look, this is riveting!'

George crossed the newsroom, preceded by the pungent aroma of Deep Heat which was emanating from his arm.

Morag from Perth was turning metaphysical now.

'And the thing is, Sally, I suspect I seek these liaisons with tattooed strangers because emotionally I am . . . a void. A nothing. I am incapable of tenderness and commitment.'

241

'Really?' said Sally with a strangled voice.

'That's right, so I view sex as just an act of animal brutality . . .'

Sally's throat seemed to dry. She opened her mouth but no noise came out.

'I'm a monster . . . Do you think there are any other women like me, Sally?'

Sally sagged. She focused on the middle distance and spoke in a small sad voice. 'Yes, Morag . . . I think there probably are . . . and I think it's a very lonely way to live your life.'

Helen felt sorry for Sally. She watched her force a watery smile. 'Thank you, Morag. That's all we have time for today.'

In the tiny edit suite, Joy put down the phone. She thought her Perthshire accent had been pretty good. OK, so it was a massive reprisal for one miserable memo. But what the hell, it made Joy feel better. Much better.

Twelve
December 30th, 1999

Mrs Grindlay stirred her tea carefully, took another chocolate biscuit, and looked across at Jim Bliss. Of course he must know that she hadn't invited him round merely to drink tea and make small talk. But she was finding it very hard to broach the subject. So far, they had discussed the weather, the millennium celebrations planned for Trafalgar Square, England's abysmal batting against Burma, and whether Gary Bushell would recover from those dreadful stab wounds.

She couldn't put off the dread discussion much longer. Bliss looked a tiny bit irritated, and who knows, she might end up needing his services more than ever. That unhinged little Welshman was still on the loose. Knowing Spooks Division, he'd probably turn up with the tape on *Newsnight*. Yes, Jim Bliss could well be the only person who stood between Mrs Grindlay and two years in Holloway.

'Jim, by the way, I never said thanks for the little fire-fighting document you did for me on that Brecon thing.'

'My pleasure,' beamed Jim. When he smiled the skin on his face tightened and made the cosmetic surgery terribly obvious. 'And happily you didn't need any of it.'

'That's right,' said Mrs Grindlay.

'A happy ending.'

'Indeed.'

Mrs Grindlay nibbled on the last chocolate biscuit. 'Actually there's another theoretical scenario I'd like to slide past you, if that's OK.'

'Fire away.'

'Well, just supposing . . .' She paused to sip her tea. 'Just supposing the Brecon story was a little more complicated than I first thought.'

'Go on.'

'Suppose the drug company involved—'

'Phabox UK.'

'Correct. Suppose Phabox UK, having developed this new wonder drug Bovactilax, a drug designed to make cattle grow faster . . .'

Bliss nodded. He wished Mrs Grindlay would come to the point.

'Suppose that maybe when they were testing this drug the company got some results which were inconvenient, and so they omitted to mention them.'

'Uh-huh.'

'And suppose, in the light of the drug's commercial potential, the company convinced elements in central government that the licensing procedure should be, well, um . . . lubricated. No real trial period, that sort of thing.'

'Uh-huh,' said Bliss. Why was Mrs Grindlay so nervous? Drug companies did this all the time, didn't they?

'And let's say that it subsequently became apparent that the drug was harmful . . .'

Bliss cut in. 'Yes, yes, I know, like those poor army officers you told me about. The ones who ate that beef with forty times the normal dose of Bovactilax in it.'

Mrs Grindlay reached for her Nicotino stick and rolled it on her forearm. She was avoiding his gaze now.

'Well . . . I mean, what if that were just an early man-ifestation of what would happen on a much wider scale? What if, purely theoretically, of course, it became clear that even minute residues of Bovactilax could present a problem? And what if, by the time this became clear, a large section of the public had been irrevocably . . . harmed.'

'. . . In what sense exactly?'

'In the sense that any man who'd eaten meat in the last two years was almost certainly doomed to become impo-tent.'

Bliss choked on his tea. He coughed and gasped for air. After a minute or two he could speak again.

'How . . . how theoretical is this?' he asked hoarsely, dabbing his watering eyes with a paper tissue.

'Well,' said Mrs Grindlay, 'not quite as theoretical as one would like.'

Bliss looked at her aghast.

'Any meat in the last two years?'

'Basically yes, unless you're buying organic meat.'

Bliss stared ahead like a zombie.

'I won't bore you with the endocrinology, but basically it looks as if Bovactilax makes the pituitary gland misfire. Permanently.' She lowered her voice slightly. 'What I need from you is an assessment, a worst-case PR strategy, in case this theoretical story . . . became real . . . and public.'

Bliss was still struggling to take it all in. Recently he'd been having a spot of bother in the erections depart-ment. But he'd put it down to stress, not chateaubriand. He became aware that Mrs Grindlay was asking him a question.

'The political fall-out?' he stuttered, gathering his thoughts.

'Yes.'

'Well, um, I think I'd have to say that any party in power which had played a role in rendering most of the male population impotent would . . . would be, um . . . well and truly buggered. And would probably find it difficult to get re-elected for the next hundred years or so.' Bliss paused to take out two antacid tablets from a little pack. He chewed on them vigorously. 'In PR terms, I can't think of any presentational strategy that would work.' He swigged down the tablets with some more tea. 'At least, not if it had to be based on the truth.'

This was all confirming what Mrs Grindlay already knew in her heart.

'So when the man on the Clapham omnibus realises he's no longer capable of the sexual act . . . ?' she asked.

'One would have to promote a tremendously clever and convincing explanation.'

'Lie,' said Mrs Grindlay, enjoying the word's vulgarity.

'Um . . . Repackage, yes. Stressing some elements and excluding others.'

Constructing this euphemism seemed to exhaust him. He buried his head in his hands and ran his fingers through the hairpiece that had been woven into his skull.

'Perhaps you could do another document for me,' said Mrs Grindlay, 'laying out the various repackaging options.'

There was an awkward silence, then Jim sat up and looked at Mrs Grindlay.

'Of course, one option is to let all the greedy little wankers who've caused this get torn limb from limb,' he said. 'It's what they deserve.'

Mrs Grindlay expressed her sympathy for this view. Then she reminded Bliss how his PR company had han-

246

dled the launch of Bovactilax. Jim said he'd come up with the repackaging options she'd asked for.

'It won't be easy though,' he added. 'God knows it won't be easy.'

'If anyone can do it, you can,' she said, moving to the door. Jim Bliss rose and walked towards her. He walked as if his ankles were invisibly chained together. God, thought Mrs Grindlay, this is how Britain's men would react once they knew the truth.

'You are sure?' asked Bliss. 'What if you're wrong?'

'Let's hope I am.'

'Yes, let's hope.'

But Bliss had lost all hope. He'd known her many years and he couldn't remember a single occasion when she'd been wrong.

'I'd like the options by tomorrow, please.'

He nodded weakly.

He seemed in such a state she wondered if his thoughts would be of any use. Oh, well, they'd be a starting point. She patted him reassuringly on the shoulder.

'Give my love to Melissa.'

He looked at her in alarm.

'You mean Melanie.'

'Oh, of course, Melanie.'

She patted his shoulder again and he drifted out of the door. It had been a mistake on her part, but a happy one. Now Jim was aware that she knew about his mistress, Melissa. It would be one more way of ensuring his silence.

She closed the door behind him, went back to her desk and immediately lit up a cigarette. She hoped she wouldn't have to resort to a PR strategy from Bliss.

The door flew open and Mitchell stood there. She noticed how the draught from the corridor made his tie

247

flap but failed to disturb a single hair on his gelled head.

'Oh, sorry,' he smirked. 'Thought I could smell burning . . . Worried about fire and all that.'

Mitchell's smile was unmistakably triumphant. He'd got her. He'd caught her smoking. She was dead in the water, he reckoned.

Mrs Grindlay leaned back and pulled languorously on her cigarette. She blew the smoke in the direction of Mitchell's smiling face. 'Do you eat much meat, Mitchell?'

'Well, I like a good steak, yes.'

Mrs Grindlay's face lit up. 'Yes, I thought so.'

She blew a perfect smoke ring.

The south of England was a glowing carpet of soft blueish white. It had been snowing heavily. The snow was bathed in bright moonlight, and as he looked out of the plane window, Damien thought the whole scene looked like an illustration from a children's book. The seatbelt sign pinged on and a hologram of Richard Branson appeared in the aisle, wishing humanity a happy century.

This is the last time I fly Virgin, Damien thought to himself. He looked out of the window at the neat fields, quilted with snow, and wondered if cosy little England could ever erupt with the kind of tribal hatred that had wrecked Yugoslavia and Switzerland. Could Yorkshire claim Lancashire as part of Greater Yorkshire and bomb Burnley into the ground? Could Devon become a patchwork of enclaves besieged by the Cornish Army? It seemed impossible. But Damien's experience as a frontline correspondent told him that human beings were capable of anything.

He had witnessed some terrible acts of savagery during his stint in Montreux. Atrocities, massacres, mindless barbarism. It had been brilliant. He'd been able to file several reports packed with bodies, rubble and dazed children. The pictures had been so strong, he hadn't had to get out the blood-stained teddy once. Pity about the ceasefire, really. Damien had been looking forward to bringing in the new century amidst death and destruction. Now he'd probably end up at a boring office party.

The excitement of the Swiss civil war had erased all his interest in the Bovactilax story. He saw the chance of re-establishing himself as a fearless war reporter who exposed life in the raw in far-flung and glamorous conflicts. He would not be going to Brecon and its like again. He must obviously be back in Gus's good books now. Although on the few occasions Damien had spoken to him via the satellite link, Gus had seemed strangely subdued. And unshaven. That was extremely odd.

Damien's ears popped as the plane descended towards Heathrow. The ground was ablaze with tiny lights. Lots of little suburban houses, thought Damien, full of little suburban people, living their humdrum little lives. The lights grew more profuse. So many houses, though Damien. He wondered what it would be like if you could see inside them all.

Off to the right was a patch of especially bright lights. These were the searchlights that illuminated the Barbican. And if Damien could have found the little light that came from Gus's flat and peered in through the window, he would have seen Gus talking to the pizza delivery girl. (He had ordered a pizza and then offered her £30 an hour just to stay and talk.) She was listening to Gus, but she couldn't understand a word. It was all

249

impenetrable jargon. And what was this 'sanity down-sizing situation' he was so afraid of?

A couple of miles up the snaking curves of the Thames, there shone the dim red lights of juggernauts parked at Nine Elms fruit and veg market. And if Damien could have seen inside the car that was cruising slowly around the market he would have found Sally. This was a regular patch for her. Sally had been driving around for some time. By now she would normally have picked up some convenient bit of rough. But tonight she was driving around Nine Elms like a zombie, without any real intention of getting out of the car. Morag from Perth had opened a trap-door in Sally's psyche and illuminated a bottomless shaft of despair. Mindless sex with a muscular stranger would never hold the same attraction. Not even if he were Italian.

And as Damien's plane banked over the shimmering, moonlit Thames, he might have glimpsed the miscroscopic figure of a drunken Henry, recently ejected from a fashionable restaurant after lurching over to a neighbouring table and stubbing out a cigar in David Mellor's profiteroles.

Or he might even have seen Dave greeting the young couple who were potential buyers for his Putney flat.

There wouldn't have been much to see in Joy's flat. Just Joy looking through some faded photos of a smiling little girl, riding on the shoulders of a tall, dark-haired man.

Damien probably wouldn't have been able to see George, who at that moment was hanging upside down in a canoe as part of his whitewater rafting induction course at the Battersea Swimcentre.

The hologram of Richard Branson was now standing

near Damien, smiling as it performed asinine conjuring tricks. Damien found this hard to stomach. Ignoring the protests from a stewardess, he walked towards the back of the plane and sat in an empty seat. Through the window he could just catch a glimpse of Central London. He imagined the hundreds of thousands of ant-like creatures scurrying about in the West End. Damien laughed to himself. All those little nobodies.

Gareth Pugh felt momentarily excited to be standing in a crowded Trafalgar Square, gazing up at the distant figure of Lord Nelson, silhouetted against the gigantic Union Jack lasergram floating in the night sky. A pigeon landed for a moment on Gareth's shoulder, but realising Gareth had no food, flew off towards two American tourists who were distributing large chunks of ham sandwiches. A small crowd of tramps had gathered, eyeing the scene hungrily. But there were too many policemen around for any of them to risk snatching a piece.

The American couple were enormously fat. Gareth pondered their dimensions. If you fed those two a few grams of Bovactilax they would probably turn into planets.

Gareth fumbled in his shirt pocket and took out the dog-eared business card he'd been handed by that cocky TV reporter. God, his stag-night party in Brecon was like a lifetime ago. He'd lost everything since then. He read the address of Globelink News. Was it far from Trafalgar Square? he wondered. He didn't know his way round London at all well. What he did know was that Sir Terence's death-bed confession was explosive to a degree that was hard to conceive. So he calculated it would be right up this Damien Day fellow's street. For the hundredth time that day, Gareth felt for the video answerphone tape in his inside jacket pocket and looked around at the crowds. A gasp went up as the Union Jack lasergram transformed itself into a newborn baby over one hundred metres long. Its multi-coloured umbilical cord twisted and curled above the National Gallery, finally shaping itself into the message, 'Happy Millennium from Benetton'. The crowd broke into applause.

Gareth did not join in. He despised these little people. None of them realised that in their midst was a man who in a few days' time would achieve greatness. He alone could prove that much of the nation's manhood was condemned to eternal droop because of the abject greed of commerce and government. There would be riots in the streets. Mobs of impotent men would tear Whitehall apart. The Prime Minister would probably be hanged from the nearest lamppost. Good, thought Gareth. That was what he wanted to happen. His own life was all but over now. He had been broken on the wheel of love. Now he just wanted to punish and obliterate all those evil men who had connived at his destruction. Yes, he would be their nemesis.

In fact, he was a rather shabby nemesis. He hadn't washed or changed his clothes for over a week. His hair was matted, and his fingernails were lined with dirt. Gareth became aware that he was being photographed by two smiling Danes. He scowled at them. One of them approached and thrust a pound coin into his hand.

'Please, we are not tourists,' said the Dane. 'We are sociologists.'

Gareth felt for the tape again. He wondered whether it had been missed yet. But even if it had, who else could possibly know what was on it? Nobody. Just as well. If Sir Terence's powerful friends knew they'd be grassed on, they'd come after the tape. And, given what was at stake, Gareth didn't suppose they'd ask him for it nicely. He'd probably end up as dead as a Tuesday night in Swansea. No, they couldn't be on his trail. Could they? Anyway, according to that weirdo who'd answered the phone at Globelink ('Miserable Bastards Productions' was a very odd name), Damien Day would be back at his desk tomorrow. Then the tape in Gareth's pocket would be broadcast to the nation and the horrific tale of Bovactilax would be revealed. Everybody would know. And Gareth would definitely be safe. And famous.

Gareth slowly turned through 360 degrees, examining everyone very carefully. He didn't like the look of that dark-haired man with the green suede shoes. He was leaning against the statue of Tim Rice and reading a paper. Or pretending to. Gareth wondered for a moment whether he'd seen him on the platform at Reading. No, he was getting paranoid now. Still, he moved away and found himself standing among a big group of Vegetarians for Jesus, who were singing modern hymns beneath the tall, artificial Christmas tree – a gift from the people of Norway (they could no longer send a real one. Acid rain had seen to that). Gareth blended in as best he could. His complexion was appalling, so he could easily pass for a vegetarian. Not that he should take the piss out of vegetarians any more, he thought. These people were about to inherit the earth. Quite soon, these whey-faced men around him would be the only ones in Britain able to get it up. Women would flock to get into bed with them. Bastards!

Out of the corner of his eye, Gareth watched the man

with green suede shoes. He'd been joined by a shorter, fair-haired one now. They were having some sort of argument. It seemed to be quite a bitter argument. In fact, it looked very much like a lovers' tiff. No, these two definitely weren't hit men.

His attention was taken by the spectacularly fat American. He was calling out to his wife and pointing repeatedly at the pigeon that had landed on his head. Squeaking with excitement, his wife unstrapped her camera. Then suddenly their squeals of pleasure turned into shrieks of fear as a tawny eagle swooped down on the pigeon, misjudged the distance, and sank its talons into the American's head. Its mighty wings beat frantically for a moment before it realised that here was a weight that could never be lifted. It let go and soared back into the night sky. The fat American fell to the ground, screaming in pain as the blood spurted from his scalp. A child screamed. A vegetarian fainted. Gareth decided he'd had enough of London's premier tourist attraction.

Towards midnight, Gareth had come to the firm conclusion that London was no fun at all. He'd wandered around Soho for a bit, looking for a place to eat. The restaurants all had funny names, like Les Frittes or Cholesterol City or Ed's Greasy Diner or La Grasserie. Gareth hated all this fashionable new food. He longed for the good old cottage-cheese salads of home. Eventually he'd found a little Italian place, and been charged an extortionate sum for a soggy pizza with three fried eggs on top. After that, he'd gone to Leicester Square and sat on a bench for a bit to let the meal digest.

Despite the snow, which was still falling, Gareth must

have dozed off, for he woke with a start as high-pressure water hoses erupted around him. Volunteers wearing big badges saying 'Friends of London' were helping council workers hose down the vagrants. Gareth very nearly got hosed down himself, but just managed to escape through one corner of the square, sheltering for a moment in the doorway of the burned-out Swiss Centre. From there he'd watched in horror as dozens of shabby men and women were sent flying by the powerful jets of water. The hosing seemed pretty indiscriminate. One drunken man in a suit was hit full square in the chest and sent flying to the ground. His wig came off, and as Gareth fled the scene he'd caught a glimpse of the poor man scrabbling to retrieve it from the gutter.

Gareth ended up spending the night in a cramped and dismal hotel behind Russell Square. The coffin-shaped room with the peeling wallpaper cost £80. He couldn't really afford it, but he desperately wanted to get off the London streets. Gareth fell asleep to the strains of 'Moscow Nights' being sung raucously by a bunch of drunken Russians in the champagne bar across the street.

Thirteen
December 31st, 1999

The last morning of the old century dawned on a city brought to a virtual standstill by four inches of snow. Gareth Pugh, standing on the platform of Russell Square tube station, couldn't understand why the snow above ground could also halt most of the trains underground. He stared at his *A-Z* map of London as the loudspeaker announced the suspension of all trains on the Piccadilly line 'due to adverse weather conditions'. Now he'd have to find some other way of getting to Globelink. A second loudspeaker announcement informed customers that the lifts were 'temporarily non-functional'.

As Gareth plodded slowly up the circular steps to the street, he decided he would never in his life visit London again. He was still recovering from the shock of his hotel bill. He'd assumed the price of £80 included the usual thirty-five per cent VAT, so the bill of £108 that morning had come as a bit of a shock.

Gareth stood outside the tube station for a few minutes, examining the row of bus maps. There was one for each bus company, so it took him a while to work out which route he needed. He trudged through the snow (now turning to slush) and found the bus stop he needed. He was in luck. A Brown Squirrel was just pulling up. He jumped aboard. The doors clattered shut behind him. As the bus pulled away, Gareth saw two men stand-

256

ing on the pavement. One was blond. The other was dark, and wearing green suede shoes.

Gus was no longer in the habit of arriving for work at 7.30 a.m. In the last few weeks he had got later and later. Today he was one of the last in. He shuffled through the automatic doors, nodded morosely at Connie the receptionist, and headed for the lifts.

'Morning!' called one of the security men. It was Tim.

Gus merely grunted in reply. As he walked past, Tim stepped out from behind his desk.

'Excuse me.'

Gus looked at him blankly.

'Can I see your pass?' said Tim.

Gus fumbled in his pockets and then muttered something about leaving it at home. He went to walk on, but Tim stepped across in front of him.

'I'm sorry, sir.'

'What?'

Tim pointed to the sign that read 'All passes to be shown'.

'Don't be ridiculous, man,' Gus bridled, 'you know who I am.'

Tim shrugged. 'I have my instructions.'

Gus threw back his head and yelled. 'But you know me, I'm the guv'nor! You know my face!'

'With respect,' said Tim relishing the moment, 'the sign does not say, "All passes to be shown unless it's the guv'nor and I know his face".'

Gus fixed Tim with an expression of cold fury.

Two hundred yards away from the Globelink building, Gareth leaped off a Red Roebuck and scuttled into a

257

shop doorway. He'd changed buses six times in the previous two hours; surely he'd thrown them off the scent? He looked carefully up and down the street. There was no sign of the two men. With a final glance at his *A-Z* he emerged from the doorway and hurried towards his destination. As the sleek lines of the Globelink building loomed in front of him, a taxi pulled up alongside him. Gareth broke into a run. The two men piled out of the cab and came after him. Gareth clutched at the tape in his jacket pocket and sprinted for the Globelink entrance. There he collided with a bald man who was also about to enter the building.

'Sorry!' gasped Gareth.

'Moron!' boomed the bald man, picking himself up from the pavement and wiping the slush from his coat. The man looked dreadful, thought Gareth, but he had no time to worry about other people. He pushed through the revolving doors and entered the reception area. Behind him, his pursuers slammed into the bald man and all three went down on the pavement together.

Gareth realised that if he stopped at Reception to ask for Damien Day he'd be caught for sure. On the other side of the revolving doors he could see his pursuers, who were being harangued by the angry bald man. That gave him a few seconds' grace. 'Don't run,' he told himself. 'Act casual.' In fact, it was no problem getting past Reception, The security man was too busy lecturing some bloke about not having a pass. Gareth simply adopted a confident air and walked past. It felt like confirmation of his own insignificance. Nobody notices me, he thought. Well, they'd notice him after today all right.

Gus was too angry to pay attention to the wigless Henry,

who entered the building shouting something about brain-damaged louts who needed knee-capping. Gus was even too angry to notice the bizarrely pink and shiny dome. But Tim had to suppress a giggle as Henry flashed his pass and hurried through.

Gus stabbed a finger at Tim. 'Listen, you!'

Tim interrupted him. 'Tell you what, sir. We won't make an issue of it. I'll do you a temporary pass. How's that?' Tim went back round behind his desk and began to type out a pass on the computer. He typed very slowly with one finger.

'G-U-S . . . H-E-D-G-E-S'

Gus clenched his jaw and drummed his fingers on the desk.

Tim looked up. 'Purpose of visit? No, only joking.'

Gus realised he only had himself to blame for this humiliation. This was how the hirelings would rise up and torment him if he continued to show weakness. Gus hated weakness. Weakness frightened him. He had tried to express this to the pizza girl the night before.

'I'm scared to feel anything,' he had told her. 'I'm so scared of failing that I'm scared of feeling anything in case it makes me vulnerable. So I don't open any vulnerability window, oh no. There's the target, off I go. Straightline Gus, that's the right mode, defences up, yes indeedy, all the time. Never let the buggers know what you're thinking or feeling. Trouble is, I've got to the stage where I don't really know what I'm thinking or feeling . . . I'm not here, that's what I always tell them, and in a sense, I'm not . . . Perhaps I need help . . . What do you think?'

'It's gone twelve now,' the pizza girl had said. 'You owe me another thirty quid.'

259

Gus's thoughts were interrupted by Tim's cocky voice. 'There we are, your temporary document, sir. Try not to forget your pass in future. We don't want a repeat performance, do we?'

There was no danger of that, thought Gus. He had just added Tim to the list of redundancies. He made his way to the lift, glancing at the temporary pass in his hand. It felt strangely comforting. It proved who he was.

Gareth got out of the lift at the seventh floor. He was confronted by a tall sign bearing dozens of arrows pointing in myriad directions. All the destinations were in what seemed like a foreign language: VT, VTLIB, ENG, OBU, TECDEP. Which way should he go? Where would he find Damien Day? He had to hurry; his pursuers might well be in the building by now.

In fact, Gareth's pursuers were already approaching the stairs on the ground floor. Like Gareth, they'd had no problem getting past Security. The man at the desk had been on the phone, chortling to some friend about how he'd just humiliated the boss.

Gareth turned into a brightly lit corridor. Along the walls were huge colour photos of the 'faces' of Globelink News. Sally Smedley gazed out, her head tipped to one side and holding a phone to her ear in a totally unconvincing manner. Next to her was the face of a man with a forced debonair smile, like someone trying to be Errol Flynn. Below it Gareth read the name 'Henry Davenport'. He frowned. Wasn't that the decrepit baldie he'd crashed into at the front doors? What a difference a wig made. Further along the corridor Gareth saw the face he was after. Damien was wearing a trenchcoat and holding a microphone. He was smiling in a knowing way, with one eyebrow slightly arched. Gareth felt a wave of panic. Was he doing the right thing turning to Damien? The man looked like a complete prat.

A man in a large quilted jacket and faded denims came ambling along the corridor.

'Excuse me, do you think you could tell me where I might find this gentleman?' asked Gareth, pointing at Damien's picture.

'Oh,' said the man with grim recognition, 'the Angel of Death.'

Gareth didn't much like the sound of this. 'Why do you call him the Angel of Death?'

'Oh, you'd have to be a cameraman to understand.' The man pointed towards the stairs. 'I'd say your best bet is the newsroom. Second floor.'

'Cheers,' said Gareth, and set off for the stairs at the end of the corridor. As he descended to the fifth floor, he heard footsteps pounding up from below. Two sets of footsteps. Getting closer. His pulse raced. He dived through a pair of swing doors and stood still. The footsteps went past him and stopped. He emerged cautiously. Which was the safest way to go? He glanced up and saw two pairs of legs through the railings of the next flight of stairs. He recognised a pair of green suede shoes and froze. Then he sneezed. Oh, damn! The two men came running back down the stairs and saw Gareth.

'Get him!'

Gareth ran back through the swing doors, sprinted along a corridor, turned left, turned right, and dived through a door marked OBITLIB. He flicked the catch on the door and leaned against the wall trying not to breathe too loudly. He heard running footsteps get louder and then stop. The pumping in Gareth's temples

261

got quicker and stronger. There was a loud coughing from one of the men, then voices. They were right outside the door!

'Are you sure he came this way?'

The other didn't answer, but coughed and gasped instead.

'God, you're so unfit. It's pathetic.'

'I think . . . I think he came down this corridor,' wheezed the other.

'You "think"?'

'Yeah.'

'The people they lumber me with. You're not really cut out for this, are you?'

'I'm doing my best.'

'You're past it. You should be given a desk job. Before you make a hit on the wrong man again.'

'You always have to bring that up, don't you?'

'I'm amazed they didn't fire you.'

'It was an easy mistake to make. They were wearing the same colour pullovers.'

There was a long pause.

'Let's look along here.'

Gareth waited for the footsteps to fade away. He tried to clear his thoughts. His first reflex was to hide the tape. He looked around the room. It was small, just a storeroom really, with built-in shelves full of boxes of videotapes. The tape boxes were all marked with familiar names. Kenneth Clarke, Robin Cook, Joan Collins . . . He moved along the alphabet, finally realising that OBITLIB must stand for Obituaries Library. He'd heard that TV stations recorded obituaries before people had actually died. He shuddered. It was a bit creepy. He suddenly saw the name 'Henry Davenport', and took down the box from the shelf. Gareth took out the obit tape and slipped it into his pocket. He then replaced it with the video answerphone tape and put the box back on the shelf. Perfect. Gareth had got a good look at the old boy when he'd crashed into him at the front door; judging by his ghastly raddled face, Henry Davenport wasn't long for this world. When Davenport died, someone would open the obit box and the full story of Bovactilax would be revealed to the world. Gareth didn't know whether he'd get out of the Globelink building alive, but now, even if he died, the truth would not die with him.

Gareth went over to the door and listened. All seemed quiet. He eased off the catch and half opened the door. He slid out into the corridor and was making his way back towards the landing when he heard footsteps behind him. His heart leaped, but then he realised it was only one pair of footsteps. Very distinctive footsteps going click-clack, click-clack. He wheeled round and found himself face-to-face with Sally Smedley. She's different than she is on the telly, he thought. Thinner in the face. Not as nice-looking. He gave her a smile of recognition. She half nodded, in a faintly royal way, and would have kept right on walking if Gareth hadn't stepped in front of her.

'Hallo there, Sally.'

Sally frowned.

'I'm sorry, do I know you?'

'We've spoken on the phone. I'm Gareth from Brecon.'

'Oh my God,' Sally groaned.

'I need your help, I really do.'

Sally exploded. 'Look, it's not my fault you're a sexual

inadequate! I can't help you, understand! Either you just put up with it or step under a bus. How dare you come here and pester me! Now kindly step aside.'

Gareth was momentarily dazed by the verbal barrage, but as she swept past him, he cried, 'No, Sally, you don't understand!'

Sally spun on her three-inch heels and fixed him with a beady eye. She spoke with breathless speed, 'Oh, I understand all right, You're small, you're lonely and you're impotent and you think there's that nice woman off the telly, I'll go up to London and pour out my problems to her. Well, did you ever stop to think that other people might have problems of their own?'

'But—'

'Their lives are one HUGE PROBLEM!' she roared. 'They have problems you couldn't possibly imagine. Impotence a problem? Do me a favour. Are you addicted to loveless sex with Neanderthal strangers? Well are you?'

'Well, no, I—'

'No. Exactly. So just shut up.'

With this, Sally stomped her foot and shook her head, like a child having a tantrum. Her sculpted coiffeur started to disintegrate and three wisps of brown hair fell over her left eye.

'Happy now?' she yelled.

Gareth gabbled wildly at her. 'Look, please help me! They want me dead. It's the Bovactilax. Phabox UK. Sir Terence knew everything!'

Sally wasn't listening. She was already stomping up the corridor, click-clack, click-clack, click-clack. 'I'm sorry, Please address all enquiries to my agent.'

Gareth ran after her. 'But they want to kill me! You must broadcast that tape!'

'Yes, yes, whatever,' Sally replied as she swept through a set of swing doors. Gareth was about to follow her, but as the doors swung open he saw the two men coming towards him.

Helen was on her third chocolate croissant of the morning when Damien lobbed a hand grenade at her.

'Damien!' she yelled, spitting out crumbs.

'Calm down,' said Damien. 'I've removed the firing pin. It's just a little memento I've brought home from the front.' He produced a misshapen bullet. 'Along with this. And this!' Triumphantly Damien held aloft a jar of liquid with what looked like a long thin gherkin in it.

Dave peered at it. 'What is it?'

'A dead sniper's finger.'

There was a chorus of disgusted protest. Helen decided she didn't want the rest of her croissant.

'What's your problem?' said Damien. 'Our lads did that sort of stuff in the Falklands. Ears, mostly.' He plonked the pickle jar on top of his computer terminal.

'No, no, I'm sorry,' protested Dave. 'Call me old-fashioned, but I am not working with a dismembered finger staring at me.'

'Dave, fingers don't stare.'

'This one does. Now bloody move it!'

'OK, OK,' said Damien, putting the jar in his desk drawer. 'Talk about squeamish.' He launched reluctantly into his backlog of post. He was missing Montreux already. What a pain to be back in the land of the nobodies.

Joy entered the newsroom, bearing an armful of graphics. She slapped them down on to Helen's desk one by one. 'Here you go. Map of London showing route of

265

Millennium Charity Jog. Yawn, yawn. Crappy still of rhino for crappy rhino story. Boring logo for Millennium Honours' List story, graphs showing increase in violent crime. And silhouette of little old lady being bludgeoned by baseball bat.'

Helen shook her head. 'No, I'm not using that. Send it back and tell them to tone it down.'

'Right.' Joy hovered behind Helen, fiddling with a paper clip.

'Helen?'

'Yes?'

'My dad keeps ringing. He wants to come and see me. What do you think I should do?' Joy felt exposed, opening up like this. She felt even more exposed when she saw Helen giggle.

'Well, thanks for being so bloody sensitive about it, Helen!'

Then she realised that Helen was looking past her shoulder. She turned. She saw Henry's gleaming cranium and cackled coarsely.

'Oh, for God's sake,' bellowed Henry. 'Never seen a bald head before?'

All eyes were now fixed on Henry's proud, pink pate.

'Where's the rug?' smirked Damien.

'Never you mind where it is.' Henry sat down and pretended to find something very interesting on his VDU. He became aware of Damien and Joy lurking behind him. He attempted to open up a new line of conversation.

'So, Helen, are you going to accept that wedding invitation?'

Helen wiped some crumbs from her desk. 'Don't think so, Henry. Chloë's made her choice.'

Henry felt Damien lean closer.

'We'll find out in the end, Henry. You might as well tell us.'

'There's nothing to tell.'

'Then what's the problem?' enquired Joy.

'I incinerated it in the microwave, OK? Now leave me alone!'

A few bottom lips began to quiver.

'You microwaved your wig?' asked Dave in a trembly voice.

'Yes, yes!' barked Henry. 'It's perfectly simple! I fell out of a restaurant pissed, couldn't find a taxi, walked through Leicester Square to that little minicab company I know, and got vagrant-hosed by those mindless thugs employed by Westminster Council. Whoosh, off flew the wig into the gutter. I took it home, rinsed it out, bunged it into the microwave for twenty seconds, accidentally set it for twenty minutes, wig burst into flames and nearly burned the sodding kitchen down! There, satisfied?'

'Easily done,' said Dave.

When George entered the newsroom a few minutes later, the laughter triggered by Dave's remark was still continuing. This is more like it, thought George. This is how to greet the millennium. Morale was clearly on the up.

If the cacophony of laughter had not been so long and so loud then maybe someone would have heard the cry of 'Help!' There was only one cry of 'help' before Gareth's mouth was stuffed with a handkerchief. The dark-haired man with the green suede shoes had grabbed him round the throat and pinned him against the wall on

267

the fourth-floor landing near the lifts, while his colleague did the handkerchief-stuffing. Gareth thrashed with his legs but the grip on his throat simply got tighter.

Suede Shoes hissed at the blond one. 'OK. Quick. Do it.'

'Why have I got to do it?' came the reply.

'Because I'm busy holding him by the throat, that's why.'

Gareth's eyes widened in terror as the man who wasn't gripping his throat produced a syringe.

'Come on, before someone comes,' snapped Suede Shoes.

'All right, all right,' said Blondie.

'Nmmmmmmmmrrrrrrrgggggh,' said Gareth.

'Hurry up!'

'Don't rush me.'

'Stop staring at the syringe and just bloody stick it in him!'

'Yes, yes.'

'What's the bloody problem?'

'I've just never been able to handle injections, that's all. Never have. Not since I was a kid. They make me feel faint.'

'Stick it in him!'

'All right.'

'Don't shut your eyes, for Christ's sake! You might get me instead!'

'Nmmmmmmurrgh,' said Gareth.

'Oh for . . .' Suede Shoes let go of Gareth's throat for a second.

Gareth spat out the handkerchief and drew breath to shout, but was instantly knocked unconscious by a huge and well-timed blow. The two men looked down at the

268

little Welshman, who lay on the floor like a rag doll.

'Why didn't you do that to start with?'

'Shut it,' said Suede Shoes. He bent over Gareth, methodically felt in each of his pockets, and finally found the tape.

'Bingo.'

'Quick,' said Blondie, thinking he heard someone coming. He stabbed at the lift button.

They dragged Gareth's limp form towards the lift door.

'What if there's somebody in the lift?' asked Blondie.

'Don't ask me. You're the one who pressed the bloody button.'

The lift doors opened. The blond one crouched in a karate pose. His colleague sniggered. 'You look ridiculous.'

There was nobody in the lift. The two men dragged Gareth's limp form into it. Suede Shoes kept his finger on the Doors Open button.

'Go on then, stick it in him, I'll keep look-out.'

'Why can't you do it? You're not holding his throat any more.'

'Look, I killed the creep from Greenpeace, OK? All you did was drive the getaway car. So it's your turn, all right?'

Blondie closed his eyes and jabbed the syringe into Gareth's arm. 'Ow.'

'Why the fuck did you say ow?'

'I dunno, just the thought of it somehow.'

Suede Shoes felt Gareth's pulse. In the distance a pair of heels went click-clack, click-clack.

'Oh bloody hell. He should be dead by now. The guys in the lab told me this stuff kills in four seconds. Stick some more in him.'

The blond one shook his head resolutely. 'No, it's your turn. We're on the same money, remember?'

Suede Shoes put his powerful hands round Gareth's throat and squeezed hard. He wasn't going to admit it, but he couldn't handle injections either.

Gus hurried through the newsroom. He didn't like the sound of all that laughter. They might be laughing at him. Perhaps the story of the temporary pass was already doing the rounds. He scuttled into his office and closed the door behind him. When he turned round he saw a Japanese businessman sitting in his chair.

'What the hell are you doing here? I didn't hire you today,' Gus snapped.

'I'm sorry?' said the Japanese businessman.

Gus felt the ground open up beneath him. This man was not from the Oriental Casting Agency. Oh God, this was a real Japanese businessman.

'My name is Mr Yamaguchi,' he said in immaculate English. 'Please excuse the liberty of my sitting at your desk, but the sofa has a new fish tank on it.'

'Oh, yes,' flapped Gus. 'I'm sorry, I'm a bit late. Did we have an appointment?'

'No, Mr Hedges, Sir Roysten Merchant sent me. He said if I informed you of this fact I would not need an appointment.'

'Quite right,' said Gus quickly. 'Well, what output can I throughput into your input?'

Mr Yamaguchi let this pass. He didn't understand it. But he marvelled at the malleability of the English language. 'The situation is this, Mr Hedges. As you may be aware, Sir Roysten's many business ventures are all in considerable financial difficulty.'

270

'Glitches,' said Gus. 'Glitches in the floppy disk of life.'

'Let us hope so. In the meantime he has requested a substantial emergency loan from the Bank of Hosokawa. I represent this bank. They have asked me to inspect Sir Roysten's ventures in the UK to establish whether they are viable. The bank sees no point, obviously, in urinating money into the wind.'

'Indeed,' said Gus.

'So I am here to make an assessment on the ground.'

'Right, I'm just surprised Sir Roysten didn't notify me you were coming.'

'That's because he thinks I'm coming next week,' said Mr Yamaguchi with a smile. 'I like to see an operation as it really is, on a normal working day.'

Gus flinched. With the millennium only twelve hours or so away, he didn't exactly see this as a normal working day. And Mr Yamaguchi wasn't likely to make allowances; he probably hadn't taken a holiday in twenty years.

Mr Yamaguchi smiled at him. 'I could already tell from the amount of laughter in your newsroom that you run a happy shop.'

'Oh yes,' said Gus, with a merry grin, 'laughing all the time, that's us. Working hard but laughing as we go.' Gus broke into a laugh, which somehow came out resembling the barking of a seal. Behind the laugh every sinew of his being was telling Gus that this polite little Japanese visitor held the key to his very survival.

Out in the newsroom, the merriment over Henry's microwaved toupee had just about subsided. George, who had missed these revelations, registered Henry's

271

bald head, went over and pulled up a chair close to Henry's desk. 'Congratulations.'

'Congratulations?' said Henry.

'Yes,' said George. 'For learning to accept things.'

'Eh?'

'I know it's not an easy thing to come to terms with.'

'What isn't?' glowered Henry.

'But you've done it. You've accepted that you're getting older. You're going with it gracefully.'

George was warming to his theme, which meant he didn't notice Dave desperately signalling to him to stop.

'To be perfectly frank, Henry,' George confided, 'and I know I can tell you this now, I always felt that the wig looked like a rather absurd gesture of denial.'

'Did you?' said Henry.

Dave called across the newsroom. 'Can you check my copy on the rhino story, please, George?'

'Yes,' said Helen, 'that's a good idea. And, Henry, you might want to check it, too.'

Henry grumpily punched a button and the text appeared on his VDU. Dave relaxed. Henry and George were concentrating on the screen. The danger had passed.

'To be honest, Henry,' said George out of nowhere, 'I felt the same about the corset.'

Dave closed his eyes. Helen buried her head in her hands.

Henry's face was expressionless as he slowly got to his feet. 'George, stand up.'

'Why?' asked George.

'Because it's hard to head-butt someone when they're sitting down.'

George was saved by the arrival of Gus. What's more,

272

he was talking like the old Gus, the one they hadn't seen for a while.

'OK, news commandos, are we attacking the news-gathering net and pinging those winners past the opposition backhand, you bet, terrific. Now, on with these positive mindsets and listen up. This is Mr Yamaguchi.' Gus paused for a moment. 'From the Bank of Hosokawa.'

Meaningful looks shot around the room like bullets.

'He has come to witness our normal, day-to-day hyperdynamic scoop-busting operation. And I'm sure,' said Gus pointedly, 'that that is what we're going to show him, isn't it, team?'

'Oh, gosh, yes,' said Joy.

'Absolutely,' said George, delighted to see Gus back on form. 'Yup indeedy.'

Sally came in muttering something about nutters being allowed to roam the corridors of Globelink. She stopped muttering when she saw the man standing beside Gus. Gus's body language told her this man was a VIP.

'Sally, may I introduce Mr Yamaguchi.'

Mr Yamaguchi bowed to Sally, which Sally enjoyed enormously.

'Mr Yamaguchi, Sally Smedley, the supernova in our televisual galaxy,' oozed Gus.

'Thrilled to meet you,' said Mr Yamaguchi.

And he did seem thrilled to meet her. He couldn't take his eyes off her. Gus recalled the enormous success of a certain kind of Western woman in Japan: The Nolan Sisters, Sheena Easton, Audrey Hepburn. Sally was not unlike Audrey Hepburn in the right sort of light.

'Perhaps we should begin, Mr Yamaguchi, by showing you around our state-of-the-art computerised weather graphic generator. It's downstairs. Sally, perhaps you'd care to accompany me and Mr Yamaguchi from the Bank of Hosokawa.'

Sally's face lit up like a Christmas tree.

'Oh, I'd love to.'

They set off for the stairs to the basement. Gus didn't want to use the lifts as they were covered in defeatist graffiti.

As soon as Gus and his party had left the newsroom, George launched into a pep talk.

'Well, everyone, you all saw the change in Gus, he was much more like his old self.'

There were a few disgruntled murmurs.

'That has to be a good sign. Things are looking up. I can feel it in my bones. The millennium's going to be an exciting opportunity for us all, both as professionals and individuals. Now, let's crack on, and after the nine o'clock bulletin we'll have a bit of a party. Right now, I'm off up to VT to see what pictures have come through on the satellite from Cyprus.'

As George headed for the lifts, Dave raised an interesting point of semantics. 'This person George has turned into, is he a prat, a nerd or a wanker?'

'Yes, yes and yes,' said Joy,

'OK,' sighed Helen, 'what are we still missing for the business news? Dave, how's that going?'

Dave frowned. He hated compiling the business news, but he'd been lumbered with it since 1996. That was the year when all the broadcasters had finally realised that economic correspondents were pointless. Nobody knew

274

how the economy really worked. And in '96 when all the correspondents predicted recovery a month before three high street banks went into receivership, this finally became apparent, and economic correspondents disappeared for ever. Dave had always regarded them as poseurs and bullshitters anyway. The BBC's one had been so shrewd about money that for years he'd worked for Robert Maxwell apparently without noticing the slightest financial irregularity. But the disappearance of these guys meant that Dave had to sling together a summary of the day's trading himself. It never took too long. He just used to glance through the share prices and then decide whether confidence was up or down. It didn't really matter whether he was right or not, he argued. None of it really meant anything.

'Tell you what, Helen,' said Dave, 'why don't we just say "Bong! No City news tonight because it's all bollocks"?'

'Yes, I'm happy to read that out,' said Henry.

'Dave,' said Helen wearily, 'I know it's boring but—'

'Yes, it is boring, Helen. It must be boring because it's a job that's been given to me, Dave the Doormat.'

'Someone's got to do it,' said Damien smugly.

'Yes, well come next century maybe you'll have to find a new someone.'

Dave held up a letter. It bore a stamp with Cliff Richard's face on it and was addressed to Australia House.

'This is my ticket out of here.'

'You're not emigrating?' said Helen.

'Yup. That's the plan.'

'What will you do?' asked Henry.

'Don't know. Loads of things I could do. Lots of work

275

going over there. Short of manpower. I think all their men came over here in the Eighties to be dentists.' He laughed uneasily at his own joke. 'Look, I'm forty in March. I've achieved nothing here. And I don't just mean work.'

Henry felt a wave of panic. Dave was unreliable and exasperating. But he was Henry's best friend. 'This is morbid talk, old boy.'

'I'm sorry.'

'Don't be sorry,' said Helen 'but just think about it for a bit. You're not a doormat here. You're valued and . . . loved.' Helen weighed her words carefully. There had been a time when Dave had convinced himself he was in love with her. She didn't want to revive anything.

Dave smiled. 'I don't believe a word of it. But thanks for saying it. No, I need a new start. Fresh horizons. I mean, I'll miss you all here, but . . .' Dave got a lump in his throat and pretended to cough.

Henry was looking at his feet.

'OK,' said Dave. 'So, City news.' He looked up and saw Henry's eyes cloud with tears. 'Oh, come on, Henry, please don't do that.'

This emotional moment was shattered by the sound of a long, drawn-out scream, like the sound of a pig being slaughtered. It came from the direction of the lifts.

'George!' yelled Helen,

The scream was cut short by the sickening crump of flesh and bone hitting metal.

Dave was the first to reach George, who was lying in a heap by the Coca-Cola machine with blood pouring out of his nose. The rest of the staff flocked around, making helpful suggestions. Sit him up, lie him down, tip his head back, squeeze his nose, don't move him, wrap him

276

up, put his head between his legs, fetch some arnica, give him some air.

'Just shut up!' shouted Helen.

They all stopped. In the silence George could be heard babbling quietly.

'It's that lift. It hates me. It's after me. I know it is.'

'You'll be OK, George, take it easy,' soothed Helen, trying to staunch his bleeding nose with her hanky.

'Take your time, what happened? Why did you run into the Coca-Cola machine?'

George tried to explain but his jaw seemed to lock. He tried again. He looked at Helen with a stricken expression which reminded her of Munch's *Scream*.

'Oh, my God,' said Henry in a slow ominous tone. He was staring at the corpse in the lift. There were shrieks and gasps as others turned and saw the dead man's marble face, his eyes open, his tongue protruding.

'All right, all right,' said Damien, stepping forward. 'Calm down, everybody. Haven't you seen a dead body before?'

The lift doors began to close. Damien leaped into the lift and pressed the emergency button to disable it. He lifted the man's limp hand and felt for a pulse. He looked at the others and shook his head.

'Shouldn't we try mouth-to-mouth resuscitation?' asked Dave. They all gazed at the dead man,

Henry cleared his throat. 'I'm not actually very sure how to do it. I expect Damien knows.'

Damien shot Henry a look. 'He is definitely dead.'

'Should I fetch a mirror?' asked Joy.

'Look, he's dead! All right?' said Damien.

George began to hyperventilate.

Helen took charge. 'OK, take George through into the newsroom, Joy, and get the first-aid kit out.'

Joy helped George to his feet. Blood dripped from his nose on to his Timberlands. She led him back into the newsroom. Helen turned to look at the corpse. She hung on to Henry's arm just in case. Damien was lifting the eyelids to examine the pupils.

'Poor man,' whispered Helen.

'He doesn't look that old,' said Henry.

'Who is he?' asked Dave, plucking up the courage to look closely at the dead man's face.

Damien studied the stone-like features. 'He looks vaguely familiar somehow.'

Damien checked inside man's pockets for some ID. There was nothing except for an *A-Z*.

Helen volunteered to go and ring for an ambulance. She was pleased to get away from the body.

'I wonder what he died from,' said Dave.

'Heart, probably,' said Henry gloomily.

Damien, Henry and Dave stood in silence. The silence was broken by bouncy footsteps and the sound of whistling. Gus was coming up the stairs. He turned towards the lifts.

'OK, team, no standing around gossiping, I want dynamism overdrive.'

He crossed the landing towards the three mourners.

'Standing around is not a viable option. When Mr Yamaguchi comes up he . . . aaaaaaaaaaaaaaaaaargh!'

Gus leaped backwards as if he'd been electrocuted. He clutched his chest and gasped. Slowly his left arm came up and a trembling finger pointed at the corpse.

'That's . . . the . . . he's . . . is he . . . he's . . . he's . . .'

'Yes, he's dead, Gus,' said Damien. 'Well spotted.'

Gus's face was a study in terror. He had never been able to bear the thought that he would one day be hurled into oblivion. Worse still was the fear that he would not be remembered. Death would confirm him as the nonentity he suspected he was in life. The games of squash and the hi-fibre breakfasts were desperate attempts to ward off the grim reaper. But death had found him. It had left its calling card in his lift. While the others saw poor Gareth's sad face, Gus saw himself, cold, stiff and buried.

'We don't know who he is,' said Dave. 'You don't recognise him, do you?'

'No,' said Gus instantly. The last thing he wanted was to have to look closely at that face. 'Definitely don't know him.'

'Oh, well,' Dave sighed, going into the lift. He took off his denim jacket and gently covered Gareth's face. To everyone's surprise, Henry crossed himself.

'Hallo,' said the soft, female voice. 'Thank you for dialling 999, the emergency service brought to you by Fortress Assurance – Your Crisis Is Our Concern. Please say yes to the service you require. (Beep) Fire. (Beep) Police. (Beep) Ambulance.'

'Yes!' Helen shouted down the mouthpiece.

'Thank you for choosing,' said the voice.

Helen drummed her fingers on her desk and looked around the empty newsroom. The staff had been stood down for half an hour. Some of them were quite shaken.

The voice started up again. 'Please say "yes" after the kind of medical emergency for which you require assistance from Fortress Assurance – Your Crisis is our Concern: Cardiac arrest (beep). Road accident (beep).

Domestic Accident (beep). Contact injury (beep). Other (beep). If you have further enquiries please press the star button on your telephone now.'

Helen did so.

A real human voice came on to the phone. 'Thank you for calling Ultra Ambulances Angela speaking how can I help you?'

'We need an ambulance.'

'Address?'

'Globelink News, Third Floor, Merchant House, Vernon Road, SW1.'

'Phone number?'

'070710 49962238.'

Helen heard Angela tapping at her keyboard.

'Do you have a Gold Accident Account?'

'No, we don't.'

'And what is the medical problem?'

'Death.'

This time Helen heard no keys being punched.

'I'm sorry,' said Angela. 'Death is not a call-out trigger factor. Please make alternative arrangements. Thank you for calling.'

The phone line went dead. Helen looked up to see Joy waving an empty first-aid kit in her face.

She ignored Joy and looked at her watch. It was sad and shocking that someone had died in the lift. It was also very inconvenient. Helen felt guilty for having this thought.

Gus burst in. 'Ambulance on its way, is it? Good. Terrific. Well done, team.'

Helen shook her head. 'Not yet.'

'What?' yelled Gus. 'Well kick arse, Helen! We can't have dead people on the premises. Dead people are unacceptable. What if Mr Yamaguchi sees him?'

'What if he does?' asked Joy.

'We don't want him thinking this is the kind of work environment where dead people hang around in lifts.' Gus was rambling now. 'No, no, we mustn't let Mr Yamaguchi see that. I mean, we don't want to upset the man who holds our futures in the palm of his hand now, do we, no I don't think we do, no indeedy.'

Joy shrugged. 'Why should he be upset?'

Gus exploded. 'WHAT IS IT WITH YOU, WOMAN? DO YOU HAVE TO QUESTION EVERY-THING I SAY?'

'Yes, if it's cobblers,' replied Joy calmly.

'Can we keep the noise down?' pleaded Helen, who was trying to get through to the police. So far, all she'd got through to was a recording of the theme from *Dr Zhivago*. Helen groaned in frustration. 'If the police ask for a call-out fee, we'll pay it, won't we, Gus? . . . Gus?'

Gus was out by the lift, flailing his arms around at Dave, Damien and Henry. 'That . . . thing can't stay in the lift. Can't stay there. Get it out of sight. I don't care how.'

'Oh, great,' roared Henry. 'Why don't we just tip the poor bugger down the waste disposal!'

Gus stared hard at Henry. 'What the hell's happened to your head, Henry?'

It was the first moment Gus had registered Henry's baldness.

'I microwaved my wig.'

Gus was furious. 'This is no time to wind me up, Henry. Now, I'm going downstairs. In a few minutes I shall be coming back with Mr Yamaguchi. By then I want this thing gone. Dead men with coats over their heads are not image-friendly. So, move it!'

Within twenty minutes of finding the cadaver, every one of George's psychosomatic symptoms had made a spectacular comeback. His dizzy spells were coming around roughly every ninety seconds; he had a headache that felt like an axe was embedded in his forehead; his chest muscles were tight, his palms were sweaty, and he had that strange tingling sensation in his elbow which eighteen X-rays and a bone scan had been unable to explain. At this moment he could not have recalled a single line from the self-rebirthing book. The new George had been erased for ever.

George closed his office door, folded up his Arran sweater with the yellow triangles (bought only yesterday) and placed it on his desk as a pillow. Then he put his aching head on the sweater and waited for the next dizzy spell. He became aware of shouting out in the newsroom. But the dizzy spell was already in full spate and he didn't want to look up.

If he had done, he'd have seen Dave, Damien and Henry struggling with Gareth's corpse. Even though Gareth was small, it is not easy to carry nine stone's worth of dead human being. Gareth's head had banged against the photocopier and two desks before they heaved him into Sally's empty chair, just so they could have a rest.

'Not exactly dignified, is it?' said Dave grimly.

Damien, the expert on death, set things in perspective.

'He knows nothing about it. The odd biff is irrelevant when you're dead.'

Dave's denim jacket had slid off the face.

'He does ring a bell,' said Damien.

If the corpse had been clean-shaven, or wearing a glassy, drunken expression, then Damien might have remembered that pugnacious little Welshman at the stag-night party in Brecon. As it was, he gave up trying to recall the face and let Henry pull the denim jacket back over Gareth's face.

'Do you think the police will be able to identify him?' asked Dave.

'They'll DNA him at the mortuary,' said Damien.

Dave nodded. 'Yeah, that's about all they'll do. Police don't waste time and money on unidentifieds these days.'

Henry shook his head in grim disbelief. Even death was an exercise in cost-cutting these days. This poor sod probably wouldn't even get a headstone, he thought, just a wooden cross with an invoice number on it. 'I need a stiff drink,' he mumbled, and walked into Gus's office to help himself to the vintage Armagnac that Gus only ever opened for important visitors. And Masons.

Damien looked around for ideas. He pointed to a little edit suite at the back of the main newsroom. 'Let's put him in there.'

Dave and Damien were just about to lift Gareth's body when Sally click-clacked in at great speed, talking all the way.

'My goodness, but it's quiet in here. If I were you I'd at least pretend to do something. Mr Yamaguchi is clearly here to . . .' She broke off. A man was sitting in her chair with a jacket over his head.

'Oh, very funny, Henry.' Before Dave or Damien could speak, she'd whisked off the jacket. Gareth's empty eyes stared up at her. His mouth had opened wider now. Sally stood paralysed, all colour draining

283

from her face. Dave prised his jacket from her hand, which was clenched tight, and covered Gareth's face again.

If the shock inflicted on Sally had been less overpowering, there might have been a remote possibility of her recognising the dead man as the small Welsh pest who'd stopped her in the corridor. But even then it is unlikely that she'd registered Gareth's existence as a human being to the extent of remembering his features. Gareth belonged, in Sally's mind, to the 'little people', the faceless army that was the viewing public. Gareth had represented a momentary irritant in Sally's life, but he had left no lasting impression. In fact, Gareth had left no lasting impression on anyone or anything. Even his beloved Megan, down in Builth Wells, was forgetting him fast.

Damien and Dave tried to guide Sally to a chair, but Sally's feet seemed nailed to the ground. She wouldn't budge.

Joy emerged into the newsroom, looking for a box of tissues. She saw the catatonic figure of Sally. 'What's up? Have her batteries run out?'

'She's in shock,' said Damien. 'Best fetch her some blankets.'

'In a bit, I'm doing George's nose at the moment.' Joy found the tissues and headed back towards George's office. Dave found himself doing something he imagined he would never do. He had his arm round Sally and was trying to comfort her.

The next four minutes, which might have been used to find a discreet temporary resting place for Gareth, were spent trying to revive Sally. They managed to sit her

284

down, then wrapped her in a blanket. Eventually, after Henry had moistened her lips with Gus's Armagnac, she seemed to regain her senses.

'I've . . . I've never . . . I've never seen one before,' she mumbled. Her voice had a slight trace of a rural accent. The pure, controlled diction had disappeared.

A mighty roar echoed across the newsroom. It was Gus. 'Good God! What's that . . . that . . . person still doing here? I said I wanted him out of sight! Jesus wept! What is the matter with you people?'

The roaring had drawn Helen into the newsroom. 'All right, Gus, all right,' she soothed, 'shouting won't achieve anything.'

'Won't it?' Gus shouted. 'What will, then? Mr Yamaguchi wants to see the bulletin being put together. I've tried showing him everything else, but no, he wants to see us making the news because obviously he is a snooper from the bank and he wants to see if we're worth saving or whether he should just pull the plug on us and perform a mercy killing! I've told the boys in Engineering to keep him occupied. All I ask is that when he comes up, this office is working normally!'

'Yes, well sorry if we seem a bit down, Gus,' Henry said with a stern expression, 'but finding a corpse does tend to put a kink in your day. You see, unlike you, we are not emotionless ROBOTS!' Henry hit his top decibellage. 'THIS MAN IS DEAD, FOR GOD'S SAKE! SHOW SOME BLOODY RESPECT! EVEN SALLY, YOUR FELLOW ANDROID, FEELS SOME-THING.'

Gus walked up to Henry. 'Listen, mister, I have emotions too, you know. Complicated ones. So don't you dare call me a robot, because I am a complex individual.'

285

Henry laughed. 'You're as shallow as a gnat's bidet.'

'This is about our survival! Our jobs!' Gus ranted, tactically omitting the information that he was about to consign half of them to redundancy. 'All I'm saying,' reasoned Gus, 'is that . . . What's wrong with Sally?'

'She's in shock,' said Dave, 'and Henry's got no hair, so at this moment the next bulletin has no newsreader.'

'Well, get Sarah the trainee to do it,' said Gus, pleasantly surprised by his decisiveness. 'Helen, get the staff back to their desks and let's get that . . . *that* moved. Before Yamaguchi arrives.'

'I'm already here,' said Yamaguchi.

Gus wheeled and stared despairingly at his Japanese nemesis.

Mr Yamaguchi gave a slight bow. 'The members of your Engineering Department are very thorough, but when they started to show me the intricacies of the coffee percolator, I felt it was time to leave. Why has that person got a coat over his head?'

Gus took a deep breath. 'He's got a migraine! Yes, a migraine, y'know, light hurts his eyes, so he puts his jacket over his head and we leave him alone until he feels better. It's a terrible thing to suffer from.'

'Indeed. How long will it be before he feels better?'

Gus puffed his cheeks. 'Could be quite some time. I think. Now why don't we go through to my office and—'

'Do you normally allow drinking in office hours?' asked Mr Yamaguchi, indicating first Henry and then Sally, who were both holding glasses of brandy.

'Good Lord no,' laughed Gus. He kept laughing to buy himself some thinking time. The prolonged laughter made Mr Yamaguchi wonder whether Globelink's Chief Executive was psychologically disturbed.

'No, they are holding glasses of brandy for the very good reason that it . . . that it is a tradition, an olde English tradition that on the last day of the century two glasses of brandy are handed around the office and everybody takes a sip and shouts "God bless the King".'

'I have not heard of this tradition,' said Mr Yamaguchi.

'Oh, yes, it dates back to Henry the Eighth, I think, yes, a little known part of the tapestry that is our heritage.' With this, Gus took the glass of brandy from Henry, shouted 'God save the King', and sipped a very small sip.

'But you no longer have a king,' observed Mr Yamaguchi.

'Indeed,' agreed Gus. 'Very true, but at Globelink we view tradition as part of the bonding process that wields human resources into a success-friendly commercial unit.'

As Gus rambled deeper and deeper into a jungle of gobbledygook, Helen decided she could take no more.

'Excuse me, Gus,' she interrupted, stepping forward with a bright smile, 'I think I can explain everything to Mr Yamaguchi.'

'Terrific,' said Gus, relieved at the arrival of reinforcements.

Helen approached Mr Yamaguchi. She was calm and composed. 'You see, Mr Yamaguchi, Henry and Sally are drinking brandy because they're in shock, and the man with the migraine is actually dead.'

Gus had a sudden vision of Sir Roysten advancing on him with a buzzing chainsaw in his hand.

Helen continued, in an even voice. 'Now we don't know who the dead man is. We just found him in the lift.

287

But we are endeavouring to contact the relevant authorities. Obviously, discovering a corpse is a little bit disruptive, so what you'll be seeing is not a typical day in our operation. I'm afraid you'll just have to bear with us. I know you'll understand.'

Gus groaned.

Mr Yamaguchi smiled at Helen. He was impressed by this young woman. He was less impressed by her Chief Executive, who was now curled up in a chair in a foetal position. 'I understand entirely. Only last week my colleague, Mr Nakamura, collapsed and died during our singing of the company worksong. It was most distressing. I shall return on another day when you are enjoying better fortune.' He bowed politely at Helen. She bowed back.

'Can I be of any assistance regarding the deceased?' he enquired.

'Thank you, Mr Yamaguchi,' said Helen, 'but we'll cope.'

Mr Yamaguchi bowed again. He wished them all a Happy Millennium and quietly walked out of the newsroom.

Helen looked at Gus, who was mopping sweat from his brow with a handkerchief. 'I thought honesty was the best policy,' she said.

'Oh, yes, you always do,' replied Gus bitterly. 'Let's hope your Head Girl routine was well advised. I really don't know why you intervened like that, I had the situation fully under control.' Gus ignored a room full of incredulous looks. He became very aware of the outline of the corpse's head beneath the jacket. He felt as if it were mocking him. He reached for the glass of brandy which was on the desk in front of him. It went down in one gulp. Gus's eyes started to water. He pointed at Gareth. 'Can someone please do something about that?' he said, in a weak, small voice.

Mrs Grindlay slipped the tape into her multimedia centre and sat down in the nice comfortable blue armchair she had purloined from Mitchell's office. Mitchell had been dismissed the day before. They had found twelve packets of Marlboro hidden in his desk. Everyone was very surprised. Except for Mrs Grindlay, who had put them there.

She settled back and lit another cigarette. This would be the tenth one of the day, but she didn't care any more. All she had to do was check the contents of the tape that Spooks Division had just delivered to her, then destroy it. After that, she would go home and put her feet up. She would have a hot bath, unwind, and fantasise about having sex with Ryan Giggs. She might even watch the millennium celebrations on BBC (though she'd probably steer clear of *Start the Century with Jonathan Ross*).

She picked up the remote control and prepared to press the fast-forward; there would no doubt be lots of other videophone messages on the tape before she got to Sir Terence's little bombshell. She frowned as a Globelink logo came up on the screen. A moment later she found herself watching footage of a much younger Henry Davenport. The curiously sombre tones of Sally Smedley came up on the soundtrack. 'Henry Davenport, who began his career as a junior reporter on the *Pimlico Gazette*, quickly made a mark with his astute and incisive writing. Despite a formidable and, some would say, prickly personality, he rose to the position of—'

289

Mrs Grindlay leaped for the yellow phone. She fought off a grim sense of foreboding. This could be the mother of all cock-ups. If she had a tape of Henry Davenport's obituary, then someone out there had a tape giving chapter and verse of the Bovactilax scandal. God almighty, could Spooks Department get *nothing* right? She drummed her fingers impatiently on the desk. The high-security lines always took ages to connect.

'Hallo, John speaking.'

Mrs Grindlay shuddered. She *hated* that affected Oxbridge drawl of his. Of course, he wasn't really called John, but Mrs Grindlay was happy to know as little about him as possible. She'd never met him, and didn't want to. He sounded odious. Mrs Grindlay crossed her fingers and asked John whether, by the remotest chance, his operatives might have acquired *two* tapes from Gareth Pugh, as she appeared to have the wrong one. John replied in the negative. Mrs Grindlay then suggested that Gareth be contacted immediately and asked to provide the correct tape.

'Ah,' said John. 'Now that could be a teensy-weensy bit tricky. Seeing as Gareth has just had a fatal accident.'

Mrs Grindlay pulled deeply on her cigarette. She stared at the ashes from her earlier cigarettes and for a moment felt sorry for Gareth. Yes, he had known too much, but that didn't mean they had to kill him, for God's sake! They could have had imprisoned him on a trumped-up charge, or incarcerated him in a psychiatric ward.

John broke the silence. 'I think it would be not entirely unreasonable to assume that the tape you require is still on the premises of Globelink News. That's where the . . . accident occurred.'

Mrs Grindlay gritted her teeth. 'Yes, John, I think that's a not unreasonable assumption. Now, how are we going to get hold of it?'

'Ah, the sixty-four thousand Ecu question. The video answerphone tape is identical, *n'est-ce pas*, with the common or garden video-tape cassette? Of which there must be several thousand in the offices of Globelink. At a conservative estimate.'

Mrs Grindlay bit her lip. She hated this English sang froid in the face of a crisis. To her mind it was just a cover for procrastination and incompetence. She recalled working with Douglas Hurd. He had displayed the same air of Olympian detachment and composure, but Mrs Grindlay had once walked into his office and found him sucking his thumb.

She heard John give a world-weary sigh. 'Of course,' he drawled, 'for all we know the tape is already in the possession of one of the journalists at Globelink. Alas, no one has seen fit to entrust me with the knowledge of what's on the tape, but since it appears to be horribly newsworthy, they may be about to run the story as we speak.'

Mrs Grindlay had already thought of that. While John's oleaginous tones were insinuating themselves down the phone line, she had been tapping on her computer keyboard. In a few seconds she had accessed the Globelink mainframe. She scanned the draft running-order for the next bulletin. Peace talks on Cyprus, the release of Lady Thatcher, Gazza's knighthood, she could see nothing that might be connected with the tape. Mrs Grindlay cleared the screen. 'We're all right on that front.'

'How do you know?'

'I just know, all right?'

'Tapping into other people's computers now, are we? I thought you left the illegal stuff to us?'

John's lethargic tones set Mrs Grindlay's teeth on edge. She began doodling impaled heads on the back of an envelope.

'Listen,' she said, 'I think we're going to have to raid the premises. Seal off the whole place. Search it from top to bottom until we find that tape. If you can organise it, I'll provide some kind of legal pretext.'

'Ye-e-es,' said John. Was he suppressing a yawn? 'Not exactly watertight, though, is it? Not entirely to be ruled out that someone at Globelink will have seen it. Might not choose to put it out on Globelink. Might decide to hit the jackpot in the most vulgar manner by trotting along to the *Sun*. Who, as we know, would be only too happy to run any story which damaged the PM.'

This was true enough, reflected Mrs Grindlay. The *Sun* had grown tired of supporting Seb Coe and wanted him replaced. That very morning its front page had depicted Seb Coe's head superimposed on to the cartoon of a worm.

'Of course,' said John, 'if your assessment is that we should stage a raid, then so be it. But my feeling is that as long as the Globelink team are fully operational, you remain at risk. In other words, a raid is not the surest way to distance the faeces from the fan.'

Mrs Grindlay suddenly felt very cold. What was he trying to suggest? She pushed a wisp of hair out of her eyes and concentrated hard. 'I don't care for the implication of what you just said.'

'I'm sorry, was there an implication?'

'Yes, I think there was.'

292

'I rather think there wasn't.'

Mrs Grindlay hesitated. Even John wouldn't propose the elimination of Globelink's entire staff. 'I'm sorry, I may have misunderstood. I just want it to be clear that we're not contemplating any . . .' she groped for the words, '. . . that we're not contemplating any drastic action.'

'Absolutely not.'

'Oh, good, So we're in agreement.'

'Yes.'

'I'm glad.'

'So am I.'

There was another long pause. John whistled softly for a few seconds. The whistling stopped abruptly and John adopted his most languid tone. 'I must say I do find it immensely satisfying when I see eye-to-eye with my superiors. Total harmony is such a joy.'

A very loud alarm bell rang in Mrs Grindlay's head. Her voice hardened. 'John, I am not your superior.'

'Please. You are too modest.'

John's tactic was horribly transparent. The buck was being passed.

'George, I still think your nose is broken. You really ought to go to Casualty.'

George stood up and pushed Helen away. 'No, I'm going to be quite adamant on this one. The last time I was in Casualty I was left lying on a trolley for eighteen hours. In a corridor. And then some junior doctor, who obviously hadn't slept for a week, mixed up his patients' notes and tried to perform keyhole surgery on my small intestine.' The memory of this made George feel faint again. He wanted to lie down in his office, but couldn't, because the dead body was now laid out on his sofa, respectfully covered with a blanket.

Everyone in the newsroom listened as Joy made yet another attempt to persuade the police to send somebody round. 'Yes, I know you must be very busy . . . Yes, I know this is like a hundred New Year's Eves rolled into one, but . . . Yes, I am aware that you are not a corpse-collection agency . . .' Joy's patience, never her greatest asset, was by now wearing extremely thin. 'Well, I'm sorry, I can tell you're very busy, I'll let you get back to fitting up Irish people and letting rapists off with a caution.' She slammed down the phone.

Sally came over to examine George. 'Your best plan is to go private, George. I can recommend a very good nose man in Harley Street.'

Everybody stared hard at Sally's nose.

'A friend of mine was treated by him,' she added hastily, and went back to her desk.

George was still gingerly prodding at his nose when he felt someone looking over his shoulder. It was Gus. A thin film of sweat glossed his brow and his hands were trembling.

'What's going on, George? There's no work being done on the six o'clock bulletin. Why not?'

The others decided to treat this as a rhetorical question.

Gus had other ideas. 'I said WHY NOT?'

Henry's brow furrowed dangerously. 'Because, Gus, there is a dead body in George's office and our Editor is in urgent need of rhinoplasty.'

George took the bloodied handkerchief away from his nose and attempted to defuse the confrontation. 'It's all right, Gus. We'll be back on course soon. It's perfectly natural for the team to fall apart a little when their Editor is incapacitated.'

Gus walked up very close to George. 'Listen, mister, nobody's indispensable, is that clear? I want a final running order within thirty minutes, And make sure the trailers for the *Review of the Century* are lined up and ready to go. And check on that satellite link-up with Washington. Oh, and I want an update on Gazza's response to the knighthood.' He strode across the newsroom imperiously. 'I want to see this office in dynamism overdrive at warp factor nine. OK?' He paused for a moment to look through the glass partition wall of George's office and pointed a quivering hand at the horrible reminder of his own mortality which lay on George's sofa. 'And how often do I have to tell you to dispose of that . . . that former person?'

'We've been trying,' protested Helen.

'Trying isn't achieving!' bellowed Gus.

'Where are we meant to take it?' asked Helen.

'I don't know. A hospital. A mortuary. Doesn't matter. As long as it's out of here. I want a volunteer to remove it from the building. Now.'

Nobody volunteered.

'Right,' snapped Gus. 'Dave. You do it.'

'Why me?'

'Because you're the least essential.'

'Oh, right, yeah. Good job I'm so loved and valued round here, eh, Helen? Otherwise I might just get the impression that I'm everyone's oily bloody rag.' Dave tossed a ballpoint petulantly across the desk.

'Don't argue!' screamed Gus.

'Well stop pushing me around then!'

'I'll do what I like.' Gus's voice had gone very

high-pitched. 'Just do as I say!' he yelled, flailing his arms and knocking Damien's souvenir grenade off the top of his terminal.

'All right, all right,' said Damien, picking the grenade off the floor. 'Calm down, Gus. Don't be such a wally.'

Gus's eyes swivelled in the direction of Damien. 'Would you like to say that again?'

'Yes,' said Damien. 'Don't be such a wally.'

'Right,' said Gus. 'You're fired.'

'What?' laughed Damien.

'You heard. You're fired. For persistent misconduct and calling the Chief Executive a wally. You're fired.'

Henry sighed deeply. 'Gus, you're over-wrought. Go lie down in a darkened room and take a pill. Or possibly a large, jagged suppository.'

Gus's breathing became faster. 'And *you're* fired, Henry.'

'Oh, don't be so absurd.' Henry sat down at his computer terminal and began work on the six o'clock bulletin.

Dave wearily stood up and headed for the door. 'I suppose I'd better deal with our dead friend before I get fired too. I'll get Security to give me a hand getting him down to my car. Assuming you haven't fired them all by then, Gus.' Dave gave Gus a mocking bow and left the newsroom.

Gus paused for a moment. 'He's fired too.'

'Oh, please!' said George. 'I'm feeling quite ill enough as it is without you playing this silly game.' George looked down at his Timberlands and tried hard to stand tall. It was no good. The Timberlands suddenly looked ridiculous on him. (In actual fact, the Timberlands had always looked ridiculous on him, but George didn't know that.) He dabbed cautiously at his damaged nose.

'Let's get the six o'clock on the road, shall we? Your Editor may be bloodied but he remains unbowed.'

'Your ex-Editor,' said Gus.

George's shoulders slumped as only George's shoulders knew how to slump. 'Gus, please, just go back into your office and let us get on with our work. I know it's been a difficult day, but getting cross with everyone doesn't help.'

Gus appeared to be rooted to the spot. His face was no longer purple. Now it was a waxy grey. He pulled a computer print from his pocket and held it up as if about to read it out loud.

It slowly dawned on the entire newsroom that Gus was crying. He wasn't crying in the way that normal people cry, with sobs or howls or anything dramatic like that. No, Gus was weeping silently. Large, glistening tears ran down his cheeks. Nobody could think of anything to say, so for the best part of half a minute Gus continued to open and close his mouth like a distressed goldfish. Then he slowly lowered himself into a chair. He wiped his cheeks with his sleeve, and finally spoke.

'It's not my fault, I'm only obeying orders. I've been putting this off for weeks. Sir Roysten made me do it.'

Henry was the first to move. He took two swift steps forward and snatched the sheet of paper from Gus's hand. The others crowded round to catch a glimpse of the document.

Henry cleared his throat. His normally stentorian tones were distinctly muted. 'Globelink Human Resource Reallocation Programme. Final list of staff members to be rationalised consequent to non-voluntary downsizing operation.' Henry looked up. 'Which in English means, I believe, fired.'

The silence in the newsroom was broken only by a loud sniff from Gus.

Henry rubbed his hand across his bald pate as he absorbed the contents of the fateful sheet of paper. He again cleared his throat. 'It looks like . . . It looks like three VT editors are to go. And three sound engineers. Two vision mixers. Three PAs. Two secretaries. One receptionist. One security man. Oh, and the canteen is to be closed. That's one, two, three, four . . .' Henry's finger ran down the list of names. 'That's seven catering staff out of a job. Now . . . the newsroom.'

People would later claim that it was the showman in Henry that made him keep the newsroom till last. But on this occasion it was not a sense of melodrama that was motivating Henry, but a terrible sense of dread. The minute he'd seized the document, his eye had fallen on his own name. He didn't want to believe it. It was all too horrible.

He sensed the others were growing impatient, and took a deep breath. 'Newsroom. Those surplus to requirements are . . . David Charnley. Damien Day. George Dent and . . . and Henry Davenport.' Henry coughed. 'The above adjustments effective from mid-night on 31 December, 1999. Signed, Gus Hedges, Chief Executive.'

The silence that followed was broken by Damien. 'No, it's not possible. That's not correct, it's a mistake. Isn't it, George?'

George stood staring into space.

'Why would he get rid of me?' asked Damien nervously. 'I'm our star performer. He can't do this to me.'

'You'll be all right,' said Henry quietly. 'You're young. You'll find something else.'

Helen noticed that George had gone very pale. She put an arm round his shoulder and gave him a squeeze.

Gus looked up pathetically from his chair. 'Obviously I'll give you all very good references.'

Damien snorted. Henry cackled derisively.

Gus was conscious of a lot of baleful stares, so he mumbled something about ringing Sir Roysten with the news and shuffled into his office. The silence returned.

Throughout this extraordinary scene, Sally had kept her head down and pretended to work on her script for the bulletin. But she was finding it hard to contain her excitement. With Henry gone, she would be fronting every bulletin on her own. Her dreams had come true. She felt like turning cartwheels.

'I think you've been treated disgracefully, Henry,' she said. 'After your many, many years of service. It's rank ingratitude. You have my deepest sympathy. If there's any little way in which I can be of assistance, you only have to ask.'

Henry stared at her, his eyes bulging. 'Thank you, I would rather perform oral sex on a sumo wrestler with leprosy.'

Sally's back stiffened. 'You all heard that. He spurned my hand of friendship.'

'Oh, shut it,' said Helen, who had noticed George swaying slightly. 'You're not going to black out, are you, George?'

'Oh no,' said George, a little dreamily. 'But it's not the ideal way to go into the new millennium, is it? I feel . . . well, I feel really quite depressed.'

'I don't think we should take all this lying down,' said Helen, trying to forget the tide of relief she'd felt when she'd realised her name was not on the list. 'I think we

299

should take industrial action. Get everybody reinstated.'

'Don't be silly, Helen,' said Joy, who felt that the sacking of four incompetent men was not an issue to strike over.

Dave came into the room, accompanied by Tim the security man. 'Look, Tim,' he said as they crossed the newsroom, 'someone's got to do it, OK? Just imagine it's a drunk.' Together they disappeared into George's office.

'Well, isn't anyone going to tell him?' Henry was staring hard at George. George looked away.

Dave and Tim emerged into the newsroom, half carrying, half dragging the corpse towards the door.

'George,' hissed Henry. 'You're the Editor. You've got to tell Dave.'

Dave looked up. 'Tell me what?' The dead man's feet were bouncing grotesquely along the floor.

Sally found herself boxed in. 'Just keep him away from me, all right?' she squeaked.

'Up a bit your side. Mind the desk.' Dave looked back over his shoulder as he and Tim struggled towards the door. 'Tell me what, Henry?'

Henry clenched his teeth. 'Dave, um . . . Dave, I'm afraid you've just been fired.'

'Yeah, yeah, I know,' Dave chuckled. 'He's fired everybody. Us, the Prime Minister, God.'

Henry raised his voice. 'It's not a joke, Dave. Sir Roysten ordered a massacre.' Henry held up the printout. 'And you're one of the victims. As of midnight tonight.'

'Shit!' said Dave, and let go of the body. Tim, caught unawares, also let go. The dead body crashed to the floor. As it did so, one arm came up in an arc and came to rest around Sally's ankle.

300

'Ahhhh!' screamed Sally, unable to move. 'Ahhhhh! Help me, somebody, help me! There's a dead man with his hand on my ankle!'

Henry eyed her unfeelingly. 'With the passing of the years, Sally, one has to be grateful for what one can get.' Dave was now scanning the printout.

Tim spotted his own name. 'Oh, bugger. He can't do this, can he?'

'He can,' said Henry. 'He's even given us the generous eight hours' notice the law requires.'

Dave feigned indifference. 'Who cares?' he shrugged. 'I was off to Australia anyway.'

Damien, who had not spoken for some time, picked up the phone and dialled Gus's extension. He watched through the glass partition wall as Gus rubbed at his eyes and finally picked up the phone.

'Gus Hedges.'

'Hallo, Gus,' said Damien. 'Just wanted to say that I'm looking forward to the leaving present.'

Gus gazed back at Damien. Was Damien being friendly? He sounded friendly. Yes, thought Gus, maybe he ought to nip out and buy a few leaving presents. They'd respect him for that.

'Right,' said Gus, 'absolutely. Don't worry, you've not been forgotten.'

'No, no,' replied Damien, 'I mean the leaving present *I'll* be giving *you*.' He proffered Gus a cold smile.

Gus put down the phone and drew the blinds.

John's words kept echoing in Mrs Grindlay's head: 'as long as the Globelink team are fully operational . . .' She wandered over to her office window, and watched the falling snow. It brought back memories of that

301

incredibly long, white winter of 1963, when school seemed to have been abolished and she'd spent endless days sledging down Box Hill.

She opened her office window and reached out to catch a few flakes of snow. She watched as they melted in the palm of her hand. Was snow greyer than when she was a child? From somewhere on the street below, the strains of that month's hit song drifted up to her.

As the bells start to ring
Our hearts start to sing
Oh, my darling, I want you to see
While the whole wide world is romancing,
For the rest of my life you'll be dancing
The millennium waltz with me.

Mrs Grindlay hastily shut the window and wished that Kenneth Branagh had stuck to acting. He was spreading himself very thin these days. She crossed to her desk and idly picked up the silver folder containing the latest presentation from Jim Bliss. It laid out various news-management options, to be initiated when it began to dawn on people that there was a mass outbreak of impotence. None of them struck her as particularly convincing. Blaming it on the psychological impact of the women's movement was both too blatant and too vague. A virus disseminated by Islamic fundamentalists was better, but that could well precipitate a very nasty war with Iran. An infection transmitted through eating fish from polluted waters was probably the weakest of all, since nobody in their right mind was eating fish any more.

Mrs Grindlay sighed and flung the document on to her desk. Bliss had done his best, the poor lamb, but any damage-limitation exercise was doomed if there was

302

someone out there with the evidence to blow it apart. Which brought her back to Globelink News . . .

Mrs Grindlay closed her eyes and rehearsed the likely sequence of events. Globelink News broadcasts incontrovertible evidence that the government has had a hand in rendering ninety per cent of the population impotent. Senior ministers are implicated in pushing Bovactilax through without proper testing, and also implicated in the subsequent cover-up. The government falls, of course. Good riddance. A general election is held. Even with Tony Blair as leader, Labour is unable to lose. The Conservative Party is annihilated. Fine. She had always disliked working for Tory ministers with their porky, self-satisfied faces and their pointless, porcelain wives and their private jokes about micks and Pakis.

But what happens then? People lose all respect for civil authority. How can anyone trust in the idea of government when government has wrecked their sex lives? Of course, government lies were nothing new: a radiation leak here, an illegal arms deal there, but none of these events struck at the very sense of self. As British women flocked abroad in their millions in search of sexual partners, there would be mobs of angry single men loose in society, determined to avenge themselves on authority for the loss of their manhood. There would be demonstrations at first, then riots. Young men with huge libidos and limp penises would roam the streets in orgies of angry destruction. Government authority would rapidly collapse. Britain would find itself on the verge of a new Dark Ages.

Mrs Grindlay shuddered. Over the years, she had come to despise authority. At the same time, she saw how necessary it was, how thin was the gauze that separated a civilised society from a terrible anarchy. One only had to think of Yugoslavia. Or Switzerland. She remembered the little village near Bern which she and her ex-husband had visited three years running. She'd caught a glimpse of it burning on television the other night. Was Frau Zinsli still alive, she wondered? And her two beautiful daughters who used to help serve at tables in the evenings? It was all so hard to grasp. Nobody seemed capable of providing a rational explanation of how a sophisticated and tolerant society could slip so quickly into a maelstrom of murderous tribal conflicts. Why did no one stand up and stop it happening? Surely there was a moment where decisive action could have prevented disaster? Even decisive action of an unpleasant kind. What if a few of the key players had been eliminated before they could whip their followers into an ecstasy of hatred? Sometimes you just had to get your hands dirty, whether you wanted to or not. Lesser evils, greater evils . . . somebody had to make these choices.

The siren of a passing police car echoed up from the street below. Mrs Grindlay sat down and lit a cigarette. It failed to provide the usual comfort. She picked up the yellow phone. As she waited for John to answer, a sudden gust of air pushed open her office door. She glanced up, startled, and saw the portrait on the corridor wall. William Ewart Gladstone gave her a long hard stare.

Around the globe, last-minute preparations were in hand for the great millennium celebrations. Those few pedants who'd pointed out that the new millennium didn't actually start till the 1 January, 2001 had been ignored. The arrival of the year 2000 *felt* like a new millennium, and that was all there was to it. The world needed a party.

A visiting alien looking down on planet Earth would have seen how, as the globe turned, nation followed nation in celebrating the arrival of the Third Millennium. The first major country to greet the new age would definitely have been the most striking. The giant construction, which stretched two hundred and fifty miles from Alice Springs to Tennant Creek, had taken almost three years to build. At midnight Australian time, Prime Minister Hogan threw a switch, and two and a half million amps of current flooded through a specially laid cable, to illuminate the world's biggest ever advertisement for Castlemaine XXXX, an advertisement visible two hundred miles out into space. The manufacturers of Castlemaine XXXX were not planning to open up lucrative new markets in space. They simply knew that most of the satellites would pick up pictures of it and flash them to news stations around the world, thus providing millions of dollars' worth of free advertising.

The globe turned, and on the slopes of Mount Everest, tens of thousands of millennialists were preparing for the end of the world, when they would experience the Rapture and be hoovered up to Heaven. Excitement was growing, and fights were breaking out between the many different sects as to who should have the best pitch.

The globe turned, and on Mount Ararat the Pope descended from a helicopter emblazoned with Durex logos. (The decision of the Extraordinary Vatican Council to back artificial contraception had proved a shrewd move. Millions of people had instantly converted to Roman Catholicism.) As midnight struck, the Pope began an open-air communion service, which culminated in the distribution of Vatican-approved

305

spermicidal creams to the five thousand people gathered on the mountainside.

The globe turned, and in Red Square Muscovites gathered to see the new Czarina and President Zhirinovsky appear on the Solzhenitsyn Mausoleum together. At the same time, an even bigger crowd was gathering on what had once been the Lenin Hills, where they waved banners and called for the return of communism.

The globe turned, and in Vienna dignitaries gathered at the Staatsoper to witness the première of Cameron Mackintosh's new rock version of *Die Fledermaus*.

The globe turned, and at the Windsor Castle Business Centre, two thousand captains of British industry were sitting down to a Millennium Banquet of finest British beef. Making his way self-consciously through the throng was a familiar figure. This was ex-Prince Charles's first public appearance since the referendum he'd insisted should be held to prove the public's support for the monarchy.

The visiting alien may well have been so distracted by these major celebrations that he (or she) would have failed to spot a few less publicised events. In Sydney, an elderly Greek waiter was being stabbed to death by two men who didn't like his accent. In a windowless sweatshop in Taiwan, eleven children making plastic statuettes of Nick Faldo were being allowed five minutes off to celebrate the new century. In Kiev, a woman who had once lived near Chernobyl was giving birth to a child with no eyes. And in a factory in Swindon, a man in a neat white coat was checking the fuse on a 130-millimetre shell which, two months later, would blow away a family of seven in East Timor.

But these were mere details in the grand scheme of things. Governments had more important things to think about. Everybody had more important things to think about. The staff of Globelink News had more important things to think about.

'Oh God,' said Joy, slamming down the phone. She found Helen staring at her. 'My father's in Reception. Can you believe that? First he sends me postcards faster than I can tear them up, then he rings me up every bloody day, then he swans in here unannounced!'

'All right, all right,' said Helen. 'Don't get worked up.'

'What do you mean, don't get worked up? The last time I saw him was twenty-three years ago. He told my mother he was just nipping out for some milk.'

'I'll come down with you,' Helen volunteered.

Joy squeezed Helen's hand. 'Thank you.'

Helen turned to George. 'We're going downstairs for a few minutes. Be back soon, promise.'

'Oh, that's all right,' said George. 'I'm amazed anyone is still here. It was a miracle the six o'clock went out at all. I just think it's a tribute to the team's journalistic integrity that people who've been fired don't turn and walk out on the spot. But no, Henry, Dave, Damien, they're all determined to work through till midnight, exactly as the terms of their dismissal stipulate. That's what I call professionalism.'

George's touching view of his team's professionalism was tragically at odds with the truth. At that very moment Henry and Dave were unloading seven hundred pounds' worth of alcohol from the boot of Dave's car.

'This'll be the party of the century,' Henry declared. 'An Armageddon rave! Henry Davenport will go out not

307

with a whimper but with a bang. I'm going to drink a bottle of Scotch and then pull Connie the receptionist.'

'Are you sure you've got that in the right order?' Dave asked, dumping a case of booze into Henry's arms.

Henry buckled slightly under the weight. 'There's a bet to be won. Remember?'

Dave slammed shut the boot. 'I thought we'd agreed it was a tawdry little wager which reflected no credit on either of us?'

'Bollocks,' said Henry, staggering towards the Globelink entrance. 'The bet's still on. Fifty quid. And I want an accumulator on Jill from Accounts and the ginger temptress from Marketing.'

Sally stood in front of the mirror in the ladies' room, and leaned her head to the left, and scrunched her shoulder all the way up to her left ear, then dropped it. She did this ten times. She then repeated the exercise with her right shoulder. There. That eased the tension a bit. She hadn't had time for her shiatsu that day. She shuddered at the memory of that dead man's hand on her ankle. And the nine o'clock had been a bit of a trial. Henry had insisted on taking part, since it was to be his very last bulletin. To her amazement, he had gone on air without any kind of hairpiece. Even she had to admit there was a certain panache in the way he had wound up. 'And that was the six o'clock news from Globelink, the station that brings you the bald facts. Good night and goodbye.'

Sally made a few minor amendments to her make-up and pondered whether to go home before midnight. She had heard rumours of a wild party. It would probably be sordid beyond words; and she could no longer face the idea of making her usual play for some tatooed technician. No, she wouldn't stay. It would be horrible. Much wiser to go home.

Perspiration was pouring from Henry's brow as he rested his case of bottles on the reception desk. He stared down at Connie. God, the T-shirt didn't leave much to the imagination. Connie looked up at him with that provocative pout which she adopted as a matter of course. Unfortunately, Henry believed the pout to be exclusively for his benefit.

'Good evening, Connie,' Henry gasped as he struggled for breath. 'We're having a party and a South African presence would greatly enliven proceedings.'

Connie tossed back her head and ran her fingers through her glossy black hair. 'Mr Davenport, you'll have a heart attack.'

Henry's breathing became faster. 'Thank you, Connie, I'm extremely fit as a matter of fact.'

Dave, observing the veins bulging prodigiously on Henry's forehead, thought Connie probably had a point.

'What's more,' added Henry, with what he imagined was a wry smile, 'I'm very supple.'

Connie gave a little giggle and covered her mouth with her hand. She did that a lot. It did not give the impression of a woman of high intelligence.

'Sorry you got the chop too, Connie,' said Dave, trying desperately not to notice her nipples.

Connie tossed her head. 'It's a bloody disgrace, man. And what about poor old Tim?' She stretched out and gave the security man a sympathetic pat on the arm. 'I think getting rid of him was wicked and wrong, to my mind, if you were to ask me.'

'Absolutely,' said Dave.

'I mean, they should have fired the Kaffir and kept the white one, not the other way round.'

There was an awkward silence.

'I couldn't agree more,' said Henry.

Dave was appalled. 'Henry!'

Henry nudged him conspiratorially with his foot and leaned towards Connie. 'I remember visiting South Africa in 1988. By God, what a fine country it was back in those days.'

Dave sighed. 'Oh, please!' He turned to Tim. 'Come on, let's get the booze upstairs and leave Connie and this old Boer to compare notes about the Great Trek.'

Connie reacted sharply. 'Oh, we hate the Boers. Very cruel to the blacks. My parents and I always treated our Kaffirs with great kindness. They're like children, you see; they need looking after. I'm afraid it's a scientific fact that their intelligence is lower than ours.'

Dave looked hard at her for a moment. 'Well, if their intelligence is lower than yours, the scientists must have had some very powerful measuring equipment. Come on, Tim.'

Connie frowned and looked up at Henry. 'What did Dave mean by that, Mr Davenport?'

'Tell me,' asked Henry, 'why do you call him Dave, whereas you always refer to me as Mr Davenport?'

'It's respect for age, Mr Davenport.'

Henry winced and picked up his case of bottles. 'See you later, then?'

'Maybe,' said Connie, reactivating her pout.

Having contemplated the prospect of spending New Year alone at home, Sally formed the view that it was her duty to attend the party. All those poor wretches who'd been

310

fired would need moral support. She would dispense generous amounts of sympathy and *bonhomie*. Yes, that would be gracious. They would appreciate that. And maybe at some point in the future *Hello!* magazine would be interested in her account of the evening. Maybe something like: 'How I Comforted my Weeping Friends'. Sally spent several minutes putting her cosmetics back in her handbag. Then she walked briskly out of the ladies' room.

Joy stood in Reception and prayed that the man sitting on the second sofa along was not her father. He was in his early fifties, with a suntan of a curious orange shade. His greying hair was carefully coiffured and the hand holding the coffee cup bore three large rings. The bright yellow of his shirt clashed horribly with the red blue check of his sports jacket. But it wasn't the colour of the shirt that held Joy's gaze, it was the fact that it was open almost to the waist. And nestling on his chest, amidst a cluster of wiry hair, was a gold medallion.

Joy took a step back, then another. She gripped Helen's arm. The man looked up and stared at her.

'Hi, babe,' he said.

Henry crashed a crate of booze down on George's desk with a grunt. 'Right. Someone fetch glasses. Dave, let's sort out the music.'

George blinked at the bottles of malt whisky that Henry was pulling out of the crate. 'I'm not sure Gus sanctioned this much expenditure on drink. He might be upset.'

Henry savagely tore open another case and pulled out a bottle of Glen Grant twenty-one-year-old. 'George, do you not grasp that you have been shafted, buggered, eviscerated, kippered and upgefucked by that man?

311

Assuming, that is, that the word "man" can be used to denote a creature who leaves a putrescent trail of slime with every step.'

'I think that's a little unfair. He's only doing Sir Roysten's bidding.'

'You need a few drinks inside you, George.' Henry filled a polystyrene cup with malt whisky. 'There, that'll open the sluices and get some healthy bitterness pouring out.'

'Oh, I'm really not bitter.'

'Me neither,' called Dave, fiddling with the CD player. 'I was about to hand in my resignation anyway.'

The newsroom suddenly filled with the voice of Kenneth Branagh singing 'The Millennium Waltz'.

'No, thank you very much,' shouted Henry above the racket, and switched off the CD player.

'Hey! We want music, don't we?'

'Precisely,' said Henry, rummaging through the box of CDs that Damien had borrowed from Grams Library. A moment later the last act of the *Callas di Stefano Tosca* rang out. A beatific smile crossed Henry's face. 'Ah. Sheer bliss.'

'Not looking forward to telling Margaret I've been fired,' said George suddenly. 'I'm going round there for New Year lunch tomorrow. And in return for lunch I'm returfing her lawn.'

Muted cheers rang round the newsroom as Damien and Tim came in carrying a video-oke machine.

'Get that thing out of here!' bellowed Henry. 'That's the devil's contraption.'

'I think they're great fun,' said Connie, as she followed them into the newsroom in a short black dress.

Henry's belligerence disappeared instantly. 'Welcome. Welcome, sweet lady.'

Connie giggled and put her hand to her mouth,

As Damien rigged up the video-oke machine, he wondered what he would be doing in a year's time. Come to think of it, he wondered what he would be doing in a week's time. 'Hey, Dave, a tenner says I get snapped up by Berlusconi Weekend Television.'

Dave wasn't listening. He was transfixed by Connie's legs. They made him ache with desire. He'd caught glimpses of them before, but she was invariably sat behind that reception desk. Now these legs were walking around the newsroom in all their lissom glory. In an attempt to prove something to himself (and to Maisie), Dave had been celibate since the widows episode in Brecon. It had been a considerable strain. And now he could feel those legs calling to him. No, no, no! He was through with all that. He tore his eyes off Connie and went to get another drink.

Damien left Tim with the video-oke, poured himself a beer, sat down on Sally's chair and put his feet up on her desk.

George came over and patted him on the shoulder. 'Well done, Damien, for taking charge of the, um, dead body. It was commendable of you to deal with it so efficiently.'

'Well, I've seen death before.'

'Where did you take him, by the way?'

'Don't worry, George, it's all dealt with.'

Connie perched on the edge of Dave's desk and Dave heard the swish of her tights as she crossed her legs. He got up and quickly walked over to the other side of the newsroom.

Sally entered. She looked around brightly. 'Large Babycham, please, Henry.'

313

Damien waited for her to tell him to take his feet off her desk. She swanned towards him. 'Hello, Damien. Why don't we get some decent music on and have a bit of a dance?'

Damien took his feet of the desk. 'Eh?'

'But first I'll just make sure everyone has got a drink. Don't go away now, Damien, because I want that first boogie.' She winked (which didn't suit her at all) and swept over to the cases of booze. 'Now. Further refreshments, anybody?'

Henry looked at Damien who looked at Dave who looked at Henry.

'Is she on something?' asked Dave.

As the party warmed up, nobody saw the pair of eyes peering out from between the venetian blinds. Gus wondered whether it was safe to unlock the door yet. He hoped his staff weren't bitter. He really longed for them to understand his position.

Although Gus didn't know it, he was living proof of the Greek Theory of Tragedy. Like Macbeth, Hamlet and George Best, he could not escape his fatal flaw. Gus Hedges' ambition to rise to the very top of British broadcasting would never be fulfilled. Not because he was useless, though being useless wasn't necessarily a disadvantage, but because he needed to be liked. He needed to be liked by those whom he served and he needed to be liked by those whom he fired.

There was a polite little knock on the door. Gus opened it cautiously. George edged into the room, holding a polystyrene beaker and a paper plate. 'Thought you might fancy some wine and a few Twiglets.'

* * *

As the lift ascended to the second floor, Helen realised it had perhaps been an error of judgement on her part to invite Joy's father to the office party. She'd only said it to break the charged silence down at Reception. Helen again tried to think of something to say. Joy obviously wasn't going to be much help. She was standing facing the lift doors, her arms folded and her eyes trained resolutely on the floor.

'So,' said Helen, 'what do you do for a living, Mr Merryweather?'

Joy's father was staring nervously at his daughter, 'Um, I'm an entertainer. Cruise ships mostly, I sing . . . You know, P. J. Proby, Tom Jones, Barry Manilow, all the greats.'

'That sounds like fun,' lied Helen.

Five cups of Glen Grant twenty-one-year-old had transformed Henry's attitude to video-oke machines. He was standing on a desk, midway through a rendition of 'My Way'. The video-oke screen showed him singing alongside Frank Sinatra in Carnegie Hall. Nobody in the newsroom minded that Henry was three bars behind Ol' Blue Eyes.

Dave was leaning against the wall explaining to Damien, in a mawkish, drunken sort of way, that he wanted to settle down with Maisie, because Maisie was a diamond, an absolute diamond. Damien nodded vaguely and looked at his watch. Dave tried to explain that he still had hopes of a reconciliation, but his flow of thought was broken by Connie's legs crossing his eyeline.

Gus nibbled forlornly at a Twiglet and peeked out again through the blinds. The party was obviously well under

315

way. Gus could see everyone chatting and laughing. He wondered what they could possibly be laughing about. Perhaps they were making cruel jokes about how he'd burst into tears in front of the whole office. He glanced at his watch and went over to his hi-definition monitor.

Henry was just starting on 'The Lady is a Tramp', when Damien switched off the video-oke machine. There was a loud chorus of disapproval.

'Time to watch *Review the Century*,' shouted Damien above the din.

Booing ensued.

'Listen, trust me, OK? I just think it could be worth watching, OK?' Damien turned to Sally. 'Um, Sal, you couldn't possibly nip up to the canteen and fetch some tonics, could you?'

'It'll be a pleasure,' beamed Sally. She left the news-room.

'Could it be cocaine she's on?' asked Henry.

Damien clapped his hands. 'Take your seats one and all.'

Gus was already settling down in his office for what would be the only bright point in an abysmal day – Globelink's prestigious look back over the century's most telegenic high points. A lot of time, effort and talent had been inputted on this one. It would show the world that Globelink had a serious commitment to quality broadcasting. Gus stifled the small, frightened voice that told him Sir Roysten was not interested in quality broadcasting. With a skeleton staff, quality broadcasting was definitely off the agenda. So what were Sir Roysten's plans for Globelink? And why had Gus been banned from asking questions about the staff pension fund?

The Globelink logo appeared on the screen. Gus

turned up the volume. The opening sequence was definitely high-impact, thought Gus. It was intended as a kind of taster, a montage of key images from the last hundred years. Henry's voice-over gave way to sombre music. Up on the screen came film of troops going over the top in the First World War. Then that incredible piece of film showing a suffragette flinging herself under the hoofs of King George V's horse. Then came the burning of the *Hindenburg*. Then Edward and the abdication crisis. Then the bombing of Guernica. Then the D-Day landings. Then that awesome mushroom cloud over Hiroshima. Then a naked pair of tatooed buttocks pounding up and down while a voice closely resembling Sally's shouted, 'Oh, yes! Oh yes! Make me come like Vesuvius!'

Everyone in the newsroom was turned expectantly towards Gus's office. Gus came out like a bullet from a gun. He sprinted through the newsroom and hurtled out through the other door. All eyes turned back to the screen. The rhythm of the buttocks was increasing now, while Sally had taken to screaming, 'Not yet! Not yet!'

Fifteen seconds later Gus burst into the transmission suite on the third floor. The monitor screens were showing footage of the Korean war. Gus was clutching at his chest and making dreadful choking noises. The engineer looked up, 'Sorry about that, Mr Hedges. Somebody must have messed around with the transmission tape.'

Back in the newsroom, people were crowding round Damien, congratulating him (except for George, who had felt dizzy and was now sitting down with his head between his legs).

'Brilliant,' roared Dave, punching the air.

'Oh, it was nothing,' boasted Damien. 'It just involved

some creative editing, that's all. I thought the high point of Dave's Christmas tape deserved a wider audience.'

'Superb,' enthused Henry. 'Let's see Gus explain that one to the Broadcasting Ethics Commission!'

Helen drifted off towards George's office.

Bobby Merryweather saw the opportunity of breaking the ice with his daughter. 'That was a giggle, wasn't it, Joy?'

'Only if you're an emotionally crippled male with the intellect of a cauliflower.'

Oh, well, thought Bobby, at least she's started talking to me.

Mrs Grindlay switched off the television set in her office and prepared to go home. She had rather enjoyed the brief obscenity episode on the *Review of the Century*. Perhaps they were all drunk? She hoped so. She put on her coat, hesitated, then decided to have one last listen to the goings-on at Globelink. Not that there was any longer professional need to do so. All the big decisions had been taken and were probably irrevocable by now. But over the last few weeks of tapping into Globelink she had, perversely enough, become faintly fond of them all. She switched the hidden microphones to 'transmit' and sat down again without bothering to take off her coat. The newsroom mike produced a confused babble of conversation. The only voice she could make out was some giggly South African woman who was saying, 'I wasn't sure if you liked me, Dave.' She switched to the mike in George Dent's office. There was still quite a lot of background noise from the newsroom, but now she could hear the voice of another woman, talking on the phone.

'Listen, Chloë,' she was saying. 'It's no use pretending. The fact is, I think Martin is a complete nerd . . . Oh, hello, Martin! I didn't realise you were on the extension . . . Has he gone now? . . . Chloë, all I rang to say is, I don't want you to have to choose between your mother and your fiancé. So . . . so, I'd like to come to the wedding . . . Fantastic! . . . Yes, it makes me happy, too . . . OK . . . Bye.'

Mrs Grindlay found herself curiously touched by this conversation. Her seventy-one-year-old mother lived in Vancouver. They hadn't spoke to each other in seventeen years. She switched off the receiver. She was about to light a cigarette, but changed her mind. She picked up the phone and tried to remember the dialling code for Canada.

Henry had been standing at the reception desk for perhaps half a minute before he realised there was no one there. He blinked and shook his head. He had come in search of Connie. Where had the wench got to? How could he pull the wretched girl if she was nowhere to be found?

Henry heard footsteps and turned round. Two burly young men in jeans and leather jackets hurried across the lobby and went out of the front door. Who the hell were they? Bloody gatecrashers. The place was falling apart. He made his way across to the front doors and locked them. He swigged from the bottle of whisky in his hand and watched the snow whirling past the streetlamps. He belched, then plodded gloomily towards the lifts. Maybe he would go out with a whimper after all.

In the newsroom, Sally was playing the hostess, politely

319

pouring out drinks for her inferiors. She noticed that everyone was smiling at her. She was obviously more popular than she realised. But why all these references to Vesuvius?

'Another drink, Joy?' she asked.

Joy didn't answer. She was gazing at her father with a look of pure hatred. He was holding the video-oke microphone and singing 'Delilah'. She looked away in disgust as he launched into a pitiful imitation of the Tom Jones pelvic thrust. This was definitely the most embarrassing, excruciating, nauseating moment of her life. She hated him for his phoney tan, his naff mid-Atlantic singing voice, his open-fronted shirt. But most of all she hated him for not having the intelligence to realise that Dave's cry of 'Give us a song then, Engelbert' had been intended as ironic.

Henry slouched his way into the edit suite where the obits were kept. He'd always felt there was something slightly grim about having to pre-record tributes to luminaries while they were alive. Still, there were compensations. Three weeks before, Henry had recorded the obit for Jeffrey Archer, and had greatly enjoyed the experience.

Morosely, Henry shuffled down the row of shelves laden with video tapes in plastic boxes. He ran his fingers over the Ds. Ah! There it was. 'Henry Davenport 1936–   '. That blank gave him a clammy feeling. He walked over to the tape machine, opened the plastic case, and shoved the tape in. He felt ready to indulge in thoughts of his own mortality. He pulled up a chair, took another swig from the whisky bottle, and sat back to watch the epic that was his life story.

The skull-like face of a very old man appeared on the monitor, Henry recoiled. Surely he didn't look like that? He peered closer, struggling to focus. Wait a minute, wasn't that Sir Terence Whatsit, the ratbag businessman? Henry had once interviewed him.

Sir Terence slowly unfolded the full, appalling story of Bovactilax. He listed all the individuals at Phabox UK who had conspired to conceal adverse results during the early trials of the drug. He named the Cabinet minister who had received half a million pounds' worth of preferential share issue in return for helping Phabox circumvent the normal licensing procedures. He named the other Cabinet ministers who'd connived at the deception on the grounds that Bovactilax would be 'good for the British economy'. He pointed out that the Chief Medical Officer, who had repeatedly asserted that Bovactilax residues in beef were 'well within proven safety limits', had mysteriously acquired two large properties in the Caribbean. Most devastating of all, he revealed that his drug company had recently discovered that even the minutest quantity of Bovactilax caused irreversible impotence in the human male. Sir Terence spelled it out: Britain's men had been emasculated by incompetence, corruption and greed. It was absolute dynamite! It was the news story of the century!

Unfortunately, there was no one in the room to hear it. The moment Henry had registered that the tape was not his epitaph, he had charged out, and stormed up the corridor, muttering imprecations as he went.

In the newsroom, George, now fortified by several beakers of whisky, was on the phone to Margaret. Damien listened in amazement as George told his

321

ex-wife to take her twenty-six square metres of turf and stick them up her arse. Damien was about to congratulate George when he felt himself being grabbed by Henry.

'All right, Damien, that's not funny!'

'What isn't?'

'It was you, wasn't it?' Henry swayed slightly. 'Humiliating Sally, that's funny. Nearly giving Gus a heart attack, that's funny. But hiding a man's obituary, that's not funny, OK? Now where is it?'

Damien stared at him uncomprehendingly. 'Henry, you're drunk.'

Henry took a Wild West swing at Damien and toppled backwards on to the floor.

Another backing track started up on the video-oke machine. Joy's father took Sally by the hand and, gazing into her eyes, began serenading her with 'Lady in Red'. Joy had had enough. She hunted for her coat. She pushed past George, who was looking into Helen's eyes and wondering why they had never become lovers.

Henry rose from the floor like Lazarus. 'And another thing,' he slurred, 'since when has it been Globelink's policy to let people record their own obits?'

Damien rolled his eyes. 'What are you on about now?'

'Just seen him. Thingummibob. Fellow that snuffed it the other day. Sir Terence . . . Sir Terence Bovactilax.'

'Sir Terence . . . Sir Terence Huntleigh?'

'That's the fellow. On tape. At death's door.' Henry struggled to recall the only line of Sir Terence's testimony that he'd actually heard. Some bollocks about "telling the whole story".'

'Whole story about what?' asked Damien, putting down his glass.

322

Henry's eyes glazed over. 'Where's Connie?'

Damien took Henry firmly by the elbow. 'The whole story about what, Henry?'

Henry's eyes swivelled round the room. 'And where the hell is Dave?'

Henry tore himself free from Damien's grasp and staggered towards the door.

'Three minutes to midnight! Charge your glasses!' shouted Helen.

Damien filled Helen's glass.

'Cheers, Damien,' she said. Damien didn't respond. There was something nagging at the back of his mind.

The empty corridor resounded to the sound of Henry's desperate pleas. 'Connie? Connie? Where are you? I love you, Connie! Don't let that swine lay a finger on you!'

Henry lurched towards a familiar-looking door. It was the stationery cupboard. This was where he'd found Dave with a girl from Dispatch during last year's Christmas party. He banged furiously on the door, yelling, 'Charn-ley!' He bent down and peered through the keyhole. All was darkness. He tottered further down the corridor before pausing at a door marked 'Shower Room – for Gus Hedge's personal use only'. Yes, thought Henry, this was Charnley knee-trembler territory all right. He kicked savagely at the door. It flew open immediately and the dead body of Gareth toppled on to him. Damien came walking briskly down the corridor, stepped over the entwined Henry and Gareth, and disappeared round the corner.

In the edit suite where the obituaries were kept, Dave and Connie were tearing at each other's clothes. As he felt Connie's tongue reach down his throat, Dave experienced a brief flicker of guilt. Would this wreck the last chance of a reconciliation with Maisie? Oh, sod it, everybody knew that office parties didn't count. He felt Connie's legs close around him. Within seconds they were both lost in a frenzy of lust, oblivious to Sir Terence's revelations still playing on the monitor behind them.

The door flew open and Damien came in.

'Get out!' shrieked Connie.

'Sorry,' said Damien firmly, sitting down in front of the screen and pressing the rewind button. 'You carry on if you want to.'

'For Christ's sake, Damien,' Dave wailed as he zipped up his trousers.

Damien kept his eyes on the screen. 'I wonder what Maisie would say about this?'

'Who's Maisie?' asked Connie sharply.

Dave looked as if he wanted to strangle Damien.

Connie moved towards the door, popping her breasts back inside her dress.

'Oh, by the way, Henry's looking for you, Connie,' said Damien.

She tossed her head. 'Where is he?'

Damien leaned forward as the tape clicked back to the start.

'You'll find him down the corridor. Embracing a dead body.'

Connie pouted and left the room.

Dave smoothed down his hair and tucked in his shirt. 'I'm glad I won't have to see you any more, Damien,' he said bitterly.

'Right,' said Damien absent-mindedly.

Dave swayed and grabbed at the door handle. 'And why exactly is Henry embracing a dead body?'

'It wasn't meant for him,' said Damien, hitting the play button.

'You're a complete nutter, you know that, Damien?' Dave shook his head and walked out, slamming the door behind him.

To the distant sound of a hundred church bells ringing in the new millennium, Damien watched Sir Terence Huntleigh unfold the complete, unexpurgated truth about a handy little pharmaceutical breakthrough called Bovactilax.

'Bloody hell!' screamed Damien as the tape reached its end. 'I was right all along! There IS a story! And God has given it to ME!'

Damien fell trembling to his knees. 'I've got the scoop of the century! No, the scoop of the bloody millennium!'

At that moment the bomb went off.

Postscript

The bomb did not achieve its objective. Due to a mix-up between kilograms and pounds, not enough explosive was used. More significantly, the device was placed in a suite designed for sound recordings, where the thick padded walls absorbed much of the blast. The explosion did, however, cause a fire, which took hold at enormous speed. By the time the emergency services arrived (some two hours later) the Globelink building had been burned to the ground.

ONE DEAD IN TV BLAST HORROR read the semi-accurate headline in the next morning's *Sun*. There was one dead, all right, but he hadn't been killed by the explosion. In fact, the charred body of Gareth Pugh was never identified, much to Mrs Grindlay's relief.

No one ever claimed responsibility for the bomb, though the intelligence services insisted that all the evidence pointed to Libya.

The staff of Globelink News felt themselves fortunate to be alive.

HENRY DAVENPORT was saved from serious injury by the dead body that was lying on top of him at the time. He received minor burns which soon healed. He never replaced his wig, after discovering that his bald head attracted a lot of salacious mail from female viewers.

HELEN COOPER spent three weeks in a hospital bed, recovering from lacerations to her legs. During that time she received regular visits from daughter Chloë and future son-in-law Martin. She later attended their wedding in a wheelchair and was seen to weep with joy when Chloë failed to turn up. She is back on her feet now, and still plucking up the courage to reveal her sexual orientation to her daughter.

SALLY SMEDLEY suffered superficial bruising to the face, spent £12,000 on cosmetic operations to restore her appearance, and made a fortune selling MY MOMENTS OF HELL IN BOMB CARNAGE to *The News of the World.*

GEORGE DENT, who suffered a broken arm, was in hospital for quite some time, after he was confused with another patient and had keyhole surgery performed on his small intestine. The resultant complications had never been seen before by medical science, and resulted in his having a syndrome named after him.

JOY MERRYWEATHER, who had left for home seconds before the blast, suffered only from shock, though her father received a piece of shrapnel in the left testicle. Joy hailed this as divine retribution.

DAVE CHARNLEY showed great heroism during the chaotic moments following the explosion. Despite his injuries, he helped locate and rescue several members of staff trapped in the wreckage of the Globelink building. He was seen on news bulletins all over the country carrying Sally Smedley to safety and, as he later said himself, 'Courage doesn't come much greater than that'. With his self-esteem restored, he decided not to emigrate after all.

He is again going out with Maisie, and every so often talks in vague terms about settling down and getting married.

Chief Executive GUS HEDGES was praised for the way in which he had taken command of a group of survivors, showing bold and decisive leadership reminiscent of Gene Hackman in *The Poseidon Adventure*. Everyone agreed that it was just bad luck that he'd inadvertently led them towards the heart of the fire. Gus suffered second-degree burns to his buttocks and had to lie face-down in hospital for eight weeks

DAMIEN DAY, who was nearest to the explosion, was blown through a partition wall and suffered several broken ribs and a fractured skull. This resulted in serious memory loss. He would never remember the events leading up to the explosion, nor anything from the previous twelve months. Brecon, Montreux, Bovactilax, all were erased from his mind for ever. During his nine-week stay in hospital, Damien was visited by many well-wishers, especially cameramen, who just came to see how he was getting on and joke with him about his injuries. He is now back at work, reporting from the brutal sectarian war in Belgium.

Connie van der Groote, a receptionist, suffered serious brain damage when a section of roof fell on her skull. She subsequently went on to become a spokesperson for The Adam Smith Institute.

Everyone agreed that, apart from the bomb, it was the best office party they had ever attended.

SIR ROYSTEN MERCHANT visited all his injured staff in hospital (having been advised to do so by his PR consultant, Jim Bliss). Fearing that his image would be damaged if he were seen firing a hospitalised workforce, Sir Roysten decided Globelink should not be closed down. All members of staff were subsequently reinstated. The station continued to be unprofitable, but Sir Roysten didn't care; he was easily able to subsidise it from the profits generated by his penile implant factory.

Jim Bliss was abandoned by his mistress, then by his wife. He later committed suicide.

Mrs Grindlay took early retirement on 3 January, 2000. She now lives with her mother in Vancouver, where she sometimes pulls lifeguards on Kits Beach.

Thanks to men's fear of admitting that they're no good in bed, the mass outbreak of impotence took another seven years to come to public attention. When people finally realised what was happening, humanity was experiencing so many environmental catastrophes that no one gave a damn about anything as insignificant as impotence. Nobody ever found out about the government's culpability in rendering most of Britain's male population impotent. The great Bovactilax scandal was a story that never broke.

Shortly after the explosion at Globelink, tabloid newspapers published graphic pictures of the Chancellor of the Exchequer in his garden, beating a mole to death with a shovel. Within two weeks the government had fallen, and Prime Minister Seb Coe was hurled into political oblivion.

As George Dent remarked in hospital at the time, 'Life's a bit of a rollercoaster, isn't it?'

❑ How was it for you?	MAUREEN LIPMAN	£4.50
❑ Something to fall back on	MAUREEN LIPMAN	£4.50
❑ Thank you for having me	MAUREEN LIPMAN	£4.50
❑ When's it coming out?	MAUREEN LIPMAN	£4.99
❑ Without feathers	WOODY ALLEN	£4.99
❑ Turn back the clock	JOYCE GRENFELL	£5.99
❑ George – don't do that	JOYCE GRENFELL	£4.50
❑ Stately as a galleon	JOYCE GRENFELL	£3.99
❑ Village People	PAULA YATES	£4.99

Warner Books now offers an exciting range of quality titles by both established and new authors. All of the books in this series are available from:

Little, Brown and Company (UK),
P.O. Box 11,
Falmouth,
Cornwall TR10 9EN.

Alternatively you may fax your order to the above address.
Fax No. 01326 376423.

Payments can be made as follows: cheque, postal order (payable to Little, Brown and Company) or by credit cards, Visa/Access. Do not send cash or currency. UK customers and B.F.P.O. please allow £1.00 for postage and packing for the first book, plus 50p for the second book, plus 30p for each additional book up to a maximum charge of £3.00 (7 books plus).

Overseas customers including Ireland, please allow £2.00 for the first book plus £1.00 for the second book, plus 50p for each additional book.

NAME (block letters) ....

....

ADDRESS ....

....

....

❑ I enclose my remittance for _____
❑ I wish to pay by Access/Visa card

Number

Card Expiry Date